Grace Burriting
and compnts in
he

Also by Grace Burrowes

DANIEL'S
True Desire

GRACE
BURROWES

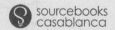

sourcebooks
casablanca

Published by Sourcebooks Casablanca, an imprint of Sourcebooks,
Inc.
P.O. Box 4410, Naperville, Illinois 60567-4410
(630) 961-3900
Fax: (630) 961-2168
www.sourcebooks.com

Printed and bound in Canada.
MBP 10 9 8 7 6 5 4 3 2 1

To the wounded healers

One

"Why must all and sundry entertain themselves by telling me falsehoods?"

Daniel Banks's teeth chattered as he put that conundrum to his horse, who had come to a halt, head down, sides heaving, before the only building in sight.

"'Ye can't miss it,'" Daniel quoted to himself. "'The only lane that turns off to the left half a mile west of the village.'"

This lowly dwelling was not Belle Maison, the family seat of the Earl of Bellefonte. Daniel had listened carefully to the directions given to him by the good folk at the Queen's Harebell. They'd sent him, in the middle of a roaring snowstorm, to a mean, weathered cottage, albeit one with a light in its single window.

"I'll be but a moment," Daniel promised his gelding.

Daniel's boots hit the snowy ground and agony shot up limbs too long exposed to the cold. He stood for a moment, waiting for the pain to fade, concocting silent epithets when he ought to have been murmuring the Twenty-Third Psalm.

"Halloo, the house!" he called, thumping up three

snowy steps. The porch sheltered a small hoard of split oak firewood. Somebody within burned that oak, for the frigid air held a comforting tang of wood smoke.

The wind abated once Daniel ducked under the porch's overhang, while the cold was unrelenting. He longed for a fire, some victuals, and proper directions, though only the directions mattered.

A man of God was supposed to welcome hardships, and Daniel did, mostly because his store of silent, colorful language was becoming impressive.

He raised a gloved fist to knock on the door. "Halloo, the—!"

The door opened, Daniel's sleeve was snatched into a tight grasp, and he was yanked into the warmth of the cottage so quickly he nearly bumped his head on the lintel.

"I said I'd be home by dark," his captor muttered, "and full dark is yet another hour away. I was hoping this infernal snow would slow down." The young lady turned loose of Daniel's sleeve. "You're not George," she said.

Alas for me. "The Reverend Daniel Banks, at your service, madam. I lost my way and need directions to Belle Maison, the Bellefonte estate. Apologies for intruding upon your afternoon."

Though, might Daniel please intrude at least until his feet and ears thawed? Beelzebub was a substantial horse who grew a prodigious winter coat. He'd tolerate the elements well enough for a short time.

While Daniel was cold, tired, famished, and viewing his upcoming visit to the earl's grand house as a penance at best.

"Your gloves are frozen," the lady noted, tugging one of those gloves from Daniel's hand. "What could you be thinking, sir?" She went after his scarf next, unwinding it from his head, though she had to go up on her toes. She appropriated his second glove and shook the lot, sending pellets of ice in all directions.

What had he been thinking? Lately, Daniel avoided the near occasion of thinking. Better that way all around.

"You needn't go to any trouble," Daniel said, though the warmth of the cottage was heavenly. A kettle steamed on the pot swing, and the scent of cinnamon—a luxury—filled the otherwise humble space. Somebody had made the dwelling comfy, with a rocking chair by the fire, fragrant beeswax candles in the sconces, and braided rugs covering a plank floor.

"I can offer you tea, and bread and butter, but then surely we'll be on our way. I'm Kirsten Haddonfield, Mr. Banks, and we can ride to Belle Maison together."

Haddonfield was the family name that went with the Bellefonte title.

"You're a relative to the earl, then?"

She wore a plain, dark blue wool dress, high necked, such as a farmer's wife would wear this time of year. Not even a cousin to an earl would attire herself thus unless she suffered excesses of pragmatism.

"I am one of the earl's younger sisters, and you're half-frozen. I hope those aren't your good boots, for you've ruined them."

"They're my only boots."

Swooping blond brows drew together over a nose no one would call dainty, and yet Lady Kirsten Haddonfield was a pretty woman. She had good facial bones, a definite chin, a clean jaw, and blue eyes that assured Daniel she did not suffer fools—lest her tone leave any doubt on that score.

Daniel was a fool. Witness the ease with which the yeoman at the inn had bamboozled him. Witness the ease with which his own wife had bamboozled him.

"At least sit for a moment before the fire," the lady said, arranging his scarf and gloves on pegs above the hearth. "Did you lose your way because of the weather?"

Daniel had lost his way months ago. "The weather played a role. Are you here alone, my lady?"

She folded her arms across a bosom even a man of the cloth acknowledged as a fine bit of work on the Creator's part.

"I am on my family's property, Mr. Banks, and they well know where I am. The weather is not only foul, it's dangerous. If you must prance out the door to die for the sake of manners, I'll not stop you. The groom or one of my brothers should be here any minute to fetch me home. We'll note into which ditch your remains have fallen as we pass you by."

The fire was lovely. Her ferocity, though arguably rude, warmed Daniel in an entirely different way. Nowhere did the Bible say a Good Samaritan must be excessively burdened with charm.

"You aren't much given to polite dissembling, are you, my lady?" For an earl's daughter was a lady from the moment of her birth.

She marched over to the sideboard and commenced sawing at a loaf of bread. "I'm not given to any kind of dissembling. You should sit."

"If I sit, I might never rise. I've journeyed from

Oxfordshire, and the storm seems to have followed me every mile."

"Why not tarry in London and wait out the weather?"

Because, had Daniel spent another night in London, he'd have been forced to call on a bishop or two and explain why his very own helpmeet hadn't accompanied him to his new post.

"I am here to assume responsibility for the Haddondale pulpit," Daniel said, moving closer to the fire. A copy of *A Vindication of the Rights of Woman* lay open facedown on the mantel. "I was given to understand filling the position was a matter of some urgency."

Her ladyship swiped a silver knife through a pat of butter and paused before applying the butter to the bread.

"*You're* the new vicar?"

Amusement made this brusque, pretty woman an altogether different creature. She had mischief in her, and humor and secrets, also—where on earth did such thoughts come from?—kisses. Fun, generous kisses.

When she smiled, Lady Kirsten looked like the sort of female who'd pat a fellow's bum—in public.

The cold had made Daniel daft. "Do I have horns or cloven feet to disqualify me from a religious calling, my lady?"

She slapped the butter onto the bread, her movements confident.

"You have gorgeous brown eyes, a lovely nose—though it's a bit red at the moment—and a smile that suggests you might get up to tricks, Mr. Banks. You could also use a trim of that brown hair. Ministers aren't supposed to look dashing. I have two younger sisters who will suffer paroxysms of religious conviction if you're to lead the flock."

Olivia had found Daniel's nose "unfortunate." Daniel found his entire marriage worthy of the same appellation.

Feeling was returning to his feet, and hunger writhed to life along with it. Lady Kirsten passed him the bread without benefit of a plate.

"It's not quite fresh, the bread, that is. The butter was made this morning. I'll fix you some tea."

Daniel took a small bite, then realized he'd forgotten to send grateful sentiments heavenward before he'd done so. *I'm grateful for this bread—also for the company.*

"Your tea, Mr. Banks. Drink up, for I hear sleigh bells."

Daniel downed the hot tea in one glorious go, the sweetness and substance of it fortifying him, much as Lady Kirsten's forthright manner had. She swirled her cloak around her shoulders, then draped his scarf, warm from the fire and redolent of cinnamon, around his neck.

"Let me do the explaining," she said, passing him warmed gloves when he'd bolted his bread and butter. "The sleigh will afford us hot bricks and lap robes, but once we get to Belle Maison, we'll hear nothing but questions. Nicholas is protective, and my sisters are infernally curious."

She crossed the room to bank the fire, then blew out the candles one by one.

Lady Kirsten had been gracious to him, and Daniel wanted to give her something in return for her hospitality. Something real, not mere manners.

An impoverished vicar had little to give besides truth.

"I'm not lost," he said. "I was misdirected by some fellows at the inn. I asked for the way to Belle Maison, and they sent me here. I did not confuse their directions, either, because I made them repeat their words twice."

He'd been taken for a fool, in other words. Again.

"The joke is on them, isn't it?" Lady Kirsten said, blowing out the last candle and enshrouding the cottage in deep gloom. "They might have entertained an angel unaware, and instead they'll have a very uncomfortable moment when it's their turn to shake the new vicar's hand. I will enjoy watching that. My sisters will too."

She wrapped up the bread and butter and stuffed it in a brown brocade bag, then set the teakettle on the mantel.

The sleigh bells went silent, and Daniel sent up a few more words of gratitude. Hot bricks and lap robes would be paradise itself compared to Beelzebub's cold saddle. After he'd tied his horse behind the sleigh, Daniel climbed in beside Lady Kirsten, who wasn't at all shy about sharing the lap robe with him.

And that was a bit of paradise too.

~

You're not George.

Had a woman ever uttered a stupider observation? Kirsten put aside her self-disgust long enough to arrange the lap robe over her knees. Mr. Banks was on her right, Alfrydd, the head lad, on her left, at the reins.

A great deal more warmth was to be had on her right.

They reached Belle Maison in what felt like moments, before Kirsten could mentally rehearse the version of events she'd offer to her siblings. Not lies.

She never bothered lying to them, though they doubt-less often wished she would.

"Come along, Mr. Banks. Alfrydd will spoil your horse rotten, and very likely the countess will do the same with you."

"I'll be but a moment," Mr. Banks said, untying his shaggy black beast from behind the sleigh. Ice beaded the horse's mane and tail, and balls of snow clung to its fetlocks. "Beelzebub has seen me through much this day. I can at least unsaddle him."

A parson who named his horse Beelzebub?

Kirsten's brothers typically handed their horses off with a pat and a treat, then went striding away to the house, there to track mud, make noise, call for their brandies, and otherwise comport themselves like brothers.

Mr. Banks wasn't George, wasn't a brother to Kirsten of any variety but perhaps the theological.

"I'll help," she said, "but you need not fear your reception with the earl. Unless you hurl thunderbolts from the pulpit and insult women in the street, you'll be an improvement over your predecessor."

Mr. Banks led his mount into the dim, relatively cozy stable, the scents of hay and horse bringing their familiar comfort. Kirsten didn't share her sisters' love of all things fine and pretty, though Mr. Banks had an air of careworn male elegance.

"If you'll take the reins, I'll tend to his saddle," Mr. Banks suggested.

Kirsten obliged, stroking her glove over a big, horsey Roman nose. "Why did you name him after an imp?" An imp of Satan.

"He's blessed with high spirits and a fine sense of humor, though little stops him when he settles to a job."

"Your owner treasures you," Kirsten told the horse. The gelding had dark, soft eyes, much like his owner's, and equally fringed in thick lashes. On both man and horse, those eyes had a knowing quality, nothing effeminate or delicate about them.

"I treasure my horse, while Zubbie treasures his fodder," Mr. Banks said, unfastening the girth and removing the saddle but not the pad beneath it.

Mr. Banks's words held such affection, Kirsten envied the horse.

"Have you had him long?" she asked, for there was a bond here, such as Nicholas enjoyed with his mare and George with his gelding. Kirsten's brothers confided in their horses, were comforted by them, and fretted over their horsey ailments as if a child had fallen ill.

Men were sentimental about the oddest things.

"Beelzebub was a gift," Mr. Banks said, taking the reins from Kirsten and looping them over the horse's neck. "A parishioner getting on in years foaled him out and saw that Beelzebub would be too big and too energetic for an older couple. He was given to me when he was a yearling, and we've been famous friends ever since."

Mr. Banks produced a disintegrating lump of sugar from a pocket, and held his hand out to his horse until every evidence of the sugar had been delicately licked away.

He patted the gelding, slid the saddle pad from its back, and led the animal into a loose box boasting a veritable featherbed of straw. The bridle came off, and some sentiments were imparted to the horse as Mr. Banks stroked its muscular neck.

"Alfrydd will see that he's properly groomed," Kirsten said, because under no circumstances would she allow Mr. Banks to announce himself. She and the vicar would storm the sibling citadel together.

Susannah would be especially vulnerable to the kindness in Mr. Banks's eyes, a patient compassion that spoke of woe, sin, and the magnanimity of spirit to accept them both. Della would like the friendliness of those eyes, and Leah, though besotted with Nicholas, was ever one for intelligent conversation.

"He likes the chill taken off his water," Mr. Banks said, giving the horse another pat, "and he's a shy lad around the other fellows."

"Nicholas prides himself on a well-run stable, Mr. Banks. Beelzebub will be fine. He's nigh three-quarter ton of handsome, equine good health, not a sickly boy on his first night at public school."

A shadow crossed Mr. Banks's features, bringing out the weariness a day of winter travel inevitably engendered.

"You heard the lady," he said, tweaking one big, equine ear. "Be a good lad, or I'll deal with you severely." He turned to go, and the horse made a halfhearted attempt to nip at his sleeve, which Mr. Banks ignored.

"Biting is dangerous behavior," Kirsten said as Mr. Banks left the stall and closed the door. "Why didn't you reprimand him?"

She'd wanted to smack the horse. How dare Beelzebub mistreat an owner who plainly loved him?

Mr. Banks pulled his gloves out of his pocket and tugged them on. "He wants me to tarry in his stall, and if I turn 'round and spend another minute shaking my finger in his face, he'll have succeeded, won't he? You must be cold, my lady. May I escort you to the house?"

He winged an arm. Bits of hay and straw stuck to his sleeve, as well as a quantity of dark horse hairs. Kirsten longed to tarry with him in the barn, to put off the moment when she had to share him with her family.

She was not a mischievous horse, however, intent on pursuing selfish schemes that had no hope of bearing fruit. She took Mr. Banks's arm and walked with him out into the gathering darkness.

"Where the hell could she be?" Nicholas Haddonfield, Earl of Bellefonte, muttered, though his countess knew better than to answer. "I've never seen it snow like this so late in the season. Why must Kirsten dash off, playing Marie Antoinette in the wilds of Kent during such rotten weather?"

Outside the library windows, snow came down in pale torrents from the darkening sky. Leah, Countess of Bellefonte, brought her husband a glass of brandy. Nick accepted the glass, then held it to his wife's lips.

"To take the chill off," he murmured, though Leah's offering was doubtless intended to take the edge off his temper—and his worry. Leah obliged by sipping the drink—she was an obliging sort of woman, until she wasn't—then held the glass for him.

"The nice thing about late storms is they're soon forgotten, Nicholas. This time next week we'll be looking for crocuses and checking on the Holland bulbs. When is the new vicar supposed to arrive?"

"I doubt he'll be in evidence until the snow melts." Nick set the drink aside. "Lovey, cuddle up. I need the fortification of your kisses."

How had he managed before his marriage? How had he managed without the constant, generous affection of his spouse? Her patient humoring of his moods? Her wise counsel regarding both family matters and the problems of the earldom?

"I heard sleigh bells before I joined you here," Leah said, tucking into her husband's embrace. "Such a cheerful sound, and you can't blame Kirsten if she wants a little privacy. Della makes her bow this year, and that has everybody rattled."

"Except Della. She has steadier nerves than the lot of us put together. I don't want to go up to Town, though." Nick loathed doing the pretty in Town, in fact.

In this, Nick could understand Kirsten's desire to hide away, to pretend the greater world had ceased to exist and the pages of a single book or the bounds of a single afternoon were all that remained.

"Lady Warne will delight in shepherding Della about," Leah said, kissing Nick's chin.

Leah would be able to reach his cheek if he reclined with her on the blue velvet sofa near the fire—a cheering thought for a beleaguered earl.

"I'll help with the socializing," Leah went on, "and it's only for a few weeks."

Lady Warne being Nick's maternal grandmother, his conscience for much of his youth, and a true friend.

"Lovey, I hate all that folderol—"

Nick's lament was interrupted by Kirsten barreling into the room. Sisters were constitutionally incapable of knocking, and thus deserved whatever awkwardness they stormed in upon. Nick kissed his wife on the mouth soundly to make that point.

Again.

"Bellefonte, Countess, we have a visitor." Kirsten had no need for dramatics in her speech or actions, for tension hummed through her very body. Nick loved her, truly he did, but she was a nocked arrow of emotion and intellect, poised to let fly in unpredictable directions.

"Kirsten, perhaps you'd be good enough to close the door, lest we lose all the heat," Nick suggested, turning loose of his wife.

Kirsten moved aside, and the fellow behind her came more fully into view.

Beside Nick, Leah drew in her breath and shifted closer, as if she needed support to absorb the appearance of their guest. Nick had met Daniel Banks on several occasions, but for the first time, he viewed Mr. Banks from a woman's perspective.

Bloody goddamned good-looking was Vicar Banks. Arrestingly so, with dark eyes that promised understanding of all a lady's woes, affectionate tolerance of her flights and fancies, and tender passion should propriety turn its head for even an instant.

The hell of it was—the confounding, almost humorous hell of it was—Banks had no idea of the impression he made.

"Mr. Banks, greetings," Nick said, extending a hand. "I had thought the storm might delay you."

"My steed is intrepid," Banks said, bowing, then

accepting Nick's hand. "I was told the manse in Haddondale was empty."

"You might have delayed while the weather sorted itself out. It's not like we've been having orgies in the absence of a parson." Nick's observation prompted a snicker from Kirsten. "It's not like we'd *know how* to have orgies, rather. Shall you have a drink, Banks?"

Nick knew all about orgies, simply as part of an Oxford education in this enlightened age. Kirsten extended him a bit of sororal mercy and didn't add that fact to the discussion.

"My feet will not thaw out until Beltane," Banks said. "A drink would be much appreciated."

Without asking, Nick poured Kirsten a small portion of brandy. She wasn't a schoolgirl, she'd been out in the god-awful weather, and small indulgences might bribe her to behave.

Leah would have something to say about serving Kirsten spirits before a guest, but the countess would save her comments for a private moment, thank heavens.

"Lovey, a sip or two for you?"

"No, thank you, Nicholas. I'll let Cook know we have one more for dinner. Welcome, Mr. Banks, and you will not think of biding anywhere except with us for tonight."

Another perfect bow. "You have my thanks, my lady."

Banks had Leah's attention too, something Nick noted with more curiosity than jealousy.

Now would be a fine time for Kirsten to announce that she had to change for dinner or must discuss the latest recipe for syllabub with her sisters, but of course,

Kirsten took a seat on the very sofa where Nick might have cuddled with his countess.

"Was the journey down from Oxfordshire trying?" Nick asked, passing Banks a healthy tot and topping up his own.

"The weather didn't help, but traveling always gives a man time to think. Has the former pastor been absent long?"

Not long enough. "Less than a month," Nick said, and because the Earls of Bellefonte had held the Haddondale living for centuries, Nick blathered on.

While Kirsten sat like a cat on the sofa and lapped up every word.

"Our previous vicar was old-fashioned," Nick said. "Full of damnation and judgment and the fires of hell, though we grew used to his style." Hard to cadge a Sunday morning nap when somebody insisted on yelling for much of the service, though.

"He was also old," Kirsten volunteered. "He didn't listen well, and his gout plagued him without mercy."

Banks managed to look elegant, even in stained riding boots, a wrinkled cravat, and a coat that needed taking in at the seams. His cheekbones conveyed derring-do, his long-fingered hands, sensitivity. What a damned silly waste on a country vicar.

"My predecessor suffered hearing problems?" Banks asked.

"He didn't *listen* well," Kirsten clarified, while Nick felt the tension of a conversational bow being drawn back right to the archer's chin.

When Banks ought to have complimented Nick on the library's appointments, or the brandy, or the fine collection of books the old earl had gone into debt amassing, Banks instead turned those dark eyes on Kirsten.

"Might you give me an example, Lady Kirsten? One doesn't want unfortunate history to repeat itself."

A miracle occurred in the Belle Maison library, while Nick looked on and sipped his brandy. Kirsten Haddonfield, Witch without Broomstick, engaged a guest in civil conversation. No hidden meanings, no veiled barbs, no slightly outrageous testing of the boundaries of propriety.

"Mr. Clackengeld suffers gout the same as Vicar did," Kirsten said, "though Mr. Clackengeld works in the livery, so he's out in all weather. When he asked Vicar how the knee was, he got a lecture about suffering giving us an opportunity for humility."

Banks considered his drink, then turned such a smile on Kirsten as would have felled Byron and all his lovelies at once.

"You didn't allow it to end there, did you, my lady?"

That smile was sweet and invited confidences—not a scintilla of flirtation about it.

"I commented more loudly than I should have that humility is a virtue best learned by example," Kirsten replied.

Some fairy prince had snatched Kirsten Haddonfield away and, in her place, left a pretty, smiling, shy young woman. The shy part, Nick had long suspected. Kirsten lobbed Latin phrases into her speech, marched about with unladylike purpose, and dispatched her opinions like a gunnery sergeant aiming shot into the enemy's cavalry charge.

In short, she repelled boarders with the few effective weapons at a lady's disposal.

Banks had needed nothing more than a smile and a certain relaxed, conspiratorial air to win a morsel of Kirsten's trust.

"Interesting approach, Lady Kirsten. What about you, my lord?" Banks asked. "Have you guidance to render as I approach this post? I've spent my life in Little Weldon, but for my years at Oxford, and my flock and I were familiar from long acquaintance. What of the people here?"

One could not lie to this fellow, not when that smile still beamed forth unchecked.

"We're the usual sort," Nick said. "Mostly hardworking, a few slackers; mostly kind, a few grouches. We aren't given to frivolity, but neither are we a flock of Presbyterians crows, poking our beaks into our neighbor's business. You should get on well with us if you're halfway decent regarding matters of faith and can dance a Sir Roger de Coverly with the occasional spinster."

"Sir Roger and I are well acquainted." Banks wasn't even looking at Kirsten, and Nick knew his sister was already mentally parading about the spring assembly beside a man who had no grasp of flirtation.

Nick went on to describe the various illuminati of the community, such as a rural village had illuminati, and all the while he mentally wrestled with a question.

Why was it the first fellow to cut through the thicket of Kirsten Haddonfield's social thorns was a poor, tired, nearly haggard man of the cloth, and a *married* man of the cloth at that?

And was this a positive development—Nick had begun to despair of Kirsten's prospects, to dread even sharing meals with her—or was it a harbinger of disaster?

Two

OLIVIA WOULD HAVE HATED THE HADDONDALE MANSE, and for that reason, Daniel viewed it charitably, despite the stench of mildew pervading every room.

"You cannot stay here," Fairly said, his boot heels ringing against the empty parlor's floor. "The place reeks of creeping damp, the roof leaks in two of the bedrooms, and the old bastard didn't leave you a single lump of coal."

An angry viscount could refer to the former vicar as an old bastard. Daniel envied his brother-in-law the casual contempt of the epithet—among other things.

"I'll sleep in the study," Daniel said. "Or in the kitchen if there's no help living in. The earl can send over some wood until the coal man happens by."

"Banks, this place will not serve," Fairly snapped. Daniel's sister had married a beautiful man: tall, blond, with a demon genius for trade and the honed facial topography of an ascetic. Daniel did not pretend to understand his brother-in-law in the general case, or in this specific instance.

"Vicars reside in vicarages," Daniel explained. "I'll

have a roof over my head, I'll be close to the church, and the village folk will know where to find me. I fail to see a problem."

Daniel's single trunk occupied the middle of the parlor, like a sarcophagus in some musty museum's back room.

Fairly planted his aristocratic arse on the sum of Daniel's worldly goods, which consisted mostly of much-mended clothing and a number of diaries written by Daniel's own father.

"You're to be vicar of Haddondale," Fairly said. "A vicar is the spiritual compass of the community. His surrounds must indicate the respect due his position. Your predecessor clearly was not respected nor was he apparently worthy of respect."

Elsewhere in the house, the women were banging open doors and cupboards, making the sort of racket women made when they invaded unconquered territory.

A headache at the base of Daniel's skull throbbed along in counterpoint to the noise from above stairs.

"My predecessor was not young," Daniel said. "His missus was not young either, and I daresay their staff was either poorly supervised or also suffering impaired faculties. Some soap and water, a good airing, proper fires in the—"

A shriek filled the empty dwelling, and Fairly was off the trunk like a boy leaving catechism class on a pretty spring morning.

"Nothing's amiss," Lady Kirsten yelled down the stairs. "Her ladyship took a fright, is all."

Fairly was halfway up the steps, while Daniel,

who'd occupied a country vicarage for most of his life, followed more slowly. Mouse droppings produced that sort of shriek, or the actual sight of a mouse could do it. Rats, perhaps because they were larger, produced fury and loathing in women instead of that startled, frightened response.

"I am losing my mind," Daniel muttered to the empty house.

The Countess of Bellefonte stormed out of the bedroom at the top of the stairs. She was a tall brunette with a pretty smile and an unfashionably affectionate regard for her earl, but at present, she was apparently in the grip of a pressing desire to quit the premises.

Fairly steadied her with a hand on each arm. "Calm breaths, my lady. You're not in danger."

"I am in danger of burning down this house," she shot back. "Nicholas will hear about this, and, Mr. Banks, you most assuredly cannot bide here."

Lady Kirsten closed the bedroom door and edged into the corridor. "We found a bat, Mr. Banks. Her ladyship thought it was dead, but was in error."

"They hibernate," Daniel said. "They live largely by eating insects, and in winter they'd starve without proper sustenance, so a good long rest is just the—"

Lady Kirsten examined her gloves. Lady Bellefonte peered at Daniel as if he'd spoken in Mandarin, while Fairly...

Fairly's gaze was pitying.

A man who'd parented a small boy for five years naturally fell into the habit of tucking biology lessons here and there throughout the day. Thus, Daniel had shared a child's innocent delight in life's wondrous designs, and kept a part of his own heart and mind young while doing so.

Daniel would have no need for such biology lessons here at Haddondale.

He endured an abrupt sympathy for the little bat, who'd likely woken in a daze, famished, lonely, disoriented, women shrieking at him, and spring nowhere to be found.

"You will stay with us until Bellefonte can set this place to rights," Lady Bellefonte said, wrenching herself from Fairly's grasp. "Lady Kirsten, come along this instant."

Lady Kirsten brushed between the menfolk, a hint of meadow grass and mint gracing the chilly air. She shot Daniel a look that might well have cindered the entire vicarage.

Lady Bellefonte had been upset, frightened, and indignant, while Lady Kirsten had been plainly furious.

Daniel was at a loss to fathom why. Surely not on *his* behalf?

"As I was saying," Fairly began. "A vicar's habiliment, his dwelling, his horse, his speech, his everything must reinforce the gravity of his station. Your horse fails that test miserably, your clothes are ready to fall off of you, and this vicarage is a disgrace. Your speech alone preserves your dignity, Banks. What say you?"

Habiliment, from the French *habit*. Danny had an excellent ear for languages. Did Fairly know that?

The vicarage had been neglected. Cobwebs festooned the corners of the ceiling, and the window at the end of the corridor was dimmed by copious flyspecking. Enough light came through to illuminate a spider, busy at her morning meal.

"I would have managed well enough here," Daniel said.

The front door slammed, ensuring that Daniel and his brother-in-law had privacy, but for the sleeping bats and the busy spider.

Fairly was a physician by training, though he'd long abandoned that calling for the pleasures of trade and viscount-ing—also marriage to Daniel's sister.

"You think you've entered some twilight status," Fairly said, "where the privileges of bachelorhood are restored to you without fear the mamas will match you to their daughters. You can eat at odd hours, wear the same neckcloth for three straight days, and neglect to clean your teeth if you've stayed too late at your reading. Don't do it, Banks."

A true physician probably never lost the tendency to prescribe and diagnose.

"I change my neckcloth regularly and take excellent care of my teeth," Daniel replied. "The ladies are doubtless expecting us to join them in the sleigh. Shall we remove my trunk to the porch?"

"We shall not. *Footmen* remove trunks to porches, Banks. Porters, grooms, those sorts of fellows risk falling on their backsides in the snow and mud before the ladies." Fairly jaunted down the stairs, lecturing as he went. "You are a man of God, the insurance provided by the Church of England that at least one gentleman resides in every village worthy of a house of worship. You do not—*Daniel, come down.*"

Daniel followed at a decorous pace, not because the spiritual leader of a rural community was supposed to trundle about at the speed of a monk in the middle of a funeral procession.

Daniel moved slowly because he was simply exhausted by the effort of making conversation and remaining upright.

"Am I to reside with *you*, Fairly?" he asked.

One grew used to Fairly's eyes, which were mismatched—one blue, one green. One grew used to his nimble intellect and his tolerant view of the world's foibles, but one did not grow used to his pity.

"I live two hours from here on a fast horse when the roads are dry, Banks. That would hardly do either."

Fairly would have gone charging out into cold, brilliant sunshine, but Daniel had had enough.

"How is Danny?" he asked.

Fairly remained with his back to Daniel, one hand on the door latch. He turned slowly, his expression as blank as a marble saint's.

"Danny is well."

Letty would have passed along news if the boy had been ill. "Is he *happy*?"

The starch went out of Fairly's posture. He ran a gloved hand through longish blond hair. This was the viscount's version of a fit of exasperation—also stalling.

"Are *you* happy, Daniel? That's what the boy will ask me."

"If I were a better man, Fairly, I'd pity you the awkwardness of your role, but that child's happiness means everything to me. *Is he happy?*"

"He is…less unhappy. He asked me to give you this." Fairly produced a folded epistle addressed in pencil to Uncle Daniel. "He gave me that when Letty was out of the room, and I haven't read it."

"Did Danny ask to accompany you?" Could the child bear to tell his mother and stepfather that he missed the uncle who'd raised him since infancy?

"I did not inform Danny of the exact hour of my departure. Consider this, though, Banks: If Danny asks me how you're faring, I will have to report to him that you're skinny, you barely speak, and your hair needs a trim. Worse, you'd be content to welcome him for a visit in a manse overrun with bats, mice, and strange smells."

Fairly stormed off, while Daniel absorbed that unexpected blow.

Danny was a little boy, and *all* boy. He'd love a place full of bats, mice, and strange smells. How could Fairly, now Danny's physical custodian and once a small child himself, not grasp such a simple aspect of normal boyhood?

❦

Kirsten had been in the company of handsome men for most of her life. Her brothers—Ethan, Nicholas, Beckman, Adolphus, and George—were handsome men. George was a stunner in breeches and boots— and probably even more impressive out of them.

Mr. Banks's good looks did not account for Kirsten's fascination with him, not entirely. He sat at the music room's escritoire, sunlight falling across his shoulders and turning his hair reddish sable, while Susannah thumped away at a Mozart sonata.

"You're rushing, Suze," Della murmured without looking up from her embroidery hoop. "You need to save back for the finale. Keep your powder dry, so to speak, or the arpeggios will be harried rather than impressive."

"Then you play it," Susannah said, rising in the middle of a phrase.

Mr. Banks's pencil stilled, then crossed something out. His pencil remained poised above the paper, his gaze focused in the direction of the stable across the garden.

"One of you play the cadence, please," Kirsten said.

Della took the bench Susannah had abandoned, and played from the middle of the phrase to the end. Mr. Banks's pencil started moving again.

Until Della stumbled on the infernal arpeggios.

"Mr. Banks, will you join me in the library?" Kirsten asked, setting aside her cutwork. "I'd like your advice on my choice of a book of sermons."

Della attempted the same passage with no greater success, while Susannah's consternation was writ plain on her face. Improving tomes of any sort did not figure prominently in Kirsten's preferred reading. Bless Susannah, she decided in favor of sisterly discretion.

Mr. Banks was on his feet, lap desk in hand. "The library, you say? That would be agreeable. The company of books soothes the soul."

He nearly pelted from the room, as did Kirsten, but he stopped halfway down the corridor.

"If you'll pardon my rudeness, my lady, once we've chosen you a book, I'll retire to my room and hope inspiration strikes me between now and Sunday."

"Hang your rudeness, Mr. Banks. Is the countess in the library?"

He took off again, in the direction of the stairs. "With his lordship."

Probably as snug as a pair of hibernating bats on Nicholas's favorite blue sofa, then.

"What about the estate office?" Kirsten asked, for a man intent on composing his inaugural sermon needed peace and quiet.

"Mr. George Haddonfield has come over to copy ledgers or sort pamphlets or some such."

"I'm surprised Elsie let George out of her sight." Why hadn't George made his bow before his sisters?

Banks started up the stairs. "I beg your pardon?"

Kirsten caught up to him easily, suggesting he wasn't hurrying away from her, exactly.

"George is newly married, and he and his lady are quite besotted. Quite."

Which was touching, surprising, and a horrible betrayal. George was the last sibling Kirsten had expected to lose to holy matrimony.

"Besotted," Banks said, as if he were choosing among a selection of hair shirts. "Besotted is a trial to behold for those not similarly afflicted. What gave away my inability to concentrate?"

"You broke the tip of your pencil twice, you scratched out more than you wrote, and you developed a fascination with a garden that is mostly bracken and melting snow. I know a place where you won't be disturbed."

Kirsten should have offered a sanctuary to him sooner, but she valued what few retreats she'd been able to fashion.

"I'd like that," Banks said, "a place where I won't

be disturbed. I usually enjoy working on sermons, but one wants a maiden effort to be memorable or even impressive, and inspiration has apparently not followed me down from Oxfordshire."

This mattered to him, this fifteen minutes of scriptural droning most people dozed through on Sunday mornings.

"Up one more floor," Kirsten said, pausing to give a footman instructions as she passed the family wing. "The room will be cold for a time, but quiet. I find quiet and solitude matter more than heat, more than comfort, when I'm in a certain mood."

"Was that why I found you alone in the tenant cottage?" Mr. Banks asked.

Kirsten had underestimated him, assuming goodness equated with a lack of perceptivity or an unwillingness to confront perceptions. To her surprise, Kirsten liked that he'd ask, liked that he'd turn his perceptivity on *her*.

She rounded the final landing on the way to the third floor.

"You found me in a former tenant's cottage," she said, "one that used to house several active children. I offered to make it habitable for a successor tenant because I enjoy fitting a space to the best use of its occupants."

Banks paused on the landing, the air noticeably colder in this part of the house. A portrait hung in the tall space of the stairwell.

"Your mother?" he asked. The lady was blond, smiling, beautiful, and cradling a baby in her arms. The infant wore a christening gown—all lace and light—and an angelic smile.

"I'm told Mama is holding me," Kirsten said, "though how I remained still long enough to accommodate a portraitist, I do not know."

Mr. Banks studied the painting far more intently than Kirsten could bear to. "Your brother explained to me about the former tenant of the cottage. My flock did me a particular insult when they sent me there, didn't they?"

"Come along, Mr. Banks," Kirsten said, taking him by the arm. "You have years to learn what mischief Haddondale's villagers can get up to on an idle afternoon."

He was a big man, but not as solid as, say, Nicholas. No human was as solid as Nicholas, though the plow stock resembled him in some particulars. Mr. Banks was leaner, but Kirsten suspected he had no less strength.

"The former tenant was a fallen woman," Mr. Banks said, accompanying Kirsten up the stairs. "When did she vacate the premises?"

Perceptive and analytical. No bats in the attic for Mr. Banks. "Addy Chalmers left the first of the week to join the household of a cousin in Shropshire. She did what was necessary and available to support her children, Mr. Banks, and her situation wasn't entirely of her own making."

A man had been involved in Addy's initial fall from grace, as a man was often at the root of a woman's worst troubles.

Kirsten had given Nicholas's workers two days to get a plank floor down in the cottage, then she'd set about making the space habitable. Her family had avoided asking her when she'd finish with the project, and she'd not volunteered a date.

"Did the villagers know of this unfortunate woman's departure?" Banks asked as Kirsten led him to the nursery wing.

"How should I—?" She came to a halt outside the schoolroom. Her sister Nita and Nita's new husband, Tremaine St. Michael, had sent Addy and her brood to Shropshire in Mr. St. Michael's commodious traveling coach. "I doubt anybody knew. Addy's departure was quietly arranged, and we're not sharing her destination with our neighbors."

Mr. Banks wore calm the way some women wore their favorite shawls, as much a part of him as his voice or his hands.

"The fellows at the Queen's Harebell were mean-spirited then," he concluded mildly. "I don't mind a jest at my expense, but for the woman who lived there, my arrival would have been awkward, indeed."

Kirsten opened the door to the largest nursery suite, the one she'd spent years in as a child. What sort of vicar fretted over a prostitute's dignity?

"You can preach to the faithful about hypocrisy and judgment," Kirsten said, "about casting the first stone, though it's a daring place to start. You might want to work in here."

She led him into the schoolroom, which had remained unchanged for years, as if waiting for the arrival of more little scholars. Nicholas and Leah used a smaller group of rooms for their firstborn, one on the same floor as the earl's suite.

Sharp sunlight illuminated a fine coating of dust on the mirror over the fireplace, but the rest of the room was as Kirsten had last left it—a small table with small chairs in one corner; a larger desk in the other; the thick, stained rug before the hearth.

A tartan blanket was draped over the settee, a battered footstool sat before the settee, and a spare lap desk had been tucked beneath it. Kirsten had also left a sewing box under the settee, and a copy of Shakespeare's sonnets graced the footstool.

So that's where I left it. Susannah had been asking.

Kirsten's knees knew the rough texture of the rug's wool, her backside recalled intimately how hard the chairs were on a fine spring day. She generally ignored those memories, but Mr. Banks's presence infused them with uncomfortable vigor.

"You can conjure a fine sermon here, Mr. Banks. You'll have peace, solitude, and a lovely view of the pastures. I've asked that the fire be lit and braziers and a tray sent up. I can even put a cat in here with you."

For cats, while independent and regal, were the quintessence of domesticity. Mr. Banks struck Kirsten as a man much in need of domesticity.

"A cat won't be necessary, but your consideration is appreciated." He smiled slightly at the scene of Kirsten's earliest attempts at scholarship. His smiles were like the rest of him—quiet, sweet, and a little sad. Attractive, but not as easy to look on as one first thought.

"If you tell me I'll make somebody a wonderful wife, I will slap you, Mr. Banks." Kirsten had no idea where that threat had come from, but then she was often at the mercy of remarks she hadn't planned.

His smile changed, acquiring an intriguing hint of…*mischief*? Or—astounding notion—approval.

"I think you would write an extraordinary sermon,"

he said. "About hypocrisy and judgment and courage. My remarks will be more prosaic, I'm sure, and bear no relation to your marital prospects."

Sunday was two days off, and Mr. Banks hadn't anything prepared. What had occupied his mind on the long ride down from Oxfordshire?

"Why not use a sermon you wrote for your last post?" Kirsten suggested. "Surely you have a few party pieces suitable for when the bishop comes calling?"

"Interesting analogy. I hadn't thought to use old material."

He had no guile, no instinct to conserve his resources for eventual hardship. Kirsten abruptly could not stand to be in the same room with him.

"I'll leave you to your Scripture, then."

He set his writing paraphernalia on the desk by the windows, the coldest but best-lit space in the room.

"My thanks, Lady Kirsten."

She popped a curtsy and left Mr. Banks to his musings. Despite Kirsten's sudden need to be away from him, she'd come back to check on him, as if he were her guest and she his hostess.

Part of what drew her to Mr. Banks was the sense that, like Kirsten, he was going slowly mad. He replied when spoken to, he complimented the countess on the meals served, he'd turned pages for Susannah at the pianoforte last night, and he had competently handled the bass part of the hymns they'd sung.

And on a handful of the infernal mopey ballads too.

And yet Mr. Banks exuded a sense of loneliness that called to Kirsten, and that was the essence of his attractiveness. He was in mourning, she knew not for what or whom. She'd look in on him, to make sure he was comfortable and to discuss his sermon.

Moral topics were great fun to debate, and even spiritual matters could hold Kirsten's interest. What intrigued her though, what had her smiling as she passed three footmen on the stairs, was the notion that Mr. Banks would make the right someone a wonderful husband.

"Daniel was the perfect husband," Fairly said, picking up Nick's favorite hammer. "He was the perfect brother, the perfect father for Danny, the perfect vicar, even. This is the largest hammer I've had the pleasure to handle."

Nick pushed his spectacles up his nose, for he was trying to sketch a birdhouse to make for his recently married sister, Nita.

"If I'm to use that hammer on your hard head," Nick said, "it needs to be stout. Banks is not the perfect vicar. I assumed Banks was married, but why didn't you tell me he's estranged from his wife?"

Fairly prowled around Nick's woodworking shop as a cat stuck in a library prowls from window to window, switching its tail. The viscount was always subtly agitated unless in the company of his lady.

"I'm not sure Daniel is estranged from the fair Olivia, though she's estranged from him." Fairly peered over Nick's shoulder. "What are you attempting to draw?"

The viscount smelled pleasantly of sandalwood, and he was like a small boy who had to touch what interested him.

"Get out of my light," Nick growled, elbowing his friend. "I need room to think. Explain what you mean about Banks. If he's on the outs with his wife, he should certainly know it."

The villagers would soon know of it too, and wouldn't that make for lively churchyard gossip? On the page, Nick had drawn a prosaic birdhouse, like a Bavarian cottage with windows, a front door, and two chimneys.

Boring, but pretty enough. Banks's looks were not boring, they were attractive. Alluring even, some sort of celestial joke, or a penance for the ladies of the flock.

"You've probably heard most of this," Fairly said, hoisting himself to sit on Nick's worktable, "but here's what Banks faces: His sister Letty, my own dear wife, was taken advantage of by her papa's curate when she was quite young, and Danny is the result of that misadventure. Banks and his wife raised the boy as their own, a common enough fiction in otherwise upright families, and one undertaken in Danny's case very successfully."

Fairly clearly wanted the telling of this story over with, and Nick sensed much was being left out. That Banks and his wife had deceived the upright Christians of Little Weldon about the boy's patrimony was probably a detail.

"Hands off my good eraser," Nick said, snatching the rubber from Fairly's grasp and smacking his lordship's knuckles. "The next part I can guess: Letty falls in love with the handsome, dashing, filthy rich Viscount Fairly, and is now in a position to quietly acknowledge the boy and shower coin upon him. What has that to do with Banks's wife? Vicars' wives are supposed to be the loyal sort, reliable sopranos, handy with the comforting platitudes, and good at baking, knitting, and embroidery."

"Olivia threatened Letty with disclosure of Danny's origins," Fairly said, "which would have cost Daniel his post, if not his calling. The child would be doubly cursed by scandal in that case, so Letty found ways to pay Olivia enough to keep her silent."

Nick ripped out the page he'd been working on. Cottages put him in mind of the Chalmers woman, whom a considerate in-law had thankfully relocated to Shropshire.

"If you tell me Banks extorted money from his sister, I'll beat you soundly, then start on him, for he'd not be welcome in any pulpit I support. What's the last thing you'd expect to see made into a birdhouse?"

Fairly snatched up three small stones Nick used as paperweights and began to juggle them.

"A bordello. The child—Danny—has been restored to Letty's keeping, and Banks has left the village where anybody might have connected the puzzle pieces. The money Letty sent to her sister-in-law has been given back to Letty, for Olivia, of course, had kept her extortion secret from her husband."

The blank page stared back at Nick while churchyard gossip nattered in his imagination like so many crows.

"Does Banks think to stash this mercenary helpmeet on some Scottish island?"

The weights whirled through the air faster. "I have no idea what Daniel thinks these days about anything. He's always been a quiet, self-contained fellow, and he's grown worse since last I saw him."

"Perhaps he needs to sort matters out with his wife. Relocate to America or Peru. I'm sure Christians are in high demand in the wilderness. I'll pay his fare, cheerfully."

Fairly caught two of the rocks. The third smacked onto Nick's blank page.

"That's a generous offer, Nicholas, but I doubt Banks would leave the boy's ambit at this point. You're in a mood. What's amiss?"

Nick closed his sketchbook. Fairly was a nuisance and an irritant, but he was also a friend. When Nick had needed an expert medical opinion—and he had, more than once—Fairly had been unhesitating and generous with his expertise.

"Kirsten has taken notice of your Mr. Banks."

"Lady Kirsten is the noticing sort." Fairly collected the third rock and set all three in a neat line at the top of Nick's workbench. "I'd be surprised if a full-grown, well-mannered, male houseguest in good looks didn't gain her notice."

"Not that sort of notice. Kirsten dislikes people in general, but men in particular get the rough edge of her tongue."

Fairly hopped off the worktable, nimble as a fox. "Intelligent women are in a difficult position when they're also saddled with high birth and fine looks. You can trust Daniel, however. He's the last man who'd take advantage of an innocent."

"Because he himself was taken advantage of by that wife?"

"Because Daniel is genuinely good, genuinely honorable. He would no more take advantage of Lady

Kirsten's friendship than he would have imposed on Addy Chalmers."

"A saint as well as a martyr," Nick groused, rising from his stool. The workshop was at the back of the stable and not exactly cozy, but it was quiet—mostly. "I'm heartily sick of damnation and Doomsday. My sisters became prone to megrims on Sundays, and my own Sabbath health was growing precarious too."

"You won't have that problem with Daniel," Fairly said, once again taking up Nick's hammer. "He's the soul of kindness, tolerant of the elderly and the very young, and his sermons are short and full of forgiveness and Christian charity. Could you make a smaller version of this hammer?"

"Of course. Why?"

"For the boy, Danny. We've yet to find much that interests him, and he's too young to be kept shut away in the schoolroom all day."

Nick stretched, hands braced on the small of his back.

"The child needs storybooks and toy soldiers. No boy should be shut away in the schoolroom all day, not even a very big boy. You've yet to tell me what Banks will do about his wife."

"He's sent her off to visit her family in the north, and that has served for the nonce." Fairly, being married to Olivia's victim, had probably advocated for criminal charges and transportation.

"Has Mrs. Banks remained docilely tatting lace in the West Riding? If she's the disagreeable sort, then her relatives are likely tired of her. I'll send her to Canada and Banks to Peru. Seems like a fine plan to me."

Fairly was considering juggling the hammer.

Nick could sense this by the angle of the viscount's blond brows.

"The problem is the boy," Fairly said, letting Nick snatch the hammer, but then taking down an awl instead.

Nick took the awl from him too. "You could put your eye out with that, Fairly."

"I'm not a child, Nicholas."

And apparently never had been, for what English peer was raised without benefit of toy soldiers?

"I cannot like this situation with your Mr. Banks," Nick said, hanging the awl on its hook and shrugging into his greatcoat. "An unhappy wife is seldom quiet in her misery."

"She need not be quiet, she need only stay far away for a long, long time."

"How will Banks, a penurious, kindhearted, tolerant Christian sort, make certain that happens?"

Fairly let Nick hold the door for him. "Prayer, I suppose."

Now that was interesting, because Banks had been under Nick's roof for several long days, and other than grace before meals, Nick had yet to catch the good vicar at his prayers.

Not even once.

Three

THE SABBATH RITUAL NO LONGER COMFORTED DANIEL, which in itself added to his unease. For nearly a decade, he'd prepared for the Sunday morning service the same way—no breakfast, plain tea, his sermon notes, and silent reflection as the sun came up and the household stirred to life.

In Little Weldon, that had meant the maid of all work putting together Olivia's and Danny's trays while Daniel used the warmth of the kitchen to aid his devotions. The kitchen had been quiet and welcoming in a way the rest of the house hadn't been.

At Belle Maison, breakfast was a lavish meal served with endless helpings of chatter in a bright, east-facing parlor.

"Nita writes from London that arrangements for her wedding journey are almost completed," young Lady Della reported. "I wish I were going with them."

"They don't wish you were going with them," Lady Susannah replied. "It's a wedding journey, after all. Pass the pot, Della, if there's anything left in it."

"But to see Paris!" Lady Della marveled.

She went off on a flight about the great capitals, and art, and culture, while all Daniel wanted was quiet. Across the table, Lady Kirsten caught his eye, raised her toast point in a silent salute, and winked.

Daniel stirred his tea, though he didn't take it with sugar or milk on Sundays. How had Lady Kirsten divined his thoughts? Divined his mood when he himself couldn't decipher it?

"What of you, Mr. Banks?" the earl asked from the head of the table. "Do you look forward to Sunday services, or does the celebrant admit to a certain relief when his duties are over for another week?"

The entire pretty, chattering table turned to regard Daniel, like so many colorful birds flitting about the park would perch on a high branch when a rambunctious child gamboled by.

"I enjoy my Sunday duties," Daniel said, though Sunday was the least of a vicar's responsibilities, "and doubly so today because I will meet my new congregation, and in such fine company too."

Bellefonte smiled, for he was peacock-proud of his womenfolk. "I share that company with you begrudgingly, Banks. A shame you won't meet our sister Lady Nita and her new spouse."

"This is the lady traveling to Paris?" Daniel asked.

Lady Della, predictably, blessedly, snatched the conversational reins and did not give them up for the duration of the meal. As luck or a mischievous Deity would have it, Daniel was wedged into the sleigh next to Lady Kirsten for the journey to the village.

A mercy and a torment, for reasons Daniel didn't examine.

"Next Sunday morning, you take a tray in your room," she murmured as she tucked the lap robe around her. "They'll natter you to Bedlam otherwise."

"One doesn't want to appear rude to one's host and hostess," Daniel said as the coachman gave the horses leave to walk on.

"You ate nothing, Mr. Banks, and you had no sermon prepared even forty-eight hours ago. Nicholas seems to think your duties consist of an hour of playing dress up on Sundays, and you did not correct him."

The horse trotted along, the cold more tiresome than invigorating. Beside Daniel, Lady Kirsten appeared not at all affected by the elements, the company, anything.

This woman disquieted Daniel in ways that had only a little to do with the greater disruption in his life. If he'd come across her in Little Weldon, she would have disquieted him there too.

"Must you always be scolding somebody, Lady Kirsten? I would not expect an earl to comprehend the routine of a vicar's days any more than I'd know how to be an earl."

"You'd manage," she said, making that sound like either another scold or a dire prediction.

She'd manage. "You are a grouch, Lady Kirsten. I haven't met a genuine grouch in some time."

The notion cheered Daniel, and proved in a small way that he was *not* a grouch. His observation apparently cheered the lady as well.

"I am a grouch," she said, patting his sleeve. "Good of you to notice. My family acts as if there's something wrong with me because I am honest and unsentimental. You have the right of it. I cannot change who I am."

Had she tried to change who she was? "A grouch is not happy company," Daniel said as the sleigh turned onto the Haddondale village square. "Or perhaps she's simply not happy?"

He could ask Lady Kirsten that in the brisk air, the church coming into view. The question was vicarly—in this setting.

"Are you happy, Mr. Banks?" she retorted. "You say I'm a grouch, meaning I deal in truth rather than appearances and gossip. What do you deal in?"

"Not gossip." Which left…appearances? "You deal in honesty, my lady, but what of kindness? Has it no place in your scheme? Truth can wound, cripple even, and should be wielded with caution."

Olivia had taken it upon herself to bludgeon Danny with the unvarnished truth of his origins, for example.

The horse slowed, though before the sleigh could pull into the churchyard, the party in the earl's traveling coach had to disembark.

"This business of honesty and kindness is not a philosophical debate to you, is it?" Lady Kirsten asked.

The word *philosophy* came from roots that implied a love of knowledge. Danny had enjoyed learning where words came from, how the Latin and Greek were related.

"Truth and kindness are not mere concepts to you either," Daniel said as the sleigh inched forward. "I like that about you. You do not mine a topic for clever remarks you can toss out in company. You embrace a matter with your intellect, and wring from it what truths or contradictions it has."

Lady Kirsten also knew how to find a man a bit of solitude to compose his sermons, and knew that a tea tray graced with a few lemon biscuits made Scripture ever so much more palatable of a chilly afternoon.

Interesting combination in a gently bred lady.

"My siblings will take forever to move away from the coach now that they've started socializing," Lady Kirsten said, disentangling herself from the lap robe.

She alluded to her sisters, who were indeed visiting merrily with other women, not even stepping away from the earl's coach in their eagerness to greet their neighbors. Daniel climbed out on his side and came around to offer Lady Kirsten assistance.

The congregation hadn't noticed him yet, so he spoke softly as he handed her out of the sleigh.

"Whatever unkind truth you've been dealt, I'm sorry for it, my lady."

She stepped down from the coach and kept hold of Daniel's hand, even when she'd gained solid footing. He'd apparently surprised the lady who regularly ambushed others with her blunt speech.

Lady Kirsten's grip on his hand remained snug. She blinked twice, staring straight ahead at the ladies chatting and smiling beside the much larger coach.

Then she tucked her scarf up higher, so it wrapped over her mouth. The gesture hid what Daniel saw only because he was studying her expression for some hint that she'd heard him.

"Thank you, Mr. Banks. Good luck with your sermon."

She strode off, abandoning him as the earl's conveyance lumbered away and exposed Daniel to the notice of his new neighbors.

"Mr. Banks!" Lord Bellefonte called. "Come meet the good souls of Haddondale, for they are eager to meet you."

Lady Kirsten marched into the church as if her brother hadn't spoken. Daniel had no choice but to allow the earl and the countess to introduce him around in the cold, sunny churchyard, until the organist began the prelude.

Daniel let himself be hustled into the building by his pastoral committee chair, and from there, routine took over. Vestments, Book of Common Prayer, a kindly, cheerful expression—Daniel assembled them all in the usual order and began the service as he'd begun hundreds of others.

Except this service was different. Lady Kirsten sat in the front row, a pretty blond well past girlhood. She occupied the same location Olivia often had, and she had Olivia's faint air of chronic vexation too.

The similarities ended there. As Daniel called his new flock to worship, he was plagued with a question, which he doubted even the forthright Lady Kirsten would answer:

What about his final observation regarding the unkindnesses dealt her had inspired the lady to blinking back tears?

⤖

For Kirsten, Sunday services were a ritual to be endured. At best, the Sabbath was a time to collect thoughts, to sit for a while on a pretty spring morning and admire sunlight coming through the church's two stained-glass windows.

Kirsten had long ago cut off any discourse with her Maker, other than before meals or when a family member was imperiled. She occasionally exhorted God to keep her siblings safe or to look after the crops and livestock, because experience had proven even the Almighty occasionally forgot the basics.

From the opening hymn, however, this Sunday morning was different. The church was packed to the rafters with a flock bent on inspecting its new shepherd, and the congregation was in good voice.

Above the droning basses and warbling sopranos, a ringing baritone led a march through melodic scriptural sentiments. Mr. Banks had a fine voice, Kirsten had known that, but he also had something—a presence—a joy in his office that enlivened even the tired strains of Mr. Wesley's music.

And—miraculous to relate—his sermon was short enough that Nicholas did not doze off halfway through.

Neither did Kirsten. Somebody deserved a moral birching this morning for directing a stranger to Addy Chalmers's cottage when that sojourner had asked for guidance to the earl's home.

Mr. Banks merely thanked the congregation for welcoming him so warmly, pledged his best efforts as their spiritual leader, and invited them to call upon him in any capacity he might be of aid or comfort.

Not a hint of a scold, not even an innuendo. What sort of vicar would they take Mr. Banks for if meekness and short sermons were his return when buffoons made sport of him?

Kirsten fairly bellowed the words to "Come, O Thou Traveler Unknown" as the service concluded, anger taking a familiar hold of her mood. Harold Abernathy shifted from foot to foot in the next pew back, and Robert Harker seemed to have developed a fascination with the back of Goody Popwright's bonnet.

A bonnet Goody had been wearing since last year's spring assembly.

Oh. Oh, yes indeed, *come, o thou traveler unknown.*

"We're supposed to share the hymnal," Susannah hissed at the end of the sixth verse. Mercifully, they'd leave the remaining half-dozen verses for some other occasion.

"We're also not supposed to flip back to the Song of Solomon during the reading," Della added from Susannah's other side. "Shall we defend Mr. Banks from the Haddondale inquisition, or will you two stand here all morning bickering?"

In other words, Della didn't want to miss a word of that inquisition.

Kirsten tucked the hymnal into the bracket designed to hold it. "I've no wish to linger here, and I doubt Mr. Banks needs defending."

Though he needed something. Kirsten recalled the lyrics of the opening hymn they'd sung that morning. Was there significance to Mr. Banks's choice of "Thou Hidden Source of Calm Repose" as the first song he'd sung at his new post?

❧

Daniel shook hands with the menfolk, bowed to the ladies, matched names with faces—he'd studied the parish rolls at length—and took note of whose Sunday finery was indeed fine and whose was much mended.

The church steps were chilly, but not even arctic conditions would have spared him this gauntlet of genteel inspection. Every pair of eyes, even the genuinely kind ones, held the same question.

Was there a Mrs. Reverend Banks, and if so, where was she?

Reprieve came from an unlikely corner, when Mr. George Haddonfield and his recently acquired spouse filed out of the church, a small boy perched on Mr. Haddonfield's hip.

"I want to get down," the boy insisted. "I won't get muddy, and I won't catch an ague, and I won't bother the earl's coachman."

"Hush, child," Mr. Haddonfield soothed. "We'll greet the vicar and be on our way, and perhaps you can hold the reins for a bit on the way home."

That bribe would certainly have worked for Danny.

"Good morning," Daniel said, addressing the child, a sturdy boy, probably about Danny's age. "Was my sermon too long, young sir? You can be honest." Danny had always given an honest assessment of his papa's—his uncle's—Sunday morning efforts.

"Not long enough, sir," the boy said. "You're supposed to tell us a story, but all you said was hello and that you'd be a good vicar. You also said thank you, but I'm not sure what for."

"Digby!" The child's mother was not pleased with her offspring's honesty. "You'll not get a turn at the reins if that's how you greet Vicar."

On the opposite side of the steps, Lady Kirsten was probably listening to every word as she retied the ribbons of her bonnet, undid them, and retied them again.

Several times.

"I admire honesty in any member of my flock," Daniel replied, "and will take Master Digby's comments in the constructive spirit in which they were intended. So you like horses, do you, Digby?"

The boy flew into raptures about the blessed day when he had his own pony and riding to hounds and joining the cavalry and taking the best, best care of his steed.

Because Daniel was a fool who missed his nephew terribly, he asked the next question certain to keep the boy prattling on.

"What will you name your loyal mount, Master Digby?"

"Something Latin, for he'll be a very fine pony. Do you teach Latin?"

Most vicars did, and history and maths, among other subjects. Daniel's pupils in Little Weldon had been few and plodding, but this boy's parents looked lamentably hopeful.

"I have been known to conjugate a few verbs and decline the occasional noun."

"Do you know about the Second Punic War?" Digby asked.

A budding military scholar, then.

"Digby, enough," Mr. Haddonfield said, setting the boy down and keeping hold of his hand. "Vicar, we'll call on you, if you don't mind. Digby has an active mind and is in want of tutelage in a number of subjects."

As Mr. Haddonfield sauntered off with his little family, Lady Kirsten affixed herself to Daniel's side, wrapping her arm around his.

"Smile politely," she murmured. "Not the genuine smile you indiscriminately shine on all and sundry. Contrive to look pained that you must escort Bellefonte's shrewish sister to her conveyance, or the good folk of Haddondale will keep you here all day. It's ten yards from here to freedom, Mr. Banks. Fix bayonets and charge."

Mr. George Haddonfield and his lady were visiting with his sisters beside the larger coach. Digby waved, and Daniel waved back.

"Did you spend time with the child because you like children," Lady Kirsten asked as Daniel handed her up into the sleigh, "or because the boy helped spike the guns of the curious?"

Daniel unfolded the lap robe and draped it over her skirts, though clearly, Lady Kirsten was not to be put off.

Ever.

"Both," Daniel said. "He seems a bright boy."

"And you're a bright man. I was particularly pleased to sing the closing hymn. Well done, Mr. Banks."

The closing... Ah. "A favorite of mine, among many."

Daniel walked around to the other side of the sleigh and climbed in beside Lady Kirsten. She obligingly flipped the woolen blanket over his knees, while the driver maneuvered the sleigh out from behind the earl's coach and onto the track around the square.

"What did you think of my sermon?"

"As Digby said, deceptively gracious. I will enjoy watching you take your flock in hand, Mr. Banks."

She was a member of that flock, though Daniel wished much luck to any fellow who sought to take her in hand.

"Have you a schoolmaster in Haddondale, my lady?"

"We have a dame school only. The vicar is expected to provide instruction to the gentlemen's sons, in exchange for proper compensation, of course."

George Haddonfield, as the son of an earl, was solidly of the gentlemanly persuasion.

"I have only the predictable experience as a teacher," Daniel said. "Digby seems a delightful child."

To Daniel the term *delightful child* was redundant, and yet little boys were the last company he wanted to keep in Haddondale.

Vicar-ing had occupational hazards, one of them being an inconvenient tendency to recall Scripture at inopportune times. *Suffer the little children to come unto Me,* flitted tauntingly through Daniel's head.

"How will you spend your Sunday afternoon, Mr. Banks?"

Normally, Daniel would eat, have a nap, then read next week's Bible passage, so the Scripture could germinate into a sermon as the week progressed.

"I've an important letter to write," he said. "A certain young gentleman needs to know how I go on, and I've neglected my correspondence for too long."

The idea—the conviction—had popped into Daniel's head, a surprise and a revelation. He'd left Danny to Letty's devices for several months. The clean break had been made, punctuated by two short visits in which Daniel had failed utterly to make the shift from papa to doting uncle.

Resulting in much awkwardness on all sides and a blooming sense of defeat on Daniel's part.

Time to make another try, then. Doting uncles

wrote to their nephews, if only to inquire as to how the boy's Latin was coming along.

❧

Papa, whom Danny was now supposed to call Uncle Daniel, had always said that unhappiness passes. Sitting between Lord Fairly, whom Danny did not know what to call, and Aunt Letty, who *was* Danny's mama, though he was supposed to call her Aunt Letty, unhappiness grew inside Danny until he nearly burst with it.

Nothing had gone right since Danny had left Little Weldon months ago.

"I hate it here."

Lord Fairly kept driving, as if he hadn't heard Danny over the trotting of the horses, but Mama— *Aunt*—adjusted the lap robe around Danny for the eleventh time since leaving the church.

"Did you say something, Danny?" she asked.

Danny grew even more miserable, for Mama had aimed that bright, anxious smile at him she so often wore.

He scrambled to find something nice to say, because "I miss Papa" would only make her eyes get shiny.

"*Hic, haec, hoc,*" Danny said. "It's Latin for—"

"*Huius, huius, huius,*" the viscount said, in rhythm with the horses splashing through the muck.

Old habit had Danny offering the dative, "*Huic, huic, huic!*"

And the viscount obliged with the accusative, "*Hunc, hanc, hoc.*"

So Danny concluded the song—Papa had said it

was a song without a tune of its own—with the ablative. "*Hoc, hac, hoc!*"

A shaft of glee pierced the dismal morning, for Papa had always been proud of Danny's Latin ability and had traded the lines with him in exactly the same way. Papa and Danny had played French games too, alternating the names of objects in a room until Danny had run out of terms he knew.

"*Hi, hae, haec,*" the viscount sang out as they turned up the lane toward the stable.

The bubble of glee inside Danny burst. "I don't know the plural. Papa hadn't taught it to me yet but said it was as easy as the singular."

That look passed between the adults. *That look* they shared whenever Danny blundered and forgot to call Papa "Uncle Daniel."

"I meant Uncle Daniel." *Papa, Papa, Papa.*

"No matter," Mama—*Aunt*—said. "You know a prodigious amount of Latin for a boy your age, and if you'd like to resume your studies, it's easy enough to arrange. Would you like that?"

More of her fierce, determined brightness.

"Yes, Mama."

The next look was harder to decipher, but Danny suspected his blunder had spread the unhappiness from him to both adults, probably even to the horses. Blunders—plural, for he ought to have called the unhappy lady beside him Aunt Letty rather than Mama.

Though *she was his Mama.*

Danny mostly liked these people. They were kind, and the viscount was an ally of a sort Danny didn't know how to describe. Papa had been that sort of ally when Olivia—Danny had *no* trouble calling her Olivia rather than Mama—had been very cranky.

Which was often.

Danny did not miss Olivia one bit. She'd been angry all the time, she'd said mean things about Papa, and she'd even been mean to Mama.

The gig came to a mucky halt in the stable yard. The viscount handed Mama down, then reached up for Danny, just as Papa had used to.

"Come along, lad. Her ladyship will alert the garrison that we're back from our devotions, and you can visit Sweetness with me for a moment."

Sweetness was the viscount's mare. She was nearly as big as Papa's horse, Beelzebub, but she was white, while Zubbie was black.

The viscount set Danny down in the slush of the stable yard while Mama strode off for the house. Something in the set of her shoulders made Danny feel bad.

"I miss Beelzebub!" The words were out, not what Danny had meant to say, but the truth—Papa would have been disappointed in him if he'd lied—for he did miss even his Papa's horse.

His Uncle Daniel's horse.

The viscount scooped Danny up, as if he were a very little boy, and took off in the direction of the stable while a groom took the gig around to the carriage house.

"We fellows must stick together, right, Danny?"

Papa had often said the same thing. "Yes, sir."

"Well then, as a loyal member of the We Fellows club, I'm suggesting you give her ladyship time. You were very patient with her this morning and she's trying hard. I thought she'd about smother you with the lap robe. I'm surprised you didn't leap from the carriage and run howling to join the Navy."

"I'm for the church, sir." Danny had known this ever since he'd come to live at the viscount's large, pretty, *cold* house. A boy couldn't slide down the banisters in such a house for fear of breaking some vase or mirror or other delicate, expensive ornament.

"You'll be very good at vicar-ing," the viscount said, "for you're a very good boy."

The viscount was the opposite of Papa. Papa was dark; the viscount was fair. Papa had Danny's brown eyes, while the viscount had funny eyes—one blue, one green, which Danny hardly noticed anymore.

"Thank you, sir. Pa—Uncle Daniel said I must try hard to be good, because her ladyship has missed me for a long time."

They stopped outside Sweetness's stall, and once again, Danny found himself affixed to the viscount's hip. Back in Little Weldon—a four-word phrase that had come to mean "when I was happy"— Danny would have gone right into Beelzebub's stall, and Zubbie would have bowed hello to earn his treat.

"Danny, my boy, you are wise beyond your years," the viscount said. "Her ladyship has indeed missed you."

The mare hung her head over the half door. She was a good horse, and clearly, the viscount loved her. He passed Danny a hunk of carrot he'd produced from some pocket or other, and Danny held it out to the mare.

She hesitated, her horsey glance passing over Danny

with silent wisdom. *You are not my master*, that look said, but to please her master, she nibbled the carrot from Danny's palm anyway.

"I miss Zubbie," Danny said again, his throat aching. He wiggled down to his feet, lest he bury his nose against the viscount's greatcoat and wail like a baby. "I miss him a l-lot."

The viscount hunkered beside Danny. "He probably misses you too."

"Yes, s-sir." *Papa, Papa, Papa.*

Danny did as Papa had taught him and stuffed his hand into his pocket and made a very, very tight fist. He used that fist to hold on to all the words he mustn't say, all the feelings he ought not to mention.

"You need a visit with your pony, Danny, my lad."

"Yes, sir." *I am not your lad.*

Danny had longed for a pony for forever, but he didn't want to visit Loki now. He didn't want to make fists in his pockets; he didn't want to worry that he'd said the wrong thing and made Ma—Aunt—*her lady-ship* unhappy and the viscount anxious.

"Come along," the viscount said, rising and patting Sweetness's nose. "And please remind me to wipe my boots thoroughly before we get to the kitchen, or her ladyship will ring a peal over my head that makes the church bells pale."

The viscount extended a gloved hand to Danny, but for once, Danny ignored it.

Did they think he'd run off to join the Navy between the stable and the house? Did they think he couldn't even walk, like some little baby who toppled to the nursery floor without warning?

Danny marched faster, the viscount trailing behind him across the mess and mire of the stable yard. Both of Danny's pockets held tight fists, and he didn't watch where he was going, which was why his good Sunday boot landed smack in the middle of a half-frozen horse dropping.

Bad words welled up behind the lump in Danny's throat, nasty bad words about horse droppings, about attending service at the wrong church, about missing Papa.

"Are we in a hurry, Danny?" the viscount asked in that kind, easy voice that Danny positively *hated*.

"I never want to be a horse," Danny said.

"Horses can gallop," the viscount replied. "They're very handsome, but they do have trouble scratching certain parts."

Handsome did not matter. Pretty did not matter, except that beauty was a chance to admire the Creator's work. Honesty and kindness mattered—Papa had said so many times.

But Danny could be only half honest.

"If I were a horse, then I could be bought and sold at any time," Danny said, narrowly missing another pile of manure. "I'd have nothing to say to it. I would *hate* being a horse. I might miss my old master until I wanted to *die*, and if I were a horse, I couldn't do anything about it."

The viscount's steps paused, but Danny barreled on.

His fists were swinging at his sides now, and if he spied another horse dropping, he'd stomp on it, on purpose, even wearing his good Sunday boots.

For Danny was not only unhappy, he was—Papa

had said to be honest, and this honesty set something awful and irresistible loose inside Danny—*furious*.

Four

KIRSTEN'S STARTLING INSIGHT CAME AS MR. BANKS assisted her down from the sleigh. All around them, melting snow dripped from eaves and tree limbs, a wet, happy undercurrent to sparkling sunshine and slushy footing.

She'd not be sharing a sleigh with Mr. Banks again for some time, alas.

"Down you go," Mr. Banks said, his hands secure at her waist. Kirsten grasped his shoulders, the same as she would have done with one of her brothers—the footing was uncertain, after all—and he swung her down, his grip solid until she had her balance.

"I'm happy," Kirsten said, the most ungainly expression of sentiment ever to bleat forth from her usually annoyed mouth. "I mean, I'm glad you got off such a subtle and sound scolding to those fellows. I'm impressed."

She was glad Mr. Banks had been kind to George's little stepson too. Glad the new vicar had been well received by the parishioners, glad he'd felt no duty to linger among them, shaking hands, bowing, and currying favor.

Glad he'd chosen instead to accompany Kirsten back to Belle Maison in the sleigh.

"You're proud of me, then?" The notion seemed to amuse him, and some of Kirsten's pleasure in the sunny, drippy day dimmed.

"Has no one been proud of you, Mr. Banks? Does the Bible proscribe an honest pleasure in another's accomplishments? If it does, then I am doomed to perdition, for I am proud of both my sisters and my brothers."

Kirsten was doomed to perdition of a sort anyway. Before she could say as much, old Alfrydd came out to lead the horse away. The sleigh's tracks cut through the slush right down to wet, muddy earth.

"You may have your pride in me, my lady, and my thanks for it. Shall we say good morning to Beelzebub?"

Kirsten's irritation melted away like spring snow on a sunny morning, for, apparently, the vicar was *bashful*.

Well then, yes. They should do whatever allowed Kirsten a few more minutes of Mr. Banks's exclusive company, for when Kirsten was with him, she was not grumpy. Not grumpy, not grouchy, not sour, not shrewish, not any of the cranky, accurate, loving appellations her siblings leveled at her so often.

Kirsten took Mr. Banks's arm—he needed a new coat, for this one was loose on him and worn at the elbows—and he sauntered into the stable with her. His gelding whickered softly, ears swiveling in the direction of his master.

"Greetings, Beelzebub, on this fine day. You wonder why I did not saddle you up for a trip to the kirk, don't you?"

Another whuffle. Across the barn aisle, Kirsten's bay mare didn't so much as look up from her pile of hay.

"Beelzebub is very handsome," Kirsten said. "Did you fear to make a bad impression on the congregation by cantering up to the church on such a fine steed?"

The vicar tugged off his gloves and passed them to Kirsten. "I feared we'd pull a shoe in this footing—the off hind could use another nail or two—and the trip down from Oxford entitles a horse to some rest. Another Sunday will arrive soon enough."

Next commenced a scratching of ears and chin, a caressing of a muscular horsey neck, and a patting of a sturdy equine shoulder. The sight of the vicar's hands on his horse provoked curious sensations in Kirsten's middle, novel sensations she did not exactly enjoy.

"You'll have hair all over your coat," Kirsten said, for horses started shedding as early as January, and the mess only grew worse as warm weather approached.

"So I will," Mr. Banks said, digging his fingers into the beast's chest, "but Beelzebub misses Danny, and allowances must be made."

"Is Danny his former groom? Another horse?"

A final caress to the gelding's ear, and Mr. Banks withdrew his hand. "Danny is my…my nephew. His situation is complicated, and I'd rather not burden you with it."

The horse made an attempt to nip at Mr. Banks's sleeve, but the effort was halfhearted, and the gelding soon turned his attention back to his fodder.

Kirsten passed the vicar his gloves, nearly every finger of which had been darned.

"I am a grouch," she said, though the word stung a bit. "Soon I will be a grouchy spinster and the scourge of the nieces and nephews bound to appear in great numbers ere long. Nonetheless, I'm a grouch with an excellent sense of discretion, Mr. Banks, and I'm loyal to those I care about."

She cared about him, in other words. Kirsten neither examined nor elaborated on that admission, for already, amazingly, wonderfully, it was the truth.

"You are not a grouch," Mr. Banks said, taking Kirsten by the elbow and leading her from the gloom of the stable into the sharp morning sun. "Or not only a grouch. You are also brave. Danny's tale is not exclusively mine to tell."

The sunshine was so bright as to hurt the eyes, but Mr. Banks did not seem affected.

"This Danny is illegitimate, then." *I did not say that. I did not say that.*

Mr. Banks dropped Kirsten's arm and turned his back to her, probably a vicar's equivalent of loud, protracted cursing.

"Don't run off," she snapped.

He stood his ground—brave fellow—while Kirsten mentally flailed about in search of words to repair what she'd just put wrong.

The stable yard lay before them, an increasingly muddy soup of snow, horse droppings, and stray clumps of new grass. But for that morass, Mr. Banks would likely be striding off for the safety of the manor house.

"Please don't let me chase you off, I mean. Illegitimacy is no great rarity. Sooner or later, you'll hear that Della's circumstances are irregular, and

Nicholas was not a saint as a younger man. I'll thrash you if you judge either one of them harshly."

Mr. Banks faced her, and apparently Kirsten had stumbled on the right thing to say—a miracle, surely.

"You could do it," he said. "You could thrash me, and I've at least three stone on you and considerable reach. You are formidable, Lady Kirsten."

Her siblings called her contrary, stubborn, wrongheaded, and curmudgeonly. Nobody called Kirsten formidable, much less in an admiring tone of voice.

"I've never thrashed a vicar," she said. "I don't believe the Commandments expressly forbid it. Would you defend yourself with another hymn?"

Mr. Banks turned his face to the sun. His physiognomy was an excruciatingly attractive assemblage of the same parts assigned to most creatures at birth, but paired with the understanding and compassion in his dark, dark eyes…

"Come," Kirsten said, leading him around the edge of the mire. "We will sit in the gazebo where all can see us, and you will explain about your nephew. If he's your son, you needn't hide that. I'd be surprised if some female or other hadn't thrown herself at you. Scores of them, in fact. You're human, Mr. Banks. The best vicars generally are. You're also indecently handsome, through no fault of your own, of course."

She was babbling, and Mr. Banks was coming along docilely. Kirsten shut her mouth before he called her something less flattering than formidable.

He sat across from her in the octagonal gazebo, which meant she could visually gorge on the myriad nuances of his expression without staring too obviously.

The vicar was tired, he could do with more weight, and he'd tried to hide a frayed seam on his cravat by tying the bow off center.

The man needed a wife.

"The aristocracy can be tolerant," Mr. Banks said, leaning back and resting an arm along the back of the bench. "One shouldn't be astonished at this, but I am. My brother-in-law is a viscount, you know."

That situation seemed to puzzle Mr. Banks.

"Viscount Fairly is one of Nicholas's dearest friends," Kirsten said. "He and his viscountess have joined us for an occasional meal." How odd that Lord and Lady Fairly had never said much about her ladyship's brother. A vicar in the family was usually an opportunity for boasting. "Lady Fairly bears a resemblance to you about the eyes."

The viscountess also shared an air of sadness with Mr. Banks, and Kirsten suspected the boy, Danny, was the common element to their unhappiness.

Unfortunate for the child. Fairly would sort them out, though. His lordship was a toweringly competent man who cared not one fig leaf for social convention.

"The child is not mine, though I've wished he were," Mr. Banks said as a turtledove landed on the back of the bench not a foot from his outstretched arm. "Danny is the dearest boy who ever winked at his—*his uncle*—in church. My sister fell into difficulties at a young age, and when she removed to London in search of work, I raised the lad at the vicarage in Little Weldon. Letty, as Fairly's viscountess, now has the social standing and means to accept Danny into her household, and I have no reason to gainsay her. A mother should be with her child."

The story was prosaic on the surface. Many a child was consigned to the care of a local vicar, either because the child was an extra mouth, slow, or otherwise in need of charity. Any vicar with extended family became a convenient place to stash a stray child. In a tolerant village, Danny's origins might not have been held against his uncle.

The church's attitude toward that arrangement had likely not been solicited.

"You took a risk, keeping the boy in your home," Kirsten said as a second dove joined the first—a dangerously precocious pair, considering the weather. "A fussy bishop would have taken a dim view of your decision. Your sister owes you."

"Letty owes me nothing."

Another revelation: Mr. Banks was capable of anger. On him, ire was cloaked as barely discernible irritation. Did he even *know* he was angry? Did he know he was handsome in an entirely new way when fire flickered in his eyes?

The doves settled, as if waiting for the tea tray to be brought 'round. They were the first pair Kirsten had seen that year, and probably they wished they'd not arrived so early. Mr. Banks didn't seem aware of them or their gentle cooing.

"In any case, you miss the boy," Kirsten said. "Why not visit him?" Kirsten was meddling, but Mr. Banks's saintly tendencies, if unchecked, would result in pointless suffering.

"I have visited him, Lady Kirsten, and the time spent

together neither eased my worry for him, nor comforted the lad. The situation wants time is all, but until I know Danny can thrive in his mother's household, I will not accept a missionary post for parts distant."

The *situation* wanted a great deal more than time. "How distant?"

"Cathay has some appeal, or Peru."

Kirsten rose and the doves fluttered away. Neither Cathay nor Peru was in her plans, and they shouldn't be in Mr. Banks's plans either.

"Danny will love that—waiting months for a letter from you, worrying that a dread disease has carried you off or that you've been eaten by cannibals or tigers. An excellent plan, Mr. Banks, for those who must have privacy for their holy pouting."

He rose slowly, and for the first time, his size struck Kirsten as masculine and powerful.

"You don't know the half of it, my lady. I'd counsel you to limit your comments."

Oh, not him too. Life was just full of disappointments. Kirsten tucked the frayed end of his cravat under the seam of his waistcoat.

"Everybody counsels me to limit my comments, and then nothing of any import is resolved. Della is terrified of her reception in Town later this spring, but we don't talk about that. Nicholas has a grown daughter, one of marriageable age but unfortunate pedigree, and we don't talk about that either. He misses Leonie to pieces while she's trying to learn how to serve tea at his grandmother's in Town. Nobody talks about that."

"You miss this Leonie as well," Mr. Banks said, seizing on this insight a little too enthusiastically.

"*Of course* I miss her. We hardly know her, and she's the dearest soul, and Nicholas should not have let her go, but she wanted to see London and he can deny her nothing. She writes to me, but her penmanship—" Kirsten hauled up short on the reins of a confidence not shared outside family.

Mr. Banks excelled at provoking expressions of sentiment, and all the while, he paraded around, a rascal in vicar's threadbare clothing.

"You miss Danny," she said. "He's barely two hours' ride from here if he's dwelling under Lord Fairly's roof. Trot over there and see him. You can be back in time for supper."

The lift of Mr. Banks's dark brows said she'd tempted him. Kirsten would rather have tempted him with a kiss, so she went up on her toes and bussed his cheek.

I did just do that. She'd like to do it again too.

"The love of a child is fragile and precious, Mr. Banks. Some of us will never earn such a love, but you have. Take your horse out for a gallop, see the boy, and let him know you're settling in here well."

When Kirsten gave her family orders in triplicate, they invariably ignored her or argued with her. Mr. Banks touched bare fingers to his cheek, his expression hovering between bemused and bewildered.

Kirsten left him in the gazebo, pleased with herself for once.

And pleased with him too.

❧

"You owe me," Olivia said, though embarking on a harangue on a pretty Sunday morning was a chore even for her. "I would never have married that man if you hadn't trifled with me."

Bertrand Carmichael set the tea tray on a stool beside the bed. Sunlight reflected cheerfully off the silver service—Bertrand hadn't used the everyday since Olivia had arrived three days ago.

The notion that some menial had extra polishing to do pleased Olivia nearly as much as Bertrand waiting on her did.

"The trifling was at least a mutual undertaking, Olivia, and long ago. You truly should not tarry here much longer, my dear. If you hang your head, dredge up some Scripture, and tearfully confess to the right bishop, Banks will have no choice but to take you back."

Bertrand sat on the edge of the bed, not as lean as he'd been as a younger man, his red hair thinner. His features were the same though—refined, almost aristo-cratic, his hands always in motion and free of calluses.

Of necessity, Olivia had allowed the trifling to resume the morning after her arrival weeks ago. Needs must. Daniel Banks, wallowing in piety and honor, had never understood that.

"You don't want me to go back to the vicar, Bertrand. I'll take a cottage in the Orkneys before I resume a sentence under Daniel Banks's roof."

Bertrand poured out as gracefully as a duchess, the steam adding a black tea fragrance to the bedroom.

"Olivia, you'd be *lucky* to live under his roof again."

God spare me from martyred men. "I'd be worked to death without the first luxury, expected to spend half my life in some dusty old church, my knees aching through every winter." She'd also have to endure

Daniel's forgiveness, because Daniel would forgive Old Scratch himself. "I won't do it."

Bertrand tugged her braid from between the pillows and brushed the end across her mouth.

"You know I can't force you to do anything, Olivia. I do fear for your immortal soul, though."

Oh, *that*.

"I couldn't keep the money Letty sent," Olivia spat. "Daniel has it. If he hasn't given it to his titled sister, he'll put it aside for the boy and live on locusts and honey. My immortal soul is not so very imperiled."

Yet.

Bertrand leaned down and took a sniff of Olivia's cleavage. "You were wicked, Olivia. You took advantage of another's misfortune, and you've done nothing to make it right. I love how you smell in the morning."

Olivia petted Bertrand's hair, not particularly concerned with his overture. Bertrand was elegant, refined, and biddable, entirely unlike Daniel's hulking darkness. Daniel's worst transgression by far, though, had been a stubborn independence Olivia had never found a way to curb.

That, and he'd failed to give her children of her own. Olivia was no great admirer of sniveling brats, but to have to raise another's child, without any of her own to show for years of marriage, had galled bitterly.

Bertrand teethed her nipple through her nightgown. "Shall I take off my robe, Olivia?"

Olivia's family in Yorkshire believed she'd come south before Christmas to rejoin her husband after an extended holiday among relatives. Daniel believed she still tarried in the West Riding, of all the godfor-saken purgatories.

Bertrand, having had the good sense to survive a wealthy wife, was a comfortable—and biddable—port in a storm.

"Finish fixing my tea first, Bertrand. I have plans to consider."

He left off bothering her, his gaze alit with lust and longing as he stirred a quantity of sugar into Olivia's tea.

⁓

Immediately after kissing Daniel, Lady Kirsten had churned off toward the house, while he'd remained sitting in the gazebo, his emotions as tangled as the thorny hedges encircling the nearby knot garden.

Pleasure demanded his notice—the lady had *kissed* him. A friendly, presuming, confident buss to his cheek, such as a woman bestowed on a familiar.

Bewilderment marched forward as well, because, for the merest instant, Daniel had longed to put his arms around Lady Kirsten and turn that kiss into the beginning of a conversation that could go nowhere.

He was married, and a godly man. End of sermon.

So resentment also rustled in the bushes of his emotions, because he had no wife, no marital companion, no helpmeet at his side. As his father had warned him before the vows had even been spoken, Daniel had chosen poorly.

And finally, Daniel endured weariness of the spirit. He'd told Lady Kirsten the sad truth: visiting Danny only seemed to make the boy sadder, because every visit ended with Daniel turning his back on the child and riding away. Every choice led to sadness, and thus Daniel would not be visiting the boy again in the immediate future.

A horseman dismounted in the stable yard, a tall fellow on a fine gelding. He doffed his hat and tarried for a moment with the groom, sunlight glinting on the golden hair common to many a Haddonfield.

Mr. George Haddonfield came striding across the garden, his posture and pace suggesting his visit was not a mere social call upon his siblings.

"Have you been put out in the garden like a rambunctious hound, Mr. Banks?" Mr. Haddonfield asked, thumping up the steps of the gazebo. He lounged against one of the supports, all fine tailoring, gentlemanly bonhomie, and energetic good health.

"I expect in a few weeks, this will be a lovely garden," Daniel replied, summoning small talk. Today was Sunday, after all. "A hound would enjoy being banished here. Have you come to call on your family?"

Mr. Haddonfield's smile dimmed to a rueful and slightly puzzled expression as he appropriated the bench beside Daniel.

"That's what I told my wife, but I lied, Mr. Banks— your first confession from the sinners of Haddondale. I lied to my new wife."

"The early days of a marriage are difficult," Daniel said. "One wants to be kind but also make an honest beginning. Why did you tell your wife this great falsehood?"

The middle days and end days of a marriage could also be laden with difficulty. A merciful deity would spare Mr. Haddonfield that insight.

"I'm on a reconnaissance mission, Mr. Banks. Your conversation with Digby got me thinking."

Digby, the budding military scholar. Daniel sat up. "I can't absolve you of a prevarication if I don't know its nature, Mr. Haddonfield."

"You will make a first-rate tutor, and it's about that I wanted to speak with you. My stepson is developing rotten tendencies. I can spot these three leagues off because, as a lad, I had more than a few myself."

"As lads, we all did." Many a sound birching had persuaded Daniel to put his aside—for the most part.

"Digby, the apple of his mother's eye, and my pride and joy, shut the pantry mouser in the linen closet."

To Mr. Haddonfield's credit, he was worried about this little domestic contretemps. The scent of cat on clean linen would drive any mother to screeching.

"The boy's mother dotes on the cat?" Daniel asked.

"How did you guess?"

"Digby struck me as having an academic bent. His rottenness will have a strategic quality. The cat works his mischief, Mama flies into the boughs with the cat rather than the true culprit, and Digby has eliminated a rival for Mama's affections. How recently did you marry?"

Now Mr. Haddonfield sat up. "Very. I rather like being married to my Elsie, but the boy is becoming a problem."

Mr. Haddonfield probably liked being married to his Elsie several times a day, exactly when young Digby wanted assurances that Mama was still exclusively devoted to her son.

"What did Mrs. Haddonfield think of this stunt with the cat?"

"She declared it an accident, but a six-year-old boy

doesn't stuff a cat weighing well over a stone into the linen closet by accident."

"Malice aforethought, then." Also excellent planning skills. "Are you asking me to pray for your budding felon?"

Daniel could do that easily. Every rotten boy should have somebody praying for him, as should the boy's parents.

"I want you to teach him Latin, Mr. Banks, and ciphering and geography and so forth. Prior to marrying me, Elsie had to allow Digby to attend lessons with the local vicar, because the boy's former guardian insisted. I can argue that Eton is now within Digby's grasp, and a proper foundation is necessary if he's not to be humiliated. Digby will leap on this proposal because I'll get him his own pony for shuttling back and forth to his lessons."

Strategic indeed. "You were truly once a rotten boy, sir."

Mr. Haddonfield's ears turned a shade of pink common to the newly married. "Elsie seems to like that about me."

Another tall, blond fellow emerged from a Belle Maison side entrance, the Earl of Bellefonte himself. Had he seen Lady Kirsten kissing the new vicar's cheek? Did Daniel mind if he had, when the kiss had been the merest gesture of friendship?

"Bellefonte has spotted me," Mr. Haddonfield said. "We used to seek cover in the library together on Sunday afternoons. Nicholas put it about he was doing accounts, I purported to tend to my correspondence, and we both got a fine nap."

Another confession, this one betraying concern for

the earl, because Mr. Haddonfield had found a cozier place to nap of a Sunday afternoon.

"You are a good brother," Daniel said. "Recall that Bellefonte has a countess, just as you have Digby's mother to while away an idle hour or two with."

"Or three."

The earl's coat was open, suggesting he'd departed the household in some haste. He took the gazebo's opposite bench with the air of one escaping a madhouse.

"They're already planning the next assembly," he said, darting a glance toward the grand edifice flanking the garden. "Witches never stirred their cauldrons as gleefully as those women plan a lot of stomping, twirling silliness. Banks, what would a sermon expounding on the evils of dancing cost me? Frame your answer carefully, for I hold the Haddondale living."

George nudged the earl's boot with his own. "Last I heard, the manse was riddled with bats and creeping damp, Lord Sober Generosity. Mice droppings on the pantry floor, spiders in the stairwells. You'll be lucky to get a drunken Dissenter to minister to the flock when that gets out."

His lordship thwacked a large boot against his brother's toes, a beat and rebeat of the fraternal variety.

"Oh, you're a great help, George. Mr. Banks, you see the disrespect a belted earl endures from his own siblings. The manse can be set to rights when the weather warms up."

"Replacing rotten wood will take forever, Nicholas," George retorted. "Mr. Banks needs accommodations now if he's to tutor the young scholars of the parish."

"I beg your pardon, Mr. Haddonfield," Daniel interjected, "I haven't agreed to tutor anybody." Particularly not a troop of little anybodies who'd make Danny's absence from Daniel's life even more painful.

But then rattling around the earl's house for weeks, dodging the scolds—and kisses—of a certain forthright lady wasn't a wise plan, either.

The long-dormant rotten boy in Daniel stirred to life: dodging Lady Kirsten's scolds—and kisses—might be *enjoyable*.

Not dodging them would be even more enjoyable—also wicked.

"I'm happy to explain Latin to the youth of the parish," Daniel went on, "but one typically undertakes that effort at the vicarage, where the occasional boy can live in. His lordship can't have a pack of juvenile miscreants running tame about the earldom's very seat."

"I can't?" Bellefonte asked—wistfully?

"You can't," George said. "Get your own little miscreants, Nicholas. You can't have mine. Besides, Banks isn't after making tree forts, dams, and tin soldier battles with these boys, he's to educate them."

"*Banks*," Daniel said repressively, "has agreed to teach Latin to one small, most well-mannered child, not bring discipline to a Highland regiment."

Both brothers peered at him, and before Daniel's eyes, fraternal schemes blossomed in the sunny, muddy garden. A precocious turtledove cooed from the direction of the stable, then the earl and Mr. Haddonfield spoke at once.

"The dower house," they pronounced.

The earl took the conversational reins and set off

at a brisk trot. "Harold Blumenthal asked me when you're removing to the vicarage because he has two boys, right terrors, both in need of preparation for public school. He wanted to make sure you were settled in among us before he sprang the boys on you."

Harder for an unsuspecting vicar to blow a hasty retreat after he'd set up camp, in other words.

"Are these young gentlemen twins?" Twins had the ability to anticipate one another's thoughts, in Daniel's experience. This gift in the hands of mischievous boys boded ill for tutors, governesses, and sleeping dogs.

Boys like that would love a manse infested with bats and spiders.

"They're the kind of twins you can't tell apart," George said. "Every other generation, the Blumenthals produce a matched set. The last time it was a pair of girls, and they were said to have turned Mad King George's head in their day. Both of them. At the same time, as it were."

While the Haddonfields had produced half a regiment of attractive blonds, some of whom were indiscriminate kissers.

"As pleasing a prospect as instruction of these budding ne'er-do-wells might be," Daniel said, "we have yet to settle the matter of a venue for their education."

"Oh, we've settled that," his lordship said, crossing a pair of worn riding boots at the ankle. "A little vinegar and scrubbing, some beeswax and lemon oil, and the dower house will provide as much room for the little dears as you please. And just think, if they've a notion to build a tree fort, I'm on hand to assist."

The aristocracy must be allowed their queer starts. Both brothers were grinning hugely.

"Nicholas builds the best tree forts," Mr. Haddonfield pronounced, "but don't let him start on any tunnels. Our papa had nightmares about Nick's brilliance as a sapper."

Mr. Haddonfield and his brother were grown men, raised with every privilege, and yet, hiding from their womenfolk on a crisp afternoon, they were also simply a pair of brothers, shamelessly fond of each other, fiercely loyal, and trying to adjust to Mr. Haddonfield's recent departure from the earl's household.

Danny deserved the same sort of allies in adulthood, not simply the impotent protectiveness of an uncle aging in the solitude of some moldy vicarage.

"Shall I remove my effects to this dower house?" Daniel asked, rising. He could be packed up and gone from the Belle Maison manor within the hour—a sensible prospect, surely. A prudent man removed himself from temptation rather than repeatedly imperiling his honor and his immortal soul. '

The earl and his brother rose as well, his lordship leading the exodus from the gazebo.

"My countess won't have you moving out just yet, Banks," the earl said. "The dower house will need some attention first."

"A lot of attention," Mr. Haddonfield added, bringing up the rear. "Lady Bellefonte will want to see the undertaking done properly."

"Not Lady Bellefonte," his lordship replied, wrinkling a splendid nose. "She's consumed with the details of Della's come-out. I would say Nita is the one to take on the task, but she's abandoned us for her sheep count, so that leaves—"

"Kirsten," Mr. Haddonfield concluded. "She's the best one for the job, if you ask me. Kirsten could domesticate a dungeon so a man would want to linger among its comforts. A pity, really."

"This way," Bellefonte directed, leading Daniel around the side of the house. "We can enter the library directly, and George can dodge the pickets."

Mr. Haddonfield halted in the knot garden. "I ought to say hello to the ladies, Nick. I can't exactly claim I came over here to tend my correspondence."

"They'll hold you prisoner until supper," his lordship groused. "Then I will have to work on my accounts, which Vicar will frown upon because it's the Sabbath."

Daniel had been known to glance at his accounts of a Sunday—a brief exercise, in his case.

"My guess," Daniel said, "is that Mr. Haddonfield came to borrow a few children's books from the library. Digby has a restless imagination, and will benefit from new material. Mr. Haddonfield stayed to play a game or two of chess with me—he's the courteous sort—and to discuss his stepson's education."

"That's not even a lie," the earl marveled. "Banks, you're good. You're virtuous, but you're also good."

"The Archbishop of Haddondale gets the sofa nearest the fire," Mr. Haddonfield allowed, resuming their progress. "His Reverence needs his rest if he's taking on the Blumenthal Brats."

When all three men had dispensed with coats and boots, Daniel lay back on the sofa of honor nearest the blazing fire. The earl was already snoring in a capacious wing chair, stockinged feet up on a hassock, while Mr. Haddonfield had grabbed a pillow and sprawled on the blue sofa against the inside wall.

The library was quiet, peaceful, and cozy—a fine place to begin contemplation of next week's sermon.

Or to recall a soft, sweet kiss that must not, for any reason, be repeated. Ever.

Five

Kirsten's Sunday afternoon followed a pattern: the ladies embroidered, knitted, tatted lace, and otherwise avoided doing anything interesting, while the menfolk snored for an hour or so in the library, then stole off to Nicholas's woodworking shop to tipple and whittle.

The enforced inactivity grated on Kirsten's spirit, but because Sunday was a half day for the servants, she could at least escape to the kitchen in the name of assembling a tea tray.

A footman would bring the tray up for her—she'd committed the mortal sin of poking her head into the servants' parlor to ask for that assistance—so when her errand was completed, Kirsten simply barged into the countess's parlor unannounced.

"Mr. Banks reminds me of Christopher Sedgewick," Della was saying, "though I daresay Mr. Banks's charm is more enduring than Mr. Sedgewick's proved to be."

And there, predictably, the conversation went headlong into the nearest muddy ditch.

The countess's expression turned resolutely cheerful. "Kirsten, were you able to find us a fresh pot and some biscuits?"

Mr. Banks isn't anything like Christopher Sedgewick.

"You have a point, Della," Kirsten said, mildly of course. "Both Mr. Sedgewick and Mr. Banks are tall, dark haired, brown eyed, and well-favored, if you don't mind a bit of a nose on a fellow. Mr. Banks has the more pleasing voice, probably developed of necessity when one frequents a pulpit."

Kirsten took a seat near the window, where Nita had liked to sit. What had Nicholas imparted to his spouse regarding the estimable Mr. Sedgewick or the estimable Viscount Morton?

Or any of Kirsten's former beaus and suitors?

"Was your mission successful?" Susannah asked. "George will doubtless be over to look in on Nicholas, and there's an end to our ginger biscuits."

Hang the damned biscuits. "The tea tray will be along directly," Kirsten said, and because her sisters were looking anywhere but at her, she added, "I expect we'll see Mr. Sedgewick and his lady in Town this spring. I understand her confinement concluded happily before Christmas."

With a son, of course. A son at Yuletide in the biblical tradition, to ensure that the earldom to which Mr. Sedgewick himself was heir continued for yet another generation.

"Now that we've run Nicholas off with talk of dancing and punch recipes, we need poetry," Susannah announced. "Wordsworth, to hasten spring with thoughts of lambs, daffodils, and new life."

That comment hurt, though Suze was simply trying to leave Sedgewick in the conversational dust.

Kirsten rose, lest she put her fist through the nearest window. "I'll find us some cheerful verse, though I doubt the snow will last even another day. The sun has already turned the churchyard nearly to a bog."

The sun had also brought out red highlights in the new vicar's hair as he'd stood on the church steps, visiting with his flock. Kirsten had particularly liked the look of him in earnest discussion with George and Elsie's boy, Digby.

Not many pastors would take the time to converse with a child when a pat on the head would have sufficed.

Kirsten let herself into the library and came to an abrupt halt.

Nicholas had last been spied striding across the garden, presumably on the way to his woodworking shop in the stable. Neither he nor George, who might have been expected to come calling, were in evidence.

Kirsten's brothers had apparently been a corrupting influence on Mr. Banks, though, for he lay on the sofa closest to the fire. In the entire library, that spot enjoyed the greatest warmth and privacy, for the sofa's back faced the room.

She closed the door soundlessly and prepared to trespass, for Mr. Banks in repose was an intriguing sight.

Dark lashes fanned his cheeks, which in sleep underscored his leanness. One hand was flung back over the sofa's arm, his lips were closed in a sculpted line, and his hair—why hadn't Nick's valet trimmed Mr. Banks's hair?—lay in soft waves around a tired face.

A fallen angel, one who didn't quite fit on the sofa,

for a stocking-clad foot was propped on the sofa arm
nearest Kirsten, the toes heavily darned. In a well-
fitted riding boot, that much stitching might lead to
blisters. His knee was bent, so his second foot was flat
on the velvet cushion of the sofa.

The state of Mr. Banks's stockings offended
Kirsten's domestic sensibilities, but the rest of him was
breathtaking in repose, all of the caution and reserve
abandoned, the healthy beast on shameless display.
Kirsten's sisters would have withdrawn quietly, rather
than intrude on Mr. Banks's privacy, but her sisters
were destined for good matches and happy marriages.

Mr. Banks stirred, so the hand resting across his flat
belly drifted lower, over his falls.

Leave. I must leave this instant.

His thumb moved, and Kirsten's middle became a
quagmire of fascination, guilt, and troublesome stir-
rings. That thumb took up a rhythm, stroking slowly
over the dark wool covering his breeding organs, back
and forth, back and forth.

His lips parted. Kirsten took a soundless step closer.

He is aroused. That thought barely had time to
coalesce before another crowded in behind it. *He is
arousing himself while yet asleep.*

Men actively embraced even solitary sexual pleasures. Thanks to Sedgewick and Morton, Kirsten knew
more than she should about the male body and what
passed for the brain assigned to manage it. She hadn't
known men were prone to these urges even in sleep.

Mr. Banks moved on the sofa, undulating his hips
up against his hand. The movement caused upheaval
inside Kirsten that was in no wise moral. She wanted

to kiss him. To undo his falls, to sin with him in general, though specifics were threatening to swamp her imagination.

She'd taken an entire step in retreat from her own wickedness when Mr. Banks groaned softly and cracked open his eyes. Not a vicar but a satyr beheld her, passion, power, and fire in his slitted gaze.

His hand did not pause, but he rasped one word.

"Go."

Kirsten fled, making not a sound, and she did not return to her sisters' company in the parlor.

❧

"Letty, I love you more than life itself, but that boy needs to spend time with Daniel."

Fairly's wife made a beautiful picture, the baby in her arms, Sabbath sunshine streaming in the window. Mother and child shared dark hair and flawless skin, though the infant grinned merrily, while Letty's expression was mulish.

Lately, Fairly's viscountess had been a study in mulishness, as had his quasi-stepson.

"Danny needs more time to become accustomed to us," her ladyship said, shifting the baby to her shoulder. "He's been here only a few months, and children don't adjust as easily as adults do."

Children often adjusted more easily than adults. Letty had raised no children once Danny had been weaned, that she should be an expert on them, but she loved both of her offspring ferociously.

"Let me take her," Fairly said, plucking the baby from her mama. "She'll drool on your gown, shameless little wench." The weight of the child soothed and comforted but didn't make the next words any easier.

"Danny has been here nearly six months, my love, and he's becoming more unhappy. He threw his porridge this morning, and he's not a boy to waste food."

"All boys throw their porridge from time to time."

No, they did not. "All I'm suggesting is a visit, Letty. A call on a family member, no more than an hour. Danny needs to know his uncle is getting on well and has a good living not far from us."

Fairly had called in favors from the Earl of Bellefonte without mercy to ensure Vicar Banks didn't heed a saintly impulse to take up missionary service in Darkest Africa.

"The weather is still quite brisk," Letty said. "In a few weeks, we can consider a visit. The children might take a chill if we make the effort now."

Nobody had said anything about bringing the baby along. Fairly took a seat beside his wife, while his daughter banged happily on his shoulder.

"You are afraid if Danny sees his uncle, he'll want to bide with Daniel and you'll never have your son under our roof again. I understand your fears, Letty, but many boys Danny's age are preparing for public school. He's not a baby. He is, in fact, very bright, and he's a young fellow who will want a profession."

With the vicar as Danny's pattern card of male virtue, the boy was doomed to a life of industry and integrity, perhaps even a life in the church.

Thank God, as it were.

"Danny isn't you!" Letty snapped. "He's not six years old, living in some dirt croft with his mother, thinking himself a poor Scottish lad, when an auntie snatches him away to a wealthy household in the south of England. Danny is *my son*, and for five years, I left him in the care of *that woman*."

Letty rose and started a circuit of the parlor, skirts swishing, while Fairly patted his daughter's back. Once *that woman* had been mentioned, Letty had to wind down on her own, or tears were sure to follow.

"She didn't love the boy," Letty wailed softly. "She never loved him, and Daniel did the best he could with the situation, for which I am grateful, but I'm now in a position to be the mother I always ought to have been. One bad morning in the nursery won't change my mind."

The third bad morning in the nursery in a week, though Fairly hadn't the heart to tell his wife as much. He hadn't the heart to take the birch rod to Danny's backside either, which boded ill for tomorrow's porridge.

And everybody's nerves.

"As far as the world is concerned, you are the boy's aunt," Fairly said, trying a new tack. "Daniel is his father, and the sort of father who'd want to see his son more than every six months."

"Daniel has been to visit us," Letty sniffed, tugging a handkerchief from her sleeve. "He's written, and he's hardly arrived to Haddondale. I'm not saying no, David. I'm saying not yet. Please, please, not yet."

The baby pounded merrily away, occasionally landing a blow on Fairly's ear, while Letty collapsed, weeping, on his other shoulder.

Not yet was progress, but grudging, small progress.

Fairly sent up a prayer that Danny wouldn't run off to join the Navy before the adults in his life sorted out their various guilts, obligations, and options.

With that thought, the baby landed a stout smack on Fairly's cheek.

❧

The dower house loomed in Daniel's awareness like a promised land, solitudinous for the immediate future, and agreeably free of luxuries, comforts, and distracting kisses. Like all promised lands, however, establishing residency there was taking time and effort.

"Books, Mr. Banks," said the footman, Ralph, setting a wooden box on the desk that served as Daniel's command post at the dower house. "Lady Kirsten says boys need books, and this lot of duplicates from the library will get you started."

"Did Lady Kirsten indicate when the moving process might be complete?" Daniel asked.

Daniel had avoided her ladyship outside of mealtimes. Her gaze had taken on a speculative, analytical quality, as if she were mentally weighing him on some scales known only to her.

Or perhaps she was planning another kiss to his cheek.

"Her ladyship does things in her own time," Ralph said, putting a half-dozen books on shelves built into the opposite wall. "Lady Nita kept us organized, but Lady Kirsten knew who was slacking. Can't abide dust and fairly hates cobwebs, does Lady Kirsten."

Another half-dozen volumes went up on the shelves, right next to the diaries written by Daniel's father. Daniel had placed the journals where they'd be in his direct line of sight, hoping that gazing upon them regularly might inspire him to actually read them.

"You admire Lady Kirsten's priorities?" Daniel asked.

Ralph paused, a volume of Wordsworth in his hand. He was a young man, probably not yet twenty, with sandy hair and a friendly countenance. Like most footmen, he also filled out his livery with a complement of muscle.

"It's like this, Mr. Banks. The Quality can live in a house their whole lives and not see the very place that shelters them. Lady Kirsten sees the house and the people who work there. If she says the chimney lamps are to be cleaned, she'll notice if they're cleaned—and if they're not."

Wordsworth was followed by Blake, Burns, Pope, Sheridan—many winters' worth of fine reading.

Though young boys would enjoy these selections in only small doses.

Ralph took the now-empty box from Daniel's desk. "Luncheon be ready, Mr. Banks. We can bring a tray up from the kitchen if you'd like to take your meal here today."

A sleety rain had turned the garden to mud, and the thought of traversing that mud to join the Haddonfield family for the midday meal daunted.

"I'll come down to the kitchen shortly," Daniel said. "If you'd send word to the manor house that I'll bide with my books until supper?"

"Consider it done, sir."

Ralph withdrew, a young fellow content to be of service to others. Had he any scriptural bent, he'd have made a fine curate.

Daniel put the two dozen volumes in alphabetical order by author, then repaired to the kitchen. An army of maids had been busy for two days on the lowest floor, scrubbing every room from the corners out, shining up windows with vinegar, rubbing beeswax and lemon oil into the woodwork, and hanging lavender sachets by the score.

Footmen had been dispatched to the top floors, though Daniel had decided against turning the maids' quarters into a schoolroom. The top of any house was hard to keep warm in winter or cool in summer, so the former music room was pressed into service as a place of learning.

The dower property was a sizable dwelling, as would befit a lady with the rank of countess. In only two days' time, a sense of happy industry had settled over the building.

Would that Daniel could attain such an air himself.

The kitchen was at the back of the house, in proximity to the gardens, the summer kitchen, the henhouse, and the dairy. As Daniel approached, he heard a female voice coming from the hallway that led to the pantries and a back entrance.

"They were my father's boots," the lady said. "I would not entrust them to just anybody."

"The old earl's boots?" came the wondering reply. A child's voice, a small boy, probably the boot boy.

"His lordship wore his riding boots even when he could no longer sit a horse. They were special to him, and I know you'll do a good job with them."

Lady Kirsten, though her tone held none of its

customary starch. From the shadowed corridor, Daniel ventured a peek into the nearest pantry.

Her ladyship sat on a rough plank bench, a small blond boy beside her, a pair of handsome field boots in the boy's lap.

"They're already clean," the child said. "They want a bit of polish though. Cook says I'm lazy, because I'm not fast, but I'm not lazy. When do you need these boots, milady?"

"You must be patient with Cook, Jeremy. She's never polished a pair of boots and doesn't know how long the job ought to take. A roast won't cook faster merely because the master is hungry, will it?"

"No, milady. It's the same with boots. The leather should dry first, and the oil has to soak in, and the polish can't go on too quick after that. Ralph taught me, because he was the boots once, when he was young. He said to always try my best, and so that's what I do."

Her ladyship wore no cap, her full-length apron was streaked with dust, and her blond hair was sagging free of its bun on one side. She looked like a senior maid after a hard day's cleaning, not like an earl's daughter. Sitting beside the small boy who was beset by a small boy's challenges, she also looked like a kindly older cousin or an aunt.

Or like…a mother.

"That's all any of us can do, Jeremy," she said, "is try our best, even when people forget to say thank you. You can work at these boots on a day when it isn't raining, because I know the present earl will always have muddy boots for you on the rainy days."

"And he has big, muddy boots," Jeremy replied, hopping off the bench. "The biggest in the shire, Ralph says. Good day, my lady!"

Jeremy scampered off, nearly knocking into Daniel with his prize. Lady Kirsten remained on the bench, though it was too late to pretend she hadn't seen Daniel.

"Mr. Banks, hello. I told the kitchen to send your luncheon up on a tray if you were inclined to bide here rather than join the family."

She wouldn't meet Daniel's gaze, and that bothered him. The lady who offered a slightly imprudent kiss to her married vicar, the lady who always spoke her mind and made war on cobwebs, should not feel any awkwardness on Daniel's account.

He took the place formerly occupied by young Jeremy. "Are you missing your midday meal, my lady?"

"I hadn't planned on it, but then one of the maids closed a door on her finger, and a footman dropped a trunk on another fellow's foot. For the past few years, my sister Nita took on the running of the household, but the dower house never received much attention."

"I thank you, then, for your efforts. I'll enjoy biding here until the vicarage can be put to rights."

Silence, awkward and unusual, sprang up between them.

Daniel waded back into the conversation, because that's what a vicar did. "Thank you for the books. I'll enjoy those too. I'll have a look around the vicarage later this week and see if I can find any Latin grammars or extra copies of *Robinson Crusoe*."

Some sentiment was boiling through Lady Kirsten. Daniel could feel it, like when an outburst would well up from Danny if he'd been overtaxed and hungry for too long.

Daniel waited, because that was also what vicars did.

"I saw you," Lady Kirsten said, brushing briskly at a smudge on her apron. "In the library yesterday. I came upon you."

The library—? One of the loveliest naps Daniel could recall. Dozing off in a public room wasn't exactly proper, but neither was Lady Kirsten a Puritan spinster.

"You found me napping? I'm sorry if my manners deserted me. Perhaps I snore? Your brothers led me to believe the Sabbath nap in the library was a fraternal institution. When I awoke, I was alone."

And well rested, for a change.

"You weren't snoring. Your boots were off, though."

Whatever was she getting at? "My apologies, both for being unshod and for the shocking state of my stockings." Olivia's skill with a needle had been limited, at best. Even though Daniel could afford new stockings, he inflicted her workmanship on his feet as a penance for not admitting Olivia's true nature to himself far sooner.

A vague wisp of a half-remembered dream brushed Daniel's awareness. He recalled being angry and gleeful at the same time, like an adolescent boy.

"You'll not find me asleep in the public rooms again, my lady. I'll have chambers here, and my napping can be done in a proper bed." Or at the church offices. Daniel had long ago developed the ability to nap sitting at his desk or stretched out on a church pew. Anywhere but his own home.

"All you recall is napping?" her ladyship asked.

What else would he have been doing? "Your brother Nicholas snores. That's the last thought I recall before dropping off. Why?"

The smudge on Lady Kirsten's apron had been spread, not diminished, by her attempts to brush it off, and still she fussed at it.

"No reason, Mr. Banks. I often find my brothers at their slumbers in the library. My father had the same habit. I expect the next earl will too."

Why did you kiss me? Except Daniel knew why: she'd kissed him because she'd wanted to.

"Do you like children, Lady Kirsten?"

The batting and brushing stopped. She smoothed her apron flat over her lap. "Very much. Children are honest and want little from us. I prefer them to most adults. I intend to be a relentlessly doting aunt, and my siblings will have no say in the matter."

She popped to her feet, so Daniel also stood. "Are you playing truant from the midday meal at Belle Maison, my lady?"

From the kitchen, the scent of hot food cut through the faint odor of lavender and lemons. Beef stew, perhaps, or a cottage pie. Heaven, to a man who'd bolted breakfast and spent the morning rearranging furniture.

"I dread crossing the garden," Lady Kirsten said. "Susannah has taken to reading old issues of *La Belle Assembleé*, Della is memorizing *Debrett's*, and the countess talks only of fashion. Nobody *does* anything. With all the tea and cakes they consume, my sisters ought to be the size of Nicholas's mare."

"Most would envy them their idleness," Daniel said, though he did not. The earl gave a good account of himself, tending to significant acreage and mercantile interests, but the women were bored.

One of the women was mortally bored, though never boring.

"I want to take the vicarage in hand," Lady Kirsten said, marching from the pantry. "I doubt I'll have time before we leave for Town. Lemon and beeswax won't cure rising damp anyway."

Nothing cured rising damp save for replacing every scrap of affected wood. "You're leaving soon, then?"

The prospect of distance from Lady Kirsten should have been a relief. She was unconventional, discontent, and unpredictable. Worse yet, she was patient with small boys, had a strong streak of domestic competence, and could not dissemble even to appease appearances.

Most troublesome of all, Daniel *liked* her. A lot.

"Leah hasn't chosen a date for our departure," she said, jamming the errant loop of hair back into her bun. "But leave we shall. When we're assured the roads are passable, we're off to London. You will have started with your academy by then."

"My scholars? Three small boys taking the odd swipe at Latin does not an academy make."

"I smell fresh bread." Lady Kirsten's pace increased, then she halted to twist a sachet from behind a curtain. "Nicholas told George that in addition to Digby and the Blumenthal brats, you're to take on both of Squire Webber's sons. He aspires to send them to public school, but they lack a foundation."

And years of dedicated tutors had been unable to remedy that lack? "I think you had better join me for lunch," Daniel said, resuming their progress toward a hot meal.

"I believe I shall. I adore a hearty beef stew with bread and butter on a cold, rainy day. Cook uses Mama's recipe, and I'm partial to it."

Peasant fare for an earl's daughter. Daniel liked her entirely too well.

A scullery maid set places for them at a wooden table heavy enough to double as a threshing floor, while Lady Kirsten served up bowls of steaming stew and Daniel sliced the bread. Daniel held the lady's chair, and then, without even a nod in the direction of further small talk, took shameless advantage of his companion.

"I want to know every detail you can share about my scholars, Lady Kirsten. They're shaping up to be a pack of ne'er-do-wells, scamps, and scapegraces. One wonders if the parish isn't attempting to run me off rather than welcome me."

She snapped her serviette across her lap. "They're out-and-out rotters, every one, save for Digby, but George says he's showing dubious potential. Don't steal all the butter."

Daniel passed her ladyship the plate of butter, small golden molds in the shape of roses.

"Your butter, and Lord-we-thank-Thee-for-this-food, amen. Now tell me about these scoundrels."

Lady Kirsten sat back, her smile indulgent. "I've known these boys since they were babies, Mr. Banks. They're full of energy and mischief, and there's not a Latin scholar among them. They are truly, truly awful."

❧

"Mama's husband wants to send me away to school," Danny informed Loki. "He doesn't know what to do with me."

Danny undid the braid he'd twisted into his pony's mane, for he hadn't made a very tidy job of it. Loki was the best part of living with Mama—Danny *would* remember to call her Aunt Letty if anybody came by.

Sometimes Loki was the *only* good part of living here. He was black and white and nearly as fast as a full-grown horse.

"I like Mama's husband well enough," Danny said, making another try for the braid while Loki munched on a pile of hay. "But the viscount likes Mama best of all, and I don't know what to call him."

The viscount—David, Viscount Fairly—wasn't Danny's papa and had said Danny must not call him Papa. Danny's first papa had died, before.

Before life had gone all widdershins, and Papa—Uncle Daniel—had given Danny back to Mama—who had been plain Aunt Letty until then—before Danny's previous mama, Olivia, Papa's—Uncle Daniel's—wife, had gone away.

Before now, when Danny no longer knew what to call anybody or where a boy could hide when he needed time to think.

"My mama from before was always mad at me," Danny said. He'd again tried to braid too much coarse mane together, and the braid was too short and wide.

"I hate it here," he whispered to his pony. "Mama's husband never takes me up before him because I have you, but I'm not allowed to jump anything when I ride you. Don't worry. We'll jump soon. Mama's husband has said when the ground is firmer, that's the time to jump."

Loki lifted his tail and broke wind with the casual ease of a well-fed equine.

"Beelzebub's farts stink worse than yours," Danny said, and abruptly a lump formed in his throat and he leaned into his pony's neck. "You're my best pony, but I miss Zubbie."

He missed Beelzebub's farts, which had always made him laugh because they were so awful. Papa had laughed too and said to thank God for the horse's good health.

"Papa doesn't want me either, and he won't come visit ever again. Mama won't take me to visit him, and I'm mad at him too."

And Danny missed his papa so, or his uncle Daniel or whatever he was supposed to call the person who'd loved him and raised him for five years.

"I hate it here," he said as a hot tear slid down his cheek. "I hate to cry too, and I hate porridge— Papa always let me share his buttered toast. And I hate chocolate, and I hate not jumping, and I hate the stupid old vicar here who says the stupid service forever and ever."

Loki shifted, nearly mashing Danny's toes with a pony hoof.

"I'm sinning," Danny said, "and I don't care. What's the point of honoring my father and mother if my days upon the earth are miserable? What's the point of going to the service if it only makes me bored and have to use the necessary?"

What was the point of anything?

When Papa wrestled with a problem, he prayed about it.

Prayer hadn't done anything to make Danny's heart ache less.

"Papa also went for a long ride," Danny said. "He galloped and jumped and galloped some more, until Beelzebub had the fidgets worked out and was all muddy and ready for a nap."

Outside the viscount's vast stable, the rain had finally stopped, but the grooms were bustling about, and the ground was all over mud.

Danny wiped his cheek on his sleeve—crying was for babies—and whispered into his pony's hairy ear.

"Tomorrow morning, after your breakfast has settled, we'll go for a mad gallop, and then we'll feel better."

He patted his pony before he left the stall, though like any equine, Loki was mostly interested in his hay. Danny didn't bother undoing the last attempt at a braid, for it had come undone all on its own.

Six

"START WITH THE WEBBER BOYS," MR. BANKS SAID, passing Kirsten a slice of bread. He'd cut the loaf thinner than it was served at the manor house, suggesting a man raised with economies learned to conserve the kitchen resources.

He wouldn't let half the chocolate grow cold in the pot, wouldn't waste the first hour of his morning choosing which knot to put in his cravat.

"The older Webber child is Thomas," she said, "the younger Matthias, and there's barely a year's difference between them. Matthias is the more diabolical, for he's fair and has a sweet countenance. His mother indulges him because he did not thrive as an infant. Thomas is the more physically robust and is protective of his younger brother. They've been through three tutors that I know of in the last year."

Mr. Banks looked intrigued. "I wonder if they use the same scheme to get rid of every tutor, or if they invent new ones suited to the occasion. What about the Blumenthal twins?"

He didn't call them brats. Kirsten engaged in some

dilatory buttering of her bread because Mr. Banks either would not acknowledge that shocking moment in the library the previous day, or he simply did not recall it. Leah swore her infant son could sleep with his eyes open, and Kirsten had no grounds to doubt her.

"The Blumenthal boys are said to be indistinguishable," Kirsten replied, "but that's not so. Frederick's face is narrower than Frank's, and Fred has a small scar on his left earlobe. The nursemaid who figured that out earned Mrs. Blumenthal's undying gratitude."

"What sort of mother can't tell her own children apart?" Mr. Banks asked.

"One with ten children, five of them boys. I'm not sure they hold still long enough to be counted, much less sorted."

Kirsten could tell the twins apart irrespective of scars. Frederick was quick to use his fists, which probably accounted for the scar, while young Frank was a schemer. He'd hang back, plot and plan, and then hatch up mischief when nobody expected trouble.

"You'll have your work cut out for you," she said, reaching for another slice of bread.

Mr. Banks reached at the same time, their hands collided, and for a funny little moment, they each held a corner of the same slice of bread.

"My apologies," Mr. Banks said, relinquishing the prize. "Let's start with Frederick Blumenthal. If you could elaborate on his strengths first, I would be obliged. Everyone has something they take pride in or do with natural ease, and emphasizing those areas often allows a child to progress in more difficult undertakings."

Kirsten used the knife to lift a rosette of butter from

the dish for her next thin slice of bread, and abruptly she was angry.

And very near tears.

This was what she did well. Organized maids and footmen, kept track of which child favored licorice and which parlor needed new sachets. Made sure the good recipes were kept on hand, however humble the resulting fare. Nita could keep the accounts, organize schedules, and monitor the pantries, but Kirsten had monitored the home.

Mr. Banks would value a woman who brought that much to a marital union. He wouldn't view his lady as a broodmare who paid with her liberty for the privilege of serving his title.

"Lady Kirsten? Have I given offense? I can take my meal back to the office and spend the hours with my father's diaries if your ladyship prefers. A son ought to read his father's words, but in the years since my father's death, I haven't made the time. Haven't wanted to endure any posthumous scolds, if you want the truth."

Mr. Banks came close to babbling, while Kirsten managed to shake her head. Her bread was gently pried from her hand, and Mr. Banks finished applying the butter, such as he might have for a young child.

"I hate London."

Yes, Kirsten had said that, like a sulky, if honest, girl. Her expostulation was Mr. Banks's cue to recall overdue correspondence, pressing business with the earl, or whatever excuse from the well-stocked arsenal of polite male excuses he chose to fire off in return for Kirsten's complaint.

He tore the buttered bread in half and passed the larger portion to her.

"My father referred to Town as Sodom-on-Thames, among other less savory appellations," he said. "I gather London's propensity for vice is not the source of your dislike?"

Kirsten took a nibble of bread, which was better for having a larger quotient of butter to bread.

"You are very brave, Mr. Banks. You might fool everybody else, but you are a brave man. I will reward your courage with gossip you'll likely hear in the churchyard: on two notable occasions, I failed to bring my devoted suitors up to scratch."

Mr. Banks was even a fierce man, though the first glimpse Kirsten had seen of his ferocity had been unnervingly erotic.

Also unforgettable.

"I am a good listener," he said, smiling at his half piece of bread, then biting off a portion. "An occupational necessity for a vicar, but also one of those natural abilities I mentioned earlier. I like knowing how things function and how people work. With familiarity comes greater insight into why this one stumbles, and that one can't forgive. Won't you tell me about London, my lady?"

Daniel Banks had good, strong teeth and an ability to make a command feel like an invitation.

"I am not a good listener, Mr. Banks. I am impatient, nervous by some accounts, and lacking in charm. While I am not homely, my greatest attributes, as far as Polite Society is concerned, are a larger dowry than my sisters can claim and a certain pragmatism that will serve me well in a good match."

All true, though not the entire truth.

"A loveless match, you mean?" Mr. Banks asked mildly.

"A loveless, advantageous match." Advantageous for the man, who could improve his fortunes and his cachet by marrying an earl's daughter.

Mr. Banks patted her knuckles. "To know one's own value is a strength, my lady. If you'd settled for some viscount's spotty, self-important heir, you'd have murdered the young wretch within a year of the nuptials."

Mr. Sedgewick had been prone to spots, and he could have written odes to his own consequence. Viscount Morton, however—"Call me Arthur, won't you please?"—had been Kirsten's every secret longing adorned with a dashing smile.

She nearly hated Arthur Morton now.

"You've seen bad matches?" Kirsten asked.

"All vicars see unhappy matches," Mr. Banks said, dusting bread crumbs from his hands. "I've studied marital discord from a much closer vantage point than I had anticipated when I trained for the church. How might you make London more bearable?"

By burning down every ballroom in the West End.

"Two years ago," Kirsten said, "I developed a slight cough that served me well and was only half-feigned. The air—particularly early in the Season, while the coal fires are roaring—is foul. Another year, I was prone to sick headaches. The year of my come-out, I contrived to sprain an ankle as soon as I'd been presented, but my sisters won't tolerate those ploys now. If I cross the line to eccentric, I could queer Della's and Susannah's prospects."

"Loyalty to your loved ones is a cardinal virtue," Mr. Banks said. "That loyalty should go both ways."

His observation lay between them, and like the empty soup bowls, half-filled tankards of ale, and bread crumbs, it wanted tidying up.

"My sisters love me, as do my brothers." Only Nita, though, had been truly loyal, and she was off with her new husband to tour the wonders of the Continent—or the marriage bed.

"I love my horse, Lady Kirsten. Adore every hair on his handsome head and fret over his digestion the way a new mother frets over her baby, but when his oats are poured into his bucket, his awareness of me ceases."

"He's a horse," Kirsten said, though Mr. Banks was not making an equestrian point, and the oats of an approaching Season had indeed been poured into her sisters' buckets. "Do you miss your former congregation?"

The scullery maid—a cousin of Jeremy's who'd alerted Kirsten to the boy's earlier upset—cleared away the dishes, which meant Kirsten had to wait for an answer to her question. She was certain Mr. Banks was missing something, or possibly somebody.

A lowering thought.

He tipped his mug of ale and studied the contents—winter ale, though Kirsten preferred the lighter, sweeter summer ales.

"I miss being secure in my place in the world," he said, setting the ale down untasted. "I miss taking on the challenges I've chosen, not those that rise up, unwelcome and unannounced, to disturb my very concept of myself. I'd thought myself a decent enough fellow, competent to fulfill my calling, an asset to my community. Those convictions were shaken, and I will not take them for granted again."

Mr. Banks was leaving much unsaid, though both regret and determination echoed loudly in his words.

"Not a pleasant time, when one's convictions about oneself are shaken." Christopher Sedgewick's behavior had started that process and Arthur Morton's had finished it. "One can emerge wiser for the upset."

Though what could shake a man of Mr. Banks's fiercely decent nature?

"Wiser, perhaps." Now Mr. Banks drained the last of his ale. "I've begun to wonder if wisdom isn't overrated. Nowhere in the Commandments are we exhorted to be wise."

He came around to assist Kirsten with her chair, something her brothers would have neglected to do unless company were present.

"The Commandments don't exhort us to be happy," Kirsten said, "and yet I cannot cease wishing happiness for myself and for those I care about." She wished happiness for Mr. Banks too, though why hadn't she seen sooner that he was sorrowing for something or for someone?

Kirsten rose and Mr. Banks remained where he was, lips pursed, gazing into the middle distance. This close, she could see that he'd again turned his cravat to hide frayed stitching, and a seam on his collar was threatening to unravel as well. He'd worn the plain, clerical collar on Sunday, but apparently eschewed that affectation when at home during the week.

"Mr. Banks?"

"You've given me an idea for a sermon, my lady, and it's only Monday. My thanks, for you've made my entire week a more cheering prospect. If I take my horse out for a good gallop tomorrow, by Wednesday, I'll have the Scripture to go with the message."

Should Kirsten, the least Christian of any Haddonfield in the centuries-long history of Haddonfields, be pleased to have inspired a sermon?

"I've made you happy?" Kirsten asked.

His focus shifted back to the present moment, probably torn from the glories of Psalms or Deuteronomy.

"You have, my lady. My thanks."

His smile was so gently, radiantly pleased, Kirsten wanted to be wrapped in his arms and in his joy, to give him many inspirations and to give him her heart.

I shall not subject myself to the farce of a London season this year. The notion settled in her mind as a fait accompli, and the relief was enormous. Mr. Banks was right—she'd have murdered either Sedgewick or Morton had she married them.

"You've made me happy too, Mr. Banks, and I assure you, few can say as much." She kissed his cheek, a second transgression against strict propriety, though the maid was busy at the sink, and Mr. Banks hadn't taken any great exception to Kirsten's first such trespass.

He said nothing now, either, no scold, no remonstration, so Kirsten patted his worn cravat and sailed from the kitchen. As she flew up the maids' stairs, sunlight illuminated a coating of dust on the newel post, for the sun had finally, finally come out.

When she'd finished turning the music room into a classroom, she'd have the maids get after the stairway. Mr. Banks deserved a clean, pleasant place to undertake the challenge of educating a pack of rascally boys.

To undertake all of his challenges.

❧

"She did it again," Daniel informed Beelzebub as the horse toddled away from the mounting block. "Lady Kirsten kissed my cheek, and I was so taken aback, so ambushed, I could not chastise her for her boldness."

Beelzebub trundled along the damp lane, though already, the puddles were drying and the morning sun had chased the dew off the grass. A beautiful day, really, well suited to galloping off the fidgets.

"I did not want to hurt her ladyship's feelings. One should be kind."

Zubbie shied, of course. His former owner had called the gelding "high-strung," though others termed it "full of the devil." His spooks, shies, dodges, and bucks were not intended to jeopardize his rider, but rather were intended to ensure the rider was paying attention.

As a conscientious rider ought to, at all times.

"At least wait till we get to the road before you start quizzing me on my equitation," Daniel said, patting the beast's shoulder. "Some families are simply friendly, you know? They hug and kiss in the normal course and it doesn't mean a thing. The earl is quite a friendly fellow."

With his countess. With his sisters, Bellefonte was more circumspect.

"If you want the truth," Daniel said, guiding Beelzebub around a puddle in which the horse would have splashed and pawed away half the morning, "I don't want to hurt Lady Kirsten's feelings. Somebody already has—hurt her feelings or offended

DANIEL'S TRUE DESIRE 107

her sensibilities. I needn't court her disfavor by taking issue with a pair of harmless, friendly kisses."

Daniel's personal test for what was acceptable conduct had once come down to: Would he have behaved in a given manner if his wife or son were present? He'd tolerated many kisses and embraces from parishioners in Little Weldon as Olivia and Danny looked on, but his test failed him in this instance.

Beelzebub indulged in another of his favorite tactics for riveting his rider's attention, and came to an abrupt halt.

"Walk on, you naughty boy. He who craves a good gallop must walk and trot first."

Daniel had spent yesterday trying to distract himself from thoughts of Danny. The dower house would easily accommodate a herd of small boys in addition to one unsettled vicar, and the dwelling was becoming a pleasant place too.

Lady Kirsten had issued a decree to that effect, and so it would come to pass.

"I'm to look after other people's small boys again," Daniel said as his horse minced along the lane. "I miss Danny."

Daniel could say the words now without wanting to destroy the nearest fragile object, could say them without wanting to throttle his lawfully wedded wife, or even rant at her for very long.

"A rousing go-to-the-devil or two," he murmured as they turned onto the road to the village. "A few I-never-want-to-see-you-agains, and the usual how-could-yous at full Sunday volume. For form's sake only, you understand. I can accept that Olivia was disappointed in me as a spouse, but Danny and Letty did nothing to deserve her betrayal."

Anger joined Daniel in the saddle, a dangerous, raging flood of it that had grown more powerful with the passing months rather than ebbed.

"My lawfully wedded wife will not cost me my calling," Daniel said, sinking his weight into his stirrups. Beelzebub, a veteran of many steeplechases in pursuit of spiritual clarity—or something like it—knew what that weight shift meant. He settled, collecting back onto his haunches in anticipation of a great leap forward.

"Of all the losses Olivia has inflicted on me—my home, my dignity, my position in Oxfordshire, my relationship with my only sibling—she will not also rob me of my vocation."

Then they were away, flying across the spring countryside, a flat streak of dark horse and determined man, throwing up mud, turf, psalms, and anger behind them.

❧

"Trouble afoot," Alfrydd muttered.

Kirsten followed his gaze down the lane, to a man on a sizable, muddy horse, a small child up before him, and a riderless black-and-white pony beside the horse.

"The pony looks sound enough," Kirsten replied, but Alfrydd was right that trouble approached, for the pony had a grass-stained, bloody knee.

"Mr. Banks left more than two hours ago," Alfrydd said, tugging at the girth of Kirsten's saddle. "That black of his is winded. They had a good romp before turning up Samaritan."

The Samaritan was furious. The line of Mr. Banks's jaw and the absolute dignity of his posture shouted of rage. The child, curiously, was in no better mood.

"You can put up my mare, Alfrydd," Kirsten said. "Better still, have one of the grooms take her for a hack. I apparently won't be raiding the vicarage's library shelves today after all."

Kirsten could still climb on her mare, salute the approaching pair as she cantered past, and leave them to sort out their differences, but the child was barely school-age, and he was muddy down one side of his breeches.

Kirsten could not turn her back on the boy, for nobody's outlook was improved by a trip through the mud.

"Mr. Banks," she called cheerily. "A pleasant day to you and to your companion."

The vicar stared down at her from the back of his black destrier, a portion of that ferocity Kirsten had seen in the library lingering in his expression.

"Lady Kirsten, good day."

Nothing more, as if all manners, all civility even, had fled his grasp. The boy, however, remained snugly secured by Mr. Banks's arm about his middle.

"Won't you introduce us?" Kirsten asked, taking the pony's reins and passing them to Alfrydd.

"Master Daniel Banks, ma'am," the child announced, his little chin quivering. "All I did was take my pony for a gallop. Loki is *my* pony. The viscount said."

Banks swung down, the child leaning forward in synchrony with the adult's dismount, as if they'd ridden together many times in the past.

"You left without permission, Danny," Mr. Banks said. "You didn't take a groom, you told no one where you went, you took risks, and Loki came to harm as a result. I am very, very disappointed in you."

Mr. Banks was beyond disappointed, beyond even enraged, and galloping into the nearer reaches of despair. Kirsten knew that territory well, knew both its briar patches and the high hedges that obscured all exits.

"Well, come along," she said, reaching for the boy, though his muddy boots might do permanent damage to her riding habit. "Mr. Banks's horse must be walked out and groomed, and the lads can't see to that if you two must air your differences in public."

She'd snapped the fingers of good manners beneath Mr. Banks's nose. He passed his horse's reins to a waiting groom and reached for the child.

"I'll take the boy. He's heavy."

"I have him," Kirsten said, stalking away. The child was substantial, as a healthy little boy ought to be, though Kirsten was plenty sturdy enough to manage his weight.

Besides, how often did she get to hold any child?

Mr. Banks, as Kirsten had known he would, followed. He would have followed this disappointing boy anywhere, of that she was certain. To avoid the midday bustle in the Belle Maison kitchens, and to keep the miscreant to herself for a while longer, Kirsten headed for the back entrance to the dower house.

"Are you hurt anywhere, Danny?" she asked.

"No, ma'am. I scraped my arm, though."

"Scraped it bloody?" Kirsten had five brothers, and

as sure as they must break wind and burp, boys loved bloody mishaps.

"I haven't looked. It stings something powerful, ma'am."

Mr. Banks stalked along beside them, his lips were nearly white and his hair was tousled in all directions.

"While I tidy you up, Mr. Banks can have Alfrydd send a groom to let others know you're safe," Kirsten suggested, because a period in neutral corners was necessary for these two. A short period.

"An excellent suggestion," Mr. Banks retorted, turning with military precision and marching double time back toward the stable.

"He's very angry," the child said. "I've never seen him this angry. I'm angry too."

"Anger often works that way. We go at it in pairs." Kirsten's worst rages had been solo endeavors, though. "Tell me the truth. Are you hurt?"

As they reached the dower house, Kirsten dipped at the knees and the boy lifted the door latch.

"I'm not really hurt, not like you mean."

"Then like how?" Internal injuries had killed many a rider with more experience than Danny, but boys were tough creatures.

So were girls. Ladies were perhaps toughest of all.

"My belly aches all the time," Danny said. "I want to shout and run, but that doesn't help either. I don't want to play with my soldiers, but I'm neglecting my studies too."

Neglecting his studies was some adult's phrase for those fidgets and megrims.

"You thought to gallop off the dismals?" Kirsten asked.

The boy turned his head away. His small shoulders hitched, and then he buried his face against Kirsten's neck.

"I was mad at—at *him*. Will Loki be all right?"

Kirsten sat the child on the worktable—he was heavy—and kept her arms around him.

"Your pony will be spoiled rotten in my brother's stable. You were angry at Mr. Banks?"

A nod against her collarbone. Silky dark hair the exact same shade as Mr. Banks's tickled Kirsten's chin. The boy had the same name as the vicar. His eyes were the same chocolate brown, his jaw…

Nobody would doubt this boy was Mr. Banks's child, despite the reality of his origins.

"Let's get you cleaned up before Mr. Banks rejoins us. A good scrap is best undertaken with a full belly."

The two-inch laceration above the child's wrist was indeed bloody and would bruise handsomely. Kirsten tended the wound, bound it, and then brushed the boy's clothing clean as best she could with a damp cloth. His boots received a cursory washing down as well, more for the sake of the floors and furniture than for the boy's dignity.

She fixed him buttered bread with jam and a mug of milk. When Mr. Banks stomped through the back door, Danny was ensconced at the table, looking none the worse for his ordeal.

Kirsten intercepted the Wrath of St. Jude's Pulpit before he could tear into the child.

"Mr. Banks, perhaps you're feeling peckish too? Danny's wrist will be fine, though he has a nasty scrape. Because he's worried about the pony, I've assured him Loki will be well cared for."

"Danny should be the one looking after his pony," Mr. Banks growled, trying to dodge around Kirsten. "Danny is the one who put him at risk."

Horses slipped, they misjudged stiles, they were horses. The rider wasn't necessarily at fault for any of it any more than Kirsten's father could have stopped his sons from their various misadventures.

Kirsten put both hands on Mr. Banks's shoulders. "When you've *had something to eat*, you can take Danny to the stable to look in on the pony."

"I don't want any—"

She shook him by the shoulders, rather like trying to shake a stout oak. "You could do with some ale, and a bit of bread and cheese, Mr. Banks." Must she shout at him? Danny was hurting, upset, and *a child*.

Those broad, strong shoulders slumped.

"The boy was lost," he said softly near Kirsten's ear. "Anybody might have come upon him, stolen the pony, or worse. My own father railed endlessly against my independent nature when I was a boy. I now see why. Danny was a good two hours from home by the lanes and that pony could have come up lame at any moment. The child was completely bewildered, and I'm much afraid nobody even knows he's taken off."

Afraid. A trip through the mud was far preferable to being afraid. Kirsten slipped her arms around the *bewildered* man before her, and his stole around her too.

"I love that child," he nearly whispered. "I love him until—I love him more than life, and he was bleeding and lost, far from home, alone, and—"

All the fierceness Kirsten had seen and sensed in Mr. Banks shuddered through him, on behalf of a small boy who sat munching bread and jam two yards away.

"He's *fine*," she said, stroking a hand over Mr. Banks's hair. "The child is fine, though he needs a stern talking-to and some sorting out. You'll be fine too."

Though sending the boy back to his negligent caretakers would hurt Mr. Banks terribly.

The vicar stepped back, tugged down his waistcoat, and ran a hand through his hair.

"Have we ale?" he asked.

Yes, *we* did. "Of course, and bread and cheese. No biscuits for the boy, but I might find some for you."

Kirsten smoothed down the hair Mr. Banks had just disarranged, winked at him, and repaired to the larder in search of his ale. Once there, she poured a small pint, settled herself on a stool—her skirts were indeed a muddy fright—and prepared to indulge in a bit of eavesdropping.

❧

"The new vicar is quite tall," Matthias said, pushing his spectacles up his nose. He wore an old pair that had been his papa's, and Digby thought they didn't fit him. "Tall is bad."

"Tall means he can swing a birch rod," Thomas agreed. Around the small circle of boys sharing an empty stall in the livery, heads nodded in agreement.

"Vicar—the old vicar—would fall asleep if I asked him a question about the Roman armies," Digby volunteered, though inside he didn't feel nearly as hopeful as he tried to make his words. He abruptly missed the old vicar, who'd been gruff, smelly, and long-winded, but he'd never taken the birch rod to Digby's backside.

"This vicar doesn't look sleepy," Frank Blumenthal said. Frank was a quiet boy, often in his twin's shadow, but the scholar hadn't been born who liked a birching.

"My new papa promised me Vicar Banks is nice," Digby said.

Frank and Fred exchanged a look that suggested Papa had lied, which Digby would not believe, though the Blumenthal Brats were a formidable pair. They'd chased off three governesses and three tutors, after all.

"Every one of them is nice when they're talking to your parents," Matthias explained. "Then you're shut up in the schoolroom with them, and it's 'Master Blumenthal, have you misplaced your brain?' *Whack!* 'Master Blumenthal, do you take me for a simpleton?' *Whack!* 'Master Blumenthal, fetch my cane!'"

Matthias's imitation of adult speech was not funny at all.

"Governesses were ever so much easier." Thomas sighed. "A few frogs here and there, tea poured on her mattress just before bedtime, a nice big spider in her slippers... I miss our governesses."

A respectful silence descended in the name of bygone governesses, though Digby could hardly recall the one governess he'd had before his first papa had died.

"I think we should give the new vicar a chance," Digby said. He was the youngest, though of a size with the Blumenthals. "He asked me what I thought of his sermon on Sunday, and then he listened to my answer."

"What did you tell him?" Matthias was fiddling

some straw into a braided design. Matthias was clever with his hands.

"I said he didn't tell us a story, and then he asked me about my pony."

"You haven't got a pony," Thomas retorted, looking up from retying the laces of his boots. He needed new boots, judging from the cracks in the leather near his toes.

"I don't have a pony yet, but my new papa has promised—"

"They do that," Matthias said, pitching his straw doll aside. "They promise, but then the rents aren't enough, or your older sister has to go up to Town, or your mama wants a new gig. No pony, *ever*. And then it's off to public school where you must fag for the older boys or get beaten to within an inch of your life."

Digby hadn't an older sister, his new papa had already taken Mama up to Town to shop for dresses, and these boys were entirely too glum.

"I can't worry about public school now," Digby said, "and my new papa will get me a pony, you'll see."

This might have been an invitation for Thomas to sit on him. Thomas was very good at sitting on smaller boys until they yelled whatever nonsense Thomas demanded from them. Worse, Thomas had a talent for pushing his victims down amid the horse droppings and the mud.

The arrival of the new vicar had shifted everybody's priorities, apparently. No time for horse droppings or mud now, not when a genuine, birch-rod-wielding menace had taken up residence among them.

"We need a plan," Matthias said, folding his glasses and putting them in a pocket. "We got 'round our governesses, we got 'round our tutors, we got 'round the old vicar, and we mostly get 'round our parents. We'll get 'round this Mr. Banks too."

Seven

LADY KIRSTEN HAD DISCREETLY WITHDRAWN TO THE pantries, but to know she was within earshot steadied Daniel. If young Danny lost his temper, she'd intercede.

If Daniel lost *his* temper, she'd also intercede.

"Are you enjoying the bread?" Daniel asked, taking a seat across from the boy.

"I said grace," Danny shot back, a smear of jam on his stubborn little chin.

His dear, impossible, stubborn little chin that might have been dashed on a rock that very morning. Daniel helped himself to a slice of bread—cut thicker than he was used to—and applied butter and jam mostly to buy time.

"How is your arm?" he asked.

Boyish lashes lowered bashfully. "Lady Kirsten said I had a prodigious, terrible gash, and the blood nearly made her faint. When she'd wrapped my arm in linen, she kissed it better, but the cut smarted awfully when she cleaned it."

Olivia hadn't ever kissed the child's hurts better. She'd scolded Danny for his various scrapes instead.

Remorse nearly choked Daniel, for all the child had suffered, for all he was still suffering.

"I'm sure you were very brave," Daniel said, tearing his bread in two and passing Danny the larger portion. They'd developed this habit long ago, and Danny took his share without hesitation.

For a moment, the bread and jam forestalled the next part of the conversation, but only for a moment.

"Danny, I have to take you back. Your mother and the viscount will be worried sick. You owe them an apology for running off, and I'm none too proud of you for this morning's frolic myself."

Danny set his bread and jam down. "I *wasn't* frolicking, Papa. I was galloping off the dismals, as you and Zubbie do. All Mama does is hug me and mess up my hair and tell me how glad she is that I'm with her. The viscount at least got me a pony, but I've stopped asking them about you because they always change the subject. I *hate it* there, and sometimes I think I'll soon hate them."

Beneath the table, Daniel sensed the rhythmic kicking of a small boy's boots against the rungs of his chair.

"*Hate* is a serious word, Danny."

A dangerous word, an unchristian word. The last word Daniel had wanted the boy to learn under his mother's roof.

"I shouldn't hate, I know that," Danny said, "but *nobody* listens, and there's *nothing* to do. My tutor falls asleep, we *never* have buttered toast for breakfast, the vicar there shouts at everybody on Sundays *forever*, and *I miss you!*"

Daniel barely had time to push his chair back as the

boy pelted around the table. Small arms lashed about Daniel's neck, and the comforting weight of the dear child scrambled into Daniel's lap.

"I *hate it* there," Danny wailed, tears flowing. "It's *not* home, it will *never* be home, and *I want to go home.*"

I want to go home too, child. Daniel recognized a tantrum when it befell the boy but hadn't been as alert to his own emotions. While Danny sobbed and muttered and generally wrinkled Daniel's linen worse than it already had been, Lady Kirsten rejoined them and began quietly clearing the table.

She didn't tousle Danny's hair, but she did brush Daniel's hair back off his forehead. At that moment, he hadn't the energy to question or take issue with her familiarity, for her touch brought him too much comfort.

"Tea, I think," she said. "And maybe some biscuits after all."

Danny subsided, exhausted, as children tended to be when strong emotion has been expressed.

"I don't want to go back there, Papa. Mama and the viscount are very nice, but it's hard to remember that I'm to call her Aunt Letty when she's always telling me how much she likes being my mama. I liked her better when she was simply Aunt Letty and you were my only papa."

Daniel had liked that better too. He'd repent of that selfish thought later.

"We have two problems, my boy," Daniel said as the scent of peppermint filled the kitchen. "First, you were wrong to leave the viscount's household without permission."

"I know, but you can't gallop off the dismals with a groom on one side and a viscount on the other when neither one of them lets you go faster than a stupid trot. *You* never took a groom or a viscount when you hacked out with Zubbie."

Children would wield logic at the worst times. Over at the slop bucket, Lady Kirsten's chin had dipped, as if she stifled a snicker.

"I've been riding for years," Daniel said, "while you're on your first pony, and when you did go for a gallop, look how your pony fared."

He'd spiked the boy's cannon with that one. Danny maneuvered off Daniel's lap onto the chair beside him.

"I'll apologize to Loki and look after him, the way you showed me with Beelzebub. I miss Zubbie too."

Said with heartbreaking woefulness—which would get the lad nowhere.

"You owe the pony an apology, you owe your mother an apology, and you owe the viscount a very big apology because you betrayed the trust he showed you when he put Loki in your hands."

Ah, a gratifying quiver of the chin.

"Do you think he'll t-take Loki away?"

If Viscount Fairly were smart—he was generally brilliant—he'd forbid Danny to ride for a few days and put him on muck cart duty.

"He might. You acted irresponsibly, Danny, toward your pony and toward the people who love you and want to keep you safe."

While Danny struggled under the weight of that avuncular pronouncement, Lady Kirsten brought over a tea tray—plain wood, with a plain linen towel on it.

Not a silver service, not even pewter, but plain, sturdy crockery. Chocolate biscuits graced a small plate in one corner of the tray.

How Daniel liked her, and how he'd have to repent of that. That too.

Sympathy for Danny assailed him, sympathy for a fellow who felt overwhelmed, alone, and without good options. A fellow who had precious little to look forward to and nobody to look forward to it with.

Except his trusty steed.

"At least you can visit Beelzebub today," Lady Kirsten said, taking the place across from Daniel. "Drink your tea, snatch a biscuit, and then away with you to the stable. Take Loki and Beelzebub some sugar and start working on your apologies. They usually benefit from thorough rehearsal."

Yes, they did. Just as a grown man benefited from time to sort out a proper course when a miserable little boy landed in his lap, all scraped up, bleeding, and famished.

Lady Kirsten drizzled a skein of honey in a cup of peppermint tea and set it in front of Danny. The scent alone was soothing, and the enthusiasm with which Danny downed his tea did Daniel's heart good too.

"Why is it," Lady Kirsten mused when Danny had bolted his biscuit and left, "the silence following a child's departure is more profound than other silences? We love the children dearly, but when they leave us in peace, we always feel a bit of gratitude."

Daniel accepted his cup of tea but denied himself a biscuit. Chocolate biscuits and peppermint tea were both rare luxuries by Daniel's standards. Lady Kirsten's company was a luxury too.

His list of repentances just kept growing longer, while his remorse grew more and more difficult to find.

❧

Kirsten had been patient long enough, and somebody needed to sort out the Banks menfolk.

"I do not share your sentiments, Lady Kirsten," Mr. Banks said. "When that boy leaves my sight, a part of my heart goes with him. I am not grateful for his absence, and I cannot imagine a circumstance where I would be."

Another glimmer of Mr. Banks's well-camouflaged ferocity shone through, also his sadness.

"You'd die for that boy," she said, her regard for Mr. Banks growing. Fathers cared for their sons that way, and cared enough to step aside when the child had a chance at a better life. Kirsten would never have been so noble.

"I would die for Danny cheerfully, my lady, and sometimes I think a part of me already has."

Such drama—and such hypocrisy?

"If spiritual well-being matters more than material security, then the child should be with you, Mr. Banks. All the wealth and position in the world does not compensate a child for a father's love."

He sat back, his tea cradled against his flat middle. "How easily you chart a course through troubled waters, but a child also needs his mother's love, Lady Kirsten."

That was her cue to stand up, wish him the best with a complicated family issue, and make that trip to the vicarage in search of adventure stories for little boys.

"A voice in my head is clamoring for me to mind my own business, Mr. Banks, but you and I are friends of a sort, so I will, in my usual fashion, ignore the voice of common sense. A mother is as a mother does, Mr. Banks, and when Danny was troubled and upset, he did not confide in his mother or his wealthy viscount step-papa, did he?"

As far as Kirsten was concerned, that decided the matter. If the child had no allies, then he might as well be in enemy territory.

With no good options and a long, bleak future ahead of him.

"Fairly has the means to open many doors for the boy, despite irregularities in Danny's pedigree." Mr. Banks's reply had the weary quality of an oft-recited prayer.

Lord Fairly was a canny sort. Kirsten liked him, but she didn't entirely trust him. He moved too quietly and had a tendency to pop up unannounced in odd company. Then too, he was a physician, and she did not care for physicians as a breed. Nicholas considered him a friend though, and Nicholas, for all that he was friend*ly*, was parsimonious with his friendships.

"Have you resigned yourself to the idea that Danny must adjust to his mother's household?" Kirsten asked, taking a sip of her tea. How would that feel, to surrender a much-loved child into uncertain circumstances and know the child was unhappy but probably better off?

Awful, that's how it would feel. And for the boy, to

be taken from a beloved father figure and everything familiar and dear?

Worse than awful.

"Danny has been with his mother for some months," Mr. Banks said, "though of course she must publicly remain Aunt Letty to him. Through inadvertence, the entire, complicated, unfortunate reality of Danny's birth was made known to him. He thus also struggles with truths he should have been spared, at least for a time."

Like Della, who'd figured out too early that the late earl was not her papa. She'd become a fierce, sad, bewildered little girl as a result, and a fiercer young woman.

"What will you do, Mr. Banks?"

Mr. Banks sipped his tea, though Kirsten doubted he tasted it. He hadn't touched any biscuits either, while she was tempted to eat the lot of them.

"I've told myself," he said softly, "that Letty is a good mother. She made sacrifices for that child no mother should have to consider. She visited as often as she could, she protected Danny from much. She and her viscount love the boy and will spare no expense to see him well situated." Mr. Banks set his mug on the tray, next to the untouched biscuits.

"You are trying to convince yourself to leave matters as they are," Kirsten concluded, disappointed, but also unhappy for him. The child would be better off in the home of a wealthy lord than in a makeshift vicarage—in the eyes of the world.

Then too, how had Mr. Banks explained the boy at his previous posting? A cousin's child? A foundling? All he'd said was that he'd raised Danny "at the vicarage."

"I'm trying to convince myself to leave well enough alone, and failing," Mr. Banks said, pushing the biscuits closer to Kirsten's elbow. "The sacrifices Letty has made or any imposition on me don't signify. What matters is that Danny have the best start in life."

"Then you'll send him back?" Kirsten did not like that option, but Mr. Banks faced no real choice, did he?

Mr. Banks rose, and though his boots were worn and his cravat wrinkled, he made a fine figure in his riding attire, particularly when resolution sat upon his broad shoulders and a smile illuminated his features.

"I will send Danny back, for now, but he has arrived to an age where he should have regular instruction, and many boys live in with their vicar prior to public school. They leave home in manageable stages that way, get an education, and ease their path into wider company than one household, however wealthy, allows."

Kirsten rose too, biscuits and tea forgotten. "You'll add him to your collection of rotten boys?"

Marvelous notion, and what a marvelous man, for coming up with it.

"Legally, I still have authority over the child as his guardian. I can argue for Danny to join the boys here, where he has both company and studies to distract him from what bothers him." Mr. Banks's smile was pleased and determined, also relieved.

Kirsten was still casting about for adjectives to describe that smile when he took her hand in a warm grasp, cradling it in both of his as he bowed.

"Thank you, Lady Kirsten, for helping me sort through my priorities."

His priorities? Kirsten seized the initiative and seized his mouth with her own as well, for she had a few priorities too.

❧

Gracious, merciful, everlasting, confounded, sweet…sweet, so very sweet…

The sheer perfection of Daniel's plan for Danny, the lovely rightness of it, had inspired a friendly gesture of thanks toward the woman who'd done much to bring order to a difficult situation.

A foolish, friendly gesture, for Lady Kirsten's kisses were inspiring Daniel to nothing less than despair now. She plundered delicately, stole a man's good intentions with a tender pressing of lips to lips, and made off with his honor by replacing it with pleasure.

Daniel got a half-inch purchase on virtue. "My lady, we mustn't—"

She found him again with her mouth, with peppermint and with eagerness—a spice Daniel had not tasted in a kiss since before his marriage.

"Must," her ladyship muttered, her arms wrapping about his waist. "You even taste *good*."

For a procession of instants, Daniel's resolve hung suspended between the mesmerizing pleasure of a woman's honest, passionate desire for him, sorrow for what must be ended in the next moment, and horror.

He was not horrified to have lapsed—he was bitterly amused and mildly ashamed, and would find a proper penance for his misstep. He was horrified to realize that Lady Kirsten was no conscienceless strumpet, no overly bold aristocrat trolling for an illicit assignation.

She was innocent, the next thing to inexperienced, and with her inexpert kiss, she sought to invite Daniel to the very opposite of sinning. For that reason, he allowed the kiss to gentle, then subside into an embrace, the lady resting against him in a posture of wrenchingly misplaced affection.

Daniel gave himself one moment of sweet self-torture to imprint the embrace on his memory, then let his arms drop away.

"Lady Kirsten, I owe you the most abject, sincere, and remorseful apology a man can make."

The dear, dratted woman cuddled closer. "Kissing takes practice, Mr. Banks. I expect we could both benefit by refreshing our skills with each other regularly. We're off to a promising start, don't you think?"

Women had breasts. Daniel had somehow misplaced that fact in the last few years. Misplaced the delight a man felt when a well-endowed woman in a friendly mood snuggled up to him simply because she chose to.

He would never again be able to forget that.

"You will hate me," he whispered, and that was penance enough for any sin, for he never wanted to disappoint Kirsten Haddonfield, never wanted to earn her enmity. She was good-hearted, if lonely, and she liked children.

She liked Daniel. Though he had little coin, no ambition, and less sophistication, she liked Daniel.

"I might have hated you if you'd lectured the boy and sent him back to his mother in disgrace," she said, "but I'd have got over it, eventually. I'm much better at appearing angry than I am at remaining angry."

Lady Kirsten bore the scent of lavender. Daniel endured her patting his lapel, when he should have stepped back.

Some dark angel of mercy popped a painful, help-ful thought into Daniel's reeling mind: Lady Kirsten's brother held the Haddondale living. Should Daniel find disfavor with the earl, the clerical calling was all but forfeit.

Daniel's vocation was all he had left, and as of a few moments ago, was a means of reuniting somewhat with Danny.

"My lady, there has been a misapprehension of my situation," Daniel said, taking Lady Kirsten's hands in his and putting a foot of distance between him and temptation. "Your regard, even your friendship, will always be among my greatest treasures, but you must save your affections for another."

Her pretty blue eyes clouded with an instant of hurt before her expression cooled. She slipped her hands from his—no dramatic gesture, just a quiet, tragic, inevitable untangling of fingers, sentiments, and lives.

In that moment, Daniel finally, finally knew what it was to hate his spouse. He'd been angry at Olivia, hurt by her, embittered and bewildered by her betrayals, but as all hope and warmth dimmed from Lady Kirsten's gaze, Daniel caught a tantalizing glimpse of hatred.

And liked what he saw. Hatred was so simple, so *easy*, and as tempting as a succulent red apple.

"My apologies to you, Mr. Banks. I presumed on what was merely polite friendship. I am so sorry. It won't happen again."

She turned to leave, probably to curse him in the ladylike solitude of her private sitting room. Perhaps to weep. If Daniel were lucky, she'd dredge up scorn for the new Haddondale vicar, a task with which he could offer a bit of assistance.

"My lady—*Kirsten*, I am married."

Her ladyship had ample stores of indignation, but if Daniel sought to inspire their display, he was disappointed.

Also consoled, for she was not so wroth with him as to storm away upon hearing his confession.

"*Married*, Daniel?"

Not Mr. Banks. "I did not choose wisely, as my own father often remarked. My wife and I live apart. She was unkind to Danny and betrayed my trust as well, but I will not dishonor my vows."

He'd once thought he *could not* dishonor those vows, not in any serious or sustained manner. Even before leaving Little Weldon, he'd admitted the error of that assumption. He was still a man, and worse, he was a lonely, virtuous man.

"And if you were not married, Mr. Banks?"

What sort of mistaken, misled, rejected woman asked that question? A brave one, one entitled to honesty.

"I am not free to describe the sentiments that might befall me concerning you were I an unmarried man," Daniel said, "but I spoke honestly earlier. Your regard, even your friendship, will always be among my greatest treasures if would you leave them in my keeping."

He could have loved her.

Because Daniel could have loved Lady Kirsten as a man loves his intimate companion, and because he did esteem her, he spared her a recitation of sentiments that could not flatter her coming from him.

"I spoke honestly earlier too," she said. "*Daniel, I am so sorry.*"

Not an apology, but rather, a condolence to a man bereaved of companionship and yet yoked to his solitude. On a soft swish of skirts, Lady Kirsten was up the maids' stairs and gone.

❧

Susannah peered over the top of a volume of Shakespeare's sonnets. "Something's wrong."

Yes, something was wrong. Susannah wasn't supposed to haunt the old nursery suite, because this was Kirsten's preferred place to be alone and think.

Also to grieve.

"How many versions do you have of those sonnets, Suze?" Kirsten asked, poking up the desultory fire. "Are you trying to memorize every one?"

"I own six different editions, and Nicholas keeps one more in each library," Susannah said, closing the book around her finger. "What is bothering you?"

Why now, of all times, did Susannah have to take her pretty nose out of a book?

"You'd freeze in here and not even notice," Kirsten said, perching on a hassock before the hearth. "You might eventually notice if it grew too dark to read."

Susannah did not rise to the bickering bait.

"You have the same look you used to get when

we made our come-outs," she said, "when Lady Warne would discuss the gentlemen with whom we should dance and how to finagle them onto our dance cards."

Bad moments, those, when Nick's grandmother had prevailed on friends, goddaughters, whist partners, and passing marchionesses to ensure Kirsten and Susannah never sat out a dance.

"I hate London," Kirsten said, though she hadn't intended to announce that.

"If it weren't for Hatchards and Gunter's, I would too," Susannah replied, putting her feet up beside Kirsten on the hassock. "Her Grace the Duchess of Moreland lets me borrow from her library, and Lady Louisa is always willing to talk poetry with me."

"Are they your friends, Suze? The duchess and her daughter?"

Susannah was so pretty. Mellow afternoon sunshine slanted through the windows and gave her fair countenance a glow Kirsten associated with illuminated manuscripts and Renaissance Madonnas.

Susannah was also lonely, which might explain her devotion to Mr. Shakespeare.

"The Windham ladies are excellent company," Susannah said, "but no, I would not say they are my friends."

"Are we friends?" Kirsten's mouth was marching off in all manner of unintended directions today—as usual.

"We're sisters," Susannah said. "That's better than friends. What's amiss, Kirsten? Your expression is distracted, and you've settled on that hassock like a broody hen when you'd normally be inspecting the mantel for dust and the window for smudges."

"I'm not sure anything is wrong, exactly. Did you know Mr. Banks is married?"

Susannah toed off a pair of pink house mules embroidered with blue birds. Her feet were clad in white silk stockings, and even her feet—slender and narrow—had a graceful quality.

"Marriage would explain Mr. Banks's domestication," she said, wiggling her toes. "A man that good-looking oughtn't to be so nice and well mannered, even if he is a vicar. He ought to be arrogant or silly."

Men could be both. Sedgewick had managed it handily, while Arthur… Maybe he'd been arrogant and silly and Kirsten had been too heartbroken to notice.

"Mr. Banks and his wife are estranged," Kirsten said, though she suspected the situation was worse than that. "A prodigal wife has to be awkward for a vicar."

"Impossible, I'd say. We'll be hearing stories next about how Mrs. Banks is off tending to her widowed mother or her sister's difficult lying-in, until people give up asking directly. Nicholas did say Vicar might not be in the Haddondale pulpit for long."

Mrs. Banks. Ouch. "When did Nick say that?"

"I was in the library, looking for my Sappho, and Nick came in with Leah."

"The blue sofa?"

Nicholas claimed the blue sofa had the sturdiest construction and the deepest cushions. The blue sofa did not squeak, in other words, or shift about when a certain randy earl got to frolicking with his countess. Adolphus, the Haddonfield brother who could rarely be torn from the scientific blandishments of Cambridge, had said Nick's son ought to be nick-named "Blue."

"Not the blue sofa," Susannah said. "Nick and Leah were making a biscuit raid, during which Nick mentioned that Mr. Banks might be bound for Cathay if Haddondale doesn't suit. Our vicar must be *very* estranged from his spouse if Cathay beckons, though a spouse is a spouse, estranged or not. Sally Blumenthal was quite certain Mr. Banks would soon be holding her in a special regard. She will be devastated."

Danny would be devastated if Mr. Banks decamped for missionary martyrdom, and for that reason, the Haddondale pulpit and Danny's well-being were temporarily secure.

"I like Mr. Banks," Kirsten said, nudging her sister's discarded slippers so they were aligned with each other on the carpet. "I respect him and I like him."

What a relief, to be able to respect a man again. An ironic relief.

Susannah set her book aside amid a considering silence.

Kirsten liked Mr. Banks exceedingly well, and learning that he was married only made her feelings more complicated.

"I'm sorry, Kirsten. You seem to have the worst luck with the fellows. Is Mr. Banks very set on a career with the church?"

An extraordinary question in the middle of an unusual conversation.

"I wouldn't run away with him," Kirsten said, "if that's what you're asking."

Mr. Banks would not ask Kirsten to turn her back on propriety, not even for true love, because of all the vicars in all the parishes in all the shires, Daniel Banks's vocation was genuine.

Confound the luck.

"But you're disappointed," Susannah said, crossing her ankles. "Mr. Banks is worth being disappointed over, while your beaus did not impress me."

"Nobody impresses you except for Shakespeare, and even he must be at the top of his form." Had Kirsten's beaus impressed Kirsten, or had she merely wanted to be impressed?

She left her tuffet and flopped down beside her sister. "I flirted with Mr. Banks. I feel like an idiot." A sad, bewildered, lonely idiot. If Kirsten were smarter, she'd muster disdain for him and his soft, sweet, passionate kisses.

"He did not flirt back, I gather. Disobliging of him. Vicars can be awful flirts. Recall that fellow with the beard we had five years ago. Perhaps Mr. Banks doesn't know how, or perhaps Mrs. Banks has soured him on anything approaching warmth where the ladies are concerned."

Mr. Banks *had* kissed Kirsten back, for a few glorious, intriguing moments. Those few moments preserved her from fury with him—and the Almighty—because those tender, beguiling moments had confirmed that her sentiments were returned.

On the third try, she'd chosen a good fellow to lose her heart to, but she'd chosen him at the wrong time. One set of vows too late.

A sorry sort of progress.

"London will at least distract you," Susannah said, patting Kirsten's hand.

"London will keep me busy. That's not at all the same thing."

"Then don't go."

As soon as Susannah said the words, Kirsten mentally shoved them aside, for they had the same painful, dangerous allure as memories of Mr. Banks's kisses. Kirsten had been all but determined to avoid London *before*.

Now she'd tasted forbidden fruit and must remove herself from temptation. She knew this, not because she was pious and virtuous, but rather, because a fool should not be made to suffer unnecessarily.

"If I remain in the country, there will be talk," Kirsten said. "Della doesn't need talk for her first Season." Every debutante occasioned gossip, and Della, lacking the Haddonfield fair coloring and height, would come in for plenty of unkind speculation.

"Della doesn't need me, Lady Warne, Leah, and you to escort her, Kirsten. Nita won't be here to oversee the household, so you could credibly claim that role. Come up for the last few weeks of the Season, and nobody will think anything of it."

"You're saying whether I'm in Town or here in Kent, Della will have to endure gossip." The very thought of London and fittings and waltzing made Kirsten feel weary and mean.

"I'm saying you shouldn't have to fuss and coo over Mr. Sedgewick's heir when his proud parents show him off at the fashionable hour."

Oh, that. Arthur—quick off the mark, was Arthur— already had two sons.

"The Sedgewick heir is just a baby," Kirsten said. "One hopes the poor boy inherited his mother's chin rather than his father's." And that, oddly, was both a sincere hope and the extent of Kirsten's sentiments regarding the child.

"He'll inherit his grandfather's title eventually, and thus will be forgiven a receding chin, or three chins. Think about staying here at Belle Maison, Kirsten. You've faced down the tabbies for enough Seasons, and Della will have all the support she needs."

"You're being nice, Suze. I'm not sure how to respond."

Remaining at Belle Maison would spare Kirsten much, but also keep her in proximity to the lamentably married Mr. Banks. *How* could she have not known he was married? Though Susannah hadn't known, which was some comfort.

More likely Susannah hadn't cared. Mr. Shakespeare was a formidable rival, though he'd been estranged from his spouse too.

"You should respond to my show of support by following my example," Susannah said, picking up her sonnets. "You be nice to you too."

"I should go to London." Away from Mr. Banks, and his *regard*, and his lovely, sad eyes and wrinkled, mended cravats. Besides, Nicholas would never allow Kirsten to remain at Belle Maison. Della's come-out was a responsibility owed her by her entire family.

"You should for once do as you please," Susannah said, turning a few pages. "I think Mr. Banks would give you the same advice. Besides, if you're here, then

I can claim I'm repairing to the country to visit you every few weeks. I like that notion."

"I like you." Kirsten truly did like her sister. Lovely.

She also truly liked Mr. Banks, which was…difficult, sad, and inconvenient.

But, somehow, also lovely.

Eight

"HAVE YOU DISCUSSED THIS WITH DANNY?" FAIRLY asked. He and Banks hadn't much time to sort the situation out, because Letty would come flying into the stable if the boy didn't soon present himself in her ladyship's private parlor.

"Do you think me daft?" Banks shot back as they strode out of the stable yard. "I've spoken not a word to Danny about changing households. I haven't even told him I'm providing instruction to other boys, though that was normally part of my day in Little Weldon."

Part of Banks's income, in other words. Most vicars supplemented their stipend with some tutoring.

Fairly assayed a grand understatement. "Letty won't like it."

Banks stopped amid a garden where daffodils were trying to push up along east-facing walls and the occasional precocious tulip was sending a tightly furled green bud skyward.

"Letty doesn't have to like it, my lord. You don't have to like it. I'm not even sure having my own son among my pupils is a scheme I will like."

"Banks, Danny might be your son according to every soul in Little Weldon and the dictates of your own pure heart, but Letty will not thank you for referring to the child that way."

"Papa!" Danny came churning into the garden. "Papa, wait for me! Hibbs says Loki will be right as rain!"

Banks had the grace not to smirk, but he did catch the boy up and affix him to his back, where Danny settled in with the ease of long familiarity—and strong preference.

"You are thankful, then, that your pony will be fine," Banks said, "but I haven't heard you apologize to the viscount."

"I'm practicing," Danny said. "Lady Kirsten said apologies go better if you practice them. Hullo, sir."

"Hullo, Danny. I'm glad *you* are right as rain. Her ladyship and I were very worried."

Fairly tried to sound severe because Letty had been beside herself when the child had turned up missing. When his pony had been discovered gone from its stall, she'd grown troublesomely quiet.

"I knew she'd worry," Danny said. "I will apologize, because I was bad. I missed Papa."

"Danny," Banks murmured.

"Well, I did, and I don't like it here at all, but I'm sorry Mama worried and sorry I took Loki without permission."

A very grudging sort of sorry and a very sincere I-don't-like-it-here. This could not end without somebody in tears, again, and yet with Banks on hand, the child had finally been honest.

Danny hated it under his mother's roof. Fairly had needed to hear the words to admit that happy little boys did not throw their porridge every other morning. Happy little boys didn't answer in two-word replies, one word of which was "sir" or "ma'am." Happy little boys did not ghost about the nursery, pale and quiet, gaze ever straying to the windows.

Even the pony hadn't set the child to rights.

"Papa has a nice house in Haddondale," Danny said, "and the earl's stable is as tidy as the viscount's. Lady Kirsten kissed my bandages too."

Danny shot out a skinny wrist, revealing fresh white linen.

"We'll have no talk of bandages before her ladyship," Fairly said. "No talk of coming off your pony, no talk of cuts, bruises, *or Lady Kirsten's kisses.*"

"You want me to *lie* to *Mama*?"

Banks swung the child down, for they'd reached the back terrace. Danny took the vicar's hand as naturally as Fairly might have cuddled his own infant daughter in his arms.

Yes, Fairly wanted the boy to *lie*. Letty would have enough to deal with if Banks remained set on his scheme to take Danny away.

"You will not tell a falsehood, Danny," Banks said gently. "Out of compassion for your mother, you will also not flaunt your injury, nor will you dwell on the fact that another lady took care of you and comforted you. You will tell the truth as kindly as you can."

"Yes, sir."

A very different "yes, sir" from the ones muttered in Fairly's direction. Between one moment and the next, Fairly's allegiance shifted, or rather clarified.

Letty would smother the boy with her guilt and love, wrap him in moral and figurative cotton wool, earn his undying resentment, and possibly spoil him. She'd mean only the best, while making a bad situation worse. Banks knew how to be a parent to this boy, and Danny sensed this.

Maybe, given the chance, Letty would admit she knew it too.

"Then let's not put off the inevitable," Fairly said. "You will change your clothes, Danny, and we'll have an apology from you to her ladyship."

"What's my penance to be?" Danny asked, looking as serious and dear as the man holding his hand.

Again, Banks stepped into the awkward moment with the casual ease of a confident horse splashing through a puddle.

"You must consider, Danny, what will make amends to all whom you've trespassed against. An apology is a start, but only you know if that is all you can do to repair the damage you've done."

"I will think on it, sir, and ask Loki his opinion."

"Excellent idea." Banks gently cuffed the boy on the back of the head. "Be off with you, then, but expect her ladyship will fuss over you. I'll not leave without saying good-bye."

Danny scampered away more energetically than he'd done anything in the last six months save throw his porridge.

"I had not realized that the purpose of punishment was to assuage the miscreant's conscience," Fairly said. "I thought we were routinely birched to inure us to injustice."

Or indoctrinate them into the English vice, about which Banks probably knew nothing.

"Before one can appreciate injustice," Banks said, "one must first have an instinct for justice. Penance restores our honor to us, while a birching merely feeds our self-pity."

"You should write a book of aphorisms on the rearing of children," Fairly said. "Your outlook is compelling, for all it flies in the face of convention."

But then Banks's entire situation was unconventional, especially for a churchman.

"Oh, a book. Of course," Banks said, striding off toward the nearest door. "I'll publish a book to wild acclaim, and then Olivia will come forth and announce that Danny is not my son, my sister the viscountess is a fallen woman, and I misrepresented the situation to my bishop and my entire congregation for years."

Every garden had its serpent.

"Banks, you can't run off to Peru if Danny is to become one of your scholars," Fairly said. The boy did not need to be subjected to another round of battledore between households. Fairly's nerves weren't up to that strain, either.

"No running off," Banks said. "And no more confusing the boy. We revert consistently to the terms of address he's known for most of his life. I am Papa; her ladyship is Aunt Letty, for those are the terms the world must hear from Danny and we should not have deviated from them even among ourselves."

Haddondale had been good for Letty's brother. He'd put on a bit of weight since Fairly had last seen him and recovered some of his former energy.

A lot of his former energy.

"You fight that battle with Letty," Fairly said, allowing Banks to precede him into an informal parlor. "She has loved hearing Danny call her Mama." Though upon reflection, Fairly realized that Danny avoided that form of address if he could manage it.

"Not a battle, Fairly, a discussion," Banks said. "We're reasonable adults and we'll have a reasonable discussion."

❧

Olivia Maitland Banks had been a beauty when she'd emerged from her papa's shabby schoolroom more than a decade ago, and she was lovely still, provided she avoided direct sunlight. Around her eyes, faint lines showed, and her mouth had acquired the first hint of a pinch.

Bertrand knew better than to allude to either flaw, for Olivia was vain, bless her.

"You chose the vicar over me because he's a handsome devil, didn't you?" Bertrand asked as they strolled his back garden.

She *had* chosen the vicar years ago, though perhaps she was unchoosing him now.

"Daniel is quite good-looking and always will be," Olivia said. She paid her husband no compliment, for she would have used the same tone to assess a plow horse's soundness. "He takes no notice of his appearance, though, and would never use it to his advantage. For a wife, that's an ideal circumstance. All will envy her, but her fellow won't stray. Daniel married me in part to rebel against his saintly papa, who thought we were too young. Under no circumstances would Daniel have betrayed the wife he'd chosen over his father's objection."

Bertrand did not contradict Olivia, but Daniel Banks had been prudent even as a boy. Marrying to defy his papa had likely not occurred to him. Olivia would never admit it, but she simply admired her husband's integrity—probably hated him for it too.

Olivia hated passionately, which had fascinated Bertrand as a younger man. Her antipathy still held his interest, but also made him cautious.

"You couldn't sue him for adultery anyway," Bertrand said, using his handkerchief to dust off a marble bench near the sundial. "Though he could sue you."

To end a marriage through divorce on the basis of adultery took three different legal proceedings, one of them resulting in an Act of Parliament. Bertrand had consulted with his solicitors on the matter the previous day, for having Olivia by his side had rekindled some spark that had been missing from his life.

She was complicated, brilliantly selfish, and pretty.

"Daniel would have to give up his vocation if he sought a divorce," Olivia scoffed, settling on the bench, "and he hasn't the money or the influence. He's quite, quite stuck with me."

Which meant Olivia was stuck with her vicar. Bertrand took the place beside her—they were beyond his asking permission for such a liberty—and possessed himself of her hand.

"As long as Banks has you, I cannot have you, not legally. Do you enjoy my suffering, Olivia?"

Not the agony a young man endured, though

the memory of that thwarted passion fueled some of Bertrand's possessiveness. Olivia had been *wrong* to marry the damned churchman, despite Banks's good looks and honorable character. Witness, the vicar remained a penniless, if handsome, saint, while Bertrand could shower Olivia with the material security she craved.

"I do enjoy your suffering, Bertrand. I'd enjoy making Daniel wretched even more."

Bertrand was *not* wretched; neither did Olivia's remark entirely amuse him. "How could Banks be anything but wretched, my dove? He no longer has the child upon whom you claim he doted. He's left the pulpit back in Little Hogwallow for some pocket pulpit in Kent, and at any moment, you can denounce him to his bishop for falsely presenting the boy as his son. If I were Banks, I'd be nervous."

Very nervous, for Olivia had grown thoughtful in recent days, and that boded ill for somebody.

"Daniel could always try to have our marriage annulled," Olivia said, twitching at silk skirts of a lovely pale blue that complemented her coloring exquisitely—expensive skirts but worth the investment.

An annulment was only slightly less scandalous than a divorce, though a damned sight less complicated, if grounds existed.

"No, he cannot try to have the marriage annulled," Bertrand replied, "not if he wants to keep wearing that collar, which you've assured me he does. He isn't a wealthy lord, to manufacture grounds or bribe the appropriate bishop, either. Are you planning to blackmail him? Your silence regarding his subterfuges about the boy in exchange for his complicity in your situation with me?"

England was a big place, and Bertrand had handsome holdings in Northumbria. He could present Olivia as his new wife, late of…Cornwall, say, and no one would be the wiser. His solicitors assured him such unions were commonplace among those with the means and resolve to undertake them.

And Bertrand was certain Olivia had been plotting some particularly exquisite misery for her handsome, saintly spouse.

"Daniel is a good vicar and a tiresomely virtuous man," Olivia said, smoothing her skirts the way a dowager might stroke a favored cat. "He lied to protect the boy, but he would not lie to ease his own situation. I must think on this further."

Bertrand patted her hand, though much more of this *thinking* on Olivia's part, and she'd have enough clothing to open her own modiste's shop.

"Olivia, my dear, London is situated between Kent and Oxford. Sooner or later, somebody will recognize you here, enjoying my hospitality when you're supposed to be up north. You'll be an object of pity if people conclude you've been thrown on my cousinly charity, and you'll be an object of scorn if they understand your husband has set you aside."

Pity and scorn would be as wormwood and gall to her. Life in Northumbria should appeal to her by comparison.

She snatched her hand away.

"The bumpkins from Little Weldon hardly

frequent Mayfair, Bertrand. You plague me for your own entertainment."

Every morning, the markets of London were thronged with farm wagons bringing in produce from the countryside, and nobody gossiped like the country folk when sharing a pint with their town cousins.

"My apologies for troubling you, my dear. My regard for you makes me impatient."

Then too, Bertrand wanted to know her plans. Any prudent man, however smitten, would want to know Olivia's plans if those plans in any way involved him.

Bertrand left Olivia perched on her marble bench in the bright sunshine. Her expression was one of such fierce concentration, he sent up a small prayer for Vicar Banks's continued good health.

&c%

Letty watched through her parlor window as Danny clambered aboard Daniel's back, a barnacle of a little boy, holding fast to the one he loved most in the world.

The pain of that admission was exquisite. Love was unrelenting, irrational, and so damnably unfair.

Two large, anxious men trooped into her parlor moments later. Danny had doubtless been sent upstairs to change his clothes.

"So he fell off his pony," Letty said by way of greeting to her brother. "You weren't about to tell me, but I know mud on a boy's breeches when I see it. Danny seemed hale enough."

He'd been bursting with the energy and high spirits he'd enjoyed as a smaller child.

"He's fine, Letty," Fairly said. "Contrite, but fine.

He'll be down directly and offering us all heartfelt apologies. Shall we ring for tea?"

If Letty were anywhere near a tea service, she'd smash it to bits.

"The tea can wait until Danny joins us. Have a seat, you two. I'm not on the verge of strong hysterics." She'd passed that point hours ago.

Because neither man moved, Letty set the example by assuming her customary corner of her favorite sofa. Daniel took the armchair at an angle to Letty's seat. Fairly settled beside her—within handkerchief lending range.

"I will not cry in front of my son," Letty said. She'd talked to the nursemaids, the tutor, and the stable lads, something she should have been doing regularly.

Then she'd cried at length. The situation wanted a solution, and Letty had none.

"Letty, you mustn't blame the boy," Daniel said, while Fairly slipped his hand into hers. "He made poor choices and he'll atone for them as best he can, but with the best of intentions, we've made poor choices too."

Daniel was close to pleading with her, and as much as Daniel had done to protect Letty, she couldn't bear his kindness now.

"Danny isn't happy here," Letty said. "He's miserable, in fact, and if my son is miserable, then I can't be entirely happy, can I?"

Maternal logic was at least hers to claim and always would be.

"And if my dear sister is miserable," Daniel said, "then I cannot be happy either, for she has been through too much already, little of it her own doing. We have a conundrum. I have a possible solution."

No, they did not have a conundrum. They had a little boy to look after. One little boy who deserved every happiness in life. Fairly said nothing, but his grip on Letty's hand was a comfort. Her husband was a physician at heart, a healer, and incapable of ignoring suffering from any quarter.

"Tell me this solution, Daniel, though if you admonish me to prayer, I will ask Fairly to escort you back to the stable."

They were in such a muddle that Letty was blaspheming to her brother—the kindest, most godly, selfless soul in the realm. Her heart could not ache any more than it did, but a touch of shame crowded in anyway.

"Danny is your son," Daniel said. "Nothing can change that. I'm asking to borrow him in a sense, to add him temporarily to a household of young boys who will seek instruction from me through the week in my capacity as the Haddondale vicar."

Letty's chest was one tight misery, but her ears worked well enough. "Borrow" and "temporarily" were poison darts of grief, but not the armed infantry squares of reason and guilt she'd expected.

"One does not borrow a child," Letty snapped, while beside her, Fairly had taken on that still, watchful posture that said he was ready to march into the conversation if Letty took offense at Daniel's words.

"One doesn't lend a child either," Daniel said gently, "but you did lend Danny to me for the first five years of his life. Your selflessness and mother-love were without limit then and I believe they've only grown greater since."

Letty's desperation had been without limit once Danny had been weaned, for Olivia had quietly threatened such trouble, for Danny, for Daniel, and for Letty. Letty should have turned to Daniel then, should have been honest with him.

Should have trusted him.

"Daniel, I can't let you take him." More desperation, because whatever plan Daniel had come up with, Letty owed him at least a fair hearing.

"Not take," Daniel said. "Never take. I propose that Danny be allowed to come to Haddondale as one of my scholars. I'm gathering a collection of a half-dozen small boys, all of whom want preparation for public school. Danny would fit in with them well, and he'd be only a short carriage ride away. Holidays, summers, and special occasions, he'd be home with you."

"Think about it," Fairly said. "Banks is only asking you to consider this, Letty."

"You support the idea," Letty retorted, silently accusing her husband of petit treason and, worse, common sense.

"You are not happy," Fairly said. "Danny is miserable. He has made no friends here. His studies are not progressing. He wasn't running away, Letty, not this time."

Not yet, in other words.

Daniel said nothing. He sat two feet away, relaxed as only a man in good standing with his Maker could be, nothing but compassion in his gaze. Daniel had risked everything to provide a home for Danny, had acceded to Letty's plans without hesitation, had never once reproached Letty for what she'd asked of him.

"You would only borrow Danny?" she asked, mentally testing around the edges of the question for shrieking grief, for the death of all her maternal hopes, and finding only…a mother's normal resistance to a new idea.

Daniel fluffed his cravat, which hadn't seen starch in at least a sennight, based on the limp drape of the folds.

"I chose the word 'borrow' out of diplomacy," Daniel said, "but I cannot like what the term hides, Letty. What I truly want is to share Danny with you and Fairly. I want the boy to know his family, his whole family, loves him without ceasing. If my ambition in that regard threatens you, I will take myself off to Haddondale, but you'll see me much more frequently as a visitor here."

Daniel spoke gently—he always spoke gently—but no force of nature was equal to Daniel Banks once his mind was made up. Their father had called Daniel stubborn, but to Letty, Daniel had simply lived from the courage of his convictions.

If she refused this solution of his, Daniel would be on her doorstep every other day, offering to take Danny riding, quizzing the boy on his sums, and correcting his table manners.

The decision was left to Letty, whether to be a selfish, overprotective ninnyhammer or a mother wise enough to accept that Daniel's proposal was brilliant. Danny could have them all, plus a good education and friends.

Not quite a miracle, but a solution. Letty would be grateful to Daniel soon, after she'd endured the rest of the conversation.

"On Saturday, we will bring Danny to you," Letty

said, a sense of rightness supplanting her sorrow. "He will resume his life as the vicar's son, he will call me Aunt Letty, and you shall be his papa."

"You're certain?" Daniel asked. "This will be another significant adjustment, more for you than for the boy. Nothing we attempt on Danny's behalf will work unless it has your wholehearted support, for Danny loves you too and always has."

Tears did threaten. Letty swallowed them back, for she'd cried enough for one day. Danny loved her *too*, not her best of all.

"We do what's best for Danny, and Fairly and I will dote on him shamelessly."

"You'll do more than that," Daniel said, crossing his legs and twitching at his breeches. "I have given some thought to the options, Letty, and if Danny is to resume living with me, I must have your agreement on the following terms."

Daniel was enormously relieved, that's what the leg crossing and seam straightening were about. This posturing over terms was a sop to Letty's dignity—one she very much needed.

"I'll consider terms, Daniel, but my mind is made up." As was her heart. Letty's brother had once again solved a problem not of his making. Danny would thrive on this arrangement, of course he would.

"Weather permitting, you will either visit Danny at Belle Maison or send the coach to fetch him to you at week's end," Daniel said in his most assured preacher's tones. "Titled relations are not something any boy should ignore, particularly not doting titled relations in the very same shire."

"I'll fetch him myself," Fairly said, "and look very titled as I do. My sisters are married to a marquess and an earl, and through them, I can command the accompaniment of a ducal heir, earls, barons—"

Letty put a hand over Fairly's mouth before he'd called out the Tenth Hussars and Wellington himself to escort one small boy.

"Go on, Daniel," she said, "for that is not your only condition."

"Danny will write to you weekly, and you will reply without fail. He will report his progress to you and anything else he cares to pass along. I will not read his correspondence."

Because one gentleman never read another's correspondence, and Daniel was a gentleman to his bones.

"What else?"

"If Danny should fall ill, I will send him to you here, lest he spread contagion to the other boys. Fairly is, after all, a physician."

"Of course." Oh, of course, of course. Bless Daniel, of course.

"I must tend my flock over the Yuletide holidays," Daniel said, "so Danny will spend a substantial part of the Christmas season with you. Summer holidays as well, in order that I may have time to immerse myself in ecclesiastical studies."

Daniel would spend that time charging all around the shire on his flighty black horse—and missing Danny.

"Say yes," Fairly muttered. "Please, for the love of God, the boy, and my nerves, say yes, Letty. Danny is old enough to attend public school now, to be gone from us for months at a time, but I simply could not—please, say yes. Danny will love you all the more for it."

Danny loved his mama, but he was also beginning to resent her, and that Letty could not abide.

"Yes," Letty said. Yes to heartache, but also yes to endless love, for this was what it meant to be a mother. For her son, she could be wise, brave, and fearless. For him, she could rise above the fear that she'd never see him again, the fear that he'd never forgive her for past mistakes.

None of that mattered. Daniel's smile said as much. All that mattered was the love and the child's happiness.

"I'll fetch the boy," Daniel said, springing to his feet. "By now, his apologies should rival the performances of Mr. Garrick himself. Be suitably impressed, you two. A young man's dignity depends upon it."

As did a grown man's.

"I love you," Fairly said, taking Letty in his arms when Daniel had departed. "I love you, I love you, I love you. You and Banks are the most ferocious, tenderhearted, kind, brave—I knew this about you, but Banks has surprised me."

Letty sank into her husband's embrace, as weak as if she'd run a footrace uphill the entire distance.

"People underestimate Daniel because he's handsome and sweet. Daniel even underestimates himself."

Fairly kissed her knuckles. "He came charging over here, ready to sermonize, exhort, orate, and beg for you to relinquish the child to him on any terms imaginable."

"I suspected as much once he started bargaining with me." And yet, the terms Daniel had "demanded" had been the very best possible arrangement for Danny going forward. "Daniel has been considering this, would be my guess. My brother is shrewd, but nobody expects shrewdness to align with compassion."

Daniel popped his head around the door. "Fairly, prepare yourself to be addressed as Uncle David from now on."

"Right-o," Fairly said, tightening his embrace. "Dear, doting Uncle David. I'm outrageously fond of my nieces and nephews. Ask my sisters and their husbands."

The door closed and Letty dropped her forehead to Fairly's shoulder. "Daniel is so happy, so relieved."

"While your heart's breaking."

Letty considered her husband's diagnosis and rejected it. "I'm sad but not heartbroken. If I love my son, and I do, then I don't get to choose what he needs from me. I only get to provide it. The same for my brother, the same for you or the baby. I understand that better now than I did before we married."

She sat up and yanked the bellpull, for delivering well-rehearsed apologies could be hungry, thirsty work.

"We'll spoil Danny and his papa rotten," Fairly said. "Get them a decent conveyance, at the least, and a sedate coach horse, for that black demon Banks rides is likely not trained or to be trusted in the traces."

"Daniel believes in a classical education for both children and horses, and Zubbie is a perfect gentleman in harness."

In harness. Unease slid through Letty's relief at having a decision made and a little boy's welfare assured.

"What?" Fairly asked, disentangling his arms from Letty's waist. "You've had a thought. Is it the baby?

She was napping when I looked in on her, but a mother's instincts—"

"Fairly, if I asked you to do something for me, something not entirely cricket between gentlemen, would you do it?"

"Of course."

How Letty loved him, how she loved all her menfolk. "Daniel is shrewd and he loves Danny, but he's also vulnerable. Olivia threatened to expose the circumstances of Danny's birth to the church authorities. She can still make trouble for Daniel and for Danny. Serious, rotten trouble."

"Her again."

"Yes, her."

Fairly's eyes were beautiful but disquieting. For an instant, they shone with lethal intent.

"You mustn't imperil your mortal soul," Letty said, for a physician would know poisons and how to make a death look accidental.

"Very well, I'll only imperil my gentlemanly honor, which matters little compared to your peace of mind."

"Olivia is supposed to be in the north, visiting relatives, but she was not well liked by her own family. I doubt she's still biding among them but haven't a clue where else she might be. We should know."

"Excellent point, and finding out won't put the smallest smudge on my honor. I've also been meaning to ask you about a few other aspects of your brother's situation with the fair Olivia."

The look in Fairly's eyes now was very fierce. Wonderfully fierce.

"I'll tell you everything I know," Letty said. "First we have the ordeal of apologies to endure."

Letty was still fortifying herself with her husband's passionate kisses when the parlor door opened and a small boy snickered.

Nine

THE EARL OF BELLEFONTE WAS, BY REPUTATION, A genial man who enjoyed children and doted on his grandmother. His lordship's geniality was nowhere in evidence when Daniel came upon him in his wood-working shop at the back of the stable.

"Out of my light, Banks. I'm making a birdhouse for your vicarage."

The earl sat, penciling lines onto a slab of oak, at a worktable most people would have found too high.

"You make birdhouses out of oak? Wouldn't pine be less trouble?"

Another line drawn with a sure, single swipe of the pencil over the wood. "Pine won't last as long and the bugs get into it. How's the boy?"

"I wanted to discuss him with you."

Bellefonte stared at his oak, a durable wood, true, but the very devil to saw or carve.

"You're about to explain to me that the child's situation is complicated," Bellefonte said, "and this has to do with that wife of yours we've yet to meet. I don't like messes, Banks, and you've brought one to my doorstep."

Some lessons could be learned only after ordination. "Your sister Lady Della's situation is messy. Are you worried about her, my lord?"

Bellefonte's glower was merely disgruntled, not insulted. "Worried sick, as is my countess. Della has an air about her, a 'put up your fives' tone in even the merest civilities, and she's far too knowledgeable for a girl making her bow. Too many older siblings, too many brothers, I suppose."

Daniel took a stool, because listening to the worries of his flock was one of the more important aspects of being a vicar.

His own worries could wait. "Have you discussed your concerns with Lady Della? She's probably not looking forward to the Season either."

Bellefonte tucked his pencil behind his ear. He had wood shavings in his blond hair and a pair of gold-rimmed spectacles on his nose. He looked not like an earl, but like a new father, whose concepts of responsibility and family were undergoing a significant increase in complexity.

"Della should know we have her back. I shouldn't have to tell my own sister—"

Daniel, having heard the woes of many a sulky boy, interrupted. "Tell her anyway. She grew up trusting her father and mother would be on hand when she had to face the ordeal of her come-out, and now she has neither parent. Moreover, from what I understand, your countess hasn't exactly thrived on the machinations of Polite Society, so you're likely concerned for her too."

Fairly had passed that along at some point when

discussing the Haddondale post with Daniel months ago. The earl and countess preferred a country life "for reasons," Fairly had said.

His lordship drew the pencil from behind his ear and began flipping it through his fingers, over under, over under, back. He had large hands, of course, but they were also dexterous and graceful. The hands of an artisan rather than of a gentleman or a laborer.

"Banks, you have failed absolutely to cheer me. First, you won't forbid the damned assemblies, now you're shaking the prospect of a lot of upset females in my face when I'm supposed to spread damned rainbows and moonbeams over my womenfolk."

The foul language was so woebegone, Daniel smiled. "Perhaps it has escaped your notice, my lord, but you are an earl."

The pencil came to a halt and Bellefonte got up to pace, a great golden bear in a cage of wealth and responsibility.

"Every waking moment and in half my nightmares, I'm reminded I'm an earl. I have tenants, farms, woods, mills, and interests on the Continent courtesy of my brothers Beckman and Ethan. George has me involved in a scheme to develop hybrid sheep, and Adolphus pesters me by post regularly to invest in some invention or other. Now I'm supposed to take a lot of anxious, unhappy women waltzing, and for what?"

Valid question. Lady Kirsten had probably flung it at his lordship's head more than once.

"The Season is social, my lord. Fairly has reminded me that, through marriage, he's related to an earl, a marquess, and, I believe, a viscount. Marshal their support for your sisters."

"I know those gentlemen, and they have no daughters or sisters of marriageable age."

Parish politics apparently had applicability in the great world as well.

"They have no dependent females of marriage age *yet*," Daniel said, picking up the discarded pencil. "They will eventually, and you will be the general who knows the terrain better than any of them."

The point of the pencil needed repair, so Daniel fished a penknife out of his waistcoat pocket and got to work.

"You're canny, Banks," Bellefonte said, cracking a window. The scent of mud, manure, and spring came wafting in. "This is not what I expect in a vicar."

"You probably didn't expect me to bring my son to Haddondale either, but Danny will join the boys I'm instructing." Daniel found another pencil on the worktable and sharpened its point as well.

Danny was the son of his heart and always would be.

"A few small boys won't be too much trouble," his lordship said, propping his shoulders against the wall. "Not like a gaggle of sisters. Kirsten has decided to be obstinate as usual, but I told her I'd have none of that. If I must endure silk knee breeches, then she can put up with one more Season for her sister's sake."

Daniel had sharpened every pencil in sight, and he'd announced his intention to bring Danny to Haddondale, but the conversation wasn't over.

"Lady Kirsten hates London, my lord."

"Antipathy is my sister's greatest gift. She'll go to London if I have to haul her over my shoulder."

Antipathy was Lady Kirsten's most trusted means of concealing an aching heart.

His lordship folded his glasses and tucked them in a pocket, and that should have been Daniel's cue to withdraw.

"Every man who ever stood up with Lady Kirsten, then offered his addresses to another woman is in London," Daniel said.

Bellefonte shoved away from the wall without using his hands. "They dare not say a word." The satin across his lordship's shoulder blades had picked up the stable dust on the wall, and Daniel's observation had struck some prideful nerve—or possibly a protective one.

"The gentlemen don't have to say anything to be a bitter reproach and a sorrow to your sister. The ladies who came out with her and have since married will do most of the talking. A kind brother would allow Lady Kirsten to remain in the country."

"Point of clarification, your holiness. I'm not a kind brother, I'm an earl. If Kirsten remains at Belle Maison, there will be talk."

Daniel did not believe in bargaining with God, nor in tempting fate. He believed in kindness and honesty. Surely, with a half-dozen boys underfoot, he'd be too busy to notice Lady Kirsten, should she remain in Haddondale.

Moreover, what mattered was not Daniel's sleepless nights, but that Lady Kirsten was in need of a champion, for Bellefonte was bungling that job.

"Your lordship is fretting over his own come-out as the new Earl of Bellefonte, and while that anxiety is understandable, the earldom should not come before your family's well-being."

A silence spread, though overhead, grooms were tromping around in the haymow, and a fat, white dove fluttered along to perch on the windowsill.

"Banks," his lordship said softly, "you've overstepped."

About time somebody overstepped with Bellefonte. He was a good fellow but hadn't yet found his way in a new situation.

"Consider the Ten Commandments, my lord. Nothing in the list precludes a young lady who's tired to her soul of social inanity from absenting herself from more of same. Lady Kirsten is of age, she's stared down the gossips and rakes for several years running. In all likelihood, her presence in Town would cause more talk than would ceding the field to her younger sisters."

His lordship had good old Saxon coloring—wheat-blond hair, blue eyes, and fair skin. That skin was turning an interesting shade of pink north of his neck.

"*What damned rakes?*"

He *was* a kind brother, also a very worried brother. Daniel folded up his penknife and tucked it away. "The rakes who think a woman who remains unmarried might be interested in the connubial joys without the burdens."

Bellefonte settled back on his stool with a weary sigh. "My countess has hinted that Kirsten should not be forced to accompany us."

"Many women who made their bows with Lady Kirsten will be married and filling their nurseries, more each year." More marriages, more babies, more knowing, condescending smiles aimed at Lady Kirsten.

Bellefonte turned a keen appraisal on Daniel, while Daniel traced a finger along the patterns drawn on the oak but could make no sense of them.

"I will not have my sister made an object of pity or scorn," Bellefonte said.

Kirsten would prefer the scorn, but at least his lordship had turned up reasonable.

"She will appreciate your understanding, my lord."

Bellefonte snatched one of the sharpened pencils. "What understanding? I will simply capitulate to my countess's importuning, as I am ever known to do. Which is the one about thou shalt not kill?"

"Number six, my lord." As any English schoolboy or earl well knew. "I'll wish you good day." Daniel rose, grateful to have the announcement of Danny's arrival behind him.

"Banks?"

"Sir?"

"I love my sisters."

"I know this, my lord, and you know this, but it doesn't hurt to ensure *they* know it from time to time as well."

"I hate being an earl."

Daniel risked a squeeze to a meaty shoulder. "But you love being their brother, and they love you. Not the earl, *you*."

Daniel left as the pencil went zipping down another length of heavy, durable oak.

❧

When Mr. Banks's scholars were grandpapas dandling grandsons on their bony knees, they would still hear the long-ago tones of their vicar *amo-amas-amat*-ing in their memories.

And, Kirsten knew, they would gently quiz their grandsons as Mr. Banks had quizzed them.

Mr. Banks's voice was that lovely, that sonorous. Even over the tea tray in Mr. Blumenthal's family parlor—the walls in the formal parlor were being rehung with pink silk—Mr. Banks was lovely to hear.

"Then what time shall I expect the boys on Monday?" he asked, passing his second cup back to his hostess.

"We thought we'd send them over Sunday evening. Let you get an early start on Monday," the squire replied as another biscuit disappeared down his maw.

The boys had sat like perfect angels, one on either side of their papa, for five entire minutes. They'd spoken not a word beyond "Pleased to meet you, sir," "Yes, sir," and "Yes, ma'am."

Kirsten had smelled a plot.

"Sunday evening?" Mr. Banks repeated.

Kirsten saw the puzzle pieces snapping together in his mind, though his expression remained genial. Beside her, Susannah's teacup hit its saucer with a definite *plink*.

"Of course, Sunday evening," the squire said, taking hold of his own lapels. "They're old enough to live in, you're not two miles along the lane, and from what I hear, you're rattling around in Bellefonte's dower house, so you've plenty of space. Nothing like the patter of little feet to keep a man company, right?"

"Won't you miss those little feet right here?" Kirsten asked, for having the twins live in would not do. Mr. Banks needed peace and quiet, not armed insurrection under his very roof.

Mrs. Blumenthal aimed a look at her husband such as Wellington had likely aimed at his infantry when the French were in good form.

Steady on, or it's a court martial for you.

"Sacrifices must be made," the squire said, reaching for the last biscuit. "My boys shall have the best start, and if that means Mrs. Blumenthal and I suffer without them for the sake of their scholarship, then without them we shall do."

Mrs. Blumenthal's smile in anticipation of this hardship was a touch gleeful.

"Five days is a long time to go without seeing your own children," Kirsten said. "Are you sure the boys will manage?"

"Five days—?" Mrs. Blumenthal's question hung suspended over the tea tray, much like the Sevres pot she held poised above the sugar bowl.

"I must have Saturday at least to prepare for the service," Mr. Banks said, "and soon enough you will send your boys to public school, and then they'll be gone for months and much farther than a couple of miles down the lane. I couldn't ask you to leave them with me over the week's end as well as during the week."

"Of course you couldn't," Susannah murmured. "Mrs. Blumenthal's heart would break if she had to go all week without hugging her own little dears."

The teapot nearly crashed to the tray. "But certainly—"

"You must think of yourself," Kirsten said, taking the teapot from their hostess and setting it safely beside the empty biscuit plate. "The house will be like a tomb without their laughter and noise, the servants will go into a decline, and their sisters will bicker terribly without the boys to pick on. When my brothers went to public school, my mother grieved for months."

So had her papa. Kirsten had forgotten that.

"If the boys are to travel back and forth, they'll need to bring their ponies," Mr. Banks mused. "A fellow wants exercise after a day with Cicero and Horace."

Mrs. Blumenthal sat forward. "Ponies? But ponies cost—"

"Ponies!" the squire thundered. "Of course they'll need ponies. Haven't I been telling you that very thing, Mrs. Blumenthal? But no, you'd begrudge the lads even a puppy, and now Mr. Banks says they need ponies, ponies they shall have."

Kirsten heard a scraping sound from the corridor, then the rhythmic thud of small, booted feet.

"Have you had time to prepare their wardrobes?" Kirsten asked. "Boys going off to study need so much! New shirts, new boots, a proper jacket and coat— mornings are still quite chilly, aren't they?"

"A London season is a simpler undertaking than sending a boy away to school," Susannah added. "Your girls must have been sewing for weeks."

"A child certainly cannot ride in ill-fitting boots," Mr. Banks observed as if quoting Scripture. "He'd be neither safe nor comfortable, and an infected blister can be the very devil to heal."

"But there's not time—" Mrs. Blumenthal began.

"I'll take the boys up to Town tomorrow," the squire interjected. "London cobblers have extras, and God knows there's a tailor's shop on every corner of

Bond Street. Do the lads good to spend time with their old papa before they embark on their studies."

"You can end your day at Tatt's, choosing ponies for them!" Kirsten added.

Mr. Banks found it necessary to consult his watch. At length.

"You have much to plan," Susannah said, rising. "I don't envy you, Mrs. Blumenthal, but I so admire the sacrifices you're willing to make for the sake of your children."

"Commendable, indeed," Mr. Banks murmured, getting to his feet. "Now all that remains is to decide which week of the month you'll send the boys their baskets of sweets."

Susannah fell prey to a fit of coughing. Kirsten couldn't seem to sort out the fingers of her gloves.

"A basket of sweets?" Mrs. Blumenthal repeated, rising unsteadily. "One for each boy?"

"Of course," the squire said, finishing his tea and rising. "Fine old public school tradition, the baskets from home. Gives a lad something to look forward to. We'll send Fred's first week of the month, and Frank's the third week of the month. Won't we, Mrs. Blumenthal?"

"I'll have Cook see to it, Mr. Blumenthal."

The squire accompanied them to their carriage, Kirsten's arm linked with Susannah's, though she didn't dare meet her sister's eye. Mr. Banks handed them in, then walked off a few paces with the squire.

"Wait until we're at the foot of the lane," Kirsten murmured.

"Then we must compose ourselves before we reach

the Webbers," Susannah said. "The strain on my nerves will be considerable."

Danny would be delighted to have other boys for company, and Kirsten suspected Mr. Banks was looking forward to the challenge too.

The vicar climbed into the coach a moment later and settled in on the backward-facing seat.

"I thought the baskets of sweets rather a nice touch," he said. "The poor little mites will be away from home, and toiling away ceaselessly under my stern and wrathful eye, after all. Even my own father, a confirmed curmudgeon, sent me the occasional basket when I was at university."

Susannah giggled, Mr. Banks smiled, and Kirsten's insides rearranged themselves. This smile was not pious, sad, regretful, proper, or tender. This was the piratical grin of a rotten boy who'd had a bit of fun and was pleased with the results.

"You'll need a stout birch rod with this lot," Susannah said. "Perhaps a spare as well. Thomas Webber is big for his age, and prone to fisticuffs."

"No birch rods," Mr. Banks said, smile fading. "We have ponies and baskets of sweets, and those are ever so much more effective."

"If all else fails, the earl will show them how to build a tree fort," Kirsten said. "He's prodigiously good at it, and George will help."

"The squire would be along to inspect," Susannah said. "That poor man. I hadn't realized how trying his circumstances must be."

"He loves those boys," Mr. Banks said as the horses lifted into the trot. "But Mrs. Blumenthal is beside herself at the prospect of trying to launch the three oldest girls."

All the pink silk in the world wouldn't see that accomplished.

"They're nice enough young ladies," Susannah said, "but they've neither beauty nor great fortune to recommend them."

"Their mother also doubtless frets that they'll be overshadowed by the earl's sisters living right down the lane," Mr. Banks said, rolling up the window shade to admit a shaft of spring sunshine. "A pity that, when you ladies could well be allies to the local girls."

Why hadn't Kirsten realized that Mrs. Blumenthal's sniffy airs were a mother's desperation rather than a lack of neighborliness?

"Perhaps it's time to resurrect the choir," Kirsten said. "We haven't had one for at least five years."

"For the young people?" Mr. Banks asked. "Have we a choir director?"

When young people got to sharing hymnals of a pleasant spring evening, the presence of a choir director or even a song was of little moment.

"We'll draft Elsie into that job," Kirsten said. "She has a beautiful soprano voice, can play the organ better than passably, and will need something besides George to take her mind off Digby's absence."

"A choir, then, and scholars underfoot," Mr. Banks murmured. "Who could ask for more?"

❧

Scholars needed to eat at least three times a day and more often was better. Their ponies ate incessantly. Scholars also used clean linen, soap, dishes—young scholars were very hard on dishes—and books. They went through coal and paper like a biblical plague and could perform wonders making bread and jam disappear.

Daniel was therefore determined that his household would run on a budget. Olivia had been quick to lift that burden from his shoulders in Little Weldon, and had hoarded funds for herself even as she had begrudged Daniel fodder for his horse.

He'd been happy to indulge any sign that she supported his vocation, more fool he. The funds she'd extorted from Letty had been recovered, for they'd been banked in Daniel's name. The household funds she'd stolen from Daniel would be neither tallied nor restored to him.

Even Daniel's father, who hadn't cared for Olivia, or for matches made before a fellow had seen much of the world, could not have foreseen the misery Daniel's marriage had become.

Daniel flicked the beads of an abacus with one hand and penciled figures onto foolscap with the other. Many, many figures, for this new start in Haddondale had abruptly become important.

"Excuse me, Mr. Banks."

Lady Kirsten stood in the Belle Maison library doorway, a box in her hands. Daniel rose and relieved her of the box but did not close the door behind her.

"My lady, good afternoon."

She was in her manor-house attire—no apron, no lopsided bun. The last of Daniel's effects, the last of his father's diaries included, had been moved to the dower house that morning when he'd gone calling on his scholars' families.

Tonight, he'd sleep under the same roof as Lady Kirsten for the last time.

"Will I disturb you, Mr. Banks? I'm making a final sweep of the shelves for duplicates, especially of the children's literature."

Yes, she had disturbed him.

"Very kind of you, Lady Kirsten, and I did not properly thank you or Lady Susannah for your aid this morning. Mrs. Blumenthal is probably sewing new shirts for those boys as we speak."

"Her daughters might be," Lady Kirsten said, crossing to the desk. "You are concerned for your finances, Mr. Banks?"

"Yes." Somehow, Daniel's finances had become tangled up with his immortal soul and his enmity toward his spouse. "If I'd been more astute about money matters, more vigilant and less trusting, my wife would not have wreaked as much havoc as she did."

Lady Kirsten ran a finger down the column of figures associated with coal expenditures.

"You reproach yourself for trusting *your own wife*? If you cannot trust the one person in the entire realm who has taken a public oath to love, honor, and obey you, then what hope remains for any union?"

Put like that, the hair shirt Daniel had mentally worn for months seemed a vanity rather than a penance.

"I was a fool," Daniel said, wishing he could close the door after all. Not because he sought more of Lady Kirsten's kisses—long for them he might, but seek them he would not—but because Lady Kirsten was fair-minded, honest, and impartial.

She cast sand over his expenses. "Mr. Banks, I can

assure you, you are the only person in the history of people to have behaved foolishly, with your coin or with your affections. Nobody else has ever relied on another's promise of love, nobody else has ever misplaced trust along with common sense. You are the first."

Her ladyship remained at the desk, staring at the costs associated with keeping small boys safe, well fed, and warm.

"Who was he?" Daniel asked, though he should not have. Bad enough he liked Lady Kirsten, was attracted to her, and dreamed of her kisses. Her confidences would only make matters more complicated.

And yet, he wanted those confidences, wanted her trust when he knew he could not have her heart.

She poured the sand off the foolscap and into the waste bin.

"I mentioned them to you earlier. The first of my follies was Mr. Sedgewick, heir to an earldom, a pleasant enough young man. I did not particularly esteem him, but he was friendly, tended to his hygiene, and didn't seem to mind…me."

Daniel wanted to give Lady Kirsten flowers, smiles, a hug, anything to banish the bewilderment from her eyes. He offered her one honest question.

"You would have settled for a husband who tolerated you?"

She moved away from the desk and took a seat in the armchair flanked by the blue sofa, which, being sized to her brother's dimensions, made her look young and diminutive.

"Many women are happy to have a husband who

tolerates them. Many more avidly seek a man who will forget he's married for the entire hunt season, or while Parliament sits, or as soon as the heir and spare come along."

"You deserve better."

"So did you."

The symmetry of her logic was stunning, a direct blow to months of self-castigation and philosophizing. Daniel took a place on the blue sofa next to her armchair.

"My father tried to warn me," Daniel said. "I was young, no use to talk to me."

"You're ancient now," Lady Kirsten replied, her tone as lugubrious as Daniel's had been. "Your great age explains your facility with Latin, seeing as it was spoken in the vernacular during your boyhood. You probably cut quite a figure in your toga and sandals."

"I'm not that—" *Old.* Daniel was only a few years past thirty, in his prime—so why didn't he feel it?

Why didn't he act it?

"Pax," Daniel said. Then, because he was as amused as he was irritated as he was charmed, "You should not be in here alone with me, despite my doddering antiquity."

"The door is open, Mr. Banks, and no less than two sisters, a brother, a sister-in-law, and twenty-odd servants will interfere do I attempt to debauch you. That's what I wanted to speak with you about."

How Daniel longed to tease Lady Kirsten for that sally, but she sat with her hands folded in her lap, not a jot or a tittle of humor about her expression.

"I'd rather hear more about this Sedgewick boy first." For only a boy would have failed to appreciate the fire in Lady Kirsten.

She rose and wandered off along shelves that held books older than she was.

"I referred to him earlier as a suitor, though in truth he was a fiancé. I wasn't disappointed when he backed out of the engagement. I was mortified, and then I was furious."

"How does a man back out of an engagement without finding himself an object of scandal?" Or worse, a lawsuit. And why would he? Lady Kirsten might have her rough edges, but she was lovely, kind, loyal, intelligent…

Drat Olivia to the foulest swamp. Drat all clueless young men too, even if that sentiment made Daniel sound exactly like his own father.

"If the man is embroiled in scandal, then the lady is too, isn't she?" Lady Kirsten observed. "Papa agreed not to bring a breach of promise suit in exchange for a sum certain, very quietly exchanged while I was seen to cry off."

"But you hadn't cried off. You'd been set aside."

"Dumped like a load of refuse. Viscount Morton, who had also advanced to the status of fiancé, paid twice the sum a year later, though in defense of both men, they've kept their mouths shut and the engagements had not been announced."

The men had kept their mouths closed about their own perfidy, while Lady Kirsten had instead closed her heart, or tried to. She ran a bare finger along the bookcase's edge, then examined her fingertip and wrinkled her nose.

"Nicholas should burn peat and wood in here," she said. "The coal dust is very hard on the books."

Daniel rose and passed her ladyship his plain linen handkerchief, which she used to rub dirt from her finger before returning the handkerchief to him.

"Kirsten, I am sorry. One weasel would put any young lady off courting, but two is a reflection on them, not you."

She drew a volume at random and flipped it open. "There you would be wrong, Mr. Banks."

"You do not misrepresent yourself, such that you turn into a gorgon between the hours of dusk and dawn. You don't tipple, you aren't obsessed with fashion or gambling. You aren't silly, though you have a fine wit and copious common sense, and you are very pleasing to look upon. Those fellows were simply idiots."

She snapped the book shut and shoved it at him— Rev. Cary's recent translation of *Inferno*, from *The Divine Comedy*.

"They were idiots who needed heirs, Mr. Banks, and of all the virtues you so generously attribute to me, I could not guarantee those men the children motivating them to take me to wife. My mother did her duty by the earldom splendidly, but the simple biological gift of reproduction has been denied me."

Abruptly, Daniel was staring at a heartache beyond comfort, a sorrow without end. *I'm sorry* was insultingly inadequate, and yet, even now, even with the library door open, he could not take her in his arms.

So he shared with her a truth that had whittled away at his own joy, crushed the life from his marriage, and threatened his very faith in God.

"I hate that you've been made to suffer thus, my

lady. It isn't fair, you don't deserve it, and I'd do anything to relieve you of this curse, for I suffer it as well."

❧

"We're to have *ponies*," Fred Blumenthal said in the privacy of the livery's haymow. "What about you?"

"Us too," Matthias Webber replied. "I can't imagine what for."

Digby could. "Ponies are because we'll live in with Vicar and have to ride back and forth to home on Fridays and Sundays. My papa explained it to me."

Papa had said the living-in part would be great fun too, though Mama had blinked rather a lot at that bouncer. Living in probably meant cold porridge, regular birchings, and sore knees from praying all the time. Living in with Vicar would also put an end to meetings in the livery, where a boy could not keep clean and always ended up sneezing halfway home.

"We walk everywhere now," Matthias said, pushing his glasses up his skinny nose. "Vicar is up to something."

Schemers saw schemes everywhere, as Mama used to say about Digby's Uncle Edward.

"Vicar can't ride our ponies," Thomas Webber said. "He's quite the largest vicar I've ever seen."

"He'll sit on you," Frank Blumenthal retorted, "and squash you in the dung the way you squash everybody else."

A tussle ensued, merely a skirmish because no mud or dung was to be had in the haymow, and everybody was preoccupied with thoughts of ponies.

For each of them.

"I know something," Digby said when Thomas and Frank were done getting their clothes dusty.

"You know your new papa is blowing the ground-sills with your mama," Fred said.

Digby let that pass because Fred was likely repeating something an older brother had said. Whatever ground-sills were.

"I know Vicar has a son about our age," Digby said. "His name is Danny, and he already has a pony." Digby left out that Papa had shared this with him, and had also pointed out that Danny and Digby would be the only boys without brothers at Vicar's establishment.

"How'd he get a pony if his papa's only a vicar?" Frank asked.

"No sisters," Matthias suggested. "Sisters cost a lot of money."

On this, the other boys seemed agreed.

"Have you seen Vicar's horse?" Digby asked, lowering his voice. "It's huge and black and half-wild, and I bet that horse can kick a pony halfway to Dorset."

"Vicar can kick us halfway to Dorset too," Thomas said. "Vicars should be little old fellows who fall asleep over their tea."

"I miss our governess," Frank said. "I miss her a lot."

"Miss her all you please," Matthias retorted, standing and brushing hay off his breeches. "I'm off to catch a half-dozen warty toads. Who's with me?"

Digby had no choice but to tramp along with them, though catching toads was muddy, stinky work. Then what exactly did a fellow do with a little, helpless, blinking creature who hopped about and made funny noises all night?

Much less with six of them?

Ten

"Mr. Banks," Kirsten said, honestly staring at him. "I beg your pardon?"

Of all the empty condolences, awkward platitudes, and useless promises of prayer Daniel Banks might have proffered, Kirsten could not, in her most fevered dreams, have imagined Mr. Banks commiserating with her.

"This was the part my papa didn't know," Mr. Banks said, folding his handkerchief and tucking it away. "Might we sit for a moment?"

Not the blue sofa, where Nicholas cavorted and cuddled with his countess.

Not the sofa before the fire, where Kirsten had come upon Mr. Banks dreaming of forbidden pleasures.

Well, yes, the sofa before the fire, despite its memories. Daniel sat beside her again, a mere inch away but not touching.

Damn and blast.

"You will explain yourself, Mr. Banks, for I was under the impression a reproductive fault could only be attributed to women."

He stared at the hearth, which, for the first time

in months, had no fire. "Some expert told you only women can be thus afflicted?"

Kirsten hadn't had the nerve to ask any save her sister Nita, who wasn't a real physician.

"Papa wanted to send me to an expert in Switzerland, but Mama pointed out that all of Polite Society would know of my travels. No lady of marriageable age ever summers in Switzerland because she enjoys perfect health. Then Mama wanted to consult a French midwife."

"What did you want?"

A bold question, but Daniel Banks was fierce in ways a woman could not anticipate.

Kirsten wished she'd thought to place a huge bouquet of flowers before the empty hearth, as her mother often had. Cheerful, bright, fragrant, doomed flowers.

"I wanted to die," she said. "A young lady of good birth is raised to understand that her value lies, ultimately, in her ability to pass along her blue blood. This I cannot do. I'm destined to become an object of pity, if not scorn, a relic tolerated by my family."

A country vicar might want children; a woman in Kirsten's position needed them.

"I had measles," Mr. Banks said, as easily as a man might convey that he sings tenor rather than baritone. "A serious case, shortly before I wed. The herb woman in our village said measles can render a man unable to procreate, though the illness does nothing to interfere with the mechanics."

Daniel wasn't even blushing, and neither was Kirsten. "You discussed this with her?"

"I had my heart set on marriage, Lady Kirsten. Do you know of any childless vicars?"

No, she did not. Vicars had large families; bishops' families were often enormous. King George, nominal head of the Church of England, had sired fifteen legitimate children.

"Have you mentioned your situation to any physicians?" she asked. Daniel would suffer that indignity at least once for the sake of children.

"One. Fairly was equivocal, presumably out of kindness, which I took for endorsement of the herb woman's opinion. She was very old and had seen much. I married Olivia at least in part because Olivia was willing to overlook my possible procreative failings. To her I seemed healthy, and she dismissed my disclosures easily."

The same woman had easily dismissed her very marriage vows.

Kirsten longed to take Daniel's hand, because this conversation transcended any intimacies she'd shared with others. This was not an exchange of rutting passion on one side and beleaguered modesty on the other, as she'd tolerated with Sedgewick and Morton. This exchange wasn't about her own desire, either.

These confidences were the stuff of a friendship closer than Kirsten shared with even her siblings, though she and Daniel weren't even touching.

"I had a female problem when I was fifteen," Kirsten said, her gaze straying to the painting over the blue sofa. Flowers, of course. White roses, some of them blown, all of them lovely, none of them real.

"The problem went away after plaguing me for

months," she went on, "but my biology has remained unpredictable, and my own mother, who'd delivered many babies, assured me that combination was cause for serious concern."

"For grief," Daniel said.

The eight-day clock ticked placidly along, the scent of old coal fires and older books hung in the air. Just another prosaic silence in a library made for silence.

Without touching Daniel, Kirsten shared a variety of sad moments with him she hadn't ever thought to share with anybody, moments that brought a measure of sanity to the rage fueled by her grief. Somebody else's dreams had been struck down by cruel, celestial whim. Somebody else had been left with a sense of hopeless inadequacy.

"You told Sedgewick and Morton, didn't you?" Daniel asked.

"Of course I told them, and my parents were wroth with me. Papa insisted nobody could ever prove a lack of heirs was my fault. Mama allowed that health matters are the most frequent subject of miracles."

"But you could not lie to a man who'd meet you at the altar." While Daniel's spouse had apparently done nothing but lie to and mislead him.

Maybe worse heartaches could befall the innocent than an inability to have children.

"Don't attribute any great virtue to me," Kirsten said. "Both men wanted to anticipate the vows, which is common enough. I could not allow them that privilege without explaining the risks they took. I would not have cried off had I given a man my virtue."

Memory assailed her, of the sturdy blue sofa and

Arthur Morton's hot breath against her neck as he swore vilely and battled with her skirts to get his breeches re-buttoned.

Daniel rose but went only a few feet, to stand by the empty hearth, his elbow braced against the mantel. *Must* he look so handsome and dear?

"Why are you smiling, Lady Kirsten?"

"The timing of my disclosure to Viscount Morton wanted finesse—or maybe my timing was exquisite." Though Kirsten's timing with Daniel Banks remained one set of vows too late. "You have Danny," she said, not an accusation so much as an insight. "He's the one child you've been given, and thus your attachment to him is like a king with one royal heir."

Danny was to rejoin the vicar's household, or join the vicar's herd of reprobate young scholars. Della had passed that along not an hour ago.

"Danny needs to learn to sin," the Vicar of Haddondale said, nudging a chunk of charred kindling back into the hearth with the toe of his boot. "With Olivia for a mother and me for a father, Danny became a perfect boy. He would not offend her, because she could be cruel. He would never offend me, because though I was ignorant of her true nature, I was his sole refuge from her carping. The corrupting influence of other boys will spare him a world of self-loathing and useless reproaches as he matures."

"I wish I could shake you, Daniel Banks." Kirsten also wished she could smooth his hair back, hug him, comfort him.

And kiss him, damn it. She resisted the urge to sit on her hands.

"I'm slow to accept certain insights, Lady Kirsten, but I can assure you, my own store of self-loathing and useless reproaches is ebbing the longer I remain in Haddondale."

Daniel gave her a smile, a sweet, confiding blessing of a smile. A regret of a smile that yet connected them in their miseries and their fierceness.

"I came in here to tell you that you're safe from me," Kirsten said, lest, like an idiot, she remain beaming back at him until summer.

He settled in, so he was nearly slouching against the mantel, and abruptly, handsome and dear were joined by mischievous. Devilish, even. Kirsten tucked her palms under her thighs, as a small boy did in the presence of forbidden sweets.

"Safe?" Daniel said with mock consternation. "You'll no longer scold me for my excesses of virtue? No longer kick me under the tea table when I forget to insist on baskets of sweets for the Webber boys? This is not a form of safety I will enjoy."

He was the dearest man, the dearest friend, and Kirsten wanted to be a friend to him as well. Among other hopeless, pointless things.

"You have Danny," Kirsten said. "I want the rotten boys." She wanted their vicar as well, which probably made her rotten too.

Lovely.

"The boys have yet to fall into my reforming clutches, my lady. What fate have you planned for them?"

"Tea with me on Thursdays," Kirsten said, barely, barely resisting the urge to retie Daniel's off-center cravat. "To learn deportment, the order of precedence, the royal succession, and other drawing room tricks to impress their parents while their studies come along at a more reasonable pace."

Daniel sauntered away and propped a hip on a windowsill, almost as if he'd known Kirsten's dignity was losing the fight with her ill-timed impulses.

"You get the parlor tricks while I break the new sod with first declension nouns and Psalms? Hardly fair, my lady. Am I to join this tea party?"

Did he want to? Kirsten would love to share—

"I think not," she said, before her rotten nature could stop her. "You and the boys can't be in each other's pockets all the time. You have sermons to prepare, after all. I also suggest you appropriate Ralph as your general factotum. The family is going up to Town soon, and the staff will be in want of activity."

Outside, the day was shifting, from overcast and rainy, to sunny and damp. The sunlight was still weak and wintry, and Daniel made a lonely, wistful figure silhouetted against it.

"Every headmaster needs a general factotum," he said, pushing open the curtain wide enough to reveal the view of the dormant gardens. "I thought you were traveling to London with your sisters."

"Nicholas and I are negotiating. If the staff is to take on regular meals for small children, a great deal more laundry, and a half-dozen fractious ponies—for ponies are always fractious—then somebody had best be on hand to keep matters organized."

The household would probably enjoy the occasional stray toad, bat, squirrel, or rabbit too, and

Kirsten wouldn't miss that excitement for the world. Would that the vicar were inclined to stray.

But no. Fierceness suffused his honor as well as his kindness, and Kirsten would not for the world trespass on the kindness or compromise the honor.

"I was set on organizing the finances," Mr. Banks said, opening the window a crack. "I hadn't thought of the rest of it. You're also good at dealing with minor injuries."

Kirsten's ability to cope with a broken heart was improving as well.

"I suggest you resume your place at the desk, Mr. Banks, and jot down a few notes. I have five brothers, the privileged sons of an earl, whereas you were raised the sole boy in a rural parsonage."

"You're suggesting my upbringing had its limitations, and I can't argue that conclusion." He took a seat behind the desk, produced a penknife, and whittled a new point on his pencil. "Madam, I await your guidance."

They argued, they discussed, and when insisting that the vicar borrow the schoolroom's glass terrarium posthaste, Kirsten even raised her voice.

For Daniel Banks had become her friend, and she was helpless not to protect him, even from the herd of loose toads doubtless hopping his way.

⌘

Lady Kirsten had assigned all six boys their beds, cots in an upstairs room that had a big fireplace, a worktable, and a row of windows that looked out over the stable and pastures.

"Maybe it won't be so bad here," Thomas Webber said, climbing under his blankets. "Her ladyship didn't even mention baths, and the ladies are always going on about baths."

Digby exchanged a look with Danny Banks, who'd ridden up the lane on his own pony in the company of a big, blond lord of some sort.

Papa had brought Digby over, with the new pony on a leading line. Papa was only the son of a lord.

"We'll bathe in the laundry," Matthias Webber said. "Cleanliness is next to godliness, and vicars are the godliest bunch. At least I'll have my sweets to look forward to tomorrow."

"I'm not particularly fond of sweets," Danny said. He was wiping off his boots with a rag, probably his only pair. Vicars were poor, so a vicar's son would be even poorer.

Poor did not, apparently, mean stupid.

"I'm not one for sweets, either," Digby said. "I do enjoy cricket."

"You can forget cricket," Frank Blumenthal muttered, smacking his pillow. "This is a new pillow."

"Won't be for long if you beat it," Fred Blumenthal retorted, smacking his own pillow in an identical fashion. "We need a cricket set if we're to play cricket, and that's assuming Vicar doesn't chain us to our desks."

Danny spat on the toe of one boot and went back to his polishing. "He can't chain us to our desks. We have to look after our ponies."

An uneasy silence fell. The boys had ponies, but like Digby, they'd only recently acquired them.

"What do you know about looking after a pony?"

Matthias sneered. Without glasses slipping down his nose all the time, he looked less like a baby owl and more like a skinny, tired boy.

"Everything," Danny said easily, setting a shiny boot beside its mate. "I've been helping Papa with Beelzebub since I was very small. There's a lot to know, but the horses understand if you're trying to learn, and are patient with us as long as we mean well."

Pray God the vicar worked along the same plan, because Digby had no head for Latin.

"Tell us about looking after a pony," Fred said around a yawn. "Though I expect the earl will have his grooms look after ours."

"He won't," Digby ventured. "A gentleman knows how to look after his cattle, so we'll learn about looking after our own ponies." Papa had winked when he'd said that, though in addition to Latin, French, geography, math, history, and natural science, mucking out a pony stall loomed like one of those impossible jobs set for that big Greek fellow whose name Digby forgot.

Harold? Hairy-something?

"What's one thing we need to know about looking after ponies?" Thomas asked. "I haven't even given mine a name yet."

"The name is important," Danny said, getting into bed. "Water is more important. The first thing your pony must have is frequent rations of good, clean water."

"What else?" Fred prompted. "Nobody lives on just water."

"A fish might," Frank retorted.

"Don't think I'll share my sweets simply because

you're telling us about ponies," Matthias said, blowing out the last candle, for he'd appointed himself in charge of candles.

"I want Digby to share his cricket set," Danny said. "Though I'm sure the other boys would enjoy sharing your sweets."

A considering, perhaps even wondering silence ensued, broken by a single weak croak from under Matthias's bed.

"I'll share my basket," Thomas said, "and Matthias can be a miser. A month is a long time to go between biscuits."

"Danny will have to tell us about keeping a pony," Digby suggested, for a vicar's boy might not get a basket of sweets ever.

"You'll share your cricket kit," Danny replied. "And we'll all have sweets."

Another lone, perhaps consenting croak, and then all six boys drifted to sleep on dreams of ponies and biscuits.

⁂

Daniel's week bumped along in the direction of a new routine, one that pleased and tormented him in equal measures. For reasons he could not fathom, Lady Kirsten had bid him to fill a terrarium with moss, sticks, and leaves, and keep it out of sight.

On Monday, Matthias Webber's basket of sweets arrived, crammed full of biscuits, a wedge of cheese, a large loaf of fresh bread, and even a few candied violets.

On Tuesday, Matthias had a bellyache, which meant Daniel assigned him to say grace before all three meals, a bellyache being a known guarantee of a short blessing. Tuesday was also the day set aside for Mr. George Haddonfield to assist with lessons in horsemanship, so Daniel had the later afternoon free to work on his sermon.

Wednesday after studies, because the scholars were off to a good start, Master Digby's cricket set was pressed into service, with Ralph, the stable lads, and the under-footmen filling out the athletic ranks. Daniel used the time to call on several parishioners too ill or infirm to attend Sunday services.

Thursday afternoon, the boys were subjected to a thorough scrubbing of hands before they thundered across the garden and invaded Lady Kirsten's formal parlor. The wonders of the tea ceremony were laid before them, also the wonders of ginger biscuits and—with the assistance of the ginger-biscuit-snitching earl himself—the art of the proper bow.

More cricket ensued at the lady's request, though it hadn't been on Daniel's schedule. Her team lost but didn't seem to mind their defeat.

Friday, the day when Daniel intended to administer the boys' first examinations, all hell finally broke loose.

"I count six," Ralph muttered as the croaking in the schoolroom reached a crescendo. "One toad for each boy, and these are the biggest toads I've ever seen, sir."

"The loudest as well," Daniel replied. The boys, seated each at his desk, failed to stifle smug little grins, though Danny was making an effort. "If you open the cupboard behind the desk in my study, Ralph, you will find a large glass terrarium. You will please fetch it, though take your time. I must explain something to the boys."

A sermon of sorts organized itself in Daniel's head.

"Gentlemen, into the corridor with me." Where Daniel would be heard over the croaking of hapless amphibians. No wonder frogs had qualified for biblical plague status.

Six abruptly sober little fellows filed out into the corridor. Daniel shut the door, lest they be joined by their new pets.

"Can anybody hazard a guess as to how our studies have been disrupted?" he asked.

Silence, much shuffling of small feet, a glance between the twins. Matthias Webber pushed his glasses up his nose. Danny studied his boots. Digby stared straight ahead.

"As I thought, a simple unfortunate coincidence," Daniel said. "A half-dozen ambitious gentlemen toads took it into their little toadly minds to acquire an education in Latin. We must not disappoint them. We'll have our examination first, and then I'll leave you to round up the misguided creatures while I have my luncheon. When the toads have been returned to their natural habitat, we'll do an experiment regarding the benefits of captivity for our science lesson this afternoon. Does that sound agreeable?"

Thomas, a dear little soul with a good heart and a solid left cross, ventured a question.

"Does that mean we don't get to eat, sir?"

"Of course you'll eat," Daniel said. "But we're dealing with a matter of stewardship, Thomas. These misguided toads have likely been hopping their way into the house for days. Unless somebody has thought to feed them their accustomed diet, they're near starvation to say nothing of the miseries of dehydration, while we've enjoyed our toast, eggs, and porridge only hours ago. We must look after those who cannot manage for themselves."

"If they're dying of hunger and thirst, shouldn't we catch the poor little toads before we take our examination?" Matthias asked. The boy intended the toad catching to go on all day, of course.

Such a bright lad.

"You hear them," Daniel said. "They're unsettled, bouncing around, trying to find the fresh water and flies they need to survive. They'll quiet down while you boys tend to your examinations. I'm sure of it."

The toads, obliging fellows, did not quiet down. In the midst of Digby's academic labors, one plopped right onto his paper, provoking a screech from the boy, which resulted in a watery brown streak across the paper, before the malefactor hopped to the boy's boot and on about the schoolroom.

"Shall you start over, Digby?" Daniel asked, flourishing a clean sheet of foolscap.

"From the very beginning?"

"Afraid so. You'll keep your jacket cleaner. Toads haven't the knack of using the chamber pot."

The look that crossed the boy's face nearly undid Daniel's composure, so horrified was his hungry little scholar. The other five boys took to curling their arms protectively around their work, which was not, alas, progressing very quickly.

Ralph produced the terrarium and Daniel left him to oversee the remainder of the examination, for nothing would come between Daniel and his favorite, most dreaded penance.

Lady Kirsten had taken to joining him for lunch in his study. The door remained open, of course, and the occasional boy, Ralph, or a footman with a bucket of coal often interrupted.

She sat on her side of his desk, content with a tray of soup, cold chicken, and buttered bread.

And apparently with her vicar's company.

"My papa declared it the eleventh commandment that a sensible routine was a cure for nearly all ills," Daniel said, passing her ladyship the saltcellar. Papa had been wrong, of course. Routine might address a boy's ills, but not a man's.

Papa's journals did not go flying from the shelves at Daniel's disrespectful thoughts. He really ought to have been spending his luncheons reading those journals.

"Are the boys settling in, then?" Lady Kirsten used her fingers, not the delicate silver spoon, to add a dash of salt to her soup.

"Ralph counted six toads in the schoolroom this morning," Daniel said. "An encouraging sign of solidarity among the lads, though their academics are sadly wanting." Even Danny had lost ground in the months since Daniel had last shared a roof with him.

"Toads? Frogs are slimier. My brother Adolphus had a positive fascination with the varied effects of a frog in a sister's bed. I grew to like toads by comparison. Butter for your bread, Mr. Banks?"

Daniel had forgotten to butter his bread. Around Lady Kirsten, discussing the boys, discussing toads, discussing *anything*, he could forget his name. The primary difficulty lay not with sexual desire, though he was powerfully attracted to her.

Thwarted sexual urges were a trial of almost tiresome familiarity.

The primary torment her ladyship provided, and the greatest comfort, was her simple company. Daniel's concerns interested her, the boys interested her, and ensuring he had proper directions to each parishioner's home interested her.

Their hands bumped as she passed him the butter. Daniel sat back, wrestling a combination of loneliness, desire, frustration, and bewilderment into submission.

"Are you sure you ought not to go up to Town?" he asked.

Lady Kirsten put her spoon down and set about buttering Daniel's bread. She had such pretty hands, and yet they were capable too.

"At meals, all my family talks about is Town. Who was engaged last year but has still not married this year. Who is on her third season, now accompanied by a prettier younger sister. What fellow has come into an inheritance or a title. I cannot abide it."

So she sought refuge with Daniel and the boys.

And the toads, of whom she'd learned to be fond.

"I cannot imagine your sisters engaging in such talk maliciously," Daniel said, accepting a thoroughly buttered slice of bread from her ladyship without risking so much as a brush of fingers.

"My sisters are never malicious, but then Nicholas clears his throat. Leah sends me a pitying glance, and Della remarks on Prinny's latest foolish wager, as if anybody cares about that."

Lady Kirsten turned the topic back to the boys, all of whom had been kept too busy to get to scrapping, though they would soon.

Daniel had used the week to become familiar with his pupils and to assess their abilities, rather than apply any academic pressure.

"They're smart boys, though they've had a poor start," he said as he and Lady Kirsten sipped identical mugs of ale. "Thomas isn't as quick as the rest, but he's thorough. When he reaches his conclusions, they're well thought-out and sensible. He'll be a good influence if he can keep from sitting on the smaller boys."

Danny had let that part slip, about Thomas and his unique approach to pugilistic encounters.

"Sometimes small boys need sitting on," Lady Kirsten said. "They weren't out catching those toads last night, Daniel." She slipped more and more often, calling him by his Christian name, though only when they were private.

"I suspect the toads matriculated with the boys," Daniel said. "I leave the children the privacy of their bedroom, but the chambermaid reported a curious croaking from under the beds early in the week."

"Those poor creatures have been boxed up all week? Left without food and water? Next they'll be trussed up in ball gowns and sent to hop around Mayfair, twirling parasols."

Lady Kirsten was angry, and not exclusively on behalf of the toads.

"You were dreading the remove to Town very much," Daniel said, while he dreaded the next day—no boys, no Danny, no midday meal with Lady Kirsten. His sermon was neatly prepared, his budget completed.

"I know we're not supposed to hate," Lady Kirsten said, rising. "But, Daniel, I hate to see Della so nervous and Nicholas so quiet. Della's reception in Town will be difficult. Some will fawn because she's an earl's daughter. Others will gossip that she's a countess's by-blow. What does it matter? She's dear and smart and kind, and it's all—"

"She is well loved," Daniel said, getting to his feet. "She must learn to make her way, but she'll have supporters, your brother first among them. Bellefonte makes a formidable ally, and his countess does not suffer fools. Lady Susannah has memorized every colorful insult the Bard concocted, all in the interests of literary wit, of course."

Lady Kirsten needed reassurances and understanding.

She needed a consoling hug.

Remaining in the country was by no means a desertion of her sisters, and yet a wiser man would have chased Lady Kirsten off to London, previous positions on the matter notwithstanding. Daniel passed Kirsten the half-eaten bread from her plate, butter glistening in abundance. She took it, and again, their fingers didn't brush.

Daniel, his immortal soul, his breeding organs, and his honor were all safe with Kirsten Haddonfield. Damnation, but he could not manage to be grateful for the security she afforded his gentlemanly integrity.

"Shall we finish our meal?" he asked. "I've been meaning to ask you how the choir's first rehearsal went."

He had given the choir half a passing thought at some point.

Her ladyship took a nibble of buttered bread and sat back down across the desk from Daniel. They chatted about ailing parishioners and who should be invited to join the choir despite lack of musical ability.

The food disappeared, and Daniel's pocket watch said he'd best check on the progress of his budding toad drovers on the next floor down. He lingered another five minutes with Lady Kirsten, not because he desired her, not because academic administration required it, not because she was lonely.

And not because he was lonely, either.

Olivia had never once spent a pleasant midday meal with her husband, discussing parishioners, students, toads, or flirtatious young people. Not once. The lack of support from his wife put Daniel in mind of Lady Kirsten enduring her social seasons, beset by gossip, judgment, and emotional hazards on all sides.

London had plagues enough, even without grasshoppers or frogs.

Daniel remained those extra minutes with Lady Kirsten because he and she simply liked each other, and everybody—every single person on the face of the earth—deserved the comfort of simple friendship.

Why hadn't he known that? Why hadn't his inability to be friends with his own wife bothered him a great deal more and a great deal sooner?

When Ralph arrived to take the empty trays, Daniel bowed Lady Kirsten on her way, knowing she'd look in at the schoolroom before she crossed the garden to rejoin her family.

"All but one hop toad is tucked up right and tight in the tea-rare-ee-thingum," Ralph said when Lady Kirsten had left. "The last little blighter is quicker than the rest. All six boys together haven't been able to catch him. It's been proper entertaining, sir."

"Get some lunch, Ralph," Daniel said, for he was a country vicar, and catching even nimble, independent toads was in his gift. "We'll soon have the lone fugitive incarcerated with his fellows."

Though not for long, because toads belonged at liberty in the countryside. How Daniel envied the homely toad, who would soon be hopping free in the puddle of its lowly, warty choice.

For a few daring, useless moments, Daniel allowed himself to envision a life without Olivia. Either divorce or annulment would cost him his calling, bring scandal down on Danny, and reduce Daniel's means to that of a common laborer, for no gentleman ought to employ an ordained refugee from a failed marriage.

Daniel mentally boxed up his musings and shelved them under the increasingly broad heading of "penance."

One last feckless toad needed rescuing from its own independent nature, and six little boys were doubtless on the verge of starvation.

Eleven

"HOW CAN COUNTRY BOYS KNOW NOTHING OF horses?" George asked. "Digby was isolated from the stable by a combination of maternal hovering and his uncle's miserliness, but Squire Blumenthal loves to ride to hounds, and Denton Webber never misses a race meet."

"Not all boys are raised by the Earl of Bellefonte," Kirsten said. "Ponies are an extravagance."

George took Kirsten's arm and led her across the stable yard, which, for the first time in days, was dry.

"Did Nick cut up badly about having a herd of ponies added to the stables?" George asked.

"He said ponies were a fine notion for teaching responsibility to small boys, and if you ever tired of being the equitation master, he'd gladly step in." Kirsten had nearly hugged her brother at that offer, but Nicholas had muttered this pronouncement with his nose firmly planted in some ledger or other.

He was probably the shyest earl ever to dread the opening of Parliament.

"Nicholas loves children," George said. "As do I."

George's marriage to Elsie had come as a surprise to his siblings, and probably to George himself. Upon coming down from university, he'd cut a swath through Town that had ventured into some of the riskier shadowed corners favored by the likes of Byron and Brummel.

Della hadn't been able to unearth too many details—a certain handsome young earl's name had come up—and Kirsten hadn't wanted to hear details in any case.

She'd deal with important matters directly, though. "Will you and Elsie have children?"

"Sit with me, Kay-Kay." George was the only sibling who used that nickname for Kirsten. When he led her to a sunny bench, she took the place beside him.

"You'd be an excellent father," she said, meaning every word. "Digby worships the ground you strut about on, and you're wonderful with him."

"And I love the boy, but…Elsie said I must tell you first."

George stared at his dusty riding boots, his smile sweet, distracted, and bashful. He was a stunningly handsome man, but in the stable yard, smelling of horse and turned out in less than his company finery, George was also a radiantly happy man.

Another niece or nephew, then. Kirsten hugged her brother fiercely.

"I am so happy for you, George. So very, exceedingly, unendingly, witlessly happy for you and Elsie. I'll be a relentlessly doting auntie, I warn you. The first time I held Nicholas and Leah's baby—"

Kirsten had fallen in love, then she'd gone to her

room to cry. Lately, she'd worn a path back to the nursery and dreaded the infant's coming absence.

"Elsie said I was a fool to worry," George replied, hugging Kirsten back, "but one does."

One's brothers did because they were wonderful brothers. "I will never have children," Kirsten said, "but that only means the ones I can love are dearer to me."

She'd worked that out in the last week, while admiring the shine on Danny Banks's boots and the brawn of little Thomas's biceps. No parent kept a child close forever. Children grew up, God willing, and left home to make their way.

Nobody had a child all for her own for very long, not in the normal course of things.

George took out a handkerchief and slapped at the toes of his boots. "Elsie says I'm also not to worry about you dodging the pretty in Town this spring, either."

"Why would you worry about me when I'm—?"

He left off whacking at his boots, which would only get dirty again anyway. "I'm your most wicked, harum-scarum brother," George went on, "to hear some tell it. I'm the last person who would judge you for indulging yourself with a few stolen moments in a lonely vicar's arms."

A few weeks ago, Kirsten would have either laughed or stomped away, insulted by George's innuendo.

"George, hush."

"I see how Banks watches you across the riding arena, Kay-Kay. When he took meals with us at Belle Maison, he labored mightily to not even glance your way. I know a pair of smitten wretches when I see them."

Kirsten was smitten, but she was not wretched—not entirely wretched. "Daniel Banks is *married*, George. He'll always be married, and even Della hasn't divined the details of the estrangement between the vicar and his wife." *Mrs. Banks.* Kirsten would not refer to her thus aloud, because the woman who'd stolen Daniel's trust did not deserve that title.

"What has Banks told you?"

Without using words, Daniel had told Kirsten that he cared for her, and were he free, he'd desire her as well. A bouquet of sentiments that must always remain in the realm of wishes and dreams.

And not venture into even the realm of glances.

"Mr. Banks has told me he respects me," Kirsten said, "and that his wife misappropriated funds from both his sister and the church. I gather he blames himself." Less so than he had a few weeks ago, though. "He is devoted to that child and to his vocation."

Kirsten would never betray Daniel's confidences regarding Danny.

"You've met Banks's sister, Lady Fairly?" George asked, stuffing the now dusty handkerchief into a pocket.

"Of course."

"She bears a very close resemblance to her nephew. You might ask Banks about that."

Thus was a good man's privacy both protected and threatened.

"I'll not pry, George, and you needn't avoid the library in the coming weeks for fear you'll find the vicar and me on the blue sofa, so to speak. Mr. Banks and I are friends, and I do not enjoy Town. There's an end to it."

Across the garden, Mr. Banks led an orderly line of six little boys, each hand-walking a pony, from the stable to the large water trough near the stable's cistern.

"Elsie isn't at all impressed with my looks," George said, which odd conclusion seemed to please him.

"Both of my fiancés were accounted fine-looking men. I wasn't impressed with them either."

"I'm gorgeous though," George retorted. "Byron himself declared it so, and any number of ladies and a few gentlemen have confirmed his opinion."

"You're a handsome idiot who couldn't carry a tune in a bucket," Kirsten replied by way of support, because George's looks were a burden, not a blessing. They called attention to a man who was shy, tender-hearted, and good with children and animals.

"What I'm trying to say is that Elsie is my friend, Kirsten. She laughs at my attempts to sing and doesn't care if my cravat is frilly or if I'm even wearing one. She won't tolerate any criticism of me by others but has scolded me roundly for buying her earbobs. I thought I merely liked her, but in appallingly short order, I've fallen in love with my wife."

He'd fallen into bed with her too, apparently. Lucky Elsie, and wise Elsie.

"George, I am pleased for you and Elsie, for I've no doubt she returns your sentiments, despite your looks. What has this to do with my situation?"

"The straight path is for storybooks and sermons," George said. "I'm not suggesting you elope with another woman's husband and bring disgrace to an innocent boy. I'm suggesting you accept the gifts that are yours at no cost to others. Banks is a good fellow, even if he isn't exactly the right fellow."

"We're friends," Kirsten said again. "I could never have been friends with either Sedgewick or Morton, and yet I would have married them, and that would have been wrong. I will never marry Mr. Banks, but—"

"Exactly," George said. "Life is not always tidy and balanced. Think about that while I ride home to tell my lady that Digby has survived another equitation lesson without breaking any bones."

At that exact moment, pandemonium broke out among the ponies and the little boys trying to lead them about.

❧

Daniel blamed the mishap on his besottedness with Lady Kirsten.

While the boys had groomed their ponies, George Haddonfield had pulled Daniel to the back of the stable, where the earl maintained a woodworking shop—or private trysting site.

"Banks," Haddonfield had muttered, "you cannot look at her like that. Not in public."

Daniel left off admiring sketches of a fanciful birdhouse—or pretending to. "I beg your pardon, Mr. Haddonfield?"

The shop was roomy, but with a man Haddonfield's size pacing about, Daniel didn't know exactly where to stand.

"For the duration of the last hour," Mr. Haddonfield went on, "as six little boys went bouncing by, ponies churning up dust, and me bellowing encouragement from the center of the ring, you and my own dear sister made sheep's eyes at one another."

"You could tell this from halfway across a riding arena?"

"I could have seen those glances from the maids' quarters on the fourth floor of the manor house. Get hold of yourself, or Nicholas won't be able to ignore the situation."

Him again. Nicholas—the earl, the head of the family, the nobleman who held the Haddondale living.

"And *is* the earl ignoring the situation?"

"He exhorted me to keep a close eye on Kirsten in his absence, but not too close. Elsie and I will bide here, at Belle Maison, though my wife and I have responsibilities to see to under our own roof too."

That qualified as ignoring the situation but not the appearances.

"My own sister was led nearly to ruin by a randy curate, Mr. Haddonfield. Do you *expect* me to debauch Lady Kirsten and cast aside my marriage vows?"

Mr. Haddonfield stopped pacing. "Don't be dramatic. A discreet affair is hardly an orgy beneath the full moon. What you and Kirsten get up to in the privacy of some butler's pantry is of no interest to me, but for God's sake, exercise some discretion."

If Daniel were to violate those vows with Kirsten, he'd do it in a wide, fluffy bed, on fresh linen, behind a locked door, not in some dusty—

God help him. "Your warning is appreciated, Mr. Haddonfield, but entirely unnecessary."

"Oh, right. Forget I said anything, then, but virtue makes a cold bedfellow, Mr. Banks, and has never been known to ease a broken heart. Next week, you'll hack out with me and the boys."

Lovely. An interminable, plodding walk with six pony-sized slugs, while Beelzebub capered and cavorted his way down one lane and up the other.

"I'll look forward to it, Mr. Haddonfield."

Daniel was still pondering his newfound capacity for falsehoods when he led the boys and their steeds out to the watering trough fifteen minutes later.

Danny did well with his Loki, but then they'd had time to learn each other's habits. Thomas's mount was a solid, cobby gray, and Fred and Frank had been given matching duns.

Matthias and his little bay mare were nervous of each other, so Daniel put them at the end of the line. The mare, however, took exception to waiting for her drink, and shouldered forward of her handler, leaving Matthias holding the lead line as two ponies, indifferent to a mere boy, jostled at the trough.

"She's being bad!" Matthias screeched, hauling on the lead line to no avail. "She won't listen, and she's mean."

Loki's head came up, his hairy chin dripping. Thomas's beast barged into the mare from the opposite side, and Matthias hit the limit of his courage.

"They're squashing me," he howled, shoving at the ponies' quarters. The mare, being a mare, swung her back end into the boy. Matthias wriggled free between two wringing pony tails, and bellowed that the pony's wretched tail had nearly taken his eye out.

"Boys, hold steady," Daniel said, for Matthias had dropped the mare's lead line. "Matthias, quiet. You're frightening the ponies."

"But my eye hurts! She did it on purpose, and ponies are stupid, ugly, hairy—"

"Hush, Mattie," Thomas bellowed, and now the mare's head came up too.

She probably sensed that nobody held her lead line, though all too easily some boy or pony might step on it.

George Haddonfield came striding over from a bench in the garden, while Lady Kirsten—bless her common sense—hung back from an increasingly restive herd of boys and ponies.

"Matthias Webber," George said, "you will take yourself over to her ladyship, who will inspect your eye. You lot, look to your—"

Had Daniel been thinking, rather than envying Matthias Webber his place plastered against Lady Kirsten's waist, he might have simply tromped on the mare's lead line.

But no, Daniel was an idiot in love, and he bent down amid sharp pony hooves and little boy boots and picked up the lead. All might have gone well from there—George was sorting the boys out—but the mare had decided to take advantage of her owner's desertion at the precise instant Daniel grasped the rope.

The mare tried to bolt, the rope burning across Daniel's left palm like a hot knife as he closed his grip. He snatched the rope into his right hand and yanked stoutly.

"*Settle, drat you to perdition!*"

The mare stood docilely, blinking innocent brown eyes at Daniel, while six boys goggled and five other ponies went still.

"Come along, gentlemen," Mr. Haddonfield said pleasantly. "Put the geldings into their stalls. The mare thinks to earn attention with her misbehavior and the best we can do is ignore her. Mr. Banks has her in hand."

Mr. Banks was mentally bellowing every foul curse a vicar had ever overheard and inventing a few of his own.

"I'll take the cheeky little besom," old Alfrydd said, shuffling out of the stable. "Wants a firm hand is all, and yon boy hasn't the knack yet. Come with me, Your Highness."

The mare trailed along, lifting her tail and expressing her sentiments in Daniel's direction, as horses were wont to do. Matthias turned loose of Lady Kirsten, his spirits evidently restored by his pony's timely flatulence.

"Put her up," Daniel said to the boy. "Your eye may smart for a bit, but Freya needs to know you haven't abandoned her." More to the point, the pony needed to understand that she couldn't scare off her lord, master, and owner with a mere swish of her tail and stomp of her dainty hoof.

"I don't like her," Matthias said, his tone forlorn. "I wait all this time for a pony, and she's a very pretty pony, but I don't like her."

At least the child wasn't wed to his pretty, long-awaited pony.

"Horses are like people, Matthias," Daniel said with a patience he did not feel. "They're happiest if they know who's in charge and can respect whoever that is. She's the only mare, she's the smallest, and she's unsure of herself and of you."

Matthias pushed dusty glasses up his nose. "She

doesn't respect me, sir. It's the same at home, you know. The mares are the boss of everybody."

A swish of skirts saved Daniel from replying to that lament.

"Nobody has to be the boss of anybody, Matthias, if everybody is friends," Lady Kirsten said. "Tonight, when you've done your lessons, come out here and explain to Freya that you want to be her friend, but nobody likes a rotten pony. The other ponies will be jealous of the attention you give her."

"If you say so, milady."

He trudged off, while Daniel's palm shifted from burning to burning, throbbing, and stinging all at once.

"Come along, Mr. Banks," Lady Kirsten said, taking him by his right hand and leading him into the garden. "I was cursing on your behalf before George was off the bench. Unless I miss my guess, you'll have a proper scar for this day's work."

"The wound is uncomfortable," Daniel admitted, wrapping a handkerchief around his now-bloody palm. He'd certainly have a scar, and he'd have a stolen memory too. Holding hands with Lady Kirsten was ill-advised and stupid, and should have been awkward, but her touch was also the sweetest balm.

Alas, in all likelihood, Daniel would never hold hands with her again.

༄

For the width of one flowerless garden, past the bench, through the knot garden, around the pergola, along thorny hedges far from blooming, Kirsten held hands with her friend.

With the man she'd never call "beloved," though he was. The mare had deserved more than a scolding, and Kirsten deserved more than to simply hold hands with Mr. Banks.

Ah, well.

She relinquished her grip when they reached the back terrace.

"We're for the library," she said. "My sister Nita is very knowledgeable about medicinals and preferred not to tend wounds anywhere near the kitchen. We can use the herbal if you'd rather."

The herbal was a small, tidy room in the understory. Nobody would disturb them there.

"The library will do, but I can tend to myself if you'll show me to the supplies."

"You'll not make a proper job of it, or have a grasp of Nita's labels," Kirsten said, opening the French doors that led directly to the library. "Let's use the desk."

Mr. Banks took a seat at one of the chairs facing the desk. The linen he'd wrapped around his hand had become bloody, and the wound had to hurt.

"I know better," he growled, glowering at his abused palm. "One always wears gloves when working with horses for just this purpose. Any horse can spook, bolt, rear, and otherwise put the handler at risk for injury to the hands. Stupid of me to forget a basic rule."

Kirsten fetched the box Nita kept for household doctoring, along with some bandages made from old sheets.

"How often can you use yourself as a bad example, Mr. Banks? Surely the novelty alone has some appeal?"

"But gloves are a basic part of a horseman's attire, like boots to keep his toes safe and prevent chafing of the calves or tearing by brambles. Like a riding stock tied about the neck, to use as a bandage if a mishap occurs far from home. Like a hat he can use to water the beast if—"

Kirsten set the box on the desk. "Well then, let us agree that like Matthias's mare, you are without any redeeming features, a disgrace to your species, a thoroughgoing miscreant who should never be allowed to set foot in the stable."

Daniel fell silent, likely to continue his self-castigations where Kirsten could not hear them.

She took the chair beside his, spread several thicknesses of linen in her lap, and appropriated his injured hand, which was a right bloody mess.

"Keep your hand low," Kirsten said, "and let it bleed freely. Nita found that if a wound had bled for a time, infection was less likely."

Daniel submitted to this direction, though Kirsten could feel all manner of fresh remonstrations boiling through him. They'd entered the library from the terrace and thus the almighty, infernal Door of Propriety was closed.

While the blasted Sofa of Indecent Memories lay directly in Kirsten's line of sight.

"How badly does it hurt?" she asked.

"I've suffered worse. The pointlessness of the injury is more painful than the wound itself."

Daniel's words were a metaphor for some other aspect of his life. Had he intended to refer to his marriage? His hand bled sluggishly now, and yet Kirsten did not want to move on to the part where she bound it up and sent him on his way.

"This will sting," she said, uncorking a brown bottle Nita swore was another weapon against the horrors of infection.

A man could lose his hand to a wound like this if he were careless. Lose his life if he were careless and stubborn both. Kirsten dabbed blood away and applied Nita's distillation directly to the injury. Daniel drew in his breath swiftly.

"Do you never curse, Mr. Banks?"

"I try not to curse out loud, though I came very close in front of the boys."

Drat you to perdition. More than his words, the force behind them had riveted the attention of six ponies and six boys. George had doubtless been impressed with Daniel's restraint.

While for Kirsten, only his pain had registered.

"Nita says a double application is best," Kirsten said. "Though it won't sting so the second time."

"For my stupidity, for the poor example I set, I deserve to suffer."

Oh, for pity's sake. Kirsten dosed him again, allowing the concoction to pool in the bowl of his palm and thoroughly soak the wound. She tilted his hand, washing the wound with the tincture.

"The housekeeper should be doing this," Daniel said. "You're a lady, the daughter of an earl. Stable injuries are beneath—"

"Shut your mouth, Daniel." Kirsten turned his hand over, spilling the last of the disinfectant onto the cloth spread over her lap. "My mother held to the custom of the lady of the manor tending to her own people, and Nita continued it. The housekeeper would be less knowledgeable than I, for I learned from my sister while the housekeeper did not."

He'd find something else to rail against, because right now, Daniel Banks was not in charity with the world, himself, or his fellow creatures. From long experience, Kirsten knew how that felt.

She wrapped his hand in clean linen, snug but not too tight, as Nita had shown her. When she'd knotted off the bandage, she remained sitting beside him, his bound hand cradled in her own.

"What's wrong, Daniel? You're in a mood, and it's about more than a cranky mare's bad behavior."

She'd taken to calling him Daniel when they were private, and he hadn't objected. A small consolation against all the liberties they could never take with each other.

"We should not be alone here," he said, a little desperately.

"For God's sake, if you neglect a wound, particularly one suffered in the environs of a stable, you could lose your hand or your life. What is wrong with you, Daniel, that you'd lose a limb for the sake of propriety?"

His countenance shifted, from angry to rueful.

"You are so sensible, my lady, but the problem is not that I could lose my hand. The problem is that I have already lost my heart."

Even as Kirsten clutched that admission close, a treasure to be examined later in privacy, she understood that a line had been crossed. Daniel wasn't confessing his undying admiration; he was admitting to a Problem.

"I nearly wish you hadn't said that," Kirsten murmured, curling forward over his hand to rest her forehead on Daniel's bony, male knee. His riding breeches were worn to velvet softness, and the chamois bore the scent of horse.

She hoarded up those impressions too, because they were personal to him.

Daniel's uninjured hand landed on her hair, a caress any mother might bestow on a much-loved child.

"George counseled me to discretion in my sins," he murmured. "Your brother said he knew a pair of besotted wretches when he saw them."

I will kill my brother. "George is a tolerant sort and he means well. He as much as counseled me to discreet sinning too."

Another gentle, slow sweep of Daniel's hand to Kirsten's hair. He would be tenderness itself in bed.

"My lady, we tempt fate with continued proximity, and yet I know you dread the prospect of another London Season."

How gently he touched her as he closed more doors between them.

"Don't ask that of me," Kirsten said, though if Daniel needed her to leave, she'd go. Not to London, but she could inflict herself on one of her brothers. Ethan had two little boys and a tolerance for sour-natured sisters.

"I've told myself that friendship with you is not a consolation," Daniel said, "but rather a miracle, and we are friends. Nonetheless, you are lovely and dear, and I would not bring further unhappiness to you for anything."

Kirsten straightened, lest she start bawling against his knee. "Any more of your well-intended rejection, sir, and I'll be climbing into your lap for consolation."

She would not be sent back to her stall, like Matthias's naughty mare, because she hadn't done anything wrong *and neither had Daniel.* Then too, Daniel needed allies. In some manner, Kirsten needed him too, and his boys, and to never, ever be dragged into the purgatory that was London again.

"Is your wife faithful to her vows?" she asked.

"I have no idea, but a divorce based on scandal— based on anything—will cost me my living, bring gossip down on Danny, and leave me without a profession."

For a man to reject the notion of divorce, he must first at least consider it, which in some dark moment, Daniel apparently had.

"Annulment?"

"Less of a scandal, but I'd still lose my vocation."

"Have you grounds?"

Daniel studied their joined hands, his bound in white linen, Kirsten's fingers curled loosely around his in deference to his injury.

"Annulments are for the bishops to sort out. If I leave the church, employment of any sort will be hard to come by, and I cannot cast Danny back onto the viscount's charity. The boy's been uprooted enough."

Daniel had thought matters through, and so had Kirsten. She withdrew her hand, and Daniel retrieved his from her lap.

Kirsten had lost her heart as well, but her common sense remained intact. She wanted their friendship to remain intact too, for she'd never ask Daniel to choose between her and the child.

"Rather than have George and Elsie bide here," she said, "I'll visit them when my sisters go up to Town. I'll be at Belle Maison frequently to ensure the household runs smoothly. I'll not give up my Thursday tea with the boys, and I'll continue to prepare menus for the dower house."

Daniel rose. "My thanks, Lady Kirsten. I trust we'll also still travel together to services or see you at the occasional cricket match?"

His kindness moved her nearly to violence. "Of course."

Or they'd have passing moments in libraries with all doors open or at church functions while the entire shire looked on. What cheering encounters those would be.

Kirsten folded up the dirty linen and put the box back on its shelf.

"You'll find a similar box in the dower house library," she said, "and we'll make sure you have one at the vicarage too. The contents of the small brown bottle with an *R* burned into the cork should be applied daily when you change the dressing. Ralph can assist, but make him wash his hands with lye soap first."

"Has work started on the vicarage, then?" Daniel had the grace to sound merely curious rather than hopeful.

"Nicholas will see it begun before he leaves for London." Which news was another courtesy of Lady Della Haddonfield's domestic espionage service. "If you say that's for the best, I will curse, Daniel."

Or cry. Maybe both.

He rose, a fine figure of a man in his worn riding attire and gleaming virtue. Kirsten wanted him out of his riding attire, but she would not take his virtue from him.

"I ask one boon of you, Daniel."

"Anything."

"Establish whether you have grounds for an annulment. If you must negotiate the terms of an informal separation from your wife, that information could prove relevant. You give her an advantage to the extent you neglect to investigate the legal posture of your situation."

"I'm nearly certain of the answer, but I've sent a letter to my bishop already, my lady."

Not agreement, not quite. Kirsten had seen two marriage settlements negotiated and then renegotiated, and her papa had made sure she understood exactly what the parties had agreed to and why.

Bless Papa. "Daniel, would you be tempted to *pursue* an annulment if you had grounds?" And was that the greater problem?

He moved away from the desk, back toward the French doors. "I won't pursue an annulment, not if doing so would in any way further impact Danny. I can't, even if I had multiple grounds, the requisite fortune, access to ecclesiastical experts, and honorable work outside the church."

A list. A daunting list. At the bottom of that list was the one item that turned *I ought not* into *I cannot*: Daniel must not lose his standing with the church.

Despair, an old, familiar enemy, clutched at Kirsten from within.

"When I'm assured the household is running smoothly here, perhaps I'll pay a visit to Ethan and Alexandra over in Surrey. Beckman claims Three Springs is at its best in the summer, and I've a new nephew to spoil there too, but Ethan's boys are endlessly charming."

Daniel propped a shoulder against the jamb of the French door, the pose more defeated than casual.

"You are of age, my lady, as I've had occasion to remind the earl. You must do as you see fit."

More lethal kindness. Daniel would not ask her to stay.

"Surrey, then." Because Ethan would not question Kirsten's decision to go into exile.

She was at the door, her handkerchief already in her hand, when Daniel imposed one last, awful kindness.

"Safe journey, my lady. *I will miss you* and keep you always, always in my prayers."

Twelve

DANIEL KNEW THAT PAIN CAME IN VARIOUS AGES AND intensities, like spirits. The pain of Olivia's betrayal was old and enormous, like an aged yew, but like that tree, the branches had grown spindly, the leaves few, no matter how complex and far-reaching the roots.

Given enough time and determination, Daniel could chop that pain down to cordwood of regret and indifference.

He should have known better.

He should have seen more clearly.

He should have listened to his father.

He should have developed skills that allowed him employment outside the church, for a man of means had options a man of the collar did not.

Lady Kirsten's footsteps faded, though the memory of her white handkerchief clutched in a fist of sorrow was Daniel's to keep for all time.

A flag of surrender, like the white linen binding Daniel's right hand. He'd failed to protect a good, dear woman from heartache, just as he'd failed to protect his sister from Olivia's scheming.

George Haddonfield came striding across the garden, his boots dusty, his riding jacket slung over his shoulder. He could not, of course, stop on the terrace to enjoy a spring day, but must instead come straight into the library, probably to dispense more advice on how to sin discreetly.

"How fares the wounded?" George was a veteran of the London ballrooms and, like the earl, a good brother. Daniel nearly hated him for that.

"The *hand* will heal. I trust the ponies are back in their stalls, munching hay?"

"What ponies do best," George said, brushing past Daniel and continuing across the library. "Care for a drink?"

"Please."

"Kirsten put you to rights?"

"Her ladyship is considering a visit to your brother Ethan's estate in Surrey."

George passed Daniel two fingers of fragrant brandy. Daniel downed them at one go and handed the glass back. The resulting fire burned a path to his vitals, the pain righteous and soothing.

George's own glass held barely a splash, though he refilled Daniel's glass generously.

"Shall I get you drunk, Banks?"

"Inebriation is tempting, of course," Daniel said, taking the time to pass this serving under his nose. The bouquet held a hint of apples and roses underscored with wood smoke.

Dratted wood smoke. The first scent Daniel had associated with Lady Kirsten.

"You'll resist the temptation," George said, "tedious

saint that you are, because in the morning, you'll still wear that collar, Mrs. Banks will be kicking up her heels to the north, and Kirsten will pack for the first of many protracted journeys."

All true. "You forgot that my head would feel as if I'd taken a splitting ax to it."

George stoppered the decanter. "So you're not a saint. You've occasionally overindulged."

"I went to university, Mr. Haddonfield," Daniel said, determined to get himself beyond purgatory's formal parlor into the establishment's very bowels. "For myself, unrequited affection is simply another cross to bear. Nobody in this life has everything he longs for. We pine, we rage, we move on. I cannot abide, however, that a woman who has done nothing to deserve more disappointment must now endure heartache on my account."

George leaned back against the sideboard, arms folded like a patient schoolmaster.

"Banks, you impress me. Most men I know can't be that honest unless they're drunk, the hour is late, and all around them are also in their cups. Shall we take our drinks to the terrace? I'll hear about it endlessly if I track mud onto the carpets."

Daniel would hear endlessly from his own conscience if he allowed George to get him drunk. George followed him onto the terrace, though even the bucolic splendor of a spring afternoon in Kent didn't seem spacious enough for Daniel's conflicted emotions.

George half sat, half leaned against the stone balustrade, looking handsome and elegant even in wrinkled riding attire. He had the knack of holding a drink elegantly, and the breeze teased his hair elegantly.

"Have you never been in love, Banks?"

"With my calling." Or so Daniel had wanted desperately to believe.

The brandy comforted, not because it dulled Daniel's sense of frustration or rage, but because turning to drink was something a normal, mortal man did. George's commiserating company was also probably one of the comforts an everyday human would permit himself.

"You're to be pitied, then," George said, swirling his drink. "A calling can't love you back. It can't plop itself down in your lap when you're trying to develop a budget for your sheep-breeding venture and make you forget what a sheep is. A calling can't rely on you for help naming a pony. It can't ask you to look in on the prodigal vicar because somebody needs to take the poor sod in hand."

"Love one another," Daniel murmured. Supposedly the answer to every conundrum posed by the bishops and dons on the way to ordination.

Except…Daniel loved Kirsten Haddonfield and suspected she loved him, which was no sort of answer to anything.

Olivia stood between Daniel and Kirsten in a legal sense, but the Church stood between them in a more practical way, for who would employ a vicar pickled in scandal?

"Alfrydd's in a lather about something," George said, setting his drink down as the head lad came pelting across the garden.

Daniel did not care about Alfrydd. One greedy

pony had kicked another greedy pony, the boys had put toads in the feed room. Nothing of any moment.

Daniel tried to focus instead on the glimmer of insight creeping into his brain amid the brandied mists of regret. Something about loving one another and Olivia not being the true problem.

"Master George, Mr. Banks," Alfrydd panted. "A rider has come down from Town, and he brought this missive for the vicar." The stable master passed over a folded, sealed letter, the wax a dark blot against the vellum.

"I don't recognize the seal," Daniel said, though black wax was reserved for news of a death or serious illness.

"Thank you, Alfrydd. We'll let you know if we need a rider," George murmured, taking Daniel by the arm and steering him back into the library.

"Open it," George said, gently prying Daniel's drink from his fingers. "Unless you want me to read it?"

Daniel wanted Kirsten. That much clarity, he could muster. "Please, I haven't my spectacles." Nor his entire complement of wits, nor much of a sense of his calling.

That loss, however temporary, was perilously bearable.

George broke the seal on the missive. A silent moment went by while Daniel searched about for a vague stirring of interest. He was a vicar, after all. Somebody had died back in Little Weldon, or perhaps the bishop had fallen mortally ill.

He'd miss Bishop Reimer, a dear old soul full of merriment, tolerance, and the occasional colorful curse.

"Banks, I am so sorry," George said, passing him the letter. "My condolences on the loss of your wife."

The silence that ensued was at once empty of sound and full of conflicting emotions.

Daniel read the words, then read them again. Mrs. Olivia Banks, late of Little Weldon, had died in the home of her second cousin, Bertrand Carmichael, while journeying south from the West Riding. She had not suffered long and asked to be remembered to her husband.

Sunlight glinted on the glass Daniel had been intent on draining moments earlier. George Haddonfield, looking concerned, stood in the same place he had when he'd passed Daniel this epistle, and yet nothing was the same.

"Condolences, et cetera," Daniel muttered. Not a word for the boy. Not a request for forgiveness or for a blessing, not a parting sentiment of any kind for the child Olivia had known since his birth and raised as her own.

Daniel might have found a firm hold on hatred for his departed spouse for her omission, but ignoring the child was simply consistent with her endless self-interest.

"Banks, shall you sit down?"

Daniel stared at the letter as he rummaged among his emotions, trying to find grief, loss, sorrow, any appropriate emotion at all.

No matter which sober, vicarly feeling he reached for, the only sentiment within his grasp was relief.

❦

"I left our vicar in the library," George said. "If Nicholas were about, I'd fetch him, but he's off looking at a horse for Leah. I don't want to leave Banks alone, and yet one doesn't know what to say when a spouse has died under such circumstances."

Kirsten had planned on removing to Ethan's indefinitely. Had George not been so flustered, he might have remarked the disarray in her usually tidy room. She tossed a pale blue riding habit into a trunk already half-full.

Then realized she ought to have hung the damned thing back up.

"Mr. Banks will need to talk with his son," Kirsten said. Daniel would need to hug the boy and explain this upset to the child in a manner that made sense. "Don't say anything to the other children yet, but let Ralph, Susannah, and Della know."

Daniel's wardrobe would need black armbands.

"That's a fetching ensemble," George said, fingering the hem of the discarded habit. "The blue matches your eyes exactly, and yet I don't believe I've seen you wearing this one."

"Nor will you. Susannah had one much like it made up, and I didn't want to appear to ape my sister's good taste. Fetch Danny but give me a few minutes with his papa first."

Who was sitting *alone* in the library.

"You didn't want to outshine Suze," George said, hanging the habit up on the open door of Kirsten's wardrobe. "You are a complete fraud, Kirsten Haddonfield. Go fuss and cluck over the vicar, and for God's sake, let yourself gloat a little. Divine Providence has for once turned up helpful."

Kirsten was not gloating. She was worrying for a man abruptly bereaved of an indifferent spouse and a sustaining penance.

"George, don't be awful. A woman has died, and

however wrong some of her actions might have been, you mustn't be uncharitable."

Besides, gloating wasn't the right word. Kirsten was relieved for Daniel that the ordeal of his marriage was over, but beyond that, she was simply sad and concerned.

"You mustn't be a hypocrite," George said, twitching the folds of the habit straight. "Dishonesty is not in your nature, and you deserve a fellow who values you for the treasure you are. Be off with you. I'll fetch Danny by way of a cup of milk and a few chocolate biscuits in the kitchen."

One of George's favorite combinations.

"Thank you," Kirsten said, hugging her brother. "Your kind heart is as lovely as the rest of you."

"Elsie says much the same thing, though she also admires my—"

"Bother you." Kirsten shoved him toward the door. "And thank you, George."

Kirsten ought to call her maid to hang up her dresses; she ought to figure out what to say to Daniel; she ought to take the space of three breaths to find some composure and arrange her features to reflect sympathy, because Olivia Banks, who'd clearly been a troubled soul, was dead.

Daniel was a widower, something he could never, in his worst imagining or fondest dreams, have longed to be.

Because he was that good.

Kirsten, by contrast, was all in a muddle, but she'd spoken honestly to George. A death was regrettable. A light gone out, a life ended.

Nonetheless, she nearly flew down the steps to the

library, failed to knock, and when she found Daniel sitting in Nicholas's favorite reading chair, she stopped halfway across the carpet.

His expression was calm, his demeanor relaxed. He might have been waiting for the coach to be brought around for the trek to Sunday services, and that—that aloneness, that self-contained, stoic isolation—ripped at her.

"I'm sorry. Daniel, I'm so sorry."

He rose—a lady had entered the room, and manners required him to rise. "Thank you. This is unexpected. Danny will have to be told, and her—her family."

Daniel was the woman's closest family, and to blazes with Danny. "George will bring the boy to you here."

Daniel folded up a single page of vellum, and while his hands appeared steady, the paper betrayed a slight tremor.

"Carmichael wasn't sure where to reach me. Olivia has been interred in his family's plot in Oxfordshire. I left my direction with Bishop Reimer, but nobody in Little Weldon thought to forward—"

Kirsten pelted into him and lashed her arms around him. "*Stop this*. Stop being noble and rational. Stop thinking. Thinking won't serve, Daniel. Think later. It's awful of Olivia to die now, with matters unresolved and nothing forgiven. I nearly hate her for deserting the battle like this, and don't you tell me I'm unchristian. She was a disgrace and deserving of pity, but you also have every right to be angry at her."

Daniel's arms stole around Kirsten gingerly, as if she were some prickly bush alight with thorns.

"You're upset," he said.

Grief made people stupid. Kirsten had grieved for the future she'd never have, the children she'd never love, the husband who'd never sleep by her side.

"Yes, Daniel, I'm upset."

"I'm upset too, but of all the possibilities and eventualities and futures I'd prepared myself for, this wasn't one of them. All I can think about is Danny, whose every waking hour for months was filled with dread that Olivia might come for him."

Kirsten wanted to shake the man in her arms, but focusing on Danny was the act of a person drowning in bewilderment.

"Danny knows he's safe here." As was Daniel. "I gather Olivia was ill?"

Daniel's hand stroked over Kirsten's shoulder. Beneath her ear, his heartbeat was reassuringly steady and strong, though why Kirsten needed reassurance, she could not fathom.

"A virulent influenza. Carmichael summoned physicians, but some illnesses admit of no treatment. At least Olivia did not suffer long."

Olivia would probably suffer for all eternity, the poor wretch.

"You should let Danny know that," Kirsten said, stepping back. Daniel was still too skinny. All muscle and bone, no reserves such as even a fit man carried. "And you will need to write letters. Ralph and I will manage the boys tomorrow, and you will take your horse for a long gallop. I'll send George with you, if you like."

Kirsten had been having a tantrum earlier, flinging

dresses into a trunk, cursing, crying, and railing against the Almighty. She probably resembled the hag of the bog now.

Daniel stroked the backs of his fingers over her cheek, which had grown damp somehow.

"You will not worry, my lady. All will be well. I'll take Beelzebub out and visit my sister tomorrow."

"You should take Danny to visit his pony after supper."

Daniel passed her his handkerchief, a worn, plain square of white that was soft against her skin when she blotted her eyes.

"A visit to the stable is an excellent notion." Daniel's gaze lacked the distant, distracted quality of moments ago, and nothing about him seemed unsettled. "Please don't fret, my lady. I did not love my wife as a husband ought, but neither did I hate her. Her passing is a mercy to me and to Danny, but most especially, perhaps, to her. She was bitterly unhappy and had been for most of her life."

Kirsten tugged the knot of Daniel's cravat back to center as relief coursed through her.

"You've worked it out, then. What to feel, that is." And Daniel was *not* feeling guilty.

"For now, I've worked out what I *do* feel. I'm sorry Olivia fell ill, for her sake. I'm sorry matters between us reached the pass they did, but I hadn't seen my wife nor corresponded with her about anything of any substance for nearly a year. I am glad to be alive and glad *you* are alive."

Being glad to be alive was not gloating. Kirsten was casting around for a way to applaud Daniel's sentiments when George ushered Danny into the library.

"Not a chocolate biscuit left in Christendom," George announced. "Danny has a prodigious appetite."

"He gets that from me," Daniel said. "Danny, you and I have a few things to discuss. Will you visit Beelzebub with me?"

"Of course, Papa. Mr. Haddonfield gave me some sugar for Loki, but I'll share with Beelzebub."

"Good lad." Daniel extended a hand to the boy, and when Danny clasped hands, he was lifted up and affixed to his papa's back. "Mr. Haddonfield, Lady Kirsten, my thanks."

Man and boy were out the French doors and off across the garden in the next moment.

"They'll manage," George said, passing Kirsten a drink. Brandy from the scent of it—her favorite tipple. "I seem to be in the business of dispensing the medicinal tot of late."

"Join me?" Kirsten asked, settling into Nicholas's reading chair.

"Don't mind if I do." George downed his at one swallow. "Banks enjoys the greatest moral clarity of any man I know, but this has to be difficult for him."

"He's not gloating, George, and he's not wallowing in remorse. I'd say that's the sanest course he could plot." More than sane, Daniel had made a pass at saintly, recognizing that Olivia had been a suffering creature.

Kirsten downed another swallow of brandy. *She* had been miserable, and over what? A lack of ability to produce heirs for some titled, prancing ninny?

Odd, how hindsight could turn apparent disasters into a pair of near misses.

George appropriated Kirsten's drink and took

another sip. "The sanest course would be for Banks to propose to you before the month is out. Widowers often remarry immediately upon being bereaved, particularly widowers with small children."

While widows were expected to wait a year, lest their late husband's children be born bearing another man's name.

"I don't want Dan—Mr. Banks to marry me simply because he's grieving." For a wife he'd no longer loved? "I don't want to become somebody's wife merely because I'm an earl's daughter, or convenient, or well-dowered."

Kirsten wanted to marry a man who loved her, and whom she loved, a man with whom she could build something meaningful.

George threw himself onto the blue sofa. "You do want to marry Banks."

Not a question. "Yes. I want to marry Mr. Banks. I think we could be happy together." Having a small child to love as well only sweetened the bargain.

"Be a hell of a blow to a pair of buffoons up in Town," George murmured. "You, an earl's daughter, turning down an earl's heir and a viscount to take up life in a vicarage. My, my."

Sedgewick and Morton would know the truth of Kirsten's "rejections," but they would not utter a word of that truth for it reflected badly on them both.

"I don't care about Sedgewick and Morton, George. I would have strangled either one of them within a sennight had I married them. Life in a vicarage has meaning." That life would have love too, if Danny and Daniel dwelled in the vicarage.

And maybe a half-dozen rotten boys could live in. Then too, vicars were also frequently called upon to rear foundlings.

Kirsten nearly saluted that notion with her half-full glass.

"You look more peaceful than I've seen you in ages," George said. "I will take my leave on that encouraging development. I've left word Nicholas and Leah are to report to you upon their return from horse shopping. If Banks needs somebody to stand up with him, I'm available."

"Shoo, Cupid," Kirsten said. "Give Elsie my love, and mind you come around again next Tuesday, if not before."

George kissed Kirsten's cheek and left her with her brandy.

Also—after a short prayer for the soul of the departed—with dreams of a vicarage full of love and happy children.

❧

Condolences from Little Weldon came by post for the next several weeks, more than Daniel could have anticipated had he read every name from the parish rolls.

Spring came as well, the entire earth relaxing into the business of growing new life, new crops, and new hopes. Daniel's hopes grew too, an unfurling of his spirit that filled him with urgency and wonder every time his path crossed Lady Kirsten's.

His position as vicar became more real to him when he baptized three dear, squalling little souls, each of whom had likely been conceived in the course of pagan rituals celebrated the previous summer.

Daniel presided over the final obsequies for Mr. Clackengeld's aunt, who'd been so old that nobody was quite sure of her exact age, though she'd left her gouty nephew surprisingly well set up.

Daniel's scholars settled into a routine, all of them making academic progress, except for Matthias, who remained quiet, surly, and at outs with his mare.

"Come along, Matthias," Daniel said one fine Friday afternoon following another round of exams on which the boy had done poorly. "You're riding well enough to hack out, and Beelzebub needs to stretch his legs."

"Yes, sir. I'll fetch my boots." Matthias was never openly disrespectful, but neither was he happy.

The other boys took note of Daniel's overture, however. On weekends, Daniel and Danny rode out together, but the other boys never went anywhere without George Haddonfield or one of the older grooms. Daniel had planned for this ride, though, and no grooms would be along.

"Where's Freya?" Matthias asked when they arrived to the stable yard.

"Freya won't be joining us. I'll be up on Beelzebub, and you'll be on Buttercup. The earl hasn't had time to ride her much lately, and I told him my boys would be happy to help."

Matthias smudged his thumb over the lens before his right eye. "Buttercup is the earl's mare."

Also the largest riding horse in the shire. Bellefonte thwarted custom and rode a mare, because she was also one of the sweetest, smoothest-gaited exponents of her species.

"And thus somebody has to keep her in work," Daniel said, "for she must be strong to carry that much earl. Up you go."

Finding the right combination of gear to fit the enormous horse and the small boy had taken the grooms half the morning, but when Daniel and his companion rode out of the stable yard, Matthias's feet were in perfectly adjusted stirrups and his bottom in a saddle sized for a lad.

"Give me those glasses," Daniel said. "If they should slip from your nose, Buttercup might accidentally step on them."

"I'm always supposed to wear my glasses, sir."

As close to defiance as Matthias came anymore. The other boys didn't make fun of him, but neither did they respect him as they once might have.

"Have you another pair, Matthias?"

"No, sir. They are Papa's spare pair. I mustn't ever, ever break them."

Well then. "Can you see the lane, Matthias?"

"Yes, sir."

"Then we'll leave the rest of the navigating to Buttercup, and I'll have those spectacles."

The boy passed the glasses *over* to Daniel. Had he been on his pony, he'd have stretched in his stirrups to pass the glasses *up* to his vicar.

"Buttercup is much bigger than Freya," Matthias said. "I sit taller than you when I'm on her back."

"That you do. Will you be sorry when the summer break comes, Matthias?"

An unhappy silence formed as the horses clip-clopped down parallel ruts on one of Belle Maison's farm lanes. They'd soon come out amid the blooming orchard, where any normal boy would reach up, grab a branch, and shower himself and his horse with apple blossoms.

"I'm stupid, sir. Papa says so every week. He'll probably make me come for lessons even during the summer."

"Does he punish you for your marks, Matthias?"

The boy leaned forward at the last moment to duck under a low-hanging branch.

"He threatens to cane me, but mostly I go without my pudding and must copy sums. He says my hand is atrocious."

Barely legible, in fact, though Matthias was bright in a scientific sense, well-spoken, and had an ear for languages and a fine singing voice. His problems came when pencil and paper were involved, or sitting for long periods.

"Matthias, how would you grade me as a teacher?"

The boy snatched a glance at Daniel, as a poorly trained mount might snatch a mouthful of leaves when under saddle.

"You don't use the birch rod. Papa says you should. He says you should beat some brains into me."

"When Freya is trying hard to figure out what you want, but she guesses wrong, would it help to beat her?"

"She'd buck me off. I wish I could buck my Papa off."

"Do you think about running away?" Daniel had thought about it when Olivia had been alive. Though only weeks had passed since Olivia's death, the entire marriage had the feel of a sad tale told long ago in a land far away. Every time Daniel brought the boys to

Lady Kirsten for their weekly tea, that cold, dark land slipped farther over the horizon.

"I'm almost old enough for the Navy, sir."

Not only had Matthias thought about running away, he had a plan as well. Mr. Webber would probably consign Matthias to the midshipman's ranks, without any clue what the boy would endure or how much material he'd have to learn if he was ever to graduate from those ranks.

Daniel and his charge had ridden out of sight of the Belle Maison house and stable, the fragrant, greening countryside all around them. A precocious hedge of honeysuckle wore a few blooms to the right, and to the left broodmares and new foals grazed or napped on new grass.

Such a beautiful day, and such a miserable little boy.

"Do you ever consider, Matthias, that I may be failing you?"

Another glance, more considering. "By not beating me?"

"By not *educating* you. In some ways, you're the brightest of my boys. You think things through, you listen carefully. For sheer logic and problem-solving ability, you're a force to be reckoned with. You go down to defeat when you must sit still and wield a pencil."

The boy batted aside another low-hanging branch at the last moment. "Sometimes, the other boys seem stupid to me, but then they get higher marks. Even Thomas."

How that must gall, for Thomas to be bigger, stronger, *and* the one getting higher marks.

"You get good marks for recitation." Not spectacular marks—Danny had the advantage over all of them because he'd been at Daniel's side for years—but Matthias had good recall of what he'd heard.

"My exams are bad. Do you think the earl would let me trot his mare?"

"Let's try it, but only to the orchard." A hundred yards of smooth bridle path, but twelve hundred opportunities to fall, much like life. "You recall to kick your feet free of the stirrups if you're going overboard?"

"Yes, sir."

"Then ladies first, Master Webber."

Finally, a ghost of a hint of a beginning of a smile. Matthias didn't drive his heels into the mare's sides, as many boys would have. He gave a scoot with his seat and a nudge with his calves, and Buttercup lifted into a smooth, relaxed trot.

Daniel held Beelzebub back, though his gelding had an instinct for little boys and let the mare toddle ahead half a length. By the time they reached the orchard, Matthias was beaming.

"Good girl, Buttercup," he said, whacking the mare on the shoulder, as Mr. Haddonfield insisted a rider must do when a horse had performed well. "Good job, old girl! May we trot back to the stable too, sir?"

"You must always walk the last mile," Daniel said, another of Mr. Haddonfield's equestrian commandments. "We can trot a little more, once the horses have recovered their wind."

Beelzebub would make his owner pay for that bouncer, but Daniel had spotted a rider cantering through the orchard with her groom. The moment called for more than a tip of the hat—had Daniel been wearing a hat.

"Lady Kirsten's coming," Matthias said, sitting quite tall indeed. "You'll tell her I have permission to be on Buttercup?"

"Matthias, on your most rotten day, don't flatter yourself that you're a horse thief. Come along. Left boot passes to left boot."

Except Lady Kirsten drew rein amid the white blossoms, her smile adding another lovely note to a beautiful afternoon.

"Gentlemen, good day. Matthias, poor Freya will be heartbroken to have lost your custom, but you do look very fine on his lordship's mare."

"I'm exercising Buttercup for the earl," Matthias said. "We trotted."

"I'm sure Bellefonte will be most grateful," Lady Kirsten replied. "Mr. Banks, Beelzebub, good day. Did you trot as well?"

"We could barely keep up," Daniel said, because now, *now* he could flirt with Lady Kirsten. The past weeks had been a revelation, one joy followed by another. He could flirt with her, dream of her, sit too close to her as they planned menus, and wallow in the inane sense of well-being that came with growing attraction.

Normal joys for a normal—unmarried—man.

"Vicar says I can trot back to the stable too," Matthias said. "Most of the way, at least."

"A slow trot," Daniel cautioned. "You never want to rush with a new mount, Matthias, and you'll have to ride Freya home before supper."

The boy's expression clouded at the mention of home.

"You can tell your family you rode Buttercup,"

Lady Kirsten said. "I have never been allowed to ride her, and I don't think my brother George has either."

"Truly? Mr. Haddonfield has never ridden this mare?"

Lady Kirsten leaned closer to the boy. "I have a suggestion. You take my groom and head back to the stable by way of the home farm. There's plenty of room to trot in that direction."

Matthias whipped around in the saddle. "Sir, may I? May I please?"

Buttercup was nearly going to sleep, while for the first time since beginning his studies, the boy on her back was wreathed in hope.

"You may," Daniel said, "but mind you let the horse rest from time to time and tell her when she's being good." Because rewarding good behavior was ever so much more effective than punishing the occasional lapse.

"Alfrydd," Lady Kirsten said. "No wild riding, please, though Master Webber has been cooped up in a schoolroom all week. The earl sets great store by that mare. No galloping, no cantering, no hopping stiles or splashing through racing rivers. I forbid it, no matter how badly you're tempted."

Alfrydd had the grace to look downcast. "We're not to hop even a wee log, milady?"

"Only a small one if the footing is safe."

Alfrydd winked as his cob ambled past her ladyship's mare. "One wee log, then. No stiles, no mad gallops. We'll stick to the paths, milady. I give you my word."

Thus assured of only manageable challenges, Matthias trotted off happily with a smiling Alfrydd.

"The greatest steeplechase the shire has ever known is about to take place," Daniel said, "and we will miss it."

Though simply beholding Lady Kirsten had Daniel's heart leaping stiles and ditches at a great rate.

"You're worried about Matthias," Lady Kirsten observed. "Shall we walk for a bit, Daniel? It's a pretty day, and I haven't had the pleasure of your company much lately."

She'd been busy, seeing to the household as her family prepared for, then undertook, their transition to London. Then she'd removed to George Haddonfield's residence, and her presence at the dower house had become unpredictable and always focused on a task—dropping off menus, taking tea with the boys, changing the curtains in the schoolroom as the weather moderated.

"I would enjoy a walk," Daniel said, "and I'm sure Beelzebub would love a chance to crop some grass."

Daniel assisted Kirsten from her horse, tied up reins, ran up stirrups, and loosened girths, then gestured in the direction of the stone wall encircling the orchard.

"How are you, my lady?"

Daniel thought Kirsten was pausing to deal with the complicated skirts of her riding habit and was thus unprepared when she instead planted her hands on his shoulders and kissed him.

Kissed him tenderly at first, a slow greeting of mouth upon mouth, a renewal of addresses that was both a homecoming and a delightful shock.

Daniel drew her into his arms, no hesitation or second thoughts, not an instant of confusion in either his body or his heart. Holding Kirsten was a mundane liberty between single adults—also a miracle.

"I've been wanting to do that for the longest time," she said, subsiding against him.

Daniel was tall, "a hulking brute" in the parlance of his late wife, but Kirsten Haddonfield fit him well. He could admit that now, among many other things. Daniel rested his cheek against Kirsten's hair and silently gave thanks for a perfect moment long overdue.

"What I've been wanting to do requires several hours of privacy, my lady." He'd made her laugh, though his own words surprised him. "That was ungentlemanly. I apologize."

She smacked his chest. "That was honest. We can be honest now, Daniel, can't we?"

The answer beamed through him like sunlight in springtime, like water laughing down the brook to the sea, and honeysuckle offering its fragrance to the bees.

"Yes, we can be honest now." Amid the white blossoms bobbing on the gentle breeze, Daniel honestly kissed Kirsten as if his happiness depended upon her answering passion.

Bless her, she kissed him back with no less fervor, until Daniel had to stop lest he find a handy tree to hoist her against.

"You want me," she said, grazing a hand over his falls. "I would expire of frustration if you didn't."

"I will expire of frustration because I do. I've missed you." How lovely, to offer that simple, sincere sentiment. No guilt, no vicarly restraint owed a wife who'd long since betrayed her vows.

Why hadn't Daniel been able to fully admit that betrayal while Olivia had lived?

"I've been giving you time to sort yourself out. Daniel, it's been little more than a month."

He kissed Kirsten's ear, despite the uproar in his breeches. A happy uproar, an assurance that years of celibacy could be overcome in a moment with the right woman.

"The past few weeks have been an eternity," Daniel said. "The boys miss you too." Poor little devils. Thursday's tea and biscuits couldn't come around soon enough for them—for them either. "Kiss me some more."

Daniel had years of kissing to make up for, years of cuddling and petting, stroking and sighing. The apples would be ripe and falling from the tree before he'd addressed the least of the deficits caused by his marriage.

"Daniel, if I weren't wearing breeches under my habit, you would find yourself thoroughly debauched right here and now."

Somehow, they had found their way to a stout tree. Daniel reached above his head and shook the nearest branch, showering blossoms around them.

"I have a better idea," Daniel said as a soft, white petal came to rest on her ladyship's crown. "Let's get married, and then it won't be debauchery."

He'd proposed once on bended knee, an awkward, dutiful recitation he winced to recall. With Lady Kirsten beaming up at him, Daniel forgave his twenty-year-old self for that blunder. Duty had been the substance of his entire upbringing, a virtue exalted over compassion, honesty, and joy.

Duty was no sort of bedfellow at all. He knew that now.

The woman he loved brushed blossoms from his hair. "Lest we waste time arguing, I suggest a compromise, Daniel: Let's be married, assuredly, but let's anticipate our vows. Let's anticipate them early and often, starting right now."

Thirteen

"STOP THAT." OLIVIA ACCOMPANIED HER COMMAND with a stout shove to Bertrand's shoulder.

He left off nuzzling her ear, rolled to his back, and stared at the ceiling. The nearest corner of the room sported a few cobwebs swaying on gossamer currents from the cracked window.

"For a dead woman, you've become mighty contrary, Livvie dearest."

She snatched a handkerchief from the bedside table and scrubbed at her belly. "Don't call me that." She pitched the handkerchief onto Bertrand's chest. "Tend to yourself. At least Daniel was tidy and limited his base behaviors to after dark."

Bertrand was supposed to get out of the bed now, grateful to have been allowed to come on Olivia's belly after a few minutes of more intimate congress. The housemaid allowed him that much and was a good deal more cheerful about it.

He tossed aside the soiled handkerchief and got off the bed, fetching his own clean square of linen from his coat pocket.

"Olivia, it's only been a few weeks since I wrote to Banks of your supposed death. I warned you your scheme might take years."

"You don't know Daniel," she said, drawing the sheets up and subsiding onto the pillows. "He's handsome, has fine manners, and is a vicar. Vicars need wives, and Daniel never quite mastered his animal spirits, not that I allowed any of his nonsense once he thrust that child on me."

Bertrand climbed back onto the bed, mostly to annoy his ladylove. "Even if Banks remarries post-haste, what says his wealthy relation will give him the money you demand?"

"The children," Olivia retorted, flopping over to her side. "That wretched boy Danny, for starters, and whatever children the viscount and his lady will produce to ensure the succession of Fairly's title. Bigamy is still a hanging felony, Bertrand. Nobody needs a relation found guilty of bigamy, least of all a family already familiar with scandal."

Bertrand watched the cobwebs flutter and absently stroked his flaccid member. Olivia had great faith in this plan of hers: wait until Banks was on the verge of remarrying, then extort an enormous sum from him in exchange for Olivia's willingness to remain "dead." Everyone could move on with their lives, free of scandal and old entanglements.

Banks would be a fool to trust Olivia's word. She'd remain silent until her new dresses no longer pleased her, if that long, then she'd have her hand out again, or into the poor vicar's pocket.

Though the poor vicar had acquired wealthy relations—most unwise of him.

"Should I be concerned that I'm sharing a bed with a woman who will exploit children?" Bertrand asked, caressing Olivia's increasingly well-rounded fundament.

Olivia swatted his hand hard enough to sting. "My father didn't hesitate to exploit me, did he? I was his drudge for years, trying to make do on farthings with hardly a decent dress to show for it. He gambled away what little Mama left me, and of course, nobody will offer for a village girl who has no dowry. Lord Fairly is rumored to be obscenely wealthy, and Daniel owes me for raising a boy conceived in sin."

She settled into her rant—when Olivia raised topics like sin and her purloined dowry, she had the oratorical stamina of a Methodist preacher—while Bertrand murmured, "Yes, pet," and "Of course, my love," at regular intervals.

The pleasure of almost tupping a youthful rival's scorned wife had already faded, and yet Bertrand remained fascinated by Olivia Banks and her determination to arrange the world to suit her preferences. Her years in the vicarage hadn't been marked by real want, but clearly Olivia resented Banks simply because he'd offered for her.

In her imagination, those years at Banks's side were becoming a time of hardship, long-suffering, and ill usage.

Banks was in for the shock of his handsome, holy life. Bertrand felt sorry for the vicar, until a decidedly unpleasant thought came wafting down on the afternoon sunbeams: bigamy was, in theory, still a hanging felony, but what was the penalty for a woman who lied about her own death, and was her accessory to that crime as vulnerable to prosecution as she was?

Kirsten wanted Daniel to toss up her skirts and make love to her amid the apple blossoms, but she'd learned a few things in recent weeks, one of which was the pleasure of anticipation.

Of having something wonderful, dear, and delightful to look forward to.

"You tempt me," Daniel said, kissing her knuckles when she wanted to further explore the contour of his falls. "You tempt me to folly, because no sooner would I find my way past all your confounded female finery, no sooner would I indulge you in the pleasures you're more than owed, than Matthias and Alfrydd would come bouncing back up the lane. I have the boy's spectacles in my pocket, you see."

"My pleasure is foiled by a boy's spectacles?" Kirsten asked.

Daniel kept her hand in his and walked with her to the stone wall. "My dear, you deserve a more comfortable accommodation than a stone wall when first you indulge your passions."

Kirsten scooted up to sit on that wall. "When we make love, Mr. Banks, my goal will be to wrest from your grasp all manners, all consideration, all notions of gentlemanly deportment, for I have no intention of comporting myself like a lady."

Daniel took the place beside her, while a few yards away, the horses cropped grass and bees lazily sipped at pale blossoms. Kirsten would remember to keep a blanket rolled behind her saddle in future.

"When we make love," Daniel said, "I will comport

myself like a husband enthralled with his prospective wife. Shall I procure a special license?"

Fiend. "Vicars do not marry by special license, Daniel. Vicars marry with proper decorum. Besides, if we cry the banns starting tomorrow, we can be married within the month."

The stone wall was cool, even through Kirsten's riding habit. Also hard, though the height...felt about right.

"I'll have Bishop Reimer down to marry us," Daniel said, "unless you have another preference?"

He assumed they'd have a village wedding, which suited Kirsten wonderfully. No St. George's in Hanover Square, no lavish wedding breakfast, no forcing her sisters to endure all the comments Kirsten had endured at Nita's wedding.

A small ceremony, a buffet in the assembly rooms over the Queen's Harebell, and...Daniel. Hers for the rest of her days—and nights.

"As long as I end up married to you," Kirsten said, "sooner rather than later, I care not who officiates. What will you do about Matthias?"

Daniel's glance was naughty, confirming that he could be naughty—a prospective wife liked to be assured of these things—and that he knew Kirsten was changing the subject in defense of her sanity.

She wanted to touch him, wanted to lay him down in the soft grass within the sheltering wall of the blooming orchard and plunder his charms. She sent him a glance confirming the same.

Being in love was such enormous *fun.*

"Matthias is a puzzle," Daniel said. "He's a bright lad, and he's trying, but I don't know how much longer he'll try. Latin is a language of details. How a verb or noun inflects is crucial, and Matthias can't seem to keep it all straight. His figures are hit-or-miss, though he strikes me as the sort of boy who'd enjoy mathematics."

"Serious-minded," Kirsten said, like a certain vicar, most of the time. "Does he do any better with French?"

"His recitation is excellent, though we're not past *merci beaucoup, monsieur,* or *un, deux, trois…*"

Daniel's French accent was casually perfect. "Will you speak French to me when we make love, Daniel?"

Oh, Kirsten hadn't meant to ask that.

Daniel shifted off of their stone perch. *"Oui, mam'selle.* I can also regale you with passionate verse in Latin, if that would please you. My Greek isn't as facile, but for you, I'll learn to make love in Greek."

Kirsten adored that Daniel could tease her this way, no false piety, no shame about his flirtation. They were to be married, and they were already friends.

Gratitude assailed her, because she'd found the man who understood her, who would be her partner in all things and permit her the same privilege in his life.

"We should inspect the vicarage," she said, scooting down from the wall. Daniel's arm settled around her shoulders, as comfortable as a favorite quilt. "George says the work has come along at a great rate."

"I've stopped by a few times, but I didn't want to hover. Then too, the boys keep me busy."

The scholars kept him happy. Daniel was a natural teacher, and all save Matthias were blossoming in his care.

Kirsten strolled the bounds of the orchard with

Daniel, discussing the boys, the fitting out of the vicarage, the Harrises' new baby boy, who appeared to have a clubfoot.

"I wish Nita were back from her travels with Mr. St. Michael," Kirsten said when they'd made a full circuit of the orchard. "She'd know if there's anything to be done for the child."

"You worry over the little ones," Daniel said, kissing her temple. "Mostly all they need is love and decent nutrition. I wish I could give you children."

Kirsten turned into his embrace, assailed by a love so vast, so warm and safe and mighty, it needed a name other than simply *love*.

"You give me *yourself*, Daniel, and you accept me in return, which is almost more joy than I can comprehend. I wish I could give you children too."

For a sad, sweet, exquisite moment, they held each other while the horses grazed and the occasional white petal drifted down from above.

"Daniel, I want to make love with you now," Kirsten said, leaning her forehead against his chest. "I want to cast off my clothes and scandalize the apple trees."

"You do a man's vanity a power of good, my lady, but the afternoon is waning, and I should see you back to your brother's. We will tell George our good news, and I'll write to the earl before I dream of you tonight."

Brothers. Brothers must be dealt with. "Oh, very well, but tomorrow morning, I'm taking you on an inspection of the vicarage and we're bringing a picnic, Mr. Banks."

Daniel whistled for his horse, who came over at a brisk walk, Kirsten's mare following more slowly.

"Not tomorrow morning," he said, busying himself with Kirsten's mare first. He tugged the girths tighter, untangled the reins from the bridle, and ran the stirrup down the leather, while Kirsten tried to reconcile herself to a vicar's schedule.

"You have calls to pay tomorrow morning?" she asked, stroking Beelzebub's dark nose. As Daniel's wife, she'd have to accommodate illness in the parish at all hours, squabbling spouses, injuries, and visits from the bishop and traveling clergy.

Daniel would be her husband, but as a member of the clergy, his time was not his own. Nicholas, a belted earl with significant wealth, complained of the same condition, oddly enough.

"I have no visits scheduled for tomorrow," Daniel said. "I will plan lessons for the coming week, put the last touches on my sermon, write to Bishop Reimer concerning my marital good fortune, and spend some time with Ralph, who is learning Latin along with the boys."

Daniel next turned to Beelzebub, who stood patiently while girth, reins, and stirrups were dealt with.

"You have a busy day, then," Kirsten said. "We can inspect the vicarage some other time."

Disappointment curled the edges of her joy brown, which was petty of her. She'd have years of Daniel's company. What was an hour in an empty manse, more or less?

Daniel boosted her into her saddle, then arranged her skirts over her boot.

"We will visit the vicarage tomorrow *afternoon*, when the workers have left for their half day." He rested his forehead against her thigh. "I will spend a restless night, my love, for you'll haunt my dreams, I assure you."

"You want to see the vicarage after the workers have—? *Oh.*"

Daniel looked up, his hand remaining on Kirsten's thigh. "If that suits?"

She reveled in the feel of that masculine hand on her person. This time tomorrow, Daniel would have touched her bare skin with his bare hands.

"Tomorrow afternoon suits. We can take a picnic luncheon and make our visit after work for the day has ended. You'd best get on your horse now, Daniel."

Lest Kirsten tackle him and scandalize the apple trees and the horses.

Daniel kissed her knee, the wretch, then swung up on his great, black charger. "I'll look forward to our next outing, my lady. Let's be off. I'm eager to share our good news with your family."

Kirsten raced him cross-country to George's estate, because she was eager too—and not simply to share their good news.

⁓

"This doesn't make sense," Fairly muttered.

Letty looked up from a letter sent by Fairly's sister, the Marchioness of Heathgate.

"You're muttering," Letty said, glancing at the clock on the parlor's mantel. Danny would soon come trotting up the lane on his pony, dusty, happy, and ready to be spoiled rotten.

"You will recall we sent a fellow north," Fairly said,

tugging gold spectacles from his nose. "His task was to ascertain the whereabouts of Daniel's wife."

We had done no such thing. Letty had asked for a favor, and Fairly had likely dispatched a regiment.

"I assumed you'd recalled your investigator when Olivia died," Letty said.

Fairly occupied the escritoire that had been positioned by the window to take advantage of the natural light. His hair was brilliantly gold in the sunshine. So gold, Letty's fingers itched to stroke its softness.

"Between various errands, muddy roads, lame horses, and—I suspect—a comely daughter of a blacksmith, Mr. Darrow lingered in the north."

"Did Mr. Darrow learn anything of Olivia?" Letty asked.

"That's what doesn't make sense. Olivia left the north before the New Year, not immediately prior to her death. Contrary to what Daniel believes, she apparently prevailed on her cousin's hospitality in London for a good while before she died. "

Olivia had used Danny to extort from Letty sums that could not have been generated through decent employment. Just as bad, Olivia had lied to Daniel and betrayed his trust. Even in death, Olivia could apparently still cause trouble.

"Olivia would hate being a poor relation," Letty said. "Would have hated that, rather. She set great store by money."

Fairly sat back, making the curving guilt chair creak. "Why would a woman who set great store by money marry a country vicar?"

Would that Daniel had asked that question before

he'd spoken his vows. "Why would a young man whose looks and occupation could have earned him entrée into many fancy drawing rooms have settled for a dowerless village girl?"

Fairly pinched the bridge of his nose. "The usual reasons?"

"They were not smitten, but Daniel wanted to advance past the ranks of other young curates, and for that a wife was a necessity. Then too, Olivia was never very impressed with his looks, and he approved of her for that."

"I do not merely *approve* of you," Fairly said, shoving to his feet and crossing to the sofa. "I love you. I am smitten by you, in love, besotted, arse over teakettle—"

He knelt over Letty and swooped in for a kiss. His hair was warm from the sunshine, and his fingers as they traced her jaw smelled of ink.

"I am besotted with you too," Letty said, cuddling into her husband's embrace. "This is not how one usually makes use of a sofa, Husband."

"I wish Danny would get here. Will you play bowls with us in the garden?"

"Yes. I used to hate Olivia."

Fairly climbed off of Letty and drew her to her feet, straight into his arms. "I still do. She hurt you, Banks, the boy. I suspect her relations up north tossed her out and she was cast upon her cousin's charity."

"At least she didn't try to reunite with Daniel. You can hate her a little less for that."

"I'll hate her a scintilla less when Banks is happily wed to Lady Kirsten. Danny says they're quite in love." Fairly tucked Letty under his arm and moved with her to the window, which had a fine view of the drive. "There's the brilliant scholar now, cutting quite a dash on his pony."

Cantering up the drive, standing his stirrups, looking relaxed and confident—and much like Daniel.

"He's growing up," Letty said. "I miss him terribly, but I also enjoy the quiet when he departs for Daniel's household. Am I a bad mother?"

"You are such a terrible mother," Fairly said, "that though it broke your heart, you have twice left that boy in your brother's care. I'm proud of you, my love, and your son is very happy."

Which was all that mattered.

"I'm not any good at all when it comes to bowls," Letty said, resting her head on Fairly's shoulder. "Will you tell Daniel what Mr. Darrow learned?"

"Likely not. Daniel would feel guilty that Olivia's own family tired of her company. She's gone to whatever reward awaited her, and Daniel has moved on to happier choices."

For which Letty was honestly grateful. Lady Kirsten Haddonfield would be a good stepmother to Danny and a good wife to Daniel.

Letty kissed Fairly's jaw. "Husband?"

"Hmm?"

Letty loved the smell of him, the shape and size of him, everything. His voice, his silences, his ruthless, loving heart.

"I'll soon start to wean the baby. I'd like to move on to some happier choices too. We need an heir for you."

"Don't be—" Fairly was canny and possessed of a roaringly healthy and highly creative sexual appetite. "Letty? Are you sure?"

She would always have regrets where Danny was concerned, but that was probably any parent's lot. Regrets were about the past; her marriage to Fairly was about the present.

And the future. "I'm sure, David. I love you. I'm sure about that too."

Letty loved kissing him too, which was why Danny found them quite entangled when he came barreling into the parlor a few minutes later.

"I'm here! I'm—you're kissing. Mr. Haddonfield kisses Mrs. Haddonfield too. Digby says that's why we're supposed to knock on doors, so we don't catch anybody kissing who shouldn't be."

The boy was putting on some height. Someday, he'd appreciate that business about knocking on doors.

"We're married," Fairly said, turning loose of Letty. "One of the benefits of marriage is that you can kiss each other whenever you want to. Her ladyship has vowed to beat us both at bowls, Danny. Are you prepared to defend the honor of men throughout the realm with your stout right arm?"

Danny went straight for the dish of chocolates on the desk, no stopping to hug the woman who loved him most in the whole world.

"Yes, sir. As long as that doesn't involve kissing."

⤝⤞

Daniel's parish in Little Weldon had been neither more pious nor more sinful than any other; hence, he'd often baptized a couple's first child less than nine months after presiding over the couple's wedding.

Strictly speaking, an engaged couple was wiser to abstain from intimate relations, not because fornication was a sin—nowhere was fornication per se mentioned in the Commandments, after all—but because illness, injury, and other bad luck meant the groom might not consecrate his promise to marry the bride.

Leaving an illegitimate child to answer for the couple's eagerness.

Fornication in anticipation of marriage was selfish for that reason, and selfishness was hardly a virtue. Whenever Daniel was asked by a bishop to debate the matter, he murmured agreement that fornication was a sin, a first cousin of sorts to adultery, though at some important legal and spiritual removes.

Children were not an issue for Daniel and his intended, and thus theological platitudes—as was so often the case—served poorly in practical application.

"The smell of new wood always makes me happy," Kirsten said as she peered out the front window of the vicarage's formal parlor. "I associate it with Nicholas's birdhouses, and with my father. Papa learned to carve when he was soldiering in Canada."

The entire manse had donned new vestments. The earl had donated most of the old furniture to the parish, musty curtains had been thrown to the flames, and the premises had been scrubbed from top to bottom.

"Shall we have a look about upstairs?" Daniel asked.

"Please. We'll have to decide how to house the boys, and you'll want a study on the west side of the house."

To catch the afternoon light, because Daniel would teach the boys in the morning.

"You will need a parlor as well," he said. "A place of refuge from rotten boys, overly friendly parishioners, and sometimes even your husband."

Kirsten was across the room like a pony intent on a bucket of oats, arms around Daniel in a ferocious hug.

"Not a refuge *from* you, Daniel. We shall be a refuge for each other, or you'll have to recruit a different wife."

Desire leaped, as did tenderness. "You are the only wife for me. Let's go upstairs, shall we?"

Their boot heels thumped on bare floors in empty rooms until they came to the second largest chamber, which occupied a corner of the house and boasted a small balcony.

"Our bedroom," Daniel said, opening the door. "Unless you'd prefer another."

Because the room had no curtains, light flooded through windows and French doors. Some considerate soul had left a window cracked, so the scent of the recently scythed yard blended with sawdust and the faint fragrance of lilacs.

"We have a bed," Kirsten said, striding to the only piece of furniture in the room. "How is it we announced our engagement to George and Elsie yesterday, and there's a bed in the vicarage this afternoon?"

A large bed, complete with sheets, pillows, and a green-and-lavender quilt that blended nicely with the sunny location and spring day.

"I suspect George and Elsie were busy this morning," Daniel said. "When you ladies departed for the teapot last night, I was assured at great length that the earl will be pleased to get my epistle regarding our betrothal."

Sent to Town by messenger, at George's insistence, bless him.

Kirsten smoothed a nonexistent wrinkle from the quilt. "Nicholas isn't one for ceremony. I think he'd be an innkeeper were his countess willing. I'd never have suspected George had the makings of a country squire, though, and who knows where Adolphus will end up."

For Kirsten, that was nearly babbling. Daniel closed the door, and because his intended would wish it, he also locked it, though the house was deserted.

"Kirsten, come here, please."

The imperative, however polite, caught her attention. They wouldn't use it with each other often, but today was special. She crossed the room and stood before him.

"In your eyes, I see worry," Daniel said, taking Kirsten's hands and finding them cool. "You are haunted by the fiancés who have deserted you. I will not abandon or forsake you, not ever. You are everything my heart desires, and our wedding day cannot come quickly enough to suit me."

She leaned in, her forehead against Daniel's chest, her arms around his waist. "I could not sleep last night, Daniel. I'd doze off, and nightmares would find me. I dreamed you'd sailed away to Cathay, then I dreamed that I was married to Sedgewick and none of my dresses fit. I dreamed an enormous French-speaking hog came rampaging through the marriage ceremony. You'll think me daft."

Daniel's worst dream in the past month had awakened him several times: He'd dreamed Olivia was alive, they were living in Little Weldon, and this entire season in Haddondale had never happened.

"Kirsten, dearest lady, I am yours. I would offer you more than mere words as reassurance of my devotion." Daniel would offer his heart, his soul, his last penny, and—were he ever to be so blessed—his firstborn. His intimate affections were the smallest of the gifts he could share with Kirsten.

"You'll think me wicked." Said very softly to Daniel's cravat.

Daniel rested his chin on Kirsten's crown, the better to hide his smile from her. "Yesterday, you were bold and certain. Have my charms paled so soon?"

"I don't want to tempt you to sin."

"Then don't tempt me to sin, tempt me to love." Daniel kissed her, because Kirsten's practical, efficient mind was trying to scale the heights of moral theology rather than accept the assurances of her beloved.

After a moment's hesitation, Kirsten looped her arms around Daniel's neck and kissed him back. This kiss was different from any they'd shared previously, softer, sweeter.

More awestruck.

"I trust you," she said. "I hadn't realized that's what I'd lost, but you've found it for me, Daniel. I trust you."

No, she did not. Not entirely, but she wanted to, so Daniel took his time, savoring when he yearned to plunder, teasing when every male part of him shouted demands. Before he and Kirsten left the bedroom, she would trust him in ways she could only imagine now.

And Daniel would trust her too.

She went after the knot in his cravat. "I have brothers, Daniel. You needn't fear for my delicate sensibilities. I've longed to see you naked."

"Will you afford me the same pleasure?"

Sometime, ten or twenty years hence, Daniel's mind would stop automatically comparing this wife to his first one. Olivia had never allowed him to see her unclothed, had never initiated intimacies, had never sought his embrace even as a matter of simple marital comfort.

How miserable she must have been to have accepted Daniel's proposal.

How desperate he'd been to have offered for her. Daniel's father had seen the looming problem, but had conveyed judgment rather than concern to his son.

Kirsten dropped her hands. "You'll have to unlace me if we're to cavort as God made us."

"I don't believe I've ever cavorted before," Daniel said, drawing off his neckcloth and shrugging out of his coat. "You must be patient with me if I'm slow to learn. I can manage your hooks and laces, though."

Kirsten turned and swept her hair off her nape. "Perhaps you should recite me some of that Latin poetry you were bragging about yesterday. Or maybe French would get things off to a nice start."

Daniel got things off to a nice start by kissing Kirsten's nape, which provoked a lovely sigh as he undid her dress.

"You smell good, my lady, of roses and meadows."

"Your hands are warm," she countered. "And your lips…"

Daniel's lips were learning the curve of Kirsten's neck and shoulder, while his fingers tugged at the bow holding her laces together.

"I love that you let me do this," he whispered. "I love getting my mouth on you."

His mouth, his hands, his breath. Daniel went silently mad, indulging his every tactile appetite as Kirsten's clothes joined his in a pile on the floor.

She was down to her chemise and stockings when Daniel started on the falls of his breeches.

Kirsten brushed his hands aside and sat on the bed before him. "You got to unlace me. I want to do this."

Daniel paused, half-undone, entirely in love. "Are you keeping score?"

"Yes, I'm keeping score." She dispatched several buttons. "And you're ahead. You've kissed me nearly everywhere—" Four more buttons went down to defeat.

"Not nearly everywhere."

"—and you've taken every pin from my hair." The last pair of buttons surrendered to her deft fingers.

"Which is still braided."

"And you, you're not wearing underlinen. I had wondered. Your breeches always fit so perfectly."

God help him, Kirsten had been ogling his breeches. "What else have you wondered, my lady?"

"About this." She drew a particular part of him from his clothing, her hands cool and careful. "I've wondered a lot about this."

Daniel had wondered if he'd ever get to use "this" again outside of self-gratification and untidy dreams.

"I've wondered a few things myself, madam." Such

as how his voice had acquired a rasp. "What color are your nipples, for example? I've pondered that mystery at significant length."

"This is a significant length," Kirsten said, caressing his shaft. "I suppose you want to see my—all of me?"

She was blushing, not because she held his erect cock in her ladylike hands, but because she couldn't say the word *nipple*. Marriage to Kirsten Haddonfield would be interesting.

"Why don't I show you all of me first?" Daniel asked, stepping back and peeling out of his breeches. "Lady Kirsten, may I introduce you to your husband's naked form. You are the first woman to see me thus since my own mother had the privilege more than thirty years ago."

Daniel had tried for bravado, for a casual ease he didn't feel. Olivia hadn't wanted him, and there was no blustering past that. A moment of sorrow threatened, for the young man who'd married in such ignorance.

"Turn," Kirsten said, scooting back onto the mattress. "Please."

Daniel turned. Kirsten would be honest, and a man's appearance ought not to matter so very much anyway.

"You are more beautiful than I am," she groused, yanking at one of her garters and stockings. "I'm not sure how I feel about that."

The slight pique in the way she abused her lacy garter reassured Daniel as no flowery sentiments could have.

"A man can't be beautiful," he said.

"Oh, yes, he can, and you are. Worse, you'll age wonderfully." The second garter and stocking joined the first on the floor. Kirsten's gaze remained on her discarded clothing rather than on her naked fiancé. "I'm nervous, Daniel. What if I'm not good at this? It's an important part of being married."

Kirsten's honesty would be the salvation of them. If ever their marriage floundered, if ever they came to serious differences, her honesty would see them through. Daniel stretched out on the bed and hauled her against his side.

"You relieve my fears, Kirsten. For years, I told myself this intimacy, this mutual pleasuring, wasn't so very important. A marriage could survive on the basis of companionship and mutual respect, said I, but I was lying. The marriage cannot survive if the husband is dying inside a little more each year."

Dying of loneliness, rage, despair, and plain human heartache. Had Olivia been enduring the same torment?

Kirsten climbed over Daniel and perched upon his breeding organs. The silk of her chemise whispered against his thighs in a caress that nearly crossed his eyes.

"I'm sorry, Daniel. If I haven't said that before, I'm sorry. Olivia betrayed you, and you did not deserve that."

The sorrow lanced through him again, because Olivia, however miserable she'd been, *had* betrayed him, and not only by stealing money from Letty. Even before Danny had arrived, Olivia had been distant and cool in the bedroom. She'd taken vows to love, honor, and obey, and kept not a one of them.

"This is not the talk of lovers," Daniel said, shaping Kirsten's breasts through her chemise. "Tell me what will please you."

"Honest talk," she said, curling down over his chest. "Honest kisses too."

The latter Daniel could shower upon her in abundance, and so as the sun beamed down through the sparkling windows and lilacs bloomed in the yard below, he did just that.

Fourteen

KIRSTEN HAD GOT THE KNACK OF KISSING DANIEL, OF twining her tongue with his, of sinking her fingers into his hair to show him an angle, to ask him for another kiss exactly like the last one.

Of what came next, however, she was largely ignorant. Arthur Morton had groped at her breasts and attempted to couple with her in the library on a chilly autumn day. Kirsten recalled counting the beats between lightning and thunder as Arthur had muttered ridiculous endearments and mashed his face to her cleavage.

When Daniel glossed his hands over her breasts, Kirsten could not have counted to three.

"I like that," she said, hanging over him. "When you touch me."

"Like this?" He did it again, more slowly, two hands, two breasts, the silk of her chemise enhancing both her frustration and her pleasure.

"That muddles me," she said. "Like your kisses, but inside me too."

"Here?" Daniel's right palm glided lower to cup her sex.

Oh, yes. *There.* "I want to be naked with you."

Kirsten wanted to put behind her that moment when her intended first beheld her. Daniel would see his prospective wife's unclothed body, but Kirsten would know he studied a female form that could not manage the most basic of female functions.

"Soon," Daniel said. "Let me hold you."

Kirsten wasn't the only one breathless and boggled. Daniel urged her onto his chest, though she resisted.

"I want to hurry, Daniel. I don't know how to go on and I detest that. I like knowing what I'm about."

He'd undone Kirsten's braid at some point. Her hair spilled over her bare back, the sensation novel and soothing.

"Shall you hurry with your chemise on, my lady, or with it off?"

What chem—? "Off."

"Lean forward." Daniel carefully extricated Kirsten from her last article of clothing and set it aside, leaving Kirsten with a towering need to cross her arms.

Which she also resisted. This was Daniel, soon to be her husband. "Well?"

"You can't know," he said, grazing his nose along the underside of one breast. "You can't possibly grasp how beautiful your trust is to me. Your courage, your desire, all of you. I am in love with a beautiful woman."

Kirsten could not have children, but she could have Daniel's love and be abundantly happy with him. Peace replaced her anxiety, for she'd finally, finally chosen well.

"I am in love with a wonderful man."

Daniel's smile—bashful, naughty, pleased—inspired

another round of kissing. Then his bare hands were once more on Kirsten's breasts, his touch slightly callused, warm, and…inventive.

And then his mouth. Daniel provoked raptures with that mouth on Kirsten's breasts, with his fingers, stroking her in places secret and sweet. She retaliated by exploring his ribs, his belly, the trail of dark hair that met his erect cock.

A certain part of which was the same color as her nipples.

"I will like knowing what married people know," Kirsten said, touching her tongue to Daniel's nipple. "You taste of lavender."

"You taste of bliss," he said, rolling them and kissing her chin. "I'm prepared for a little hurry now, my love."

Good heavens, he was strong.

"Then make haste with me," she said, brushing his hair back. This was the wedding ceremony that counted, that made the two as one flesh. Daniel loomed over her, braced on his arms.

Not the soft-spoken vicar, but the man in his prime, sharing pleasure with his mate.

"I love you," he said as Kirsten felt the first hot, blunt nudge at her body. "I will always love you."

She encircled his wrists with her fingers, the better to brace herself against sensations so intimate, she regretted her request that he hurry.

"I love you, Daniel Banks, and I like this joining very much."

Fortunately for Kirsten, Daniel's version of haste was a deliberate, quiet advance and retreat that brought pleasure right into Kirsten's body, into her soul. A bed rope creaked as Kirsten hiked a leg around Daniel's flanks.

"You're all right?" he whispered.

"I want—that's better. When you do that."

He'd developed a rhythm Kirsten could follow. Steady, relentless, sweet, and searing.

"Like that?"

Kirsten tried to form an answer—*exactly like that*—but the reins of her focus were flapping out of her grasp, as sensations welled in a high, fast-running torrent.

"Let go," Daniel murmured, cradling her head against his shoulder. "Have your pleasure of me."

Kirsten's body understood even as her mind was uncomprehending. From inside, from her soul, a deluge of sensation crested over thought, words, will, everything. She clung, she keened, she clutched, and she panted her lover's name until she could bear no more, and still Daniel did not relent.

"Daniel, I can't—"

Oh, but she could, more intensely than ever as he drove her up again, this time hilting himself against her in his own surrender.

For long moments, Kirsten stroked Daniel's hair, his breath harsh against her ear.

Married life loomed as wondrously lovely, a new world of joy and pleasure, a perfect joining with the perfect man. Kirsten positively wallowed in the comfort of Daniel's weight, in the intimacy of breathing in counterpoint to him, breasts to chest in seamless marital accommodation.

Daniel rose up enough that cool air eddied between

their bodies. His hair was tousled, the muscles of his shoulders and arms bunched and flexed.

The pleasure had been marvelous, but the tenderness in Daniel's gaze was the more precious gift.

"We're lovers now," Kirsten said. "I want always to be your lover, Daniel Banks."

His lashes swept down, not quickly enough to hide the relief in his eyes.

He'd worried. He'd worried that his attentions would repulse her, that he'd be inadequate. Very likely, he hadn't even named those fears to himself, but they were yet another legacy of his disgraceful, departed, first wife.

"I'm sleepy," Kirsten said. "Shall we cuddle here for a moment before we dress?"

Daniel withdrew and rolled to the mattress beside her. "You don't want to hop up, dress, and finish inspecting the house?"

"You are daft. Pass me a handkerchief, Mr. Banks. I'd rather spend the afternoon inspecting you."

He reached across her, a casual intimacy that put the scent of him inches from Kirsten's nose.

"Your handkerchief, my lady. I hadn't meant to spend."

Damn Olivia Banks to the nastiest circle of hell anyway. "This business of trust is supposed to go both ways, sir. I love that passion overcame your gentlemanly restraint. I love you."

Daniel studied Kirsten's expression for the length of two slow, deep breaths, then brushed her hair back and kissed her brow.

"You are my miracle, Kirsten Haddonfield, soon to

be Kirsten Banks, whom I could not love more. Sleep in my arms in the broad light of day, and then you shall inspect me to your heart's content."

❦

"Why do grown-ups get married, anyway?" Fred asked. "My parents barely speak to each other, and when they do, they're sometimes not very nice."

Frank pushed the dirt around with his shoe, which Digby was sure would get him a scolding on the way home from church.

This meeting of the scholars was taking place in the graveyard of St. Jude's as the service let out and the serious gossiping in the churchyard began. Before the service, Vicar had asked to speak to his scholars—that's what he'd called them—alone in the church office, and he'd explained that the banns would be cried for the first time that day for him and Lady Kirsten.

He had *not* explained what would happen to his scholars after the wedding.

"Mama and Papa tease each other sometimes," Frank said. "Papa kisses Mama's cheek."

"Then Mama says he's not to," Fred retorted. "I like Lady Kirsten, but I like the way things are too."

"You like her tea biscuits," Thomas said, hiking himself onto the oldest headstone in the graveyard. Nobody knew who was buried there, some Viking fellow, probably. The Vikings were a grand lot for causing mischief, rather like the Romans and the Visigoths.

"My mama and step-papa tease each other all the time," Digby said. "They kiss *a lot* and Mama giggles."

"Blowing the ground-sills," Fred muttered.

"You wouldn't know a ground-sill if it kicked you in the arse," Thomas said.

Thomas hadn't sat on anybody in a long time, but he who said bad things about Lady Kirsten might still find himself facedown in the grass.

"I don't think anything will change," Danny said, picking at the moss on the headstone. "My papa was married before, and he taught boys at the vicarage. Last night, when he told me about marrying Lady Kirsten, he didn't say anything about you lot leaving the dower house."

"But he doesn't need to be married to teach us," Thomas said. "We were going along fine without Vicar having a Mrs. Vicar."

Danny had nothing to say to that, though Digby felt a pang for Thomas. Thomas was jealous of the vicar, which they all were from time to time. Vicar was good, smart, handsome, kind, and occasionally prone to mischief, to the extent a grown-up could be prone to mischief.

"Vicar and Lady Kirsten are in love," Matthias said, keeping his voice down as if love should not be spoken of in a place of death.

Matthias wasn't the brash schemer he'd been weeks ago, and Digby missed that other, more mischievous boy. Digby did not miss falling asleep to the sound of croaking toads.

"What does 'in love' have to do with anything?" Frank asked.

"It has to do with getting babies," Fred retorted. "I'm telling you lot, they're getting married so they can—"

Thomas kicked Fred in the arse, leaving a muddy boot print.

"Shut up, Fred," Matthias said, speaking up with some of his old authority. "I saw them in the orchard. Vicar put me up on Buttercup, because she needs exercise, but my glasses were slipping, so I gave them to Vicar."

"*You* were on Buttercup?" three boys howled at once, and Matthias paused to enjoy the moment, a rare grin lighting his thin face.

"We hopped several logs, but you mustn't tell anybody. Buttercup's a prime goer too."

Danny, who could gallop circles around them all, shot Digby a patient smile.

"What did you see?" Digby asked, because the business of Vicar taking a wife was important. Digby's mother had remarried, and within weeks, he'd been sent off to live in at the dower house.

Which, so far, had been more pleasure than work.

"I wanted to get my glasses back from Vicar, because I'm never supposed to take them off, and yet when Alfrydd and I rode up to the orchard, Alfrydd told me I would get my specs on Monday. We turned around then, back toward the home farm, but I saw Vicar and Lady Kirsten kissing."

Matthias was apparently not repulsed by what he'd seen; he was respectful of it.

Thomas looked like he wanted to sit on a certain handsome vicar.

"You can barely see past your own nose, but you can see halfway across an orchard?" Danny asked.

"I can see well far away. I can't see up close," Matthias said.

"Marrying Lady Kirsten doesn't mean things have

to change," Frank observed. "Lady Kirsten can live across the garden, and we'll have tea and play cricket, and she can watch our riding lessons. We'll stay away from the orchard is all."

"She won't live across the garden. Married people sleep in the same bed." Digby's mama had explained that with the gentle implacability she'd used when explaining Digby would live in with the new vicar at the dower house.

"Why do they sleep in the same bed?" Thomas asked.

"Because there are fewer sheets to wash," Digby said, though Step-Papa had another explanation, having to do with little brothers and sisters. Digby wasn't to bring up that topic with his mother. "Because then the lady can help with the gentleman's cravats, and he can tie her laces."

Thomas clearly hated that notion. He jumped down from the headstone, turned around, and kicked it. Danny threw a chunk of moss at Fred, who caught it and pitched it at Frank.

"Mattie, tell us about Buttercup," Thomas demanded. "Was she wild over the logs?"

"She was a perfect lady for me," Matthias said. "Vicar told the earl we boys could help keep her in work while his lordship's in London. One of you will probably take her out next."

The worrisome fact of Vicar's upcoming marriage was forgotten amid the wonder of that pronouncement. Perhaps riding Buttercup would even inspire Matthias to share his treats when next it was his turn to be blessed with a basket.

❧

"Thank you," Daniel murmured to George Haddonfield as the last of the parishioners climbed into buggies and gigs or started their homeward journey on foot.

"For the bed?" George asked. "That was Elsie's doing. Your vicarage will be furnished largely from the Belle Maison's attics. Elsie said that monstrosity needed a home."

Over in the graveyard, Danny and Digby were playing a loud version of hide-and-seek, or Norse invaders, or Visigoths, a particularly popular segment of their history lessons. The sound of Danny shrieking and disrespecting the dead like a normal boy made Daniel's perfect day even better.

"I would not have made mention of the bed, Mr. Haddonfield, though that's a lovely specimen as beds go."

The day was sunny and warm out of the breeze. Elsie Haddonfield was at the organ, playing through music for her choir, and Kirsten was with her, turning pages or simply being lovely and mischievous.

"Banks, you'll have to adjust," George said, sitting on the church steps. "When you marry Kirsten, you're marrying the entire Haddonfield family in a sense."

"The earl said as much in his letter." Daniel took a place beside George, though church steps were a hard seat. "I thank you for sending him my message yesterday. His answer came back to me by moonrise, and he welcomed me to the family."

Short and to the point. *Well done, welcome to the family. Best of luck. You'll need it. Love, Nicholas.*

Not Bellefonte. To his family, the earl was simply Nicholas.

"Hence the banns being called this morning," George mused. "Half the female populace of the parish will go into a decline, to have Kirsten of all people steal the prize from them. Well done, Banks."

"Don't do that," Daniel said, because he and George were to be family. "Don't denigrate your sister's value even in passing. Kirsten *of all people* deserves a prince, a duke's son at least. She's kind, intelligent, honest, honorable—you can't know how much her integrity alone appeals to me, Mr. Haddonfield."

Her passion was equally precious. Oh, to be engaged to a woman who turned into a Visigoth princess between the sheets!

George leaned back, bracing his elbows on the step behind him. In the morning sun, he graced the church front, a leonine son of privilege who *adorned* any place he took his ease.

"One forgets that you're fierce," George said. "Unless one sees you upon the back of that gelding. I suspect the horse has kept you sane."

"Guardian angels come in many guises, apparently." Sometimes, they came bearing beds too.

"Shall I give you the dispassionate assessment of your new in-laws?" George asked. "Elsie said that's Kirsten's job, but Kirsten's perspective and mine aren't entirely congruent."

"You'll tell me even if I ask you not to." Daniel knew this because George was already becoming something like a brother. Marvelous notion. Perhaps they'd chase each other shrieking through the graveyard next.

Love made a man so blessedly daft.

"There will be holy jokes," George said, "from Adolphus, who's a quirky lad. He's very bright in some ways and an utter buffoon in others. Kirsten dotes on him, and he hasn't decided whether he dreads that or adores her for it."

"Probably both." Daniel knew scholars as well or better than he knew sinners.

George crossed one booted foot over the other. How a man could look elegant lounging on stone steps was surely a mystery, for Daniel's backside was going to sleep.

"Our firstborn is Ethan," George went on, "but on the wrong side of the blankets, which I gather was a regular occurrence in my parents' generation. Ethan has struggled. We've all struggled."

George fell silent as the Visigoths came scrambling around the corner of the church.

"You take that back!" Danny hollered.

"I won't take it back because it's the truth," Digby bellowed, hands on his hips.

Danny's hands were fisted, a sure sign of serious upset. "I get good marks because I earn them!"

"You get good marks because your papa is the vicar."

"Gentlemen," Daniel said, rising and dusting off his backside, "if you must air a difference of opinion, please do so in reasonable tones. What is the problem?"

George remained on the steps, the blighter.

"He says I get good marks because you're my papa," Danny howled, finger pointed at his accuser.

"It's the truth," Digby retorted. "You grew up in a vicarage, and your papa teaches you because he's smart. My papa is *dead*, so nobody taught me."

Abruptly, Danny's fists uncurled. "You didn't have a tutor or governess or *anything*?"

"I had Mama, and a governess before Papa died, when I was very little."

Danny trotted off in the direction of the graveyard. "That's awful, but you're a scholar now, just like me. C'mon. We haven't played Romans yet."

And thus a lifelong friendship set down roots.

His Royal Lounging Blighterness finally bestirred himself. "That's what it's like in our family, Banks. Mama and Papa were often absorbed in their own dramas, and we learned to pretty much sort ourselves out. We look after each other too. Remember that."

Daniel accepted the lecture, because it was well intended, but as the shepherd of the local flock, the looking after would fall to him.

Kirsten emerged from the church, Elsie Haddonfield with her.

"Have we solved the problems of modern civilization?" Kirsten asked, taking Daniel's arm.

Simply by slipping her arm through his and patting his hand, Kirsten solved all manner of problems. She announced to anybody looking on that Daniel was hers, that she enjoyed touching him, that she preferred his company.

"If you'd like to walk back to Belle Maison," Elsie said, "we can take Danny up with us and meet you there."

"Daniel, may I have your escort?" Kirsten asked.

"Of course, my lady." For the rest of his life.

George rounded up the various pillaging armies from the graveyard, Elsie shooed them into a waiting coach, and Kirsten tugged Daniel toward the green.

"Belle Maison is that way," Daniel said, gesturing at the departing coach.

"The vicarage is this way," Kirsten replied.

Daniel wrapped his hand over hers and accompanied his lady in the direction of their first home, while the words *my cup runneth over* took on new meaning.

❧

All of the giddy, silly, brave words made sense to Kirsten. *Happy as a lark. Overcome with joy. A fool in love.*

Fortunately for her, she was also a fool frequently in bed with her beloved. As the banns had been cried in church on successive Sundays, the vicarage had become their... Mentally she shied away from the term *trysting place*. One had to maintain some dignity even if one's clothes had been strewn about the room more than an hour ago.

"You're awake," Daniel said, stroking her hair back. "You don't want to leave this bed, and neither do I."

Another man would have kissed her cheek and started muttering about time flying.

"I love you," Kirsten said. Daniel liked to hear the words, so she gave them to him often. She liked his hands on her, and he obliged without stinting.

"I love you too," he replied. "Deliriously, which ought to feel awkward, but it doesn't."

For Kirsten, it did, a little, while making love had become a mutual adventure in creativity.

"You're thinking of something weighty," Kirsten said, rolling to her side and tucking her derriere against Daniel's hip. He spooned around her loosely, the day being nearly warm and their exertions having been considerable.

"I'm dwelling on my future happiness," Daniel said, "which weighs a great deal indeed. Bishop Reimer has written to wish us well on our nuptials and confirm his willingness to officiate."

Bishops should matter to a vicar's wife, so Kirsten left off kissing Daniel's hand.

"He's the fellow who knew your father?"

"And knows me. Reimer is a friend. Doubtless, he thinks of himself as a father figure. I should probably pop into Town and visit him."

"One ought not to neglect one's bishops." In Daniel's absence, Kirsten might get the outfitting of the vicarage finished. Larders didn't stock themselves; flowers didn't plant themselves; the boys' dormitory wouldn't arrange itself.

Though of course, Kirsten did not want to be parted from her intended for even a few days.

"One ought not to neglect one's beloved fiancée," Daniel said, nuzzling her ear.

He was a big man, and yet he had the knack of delicacy. He wasn't outright asking Kirsten to go with him to London, but he was investigating the possibility.

"Perhaps you ought to jaunt out to Little Weldon, Daniel. Look up your old friends and pay your respects."

They didn't mention Olivia by name if they could help it. She'd been laid to rest not in the cemetery of her old parish, but in the larger town five miles closer to London. The cousin had seen to it, for which he ought to be thanked heartily.

Daniel settled onto his back. "I don't want to go anywhere near Oxfordshire."

Which meant, in the dutiful and virtuous logic with which Daniel cleaved every moral Gordian knot, he'd go.

"The boys and I will miss you," Kirsten said, shifting to plaster herself to Daniel's side. She never tired of his warmth or his touch. "Have Alfrydd send a rider to Nicholas to warn him of your visit. If you want company on your jaunt out to Little Weldon, he'll happily go. He has good memories of Oxfordshire and friends in the vicinity."

Daniel's arm came around her, as naturally as spring rain falling on flowers. "I'm to bide with the earl when in London?"

Daniel would stay at some mean inn or take a cot in a humble manse if she allowed it.

"Mr. Banks, you have family now. I realize the concept requires some getting used to, but just as I get to love Danny, my family gets to love you. You'd best accommodate yourself to the notion. You will stay with Nicholas, and you will allow him to introduce you as my prospective spouse."

Oh, the delight, the sheer, small-minded delight of contemplating the looks Daniel would earn in his evening finery. The ladies would flirt themselves into a swoon and make utter cakes of themselves. The gentlemen would be stupefied at Daniel's quiet self-assurance and contented air.

"That is an interesting smile, Lady Kirsten." Daniel kissed that smile, which turned it into a grin.

"You're about George's size, and he'll have clothes

at the town house. Leah will insist you borrow freely from them for social occasions." Particularly if Kirsten dashed off a note to that effect.

"I'll leave Monday and be back before the week's end."

The banns would be cried for the third time this Sunday, and the following Saturday, Daniel's bishop would preside at their wedding.

"Write to me," Kirsten said. "We haven't corresponded yet. I want a love letter, Daniel. You needn't draw hearts in the margin, but a few tender sentiments to tease you with forty years from now would be nice."

The letter would turn to dust long before forty years went by, for Kirsten would read it often.

"I shall exert myself to the utmost," Daniel said, while exerting himself to nuzzle Kirsten's ear, "and I'll write to the boys too."

"Excellent notion. I'm worried about Matthias." They both worried about Matthias, who was looking positively peaked and still struggling academically.

"He's making progress," Daniel said, though that progress required a lot of extra time with his instructor.

"Not enough for how bright he is, Daniel. He not only shares his basket these days, he practically takes no interest in it himself."

Daniel shifted, so he was crouching over her. Kirsten loved the sense of being sheltered by his sheer masculine physicality.

"We aren't all destined for Oxford," he said. "We can't all be bishops. Matthias has aptitude in many areas, and we'll build on those."

"Matthias is lucky to have you," Kirsten said, kissing Daniel's shoulder. "I'm lucky to have you."

Daniel moved again, pressing against Kirsten where their bodies had joined so often and so well.

"Monday will be here all too soon, my lady. Will you have me one more time before we leave this bed?"

❧

A visit to the Right Reverend Thomas Reimer was always a pleasant undertaking, though sometimes, Reimer could be pleasantly *insightful* too. Daniel extended a hand to his former mentor and was pulled into a camphor-scented hug in the foyer of the bishop's home.

"Hettie, dear, fetch us some sustenance," Reimer said to the plump maid taking Daniel's coat. "We'll be in the garden, so young Reverend Banks can admire my experiments."

"Will you be calling me young Reverend Banks fifteen years from now?" Daniel asked, though it was lovely to still be "young Reverend Banks" to somebody.

To not *be* young Reverend Banks was also lovely. A younger man would not have anticipated vows with Kirsten, placing misguided piety above Kirsten's need for intimate, irrevocable reassurances of Daniel's commitment to her.

And above Daniel's need for the same from her. Reimer was a great one for what he called practical piety. Daniel was increasingly respectful of the same notion.

He'd waited a lifetime for love to feel this right, this comfortable with another. Wasting even a month of such a gift would have been…arrogant.

"God willing, I will be calling you young Reverend Banks twenty-five years from now," Reimer said. "Come see my irises, for they've outdone themselves this year."

Reimer was passionate about his botany, but the garden was also a place no servant would interrupt or overhear. Daniel had taken years to figure that out.

The bishop's residence was neither opulent nor mean, but simply a pleasant, commodious dwelling. No testament to theology here, not to the glory of God, not to the overstated humility of his bishop.

Daniel had noticed that on his first visit.

"You're looking well, Daniel," Reimer said as they passed through the house. "Your father would be pleased to see you in such good health."

"In such fine tailoring, you mean? These clothes belong to a prospective brother-in-law, and I would have insulted his family by refusing them—or so I tell myself when I behold a pink of the *ton* in the mirror."

The finery was a joke played on London Society, for George Haddonfield's sartorial taste was exquisite and his clothes were only a little loose on Daniel. The borrowed plumage held a reassuring lesson as well: Daniel would not embarrass his wellborn beloved with his bumpkin vicar ways.

Small talk was small talk, a sincere compliment to a lady's parasol was a sincere compliment to a lady's parasol, and when Daniel wore George's evening finery, Polite Society paid him no more mind than they would a dowager duchess with her usual flirts.

Daniel emerged with Reimer into a sunny back garden, larger than the front of the house suggested, for the greenery ran a good fifty yards deep. Walls on both sides bore espaliered hedges in a looping paisley design, and atop the walls, potted pansies turned blue, yellow, and white faces toward the sun.

"Nothing wrong with cutting the occasional dash, Daniel," Reimer said. "Even the flowers are permitted a moment of vanity, and we're all happier for it. Come admire my purples, for I've never seen them as glorious."

Several shades of purple iris—lavender, periwinkle, and violet—absorbed the bishop's interest until a tray had been set out on a table flanking a sundial.

Reimer was a tall, gaunt, white-haired man, reminiscent of the saintly marble effigies Daniel had seen in many a cathedral. The bishop's voice was sonorous and stately in the middle of a service, but on the church steps, Reimer was friendly and given to frequent laughter.

How he and Daniel's father had remained fast friends after their theological studies was puzzling.

Reimer wound down the panegyric to his irises after he'd plucked a small specimen nearly the color of Kirsten's eyes and tucked it into Daniel's lapel. The scent was delicate and lovely, though Daniel would rather the flower had been left with her sisters to finish blooming in peace.

"So tell me about your young lady, Daniel, and help me with this food or Hettie will scold me about waste into next week. A veritable Puritan, is Hettie."

Daniel took a seat on a wooden bench and prepared to nibble his way through a polite interrogation. The tray bore pale slices of cheddar, buttered white bread, forced strawberries, and thinly sliced ham.

"We're having ale with our comestibles," Reimer said. "Perfect fare for a warm afternoon, and I'm weak when it comes to a good ale. Soon the summer ales will be available, and I do look forward to a good summer ale."

Reimer seemed to look forward to each day, a characteristic that had been mildly irksome previously, for Daniel hadn't shared that gift, hadn't understood it, beyond the stern conviction that life was a gift.

Daniel understood that gift now. "You asked about my fiancée, Lady Kirsten."

"Eat," Reimer said, gesturing at the tray. "And don't stand on ceremony, my boy. Just us fellows here, after all."

Kirsten would like Reimer, and so would her brothers. Daniel piled up a substantial serving of bread, cheese, and ham, but held off on the strawberries, for there wasn't room on his plate.

"Lady Kirsten Haddonfield," Reimer said, downing a swallow of ale. "Noted to be tart of tongue, comely, and disinclined to wed once addresses have been paid. You've set tongues wagging—all accord you great courage for tilting at the marital windmill with such a lady. But will she be content in a vicarage?"

When Daniel's father had railed against an engagement to Olivia, the tone had been disparaging and critical. Reimer sounded concerned and curious.

And Daniel was no longer twenty years old.

"Lady Kirsten had reasons for rejecting her previous suitors, sir. Good reasons. She is at heart nurturing and kind, though she doesn't suffer fools."

"So don't be a fool," Reimer said with a wink.

"Though where the ladies are concerned, that's easier said than done for most of us. Try the ale, Daniel."

The ale was very fine, the day was very fine, life was very fine. A stab of longing for the company— and kisses—of Daniel's very fine fiancée went through him. Riding away from her had been difficult; coming home to her would be lovely.

"So you'll marry Lady Kirsten," Reimer said. "Shrewd of you. I married my Violet not six months after Maria died. It isn't good for a man to be alone."

"Genesis, chapter two, verse eighteen. Though the Almighty apparently hasn't attributed to women a similar inability to tolerate their own company."

Reimer burst into laughter. "Correct citation, young Reverend Banks. Also the damned truth. Don't tell Hettie I'm using foul language."

Hettie was, to all appearances a maid or a house-keeper, perhaps twenty years Reimer's junior, but she was by no means youthful.

"Your naughty talk is safe with me, sir. How is my replacement doing in Little Weldon?"

They gossiped about church business for another twenty minutes as the food disappeared and a bee lazily inspected the strawberries.

"Shall we walk for a bit, Daniel?" Reimer asked when the ale was gone and the tray had been cleared away. "Beautiful day for a change. No gardener worth the name laments when the coal fires are put out in London."

"Town always has a faint stench of brimstone to me," Daniel said. "I prefer the fresh air of the countryside."

They made a circuit of the garden, Reimer pausing

to inspect this bed of leafy, thorny roses or that patch of violets. For the first time in memory, Daniel felt a thread of impatience with the bishop, for Reimer had all but commanded Daniel's appearance, and yet the encounter thus far had been merely social.

"Are you in love with Lady Kirsten?" Reimer asked as they stopped by a bed of roses still weeks away from blooming.

"Emphatically," Daniel replied. "Top over tail, hopelessly, unreasonably. I had no idea it was possible to feel this way about a woman. I even love arguing with her." Kirsten was so stunningly honest in their altercations, brangling with her was a revelation in both tactics and trust.

"One wondered," Reimer said as they passed under the shade of an apple tree. "That first wife of yours was a penance in the making."

Ah, so now they arrived to the real agenda.

Fifteen

A PENANCE IN THE MAKING. "MY FATHER USED EXACTLY that term," Daniel said. He recalled his father's appellation for Olivia because the words had been prophetic. Since becoming engaged, Daniel had started reading his father's journals in the evening, and the very same words had appeared more than once in reference to Olivia.

"I saw only a woman willing to share my lot in life," Daniel went on, "one who would not expect me to pursue pretensions above my station. I did not see clearly."

"And now she's gone," Reimer said. "I trust your new lady has shaken you free of any lingering guilt?"

Daniel considered the pious reply—some platitude about every death being a loss and sorrow needing time to sort itself out—and he considered what he'd say if Kirsten were present.

"My new lady is shaking me free of my anger, sir. Olivia was a disgrace as a wife, and I did nothing to merit her bad behavior. I presented my circumstances honestly when we courted, while she dissembled egregiously."

Lied, cheated, stole, misrepresented, betrayed, took advantage. Daniel no longer needed to dodge the truth, though it still stung. He'd lain down with Olivia and felt miserable when he couldn't make her happy.

"Give it time, Daniel, though your response answers a question that's been plaguing me. Take these." Reimer extracted a sheaf of folded papers bound with a black ribbon. "They're your papa's letters to me. Hettie is doing some spring-cleaning, and I've wondered when I might pass these along to you. I've held on to them because your father was full of vitriol regarding your late first wife."

"His journals are no more flattering where Olivia was concerned." Though they indicated pride in Daniel for sticking to his commitments, on the very same pages as Papa had fretted that the church was a bad choice for Daniel.

"He questioned your vocation," Reimer said, as if divining Daniel's thoughts.

Papa had been wrong—Daniel was quite comfortable serving the church. But Papa had also been right.

"Is there a question there, sir?" Daniel asked as the path emerged into the afternoon sunshine.

"I did not question your vocation," Reimer said, "but I've had the benefit of seeing how you bore up under the undeserved penance of your marriage. Is your fiancée in love with you?"

What business was that of Reimer's, and why wouldn't he leave it alone?

"Lady Kirsten has given me every indication that she fancies my company."

Bushy white brows rose over an ironic smile, like clouds over a cheery dawn.

"*Every* indication? You young people and your frisky inclinations. I suppose it is spring, and you're in love. An earl's daughter is a shrewd choice of woman to fall in love with, young Daniel. She'll bring connections to the marriage, wealth, a certain cachet."

That constant reference to Daniel's youth had begun to grate, though perhaps it was supposed to.

"None of which I seek," Daniel said, stuffing his father's letters in a pocket. "I value Lady Kirsten's honesty, her forthright manner, her affection, her intellect, and her loyalty. She's also quite fond of children, which helps when several boys will likely be living in at the vicarage, some of them for years."

Reimer left off twitching at a skein of espaliered ivy. "That reminds me. You have a boy."

Not a son, a boy. What had Reimer heard and from whom?

"Danny. He's with me in Haddondale after an extended visit with my sister and her husband."

"Your sister married Viscount Fairly, didn't she? His lordship is quite well fixed."

His lordship was in love with Letty. "My sister and her husband are very fond of Danny, and he returns their affection." Danny did *now* anyway.

They approached the sundial, Reimer toddling along as if he had nothing much on his mind except his irises—or teasing Hettie about her housekeeping.

"Your academic inclinations have always been superior," Reimer observed, "and your successor in Little Weldon hears so much good about you, the man wonders why you haven't been canonized. You handled this business with your late wife with a stoicism and decorum not many would have shown."

"Thank you, sir." The sundial, if accurate, showed that Daniel could still walk to the earl's club in Mayfair with ten minutes to spare before he and Nicholas were due to meet.

"The dean of Aldchester Cathedral will retire in another year or two, Daniel. He's a good sort, but slowing down. The position wants a younger fellow, one who will be with the place for more than his last few years of service. As it happens, the position of sub-dean will soon be vacant."

Possibilities floated on the benevolent afternoon sunshine. From sub-dean to dean, from dean to bishop, a typical progression for clergy who were hardworking, lucky, and ambitious.

"Are you asking me if I'm interested in the position?" Because Daniel surely was. Having left Little Weldon behind, and not yet having set down roots among the flock in Haddondale, now was a perfect time to make an advantageous move such as Reimer suggested.

And cathedrals had schools, not merely a half-dozen boys living in, but rather, an entire academic establishment, a chance to provide a good start, both morally and academically, to many, many boys.

"I'm not asking if you're interested yet," Reimer said, taking a seat on the bench flanking the sundial. "Your upcoming nuptials should be your focus for the present, but if not the sub-dean position, then a position on the staff of a bishop is not out of the question, Daniel. Ambition is a fine thing in a clergyman, provided it doesn't come at the cost of his vocation. Your vocation has been tested and found genuine, and this has been remarked."

How gratifyingly ironic that Olivia's misbehavior should become the very impetus for Daniel's advancement in the church.

"Thank you, sir. I'll keep this conversation in mind." And Daniel would discuss it with Kirsten, who would make a very fine bishop's wife indeed. *Lady* Kirsten, rather.

A sense of life coming full circle, of virtue rewarded and faith justified, filled Daniel in the quiet, fragrant garden. Life had tested him, and he'd held to his principles and was thus presented with a chance to advance. With Kirsten, he could be happy in any obscure little parish, but she'd approve of a chance for Daniel to operate in a wider church circle.

"Keep this discussion in mind. Pray about it," Reimer said with another wink, "and tend to taking a wife. See yourself out, Daniel, and let Hettie know she may now harangue me about whatever transgression I've committed most recently, or the ones I'm about to commit. The woman's a domestic tyrant."

"Yes, sir, and good day." Daniel conveyed a version of Reimer's message when Hettie passed him his hat, coat, gloves, and walking stick—in London, gentlemen carried walking sticks. Daniel was already down the front steps when he recalled that Reimer lacked specific directions to Belle Maison.

The garden had a side gate. Daniel took himself around the house in that direction but stopped before intruding on Reimer's flowers, for the bishop and his housekeeper were ensconced on the bench by the sundial.

And they were holding hands.

❧

"They miss him, your ladyship," Ralph said, as he and Kirsten tidied up the schoolroom at the end of the day. The tables and chairs had to be in straight rows, the slates cleaned, and the various books and maps organized.

An orderly classroom made for an orderly mind, according to Vicar Banks. Kirsten's prospective husband wasn't half so insistent on order in the bedroom.

"I miss him," Kirsten said, picking up Matthias's slate. The boy's penmanship was atrocious, but then Kirsten's father's had been too. "The boys miss him, and the ponies are in an utter decline."

"Mr. George Haddonfield said much the same thing, but soon Vicar will be back, and all will be set to rights."

The week so far had been half a holiday for the boys, with extra cricket games, riding lessons, and a daily botany lesson conducted by George Haddonfield, mostly based on information in a book Beckman had sent along years ago to the old earl. For tomorrow, Kirsten had organized a trip to the lending library, simply so the boys would know how a lending library worked.

And not be so fidgety for the balance of the day.

"It's Danny's turn to say grace tonight," Kirsten said, wiping Matthias's slate clean. "Fred has breakfast tomorrow."

"Right, your ladyship. Master Matthias is struggling a bit, ain't he?"

"Isn't he." Kirsten corrected Ralph at the footman's blushing request, for Ralph was learning as much in the schoolroom as the boys. "More than a bit. Mr. Banks hasn't figured out why. Matthias is quite bright, he reasons well, and he's well-spoken."

"Slow in some things, quick in others," Ralph said, closing the French doors. "Like most of us."

"You can leave those open, Ralph. The nights are mild enough that fresh air in the morning is welcome."

The room was set to rights, and yet it lacked Daniel's telling eye for a scholarly space. Had it been used as a parlor, Kirsten would have known which touches to add, which small items to put in another room, or where a vase of flowers would look best.

"Vicar will be back soon, your ladyship," Ralph said. "And you'll be exchanging your vows, and that will be a fine thing all around."

"Thank you, Ralph. Has Mr. Banks spoken to you about accompanying us to the vicarage?"

The school ran well in part because Ralph brought a perfect blend of good humor, common sense, and adult authority to his dealings with the boys, and yet a remove to the vicarage would be quite the come down for Ralph.

He gave the globe a spin, much as Thomas did whenever he passed it. "Me? To the vicarage?"

"I realize it's asking a lot, for you to leave the household of an earl, but you do an excellent job with the boys, you know their routine, and you know every cricket rule ever invented."

A gap in Daniel's education that Ralph and George were quickly addressing.

"I hadn't considered it, is all," Ralph said, bringing the globe to a halt. His auburn brows were knit, his focus on the New World.

"I've asked Annie to come with us as well," Kirsten said, examining the point of the pencil on Matthias's desk. Not sharp enough, so she traded it for one of the pencils kept in a jar at the front of the room. Fred's and Frank's pencils were in good repair, Danny's middling, and Digby's much in need of a trim.

"Our Annie's removing to the vicarage?" Ralph asked, to all appearances engrossed with the jungles of Peru.

Ralph's Annie, more like. "The wages will be comparable, though I daresay you'll have more work at the vicarage and a great deal less consequence."

Ralph spun the globe again, gently. "At the vicarage, we'll have more laughter, less gossip, and regular cricket matches. That sounds rather jolly to me. No more putting up with Mr. Sherwin's lectures on dust and sloth, no more having to knock endlessly on the library door when the earl and his countess are in— beggin' your pardon, my lady."

"I won't miss that either, Ralph. We're taking Beulah for our cook, and Parsons as the footman, and I agree with you: the vicarage will be a jolly place."

Though who would ever have associated Lady Kirsten Haddonfield with jollity? Such were the powers of Daniel's affections, Kirsten was jolly nearly all the time these days.

Also tired. Looking after the boys, preparing the vicarage, planning the wedding breakfast, all took energy.

Disporting with Daniel took a lot of energy but also resulted in the best naps.

"Think about coming with us, Ralph, because I'm sure Mr. Banks will bring it up with you when he returns. I'm off to the stable, and I'll see you again tomorrow."

Ralph bowed to her in parting, and as Kirsten left, he was humming an old hymn. She couldn't recall the name, but a snippet of the lyrics came to her.

Kirsten was humming the same tune—Elsie would know the name—when she left the house. The garden was coming to life, colors unfurling in the spring sunshine, the topiary dragons once again pruned to perfection.

They'd have no topiary at the vicarage of course, and who needed dragons when one had a fine pack of little boys?

Kirsten's excellent mood carried her into the stable, where her mount waited in a stall, already groomed and saddled. She was intent on leading the mare out to the mounting block without bothering a groom—they'd have no grooms at the vicarage—except a sound caught her ear.

A noise, a muffled distress signal from Buttercup's stall across the aisle.

The mare was nestled in her bed of straw to the extent a ton of equine could nestle anywhere. Curled against her shoulder was a small boy.

Matthias clutched Buttercup's coarse mane in one hand, his other arm was looped over Buttercup's withers, while the child softly cried his heart out.

Kirsten was assailed by a need to comfort the boy, to simply gather him in her arms and promise him all would be well. And yet Matthias was a dignified little soul. He would not want Kirsten to witness his suffering.

Daniel would know what to do. Daniel would know whether to ignore the lad, hunker in the straw with him, or retrace his steps and come whistling into the barn as if all were well.

While Kirsten had not a single clue how to help the boy.

⁓

Perhaps George Haddonfield's finery was to blame, but as Daniel headed for the St. James's neighborhood, more than one well-dressed lady—and virtually every lady's maid—gave him appreciative glances.

He wished Kirsten were there to see him—and to tell him how to go on. Did one smile back? Ignore the glances? Tip one's hat to ladies one hadn't been introduced to?

Except Daniel had been introduced to several of them. The Countess of Bellefonte, whom Daniel was to call Leah, was determined to see both Lady Susannah and Lady Della well matched, and thus Daniel had been dragooned into attending a ball, a Venetian breakfast, and a musicale.

A tedium, on top of an inanity, interspersed with silliness, followed by a trial of the nerves, and Kirsten had endured *years* of such nonsense.

On St. James's Street itself, no proper ladies were to be found at this hour, lest they attract the censure of the toffs lingering in the various windows of the gentlemen's clubs. Bellefonte had explained this afternoon stricture to Daniel—toffs remained safely abed of a morning—which had struck him as absurd.

A liveried footman at the earl's club held the door for Daniel and a butler ushered him into a formal antechamber. The walls were hung with red velvet, and a sideboard topped with pink marble sported a bouquet of red roses. On the parquet floor, a thick carpet runner absorbed sounds like a moonless night absorbed candlelight.

"The Earl of Bellefonte is expecting me," Daniel said, passing over his hat and walking stick. Daniel expected to be on the premises less than five minutes, and yet the rituals of privilege would be observed in their smallest details.

Much like a church service.

How did Bellefonte, a fellow who liked to nap and to cuddle with his countess in the library, build birdhouses, and sing to his mare, tolerate this folderol?

"Very good, sir. And whom shall we say has come to call?"

The butler's diction was reminiscent of Reimer's in full cathedral regalia, and the creases on the sleeves of his livery would have done credit to a scythe.

"Reverend Daniel Banks," Daniel said.

By the slightest pause, the butler's surprise showed. Perhaps clergy didn't frequent such lofty environs, or perhaps Bellefonte wasn't often in ordained company. The earl in all his Town finery came bustling into the foyer a few moments later, a more modestly attired older fellow with him.

"Banks, you're punctual," Bellefonte said. "A fine quality in a prospective brother-in-law. Have you met Bishop Howley?"

The Bishop of London? His official residence was only a few streets away, but Daniel would never have presumed—

Daniel bowed and found a hand thrust in his direction.

"Reverend Banks, a pleasure," Howley said. "Christ Church man, if I recall? Bishop Reimer sings your praises at every turn. You must come around for tea when next you're in Town. Bellefonte tells me you've pressing matters to see to in Kent. Mustn't neglect the pressing matters, especially the pretty ones. Bellefonte, don't corrupt him too awfully. The good ones are hard to find."

Howley marched off to do whatever it was the *Bishop of London* did when he wasn't lurking in gentlemen's clubs of an afternoon.

"The Right Reverend is rumored to cheat at whist when he's partnered with certain duchesses," Bellefonte murmured, catching the butler's eye. "And he's a flirt, in a subtle way. My grandmother numbers him among her cronies, which speaks to his credit."

Hats and walking sticks were produced and Daniel was once again strolling along fashionable streets in the mellow afternoon sunshine.

"Did you plan that?" Daniel asked.

"Oh, perhaps. Howley wanders from his palace occasionally, and being in the good graces of the lords and heirs lounging about the better clubs benefits his ambitions."

Howley's name was mentioned whenever the office of the Archbishop of Canterbury came up.

"Thank you, I suppose, but you needn't have bothered." Kirsten would be pleased though. Daniel tipped his hat at some duchess he'd been introduced to at the Venetian breakfast, then realized he knew one of the lady's sons from Oxfordshire.

A pianist, of all things.

"I did need to bother," Bellefonte countered, "else Kirsten would have been wroth with me. You're a member of the family now, Banks, and thus subject to the benefits of my titled influence. Howley would have expected me to introduce you, if nothing else. Don't suppose you lose gracefully at whist?"

"I'll work on that very skill, my lord." The fashionable hour approached, when all of Polite Society indulged in an inane parade about Hyde Park, as much a show of wealth and fine tailoring as an opportunity to socialize. The streets were thus getting busier, and the sidewalks more crowded.

"I miss Kent," Bellefonte said as they approached Piccadilly. "I miss my woodworking shop, my horse, my blue sofa, and having my lady more or less to myself. You've just heard a pathetic confession, Banks. Have you any advice?"

"Come back to Kent with me," Daniel said, though the earl's lament had sounded curiously like a fraternal whine. "You're expected to give your sister away when we wed, and the countess appears to have things in hand here."

"Why not move the wedding here?" Bellefonte

argued, all reason, when Daniel was certain the Haddonfield ladies had hatched this scheme.

Oh, it was very good to no longer be *young* Reverend Banks.

"Thank you, but I shall decline that suggestion," Daniel said.

"Decline? May I remind you that I hold the living, Banks? You refuse me at your peril."

Bellefonte bluffed well, but Daniel told the truth better. "May I remind you, my lord, I'm marrying *your sister*, and at her one and only wedding, she should not be plagued with Society's petty opinions and gossip. Moreover, neither she nor I want to put you to the expense of a Town wedding."

And finally, a vicar should be married in his own church, with the parishioners there to celebrate with him and his lady. Howley was firmly High Church, aligned with the aristocracy and the prevailing order.

Daniel was aligned with Kirsten and his flock, and until the sub-dean position was a possibility—

Cold slithered through his vitals.

"Banks, are you well?" Bellefonte asked, for Daniel had come to an abrupt halt, foot traffic flowing around him.

The woman was the right height, and she walked exactly the way Olivia had, shoulders back as if to announce her presence with her very posture. Daniel had thought Olivia's carriage dignified a lifetime ago, but he'd come to see it as self-important. Was this woman a trifle rounder than Olivia?

"Bellefonte, do you see that woman in blue, near the corner?" Because of his height, the earl could see over much of the crowd. The lady was dressed in a blue satin ensemble Olivia could never have afforded.

"I see her."

The cold in Daniel's middle spread upward and tried to wrap around his heart. The woman—*not Olivia, please, God, not Olivia*—was walking away from them, oblivious to her lady's maid, the same way Olivia had pretended indifference to the maid of all work in the Little Weldon vicarage.

"I am nearly certain that woman is my wife, the late, unlamented Olivia Banks."

❧

"A two-bishop jaunt up to Town," Kirsten marveled, because excitement quivered through Daniel and marveling was apparently in order.

"And not just any bishop," Daniel said. "The Right Reverend William Howley, Bishop of London. He said I'm to come for tea the next time I'm in Town."

Daniel was like a boy with a basket of sweets, and his animation was disquieting. He'd tarried an extra day in London, so Kirsten hadn't seen him until Sunday services.

They were alone, sitting in the front pew of the church, though the doors and windows were wide open to admit the lovely spring air. As sometimes happened, a swallow flitted in the side door and perched upon a rafter.

The boys loved it when birds blundered into the church.

"I also met with Reimer," Daniel went on. "He was in great good spirits and asked after you at length.

You'll like him, Kirsten. He isn't priggish, the exact opposite of my father. He was very understanding about my previous marriage."

Kirsten took Daniel's hand, for he'd neglected to take hers. "That would mean a lot to you, that your bishop understood your situation."

Daniel studied the bird, who fluttered from rafter to rafter, perhaps considering where to build a nest.

"Reimer's involved with his housekeeper."

Maybe husbands and wives shared that sort of gossip, but it made Kirsten mildly uncomfortable.

"You caught them in bed, then?"

Daniel left off bird-watching and pressed a fleeting kiss to Kirsten's knuckles. "I caught them holding hands."

When would Daniel tell her he'd missed her? "Your grasp of theology exceeds my own, sir, but is that classified as a sin?"

"Far from it," Daniel said, rising and drawing Kirsten to her feet. "It's not good for a man to be alone."

Genesis, Kirsten knew that much—the explanation for a woman's existence as man's *helpmeet*, and a pernicious bit of pontificating in her opinion.

In the face of growing irritation, Kirsten fell back on honesty. "Daniel, *I missed you*."

For the first time that morning, he focused on *her*, didn't simply look at her as if to say, "Oh, hullo! Lovely weather we're having!" Better than that, he drew her into his arms.

"I missed you until I nearly choked with it," he said. "The staying up until all hours, mincing about, stuffing yourself with ridiculous delicacies five times a day, parading around in the park, everybody trussed up in silk and satin—I don't know how you stood it."

Relief washed through her. Now, Daniel—her Daniel—was home.

"It's all they know, Daniel. All they want to know, and I never felt the Season was wrong morally, but it was wrong for me. How is our family?"

The bird took a winged tour of the altar, an occasion for some anxiety because where birds flew, they could also leave signs of their passing.

Daniel kissed Kirsten's forehead and dropped his arms. "The family is all in good form. They send their love. George's wardrobe fit me very well, by all accounts. Let's fold up the altar cloths, shall we?"

I am marrying a vicar. Adjusting to that perspective would take time.

Kirsten assisted with the altar cloths, while the bird perched on the pulpit as if to supervise. In repose, it was simply a nondescript avian specimen, darkish on top, lighter across the belly, and touched with russet on its little chin. In flight, it became a blue-and-cream streak, agile and lovely.

"I haven't let you in on the best part yet," Daniel said, setting the snuffed candles under the altar. "Reimer got around to telling me about a sub-deanship that is soon to become available, and the dean himself is getting on."

"Deans work at cathedrals, don't they?" Kirsten had been to both Rochester and Canterbury Cathedrals, and had never liked them. All those brooding effigies, folk buried right beneath one's feet, and a vague smell of damp throughout.

"Deans work at cathedrals," Daniel said, in much the same tones as the boys discussed the pony race Daniel had promised them at the end of the school year. "Aldchester is one of the older cathedrals, not quite the most northerly."

The bird took off, this time heading for the church's side door but veering away at the last instant to perch on the organ's music rack.

"*In the north*, Daniel? You'll drag Danny hundreds of miles from everything he's only now become accustomed to, and what of your scholars? What of the congregation just getting to know you here in Haddondale?"

What of Danny's poor mother? What of me?

Daniel left off tidying the altar. "I thought I'd drag you as well, but clearly that plan requires discussion."

His almighty plan required a trip to the jakes, there to be summarily tossed down the nearest hole.

"Daniel, this is all quite sudden. One moment I'm planning my wedding breakfast and the next we're off to the north for a sub-dean's position, whatever that is." Kirsten's entire engagement had been quite sudden, in fact, and she wasn't sure she liked this fiancé who'd come back from London.

The bird had resumed its position on a rafter, where it strutted back and forth as if declaiming a speech on a stage.

Daniel approached Kirsten, consternation in his eyes. "My dear, a vicar's life can involve a succession of different positions. If you cannot be happy with the opening at Aldchester, then I will decline it, but Reimer assured me that I have been noticed."

Kirsten had noticed Daniel too. Noticed his

compassion, his integrity, his honor and kindness. Ambition and looking good in borrowed finery had had nothing to do with anything.

Kirsten took Daniel's hands, hands that had caressed every inch of her, when his only ambition had been to share glorious intimacies with his prospective wife.

"This part of the two becoming one flesh will not be easy for me, Daniel. Everybody I have loved my entire life is here in Kent. My sister Nita and brother George are settling here. Beckman and Ethan aren't far. Ald-wherever sounds cold and far away."

Daniel took her in his arms, this embrace more settled than the previous one. "Danny and I will be with you, and a few years in the north can lead to more years in the south. Cathedrals have schools and little choristers, and all manner of beautiful services."

Kirsten burrowed closer while the swallow took another unsuccessful run at the door.

"Cathedrals frightened me when I was a child," she said. "I thought when you died, you turned to stone if you were very good, and you lay on your tomb through all the ages, looking stern and short, to inspire small children to be good."

Kirsten had amused her husband. She could feel the humor in him, sense it in the kisses he pressed to her temple. She still didn't like cathedrals, especially cathedrals in the far away north.

"You have a wonderful imagination, my lady. Lest you think my time in Town was all socializing and church connections, I did bring you something."

"You brought yourself home, safe and sound. I want nothing more." Kirsten fervently wished Daniel had left his brilliant ideas about uprooting the child and climbing the church hierarchy behind in London.

"I managed a short excursion to Ludgate Hill too," he said. "Your brother accompanied me and was quite helpful."

This time the bird made a parade ground of the bare altar, its birdy marching accompanied by a few wing flaps that struck Kirsten as exasperated.

"How was Nicholas helpful?"

Daniel extracted a small square box from his pocket. "He simply lounged about looking, smelling, and sounding lordly. I'm sure I was given a better bargain as a result. I hope you like it."

A ring. Well, perhaps the north had charms Kirsten could learn to appreciate, for Daniel hadn't forgotten about her after all.

"I hadn't wanted to ask, Daniel."

"You were willing to press one of your own into service," Daniel said, opening the box and passing her a small band of gold. "My mother's was apparently buried with Olivia. Something new was in order. Something new and lovely, if modest."

"It's inscribed." Which would have taken some doing, given Daniel's limited stay in London. Kirsten moved toward the open side door, where sunshine came pouring down at a steep angle.

All my love, Daniel. The ring was a bit of shiny metal, plain as rings went, the sentiment unoriginal, and yet Kirsten teared up, for Daniel had known not to bother with anything fancy.

"I will treasure it always, Daniel, and I will treasure *you* always."

Kirsten slipped the ring on—a perfect fit—and admired it on her hand. Her other engagement rings had been gaudy, bejeweled tokens of a fiancé's ostentation, not symbols of enduring love.

Daniel lounged against the doorjamb, the morning light showing signs of fatigue about his eyes.

"I had a bad moment, Kirsten, up in London."

Ah, this was much more interesting than bishops and cathedrals. "Tell me."

"One minute, I was walking along with your brother, quite bemused by having made Howley's acquaintance, the next, I was sure I'd seen Olivia, a well-dressed, somewhat plumper version, but her. I would have started running, not to stop her but simply to make sure. With Olivia, one always wanted to make sure."

A very bad moment, judging from the worry in Daniel's eyes.

"I used to hear my mother's voice in the corridor," Kirsten said, slipping her arms around him. "It was Nita or the maids or my imagination. With Papa, I smell his pipe tobacco, though none of my brothers smoke. You think you're going daft, but then your siblings report the same thing."

"That's what Bellefonte said. He's heard your father's laughter, but it was the footmen teasing the maids. Gave me quite a start, though. Bellefonte pulled me into the nearest decent pub, sat me down with a brandy, and let me find my balance."

Nicholas would never have said a word to Kirsten about this awful moment.

"What was it like, Daniel, in that instant you thought Olivia might still be alive?"

Daniel and Olivia had been married for more than a decade, after all, had shared parenting responsibilities, and a bed.

"When I thought I might be staring at the back of Olivia's head, I was in hell, Kirsten. Absolute, pitch-black, hopeless, despairing hell. If Olivia were alive, all that would be left to me is my vocation, and while I treasure that, I cannot abide the notion of life without you in it."

Oh, he'd said the right words. Kirsten leaned into Daniel, more at peace than at any time since he'd approached the altar to celebrate the morning's service.

"She's gone, Daniel. She can't hurt you anymore, and she's gone."

The swallow made one last dash for freedom, flitting directly over their heads, and this time gaining the sunshine of the lovely morning. A sign, perhaps, of the freedom Daniel had gained by his wife's death.

"Let's lock up here and admire the new curtains in the vicarage," Kirsten said, pulling back. "I've started on the pantries too, and much of the downstairs furniture has arrived in your absence."

"A brief inspection only," Daniel said, moving off to close windows down one side of the church. "I have much correspondence to tend to, Danny wants to hack out with me, and Ralph asked for some of my time to discuss what the boys have been about in the past week."

Kirsten finished with the windows on the other side of the church, for it was a small edifice.

"I can tell you some of it," she said. "A lot of botany walks, several cricket matches, two lessons in equitation—the boys are trotting over poles now—and several memorization assignments."

Daniel closed the back doors and locked them. "You love those boys, and I love that about you."

The interior grew dim without the natural light, so Kirsten could not see her beloved's expression.

"Anybody would love those boys. I think you should institute picnics on Fridays after exams, and teach the boys how to fish."

Daniel came up the center aisle, as he would on their wedding day. "I wish I could give you children of our own."

He still fretted over this? "I haven't given that a thought since we became engaged. I have you, I have the scholars and Danny. I am not simply content, Daniel, I am full to overflowing with happiness."

Daniel stopped directly in front of Kirsten, his smile the old, familiar, kind smile she'd fallen in love with.

"Your cup runneth over?"

"Exactly. *Now* may I show you my curtains?"

His smile became *husbandly*, then his brows crashed down. "That dratted bird used my altar as his outhouse."

Kirsten snickered. "And the boys aren't even here to see it."

They were both laughing and threatening to put the curtain sashes to inventive uses, when Kirsten recalled she hadn't told Daniel about finding Matthias in tears.

Sixteen

Unease had followed Daniel down from London, a sense of dislocation, as if he'd been dealt a stout blow to the head. Beelzebub had sensed it and taken to dodging and shying all over the shire, which had made the ride home lengthy and tiring.

Kirsten sensed it too, for she was chattering about chintz and velvet as Daniel admired all the progress made at the vicarage.

Kirsten seldom chattered, but she was well accomplished at worrying.

"You've been very hard at work while I strolled about the park with your sisters," Daniel said. The vicarage had become a place of gleaming wood surfaces, sparkling windows, and colorful rugs and curtains. The scents of beeswax and lemon oil followed Daniel from room to room, and a vase of purple irises graced the entryway.

"The boys have helped," Kirsten said, "and the staff at Belle Maison was happy to have a project in the family's absence. Elsie has been a godsend too, for she has an artistic eye."

The results said that mostly Kirsten had seen what needed doing and tended to it, as she always would. She preceded Daniel up the stairs, and as he watched the twitch of her skirts and assurance of her stride, he was assailed by two emotions.

He loved Kirsten Haddonfield. He admired her energy and pragmatism, was touched by her inability to accept praise, and even liked that she'd haul him up short when it came to his career decisions. She'd made him a lovely home in a very brief time, one both welcoming and pleasing to the eye.

But he did not want to make love with her in the next hour.

London had contaminated him with doubts. That single glimpse of the woman in the blue dress had been like an older man's first experience with chest pains.

Like a rat scuttling along the walls of a king's throne room. A stark reminder of human fallibility, of how one misstep could shape the path of any life and turn the most innocent, ebullient hopes to relentless despair.

Now, Daniel's doubts had acquired the same durability. He'd been wrong about Olivia before—wrong about many things.

Olivia hadn't replied to a letter since before Christmas, though they'd had no real need to correspond. Daniel had sent funds north for the care and maintenance of his wife, and she'd sent back...nothing.

Papa's letters to Reimer had been full of vitriol over Daniel's decision to marry Olivia. Page after page had descended into a paternal lament for a misguided boy, though at the time, Daniel had scoffed at his papa's misgivings.

"Kirsten, might we talk for a moment?" Daniel asked.

For if Daniel allowed his intended to take him into the bedroom, she'd expect intimate attentions from him he was in no condition to provide.

She came back down the stairs halfway and took a seat on a carpeted riser.

"Talk? Of course." Not a very cheering sort of "of course."

Daniel lowered himself beside her halfway up the staircase. "How are you, my dear?"

He'd overslept, nearly been late to services, and then been accosted by well-wishers on the church steps. Through the service he'd been distracted, and in the absence of a curate, he'd been responsible for tidying up after the service.

"I am engaged to be married," Kirsten said. "Though my fiancé has gone off to London and I'm not sure when he'll come back to me. I've missed him awfully."

How Daniel loved her honesty.

He put an arm around Kirsten's shoulders. "I've always had a distaste for London. My father abhorred the place, with great wealth flaunting its opulence in the face of great poverty, but this time…London is not all bad."

Daniel's unease originated in that moment when he'd been strolling along beside the earl on a pleasant afternoon, aglow from meeting Howley, and then in an instant, the greening plane trees, the well-dressed gentlemen strolling by, the pots of pansies festooning the pubs and stoops—all dross.

If Olivia were alive…

Maybe that's what kept Daniel from going up the stairs with Kirsten. Making love with Kirsten threatened to descend from a joyous anticipation of vows to the sin of adultery. Some traditions preached that a man would be better off dead than an adulterer.

And from there, every other doubt had found a toehold on Daniel's mind.

"London does include great wealth and great poverty," Kirsten said. "I suppose I'm used to it, to the charity and the venery, the beauty and the squalor. Did it upset you?"

Her question encompassed both the social chasm between a country vicar and an earl's daughter, and the bridge that love had formed, because Daniel could answer her honestly.

"In Little Weldon, I mucked Beelzebub's stall and turned him out with the milch cow. I limed the jakes. I pounded loose shingles back in place. I was only nominally a gentleman, Kirsten. What was that country vicar doing, trotting around in Bond Street tailoring and bowing to the Bishop of London?"

She laced an arm around his waist. "In this past week, I've beaten rugs, washed dishes by the score, and polished the sideboard and half the wainscoting in the house. I've enjoyed the work, Daniel. Perhaps I'm only nominally a lady."

Kirsten's answer helped but didn't entirely settle him.

"Would you be very offended if we did not make use of the bedroom today?" Daniel asked.

She rested her head against his shoulder. "You're tired and out of sorts and my family in the Seasonal whirl would be enough to overset anybody. Then too, you were cavorting with bishops. I have a suggestion."

"Suggest away."

"Why don't we eschew the bedroom until our wedding night? Build up some anticipation, some longing for the pleasures we've indulged in so frequently in recent weeks? I've dreamed of you, Daniel. Lovely, naughty dreams that have given me all sorts of ideas."

He hadn't dreamed of Kirsten. He'd had the nightmares again, of being married to Olivia. Nightmares of his father lecturing him about meekness and a godly heart in a helpmeet.

"My immediate response is to reject this idea of yours," Daniel said. "I rather like anticipating vows with you, Lady Kirsten." Or he had liked it—liked it a lot, today's demurrer notwithstanding.

Kirsten used her free hand to apply a gentle, wifely pressure to his privy parts, and the man-beast in Daniel enjoyed it. A relief, that—and a bewilderment.

"I've wallowed in the bliss of anticipating our vows," Kirsten said. "But I'd also like for our wedding night to be special."

"Our wedding night will be very special," Daniel said. "Your idea has merit, in that regard." And in others, because another part of Daniel, not the pawing, snorting fiancé part, was relieved—at least for the moment—to be spared the intimacy of the bedroom.

A firm rap on the front door forestalled further conversation on any topic.

"Who could be calling here?" Kirsten said, slipping free of Daniel's embrace. "If it's George and Elsie, then they have a fine nerve, interrupting our inspection of the curtains."

Kirsten opened the door, and there stood Letty and her viscount, attired in their Sunday finery. Fairly held a wooden box about the right size to safeguard a woman's jewelry, carved leaves and flowers twining about the sides.

"Hello," Kirsten said. "You find us quite unprepared for visitors, but do come in. We do have furniture in the formal parlor, though refreshment will be in short supply."

Letty stepped over the threshold and kissed Kirsten's cheek. "You must forgive us. Fairly said we ought not to try here, but should go straight to Belle Maison, though Lady Susannah writes that you're biding with your brother George and his household was yet farther—"

"Letty, they don't care about that," Fairly said, nudging past his wife. "We'll just drop off the spices and be on our way, shall we?"

Daniel came down the stairs. "You are our first visitors, and we're pleased to welcome you." Pleased that family should come to call uninvited, country style, and not by way of all the folded, bent, embossed cards used in Town.

"Let's find a place for this in the kitchen, shall we?" Kirsten said to Letty when the greetings were dispensed with and the spice box had been admired. The ladies bustled off, remarking on the changes to the old house, leaving Daniel in the company of his brother-in-law.

"Banks, you're looking well. Danny appears to

be thriving, and Lady Kirsten makes a wonderful fiancée," Fairly said, drawing Daniel out to the shaded porch. "Listen well, for I'm about to violate a marital confidence. You're contemplating matrimony, and a man on his way up the church aisle should be in possession of all the facts."

"Fairly, this drama isn't like you." Which only added to Daniel's unease.

"The ladies will soon rejoin us, and what I have to say is for your ears only. I sent a man north to ensure the fair Olivia was biding in the loving embrace of her family. Turns out, she left Yorkshire before Christmas, well before."

Another swallow, or perhaps the same one, came flitting through the porch eaves.

"Olivia lied about her whereabouts," Daniel said with a calm he didn't feel. "I suspected as much when she stopped acknowledging the funds I sent her."

Though Daniel hadn't admitted his suspicions even to himself. Olivia lied, that was what Olivia did. She could easily have had the funds forwarded to her by an obliging family member.

Daniel tugged Fairly a few steps to the left, so he wouldn't stand directly beneath the swallow.

"She came south, to London," Fairly went on, oblivious to the bird, "and took up residence in the home of Bertrand Carmichael."

"This is not news, Fairly. Carmichael was a relation of hers." Who had not once called upon Olivia in Little Weldon, that Daniel knew of.

"Pay attention, Banks. No physician has been summoned to Carmichael's household since the first of the year. *I* am a physician, and I'm still connected to the medical men in London. I've had Carmichael's staff discreetly interviewed, over a pint at the pub, in the mews, and so forth. They do not recall anybody suffering illness, but as of last week, they're heartily sick of Carmichael's ladybird."

This is not happening. This is not happening.

"Fairly, calm yourself. I've been in communication with my successor at Little Weldon. He assures me a burial service was held in Great Weldon for the late Olivia Banks. Carmichael has done well for himself, he's not married, and he's a London gentleman. Why shouldn't he have a ladybird?"

At mention of the word "bird," the damned swallow hopped along the rafter to once again perch over Fairly's head.

"Have you received an accounting from Carmichael of the expenses?" Fairly asked.

Death was a business. Everything, from the ringing of the church bells to the graveside recitations of Scripture, to the coffin, to the shroud, came at a cost.

"I have not," Daniel said. "Carmichael was Olivia's cousin, well fixed, and should he send me such an accounting, I would pay it. I have received no such correspondence." Daniel gestured above, to the bird. "I don't trust that one. You'd best step aside."

Fairly moved away to lean a hip on the porch railing, out of range of loose-boweled birds.

"Bigamy is a felony, Banks. Letty could not bear for you or Danny to endure any more upheaval."

To say nothing of the upheaval to Kirsten. "I've kept Carmichael's sealed missive to me," Daniel said.

"I've kept the letter from the vicar in Little Weldon confirming a burial. If Olivia is not dead, then she has done us both a courtesy by this elaborate charade. She can move on with her life, and so can I."

"To commit bigamy."

"Olivia is dead." A fervent wish, not a certainty. What was *wrong* with him? "If it's not too much trouble, I'd like to enlist your aid in procuring a special license."

For now, the need to marry Kirsten had become urgent, the position in the north a new promised land.

Fairly looked like he wanted to argue, but the ladies rejoined them, with Letty occupying the spot beneath the dratted bird.

"He's back," Kirsten said, scowling at the bird. "I'd move, your ladyship. That bird, or one very like him, was most disrespectful of Daniel's altar."

Letty stepped over to her husband's side, just as the bird again let loose, then flew off across the green.

❧

"The banns! The banns! They've read the banns!" Olivia crowed.

Bertrand had anticipated that the news would please her, but Olivia was not merely pleased. She was in transports, delighted, as suffused with glee as a mama whose daughter had just received a marriage proposal from a young, handsome, wealthy duke.

"They're not wed yet, Olivia," Bertrand said, coming around his desk to snatch back the missive that had come from Bertrand's eyes and ears in Haddondale.

Olivia appropriated Bertrand's seat behind the desk. "But they will be married soon, and then what choice will Daniel have? He either delivers a fat sum into my hands or he goes to prison for bigamy. Daniel would do quite well in a monk's cell, but he'll not bring scandal to the boy or give up his vocation."

Rather than take a seat before the desk like a supplicant, Bertrand pretended to peruse a volume on economics by the late Adam Smith.

"For a woman who hasn't seen her husband in nearly a year, you profess to know Banks quite well."

Bertrand opened his tome to a random page: *Civil government, so far as it is instituted for the security of property, is in reality instituted for the defence of the rich against the poor…*

Mr. Smith had never encountered the likes of Olivia Banks, to whom even celestial law had no significance.

"I lived in that wretched vicarage for years with Daniel Banks," Olivia shot back, taking a quill from the silver standish. She waved the end of the feather across her chin, back and forth, back and forth.

She was developing a bit of excess around that chin.

"Daniel treasures nothing and no one as much as he does his calling," Olivia went on, "and he'll beggar himself to keep it. Without the boy, the church is all he has."

Banks more or less had the boy. Bertrand had kept that information, contained in an earlier epistle, to himself. Young Danny was being raised not by the wealthy viscount, but by the lowly vicar, and was apparently happier for it.

"Olivia, you underestimate the allies Banks is gathering in Kent," Bertrand said, more for the pleasure of twisting Olivia's tail than anything else. "He's marrying the sister of an earl, and earls take a dim view of fraud, blackmail, and bigamy."

Bertrand tucked the note from Haddondale between leaves of the book and put Mr. Smith back on the shelf, for the man's prose was enough to muddle a mostly honest merchant on a fine, sunny morning.

"The Quality cannot abide scandal," Olivia said with great certainty for one who'd never shared a ballroom with the gossiping, romping, naughty Quality. "But they'll never know what I'm about. Daniel wouldn't ask for help from any but his precious, everlasting God, and look where that's landed him. No wife, no son, another village church that smells of mud, manure, and despair."

Olivia had to be the meanest person Bertrand had ever encountered, to take such glee in another's suffering. Woe unto Bertrand, though, that meanness had the power to fascinate, particularly when he held her in his arms and let a little of his own base nature free.

Bertrand drew Olivia to her feet. "So you'll let Banks march up the aisle, take a bride, and engage in felonies for the sake of your own material gain?"

"I'll strew rose petals in his path," Olivia said, "and bellow the recessional hymn from the rafters. I've waited too long for this, Bertrand."

Bertrand used his superior height and strength to back Olivia against the desk. "I've waited too long too, Olivia. It's the servants' half day, and we have privacy, and I'm done waiting."

She could fume, pout, and carry on like a thespian, but Bertrand was certain Olivia liked the intimacies they shared. She liked the pleasure, of which, to be fair, she'd known little, but she also fancied that he sought only her for his satisfaction, that his desire was uniquely for her.

Bertrand did not disabuse Olivia of the notion, though she was in error. The rosy-cheeked dairymaid who came around every other day could be persuaded to step over to the mews and provide a service in addition to the milk she brought. The housemaid was a lusty little baggage, and when Bertrand went out of an evening, he enjoyed the entertainments available to any gentleman of means.

"Why do you wear so many skirts?" he muttered, shoving Olivia back to perch on his desk. "I buy you enough nightgowns and night robes that you need never dress at all."

"I like my pretty skirts," she said. "I do not like *you* when you're in rut."

"Yes, you do, but you abhor that I can give you pleasure you can't give yourself." Because, village lass that she was at heart, Olivia had never guessed that women could commit a version of the sin of Onan as easily as men could.

"Any man—"

He kissed her, though the silence wouldn't last long enough for him to get his falls undone. Arguing with Olivia was stimulating—to them both.

"Not any man," Bertrand said, shoving her skirts aside and wedging himself between her pale, dimpled knees. "Do you know what I like? I like that Banks can't have you and I can. Marry me, Olivia, and we'll move to the north."

He joined his body to hers none too gently, which she also seemed to both crave and resent.

"Marriage is for fools," Olivia hissed, vising her legs around his flanks. "Marriage is for women with no ambition, no—"

He silenced her with hard, steady thrusting, though she would return to her vitriol and scheming before her skirts were back over her ankles. Olivia was relentlessly self-interested, devious, and in her venery, both pathetic and magnificent.

"You like this," Bertrand rasped. "Say it."

"Go to hell."

The stupid, tenderhearted village lad offered her no more argument, for while they fornicated on the hard surface of his desk, that boy longed to make love to this woman. Longed to give her his name and undo all the hurt and meanness life had thrown at her too hard and too early.

Olivia was flint-hearted and desperate for independent means because life had made her that way. As she clawed at Bertrand's back and the desk creaked beneath her weight, a last, troubling thought battled its way past his rising desire:

If Olivia would jeopardize the happiness of a child and of a vicar of spotless moral character, what would she do to that besotted village lad, should she realize his infatuation had never died?

≪≫

Kirsten sat in the back of the classroom, watching Daniel explain the Acts of Union to six rapt little boys. He made the joining of Scotland and England into one nation a colorful tale of heroes and villains, clever boys turned into clever men, and battles fought for motivations both base and noble.

"So Scotland couldn't trade with the colonies or Canada or India or anywhere?" Matthias asked.

"The English ports were closed to the Scots," Daniel said, "and yet Scotland needed desperately to trade with the larger world. Rather than fight for that privilege, the Scots who had the power to agree accepted the Acts of Union."

This was a somewhat nontraditional view of the matter, though Kirsten suspected Daniel's rendering was more honest than the version she'd been given.

Frank raised a hand. "That's like when Thomas sits on somebody. He's not beating us, so we can't say he's been fighting, but it *is* fighting without fists."

"Danny, what do you think?" Daniel asked.

"If I were Scotland, I wouldn't like this Union, and if I were England, I wouldn't trust it."

A concise summary of much of British history. Daniel stopped pacing the front of the room as his focus lit on Kirsten. She'd slipped in, not wanting to disturb the magic that happened when Daniel was among his scholars.

"Gentlemen, we have a visitor," Daniel said.

The boys followed his gaze and rose as one. "Good day, Lady Kirsten." They bowed like a patrol on maneuvers from the school of good manners.

Kirsten curtsied back, as gracefully as if she were in the presence of six little dukes.

"Gentlemen, good day. I'm impressed by your grasp of British history. In the tradition of true scholarship, you seem to be enjoying your lessons."

They beamed at one another self-consciously. Thomas's ears turned red, and Daniel looked a little bashful too.

"I'm sorry to interrupt," Kirsten went on, "but might I borrow Mr. Banks for a few moments? I left some biscuits in the kitchen, and it's nearly time for your snack."

Not a boy moved. They remained facing Kirsten, six juvenile pillars of longing and self-restraint.

"Off you go, gentlemen," Daniel said. "Don't forget to wash your hands and give thanks."

To their credit, the boys' decorum endured until they reached the door, at which point the jostling began, and once they gained the corridor, their footsteps beat a galloping tattoo in the direction of the kitchen.

"They're hungry," Kirsten said as Daniel sauntered to the back of the room.

"They're *always* hungry," he replied, lashes lowering. "I'm hungry too." He kissed Kirsten's cheek lingeringly and just like that, desire pooled low in her belly.

"I'm starving," she said, lashing her arms around him and seizing his mouth. Some idiot had declared a moratorium on anticipating the vows, but Kirsten felt exactly like that horde of little boys—self-restraint barely winning the fight against instinct.

Daniel smiled against her lips. "You've been missing me?"

She smacked his chest, then let her hand slide south. "Rotten man. Of course I've been missing you. I cannot wait for the time when I can sleep beside you through the night, though I doubt we'll get much rest."

She had news, news a stronger woman might keep to herself, though Kirsten was too *happy* to strive for reticence. All the biscuits in the world had been stuffed in her pockets, and the best pony in the barn was hers forever.

Now that she and Daniel had privacy, though, all her blunt, forthright speech deserted her.

"I long for those nights as well," Daniel said, his arms slipping from her waist. "Reimer will be down from Town the day after tomorrow. Your brothers Nicholas, Beckman, and Ethan will accompany him."

Leah had conveyed the same information in a recent epistle. In a flurry of letters, Kirsten had excused her sisters from attending the wedding, and Della at least had expressed her thanks.

"And on Saturday we'll be married," Kirsten said.

When Daniel ought to have kissed her in agreement, he instead wandered off to the front of the room and picked up the felt cloth used to erase the large slate positioned where a portrait of the old earl had once hung.

"And on Saturday," Daniel said, scrubbing away at the Acts of Union, "we'll be married."

His words held a distance, the same distance he'd maintained when he and Kirsten had first met. Polite, kind, mannerly, but fundamentally cool.

Kirsten had watched the boys' riding lesson on Tuesday and captained a cricket team yesterday. In another hour and a half, she'd join the boys for tea while Daniel put the finishing touches on the Sunday sermon.

For all Daniel had been at her side at both the stable

and the cricket pitch, he had in some regard already accepted a position in the far, chilly north.

"What's wrong?" Kirsten asked, striding after him.

His felt paused before the *U* in *Union*. "Nothing is wrong. I'm looking forward to marriage, the same as you are." *Union* was obliterated with a vigorous pass of Daniel's hand.

Alarms went off in Kirsten's heart, the same alarms she'd been trying to ignore since Daniel had returned from Town.

"Daniel Banks, look at me."

He did, after a moment's stillness facing the blank slate. He set aside the cloth, dusted his hands, put them behind his back, and turned.

His eyes held the old bleakness, the old misery and forbearance.

"If marrying me is an exercise in martyrdom, Daniel, you may have your ring back." Kirsten spoke from fear, also from the certainty that something was terribly amiss and Daniel would bear it alone unless she knocked the problem loose from his grasp.

"Does one procure a special license in anticipation of martyrdom?" Daniel asked. The question was civil, not enraged, not even quietly affronted.

"You are not being honest with me," Kirsten said, taking up the felt and beating it against the side of Daniel's desk. Dust flew in all directions, much like the particles of Kirsten's happiness.

"I love you," Daniel said, taking the cloth from her hand. "That is the truth. That will always be the truth. I love you and want only to be by your side for the rest of my life. In sickness and in health, in good times and bad, forsaking all others, as long as we both shall live."

"You mean that." The truth was in his eyes, in the gravity of his expression. "Then tell me the rest of it, Daniel Banks, because I'm nearly certain that we're the recipients of a miracle. If you do not look forward to becoming a papa as much as I look forward to bearing your children, I fear it's too late to register a complaint now."

Hardly the declaration Kirsten had meant to make, but she'd got his attention.

He took both her hands in a firm grip. "What are you saying?"

Now they were to deal in truths. An encouraging development.

"I strongly suspect, and the midwife has confirmed, I'm carrying a child, Daniel. Our child."

For a moment, he had no reaction, not even a blink. He merely regarded her. "You would never dissemble about such a thing."

A statement of the obvious. Kirsten waited, disappointment gnawing at her, for Daniel evinced no jubilation, no thanksgiving.

No joy.

"Daniel, if you do not right this minute tell me what's wrong, I will prevail on Beckman or Ethan to make a place for me in their households. Ethan has in-laws far to the north and properties on the Continent. Beckman knows people all over the world. You and I are either marrying, or we're not."

Sending Kirsten's previous fiancés on their way had been a mere inconvenience compared to the terror

Kirsten battled now. Daniel Banks was the man she loved, the man she'd given her heart to.

Daniel sank slowly before her, until he was kneeling at her feet, his cheek pressed against her middle. "There's to be a *child*?"

Finally. "It's very early days, and I may not carry well, but yes. The signs point in that direction." She, who had cast-iron digestion, was frequently queasy. She was drowsy at odd moments, she was…two weeks *late*. "I might well have already conceived."

A word Kirsten had barely been able to wrap her mind around. A beautiful word, a miracle, and yet, for all the awe in his voice, Daniel was not rejoicing.

He stroked a hand over her belly. "Merciful everlasting Powers, a *child*. A child of ours. *Unto us, a child is born.*"

Kirsten's mind seized on three thoughts. First, the boys would be back in a few minutes; second, Daniel *was* glad, but he was troubled too. Third…

"You mentioned a special license, Daniel. Shall we discuss that?"

He rose in one lithe movement, his expression impossible to read. "Yes, we must discuss that at the very least. Though, my lady, I fear the discussion will not be at all happy."

Seventeen

"MATTIE, DON'T YOU WANT YOUR BISCUITS?" Danny asked.

They sat around their table, the one in the kitchen where breakfast, lunch, and snacks were consumed. At night they had to eat upstairs, and manners were expected. Downstairs was exclusively for appeasing hunger, though Digby tried at all times to use his manners.

"You lot can have my biscuits," Mattie said, swiping at his milk mustache with his sleeve. "What's Lady Kirsten doing here early?"

Frank paused halfway through a ginger biscuit. "She's come by to blow—"

Thomas snatched the uneaten part of the biscuit. "If you say the word *ground-sills*, I will sit on you until it's time to up the swans."

Digby interceded, which seemed to be his lot lately. "I looked it up. A ground-sill is like a windowsill, but it's the bottom timber of a house's foundation. Perhaps blowing the ground-sills has to do with housecleaning."

Papa had explained that it had nothing whatsoever to do with housecleaning, proving once again that the right papa was a handy fellow to have about.

"Lady Kirsten sets a lot of store by her housekeeping," Frank conceded.

That she did. A few more biscuits disappeared. Cook came by with the pitcher of milk and topped up everybody's glass.

"They're soon to be married," Fred said. "Lady Kirsten has been fixing up the vicarage, and we'll all live together there. They've even built on to the stable to have room for our ponies."

"The vicarage used to stink," Digby said. "Old Vicar smoked pipes and had gas."

Which, of course, provoked snickers from the other boys, and a disapproving glower from Cook.

"I have gas too," Frank said, suiting actions to words despite Cook's hovering presence. Frank had a God-given gift when it came to flatulence, though he never demonstrated his talent in Lady Kirsten's presence.

Matthias abruptly rose and shoved at his glasses. "I'll be in the stable. If you think we're all moving to the vicarage, you're daft. By Swan Upping, you'll be packing for Eaton, where floggings are regular and biscuits don't exist."

He stomped out the back door, though a skinny little fellow like Matthias didn't have much of a stomp.

"What's wrong with him, Tom?" Frank asked. "He's become a wretched grouch who can't do his lessons."

"Maybe you should sit on him," Fred suggested, his tone genuinely helpful.

"Something is sitting on him," Thomas said. "He

gets up at night and goes down to the schoolroom. I've no clue what he's about there."

Matthias worked at his lessons, for Digby and Danny had followed him too. By the light of a single meager candle, Matthias stared at his slate and peered at his books, holding them so close to his nose it was a wonder he could read them at all.

"Mattie's not stupid," Danny said, "but he's surely not happy either."

And that bothered them all. A few months ago, Thomas alone might have spared a care for his troubled brother, but since then, they'd become friends and fellow scholars, and if one of them suffered, they all felt his pain.

"We'll help him," Digby said. "We'll get Ralph to help, and Vicar, and Lady Kirsten. Mattie's not stupid, and we're his friends, so we'll help him."

Thomas hoisted his mug of milk. "We'll help him."

They bumped mugs, just like the fellows Vicar had told them about who drew their swords and pledged great oaths, swords in the air.

"We'll help him," Frank echoed, "but we won't let his biscuits go to waste either."

A child. A brother or sister for Danny, a cousin to Letty's children. A child, the most tangible, glorious, irrefutable, troublesome evidence of a man and woman's intimate regard for each other.

Joy beat through Daniel on the heels of incredulity. He and Kirsten might become parents together—

Of a *bastard* child, if Olivia were alive.

"So why the special license?" Kirsten asked, crossing the room to open a window. The afternoon had grown warm enough that fresh air in the classroom was warranted.

"I'm not sure," Daniel said. "A hunch. I'm reluctant to tell you what my hunch is based on."

"Just say it, Daniel. We are all but man and wife, and weathering life's vicissitudes together is one of the privileges of the wedded state."

This was Lady Kirsten Haddonfield, purveyor of blunt truths, also the woman who'd saved Daniel's life. He simply said what had haunted him for the past week.

"I fear Olivia is alive."

Fear was one word, but rage and dread came into it too. Snippets of Scripture had plagued Daniel all week. *Thou shalt not commit adultery* figured prominently among them. *Thou shalt not kill* made the occasional appearance as well.

Kirsten might—had she been the helpful sort—have laughed heartily and told Daniel he needed more rest. She might have shrugged, she might have laid her hand to his forehead to see if fever plagued him.

But Kirsten was the honest sort. "Why do you think a woman dead and buried is yet alive?" She crossed her arms and took a perch on the table that held the terrarium, six pots of seeded acorns, and a globe.

Nowhere for Daniel to sit beside her, so he leaned against a corner of his desk.

"A vicar hears all the stories that touch on the graveyard," he said. "Death is not that difficult to fake. People do it all the time, to elude debts, the law, spouses of whom they've grown weary, or intolerable apprentice situations."

Kirsten reached into the terrarium and lifted out the toad of the week. Each Monday after lessons, Daniel took the boys on a biology walk. If a toad crossed their paths, the toad was subjected to the hospitality of the terrarium for one week, then released on Friday.

In honor of the Conqueror, who'd known a thing or two about being held hostage, the toad—for his week of captivity—was always named William.

"You thought you saw Olivia in Town," Kirsten said, running a finger over the toad's brown speckled head. "Or somebody very like her."

"I *felt* that I saw her." Daniel wondered if they'd have a boy, because a woman who could pet toads surely had the mettle to raise boys. "My body recognized that woman as the same person who'd taken shameless advantage of me, my sister, and Danny."

"Cold shivers?" Kirsten asked. "An awful feeling in the vitals, a sense that you couldn't get your breath? That's what I felt the first time I spotted Arthur Morton with his new wife—and the entire ballroom was watching me from behind their fans and snuffboxes."

The toad gave a toady chirp, perhaps of pleasure, while Daniel's world became a shambles.

"There's more," Daniel said, envying a dratted toad. "Fairly has made inquiries, and nobody recalls a woman falling ill in Bertrand Carmichael's home earlier this year. Carmichael has, however, taken in a ladybird who is difficult to please. I sent a missive to Fairly asking that he obtain the ladybird's description."

Kirsten lifted the toad to her cheek, as if she'd confide in it. "And?"

"A note arrived earlier today confirming that she is blond and blue-eyed."

"Half the women in England are blond and blue-eyed."

The other half were not. "I lived with Olivia for years, Kirsten, and she is devious enough to do this. She sowed discontent among the women of the parish, disparaged me behind my back, treated Danny ill, and all with a sweet expression at the church steps and an air of pious industry in the manse. She is not to be trusted."

Daniel rose, because the desk made a hard, awkward perch, and the present tense in reference to Olivia was hell all over again.

"And if she is alive," Kirsten said, "she is your lawfully wedded wife. We're back where we started, Daniel."

No, they were far worse off, for they'd consummated their love with the most wonderful and disastrous results possible.

"Olivia is my wife, if she is alive."

The words made him ill, sick of heart, mind, soul, and strength.

Kirsten gave the toad a final caress to its knobby brow and put it back among the dead leaves, twigs, and pond muck.

"I love you, Daniel, and if the situation involved only you and me, I'd march into London, find this woman, and have my brother institute divorce proceedings. She's committing adultery with Mr. Carmichael, and for that you could divorce her."

While a woman could not divorce a wandering

husband on the same grounds. Daniel had come across that fact in last night's research in the Belle Maison library.

"The situation involves Danny and possibly another innocent," Daniel said. "Divorce will cost me my ability to support any family at all." Also his vocation, and what did one do, as a vicar without a pulpit?

Kirsten rose and smoothed her hand over her waist. "If you don't pursue a divorce, *our* child will be a bastard, unless of course I can locate some fellow in the next eight months willing to take on used goods. Della's and Susannah's prospects demand I at least consider that course in conjunction with a remove to parts distant."

Her family had the means to send her to parts very distant, while Daniel had only the living from his present post and a few pounds in reserve.

Insight kicked Daniel hard in the gut, for Letty had given up her son to be raised by others. When faced with the same prospect—even when faced with returning the boy to his very mother—Daniel's whole being rebelled.

"I cannot allow you to marry another man, who would raise my child as his own." Daniel could not consider it, not for the child, not for Kirsten, not for himself.

Kirsten's countenance had lost all animation. She was once again the testy, withdrawn, self-reliant creature whom he'd met at the end of a long, frigid ride.

"Daniel, this is not your fault nor my fault, but most of all, this situation is not the fault of the child we've conceived. I love you, but this child deserves my entire consideration in the conundrum we face. I will not make a bigamist of you."

The boys would be back any moment, and Kirsten was hoisting sail to leave the classroom, and possibly to leave Daniel's life.

Though he was tempted to remain silent, Daniel gave her the rest of it.

"It's worse than that," he said. "If I marry you, I become a bigamist in expectation of further blackmail from my—from Olivia. She carried on her scheme with Letty for years, and once this child arrives, she'll never let up."

There, the entire ugly, sordid, hopeless truth lay between Daniel and the woman he loved. Had Olivia walked through the door that instant, Daniel would have done her a serious injury.

At least. And he would have enjoyed the violence, despite vengeance being the Almighty's exclusive province.

Kirsten remained where she was, two yards and a world of impossibilities away, a crease furrowing her brow. She took two steps toward the door, came past the desk assigned to Danny, and put her arms around Daniel.

The sensation of her embrace was homecoming, torment, Daniel's every hope, and his last prayer.

"You were my first miracle, Daniel," she said, smoothing her hand over his cravat. "I'd resigned myself to being the crotchety auntie, the outspoken relation nobody really wanted to invite for a visit. Then you came along, undaunted by my lack of charm, unwilling to be put off by a few graceless comments. I love you."

He kept the embrace loose by force of will. "I love you too." Wholly, entirely, forever.

"Then we learn that we've very likely conceived a new life. That's another miracle, and I will never be anything but grateful for it, as much as I fear consequences to the child."

Endless, miserable consequences.

Now came the "but," the pragmatic rejection, the letting go. Kirsten was strong enough to make the right, selfless choice for their child. Daniel kissed his beloved one last time before those words were spoken.

"Say the rest of it," he whispered. "Say the difficult words you've always been relied on to say, Kirsten, for if those words are good-bye, I cannot utter them."

"You are a good man," she said, giving Daniel more of her weight. "You're brilliant with the boys, devoted to Danny, sincere in your vocation, and deserving of some happiness."

Which he'd never have without her. "And?"

"And we simply need another miracle, Daniel, or something very close to it."

❧

"Lady Kirsten is your sister, and Banks is my brother," Fairly said. He'd ridden the distance to Town at Letty's demand and at the prodding of his own conscience.

"Banks is your brother by marriage," the Earl of Bellefonte replied, leading an enormous gelding from its stall. Nicholas did not sound happy to be the repository of Fairly's confidences, but then dear Nicholas was seldom happy when confined to Town.

Fairly had accosted him in the mews behind the Bellefonte town house, which meant Lady Kirsten's sisters need not know of his visit.

"You're sure this Olivia person is alive?" Bellefonte asked, securing the horse into cross ties.

"I sent a boy with a talent for sketching to lurk in Carmichael's garden," Fairly said. "He made a likeness, and Letty positively identified the woman as Olivia Banks."

Bellefonte slung an arm over the horse's withers and leaned against the horse, whose dimensions looked merely normal next to the earl.

"This is messy," Bellefonte said. "Kirsten has had enough of messes."

That Bellefonte would be protective was a foregone conclusion. "Banks has had enough of messes as well." To say nothing of Letty, the boy, and Fairly himself.

Possibilities hung in the air, some of them gratifyingly violent.

A door scraped open down the barn aisle and Ladies Susannah and Della came bustling in, attired for riding.

"Damn." Bellefonte's curse was muttered loudly enough for only Fairly to hear it.

"Kirsten has had enough of you fellows arranging her life," Lady Della said, as if she'd overheard the entire exchange. "Enough of others selecting her suitors and generally meddling. What mischief are you two getting up to?"

"Don't think to dissemble," Lady Susannah added. "Or we'll tell Leah and Letty."

Fairly watched as Bellefonte, in the time it took a horse to swish its tail, sorted through options. Charm, guile, bluster...

Not with these two.

"We have reason to believe Lady Kirsten and

Mr. Banks are facing a contretemps with few good options," Fairly said. "We're open to suggestions, but this is perhaps not the place to air them."

Bellefonte released the horse from its cross ties. "My thoughts exactly. I can hack in the park anytime, but familial discussions of fraud, death, bigamy, and mayhem only come along once a week or so."

His lordship put the gelding back in its loose box, settled an arm around each sister, and escorted them to the garden, where refreshments were ordered and the countess summoned to join the discussion.

"Divorce is not a miracle," Daniel said to the woman in his arms. "Divorce will cost me my calling, and with it, my ability to provide for you and the children. Divorce will immerse your entire family in scandal, to say nothing of the consequence to your sisters and to the children."

Daniel included his scholars among that number, for they expected him to set a standard of attainable honor, the same as he expected of himself.

Kirsten drew away. "Two jilted fiancés immersed me in scandal, and five years later, I'm yet able to find meaning in life and take joy in my blessings. Scandal is preferable to hypocrisy, blackmail, and inflicting illegitimacy on a child."

The door opened, revealing five small boys prepared to resume their study of the Acts of Union. Ralph stood behind them, trying to look as if he hadn't overheard a single word. Matthias alone was unaccounted for.

"Gentlemen," Lady Kirsten said, "I trust you enjoyed your biscuits. I'll leave you to glean what wisdom you can from Vicar's lectures about the past."

She quit the room at a brisk flounce, serenaded by William's soft croaking.

"Ralph, the boys were discussing the Acts of Union," Daniel said, intent on following his hurt, angry beloved wherever she got off to. "You'll aid them in that pursuit."

Nobody moved to take a seat, nobody left the doorway, through which Daniel intended to charge at a dead run.

"You should clean your boots, sir," Digby said.

"Clean my—?" Daniel advocated boot cleaning to facilitate contemplation of a misstep.

"He's right, Papa," Danny said. Danny never called him Papa in the classroom, only sir. "Or go for a walk in nature."

Another of Daniel's famous prescriptions for upset fellows.

"Or go for a ride on Beelzebub," Thomas suggested helpfully. "A gentleman never upsets a lady."

For pity's perishing sake. Scolded by a lot of children, *and they were right*.

"I know you mean well," Daniel said, "but you don't understand. The situation is complicated."

The William of the Week croaked, which appeared to be all the support Daniel would get.

"Her ladyship was a trifle upset," Ralph ventured. "To be expected when the nuptials are in the offing. Come on, you lot. To your desks."

The nuptials were apparently *not* in the offing.

"Tell Beelzebub to be a good boy," Danny added kindly.

"I'll do that," Daniel said, marching for the door. "I'll do exactly that."

When Daniel reached the garden, Kirsten was nowhere to be seen, so he trotted to the stable, where again, her ladyship was not to be found. The head groom, the only human life in sight, was leading Loki to the trough.

"Alfrydd, have you seen Lady Kirsten?"

"I have not, Mr. Banks, but Master Matthias has come for a visit and the boy is in quite a taking."

Confound this day. Matthias had been in a taking for weeks. "If Lady Kirsten should ask to have her horse saddled, please detain her until I join her. Where's the lad?" For Daniel was Matthias's vicar as well as his teacher, and would not abandon the boy to his misery.

"Master Matthias be in the mare's stall, but I'm pretending I haven't seen him. Crying his heart out again, poor lad."

"Please do *not* let Lady Kirsten leave without speaking to me," Daniel said, heading for the barn.

Alfrydd saluted, though Daniel knew very well that Kirsten would go where she pleased and do as she pleased. He first looked for Matthias in Freya's stall, but the pony was contentedly munching hay and spared her visitor only the briefest uninterested glance.

Which left—Buttercup?

Across the aisle, the earl's preferred riding horse was recumbent in the straw, a skinny boy affixed to her neck like a particularly large, unhappy cocklebur. Doubtless the mare missed her earl, or perhaps she was simply a kind equine soul.

"I hate being a scholar," Matthias wailed softly. "I hate Fridays, and I hate the stupid lessons. I hate my stupid self."

If the horse noticed Daniel, she might well stand and step on her visitor. But then she'd tolerated Matthias's intrusion on her solitude placidly enough.

"Matthias, I'm coming in," Daniel said.

"Go away! I hate you too!"

Platitudes about hatred eroding the soul of the one who carried it sprang to Daniel's lips, but of what use were platitudes when a heart was breaking?

"So you've given up on me?" Daniel asked, sliding down the stall wall near the mare's head. She sniffed at his knee and tolerated a scratch to her forehead.

"I hate everything," Matthias said with less drama, more misery. "I'm stupid and I wish I never had to study anything ever again. Papa says I'll be the world's oldest boot boy if I don't join the N-Navy."

"Do you want to join the Navy?"

For the first time, Matthias looked at Daniel. "You'd send me *away*?"

"Never. You are one of my scholars," Daniel said, resisting the urge to hug the stuffing out of the poor child, "and you are a very bright boy. I simply haven't found the best way to teach you yet. You should be upset with me, Matthias, not with yourself. You're trying your very, very hardest, and that's all God, your papa, or anybody can expect of you."

Though sometimes a fellow's best efforts and heart-felt dreams only resulted in a great, stinking muddle.

"I'm good at French," Matthias said, stroking a hand over the mare's coarse mane.

He was good at French *recitation*. "You have an excellent accent, better than any boy I've taught your age. You've also learned the royal succession more quickly than any other boy."

"But I'm stupid. Papa says so."

Always helpful, when a father had nothing but criticism for his son. "I say you're not. Where are your glasses, Master Mattie?"

The use of the boy's nickname provoked a brief lift at the corners of his lips, followed by a scowl.

"I lost them. They're here somewhere, but I hate them too."

"You're a man of consistent opinions, then. I think our spectacles give us a scholarly air," Daniel said, visually searching through the straw. When the child's temper faded, he'd become hysterical if he couldn't find his glasses.

"You hardly ever wear yours," Matthias replied, brushing his hand through the straw near the mare's knobby knees. "I'm to wear mine all the time."

"I wear mine only when the lighting is low or my eyes are tired," Daniel said.

"Because they make your head ache?" Matthias asked. He was on his hands and knees, systematically rifling the straw, while the mare, fortunately, lay contented as a dairy cow at her cud.

"Spectacles *prevent* my head from aching," Daniel said, joining the search.

"My head hurts all the time," Matthias muttered, working out another foot from the mare's shoulder. "I wake up with a headache, I go to bed with a headache, and then I get a headache in my belly.

That's because I can't stuff any more lessons in my head."

Daniel grasped the spectacles beneath the straw. "Found 'em. What do you mean, your head aches all the time?"

Matthias sat back on his heels. "Papa says it's because—"

"You're stupid," Daniel finished. "Your papa is wrong, Matthias, though if you tell him I said that, he'll accuse me of disrespect and he'll be right. Does your head hurt now?"

Matthias pressed the heels of his hands against his eyes. "Some. It's worse if we're doing lessons all day. I like cricket and riding, though."

Cricket and riding—*when he took his glasses off.*

Insight came between one heartbeat and the next.

Daniel held up a hand. "Can you see my hand clearly?"

"Of course I can."

He passed the boy the dratted, almighty, everlasting glasses and held out a hand again. "Put them on and tell me what you see."

"I know it's your hand, but it's fuzzy," Matthias said. "Not as fuzzy as the print on a book page, though."

Well, of course. "Matthias, do you recall when we rode out and you were up on Buttercup?"

The boy patted the mare's shoulder. "Yes! She was a very good girl too."

The mare was a saint. "I accidentally kept your glasses until that Monday. Did your head hurt then?"

Matthias's next pat to the mare's shoulder was more thoughtful. "No, sir. I thought that meant I was making room for all the lessons in my head, but it didn't last."

Daniel plucked the glasses from the child's nose, for apparently a moment of grace was to intrude on an otherwise hopeless day.

"Matthias Webber, listen to me. *There's nothing wrong with you.* The glasses are the problem. You simply can't see properly with them on." So simple, and yet so troublesome. Why had Daniel not figured this out sooner? Why had nobody figured this out?

Whatever reaction Daniel expected to his words of absolution, a small, quivering chin wasn't among them.

"I t-told Papa I didn't want to wear his glasses, but he said I was ungrateful."

And told the poor child he was stubborn, pig-headed, and disrespectful too, probably.

Daniel hugged the boy, a swift, tight, half-wrestled embrace followed with a shove to his small shoulder.

"You were right, Matthias, and your papa was mistaken. You can fit as many lessons in your head as any other boy, but *you simply couldn't see.*"

Probably couldn't see his own slate, much less the one at the front of the room that Daniel filled with learned scribblings every day.

"I don't want to be stupid," Matthias said, a tear trickling through the straw dust on his cheek. "I want to be a scholar, like the other fellows."

The mare nuzzled Matthias's hip, a reminder that the occasional pat or scratch was appreciated.

"You'll be a fine scholar," Daniel said, passing the boy a handkerchief Kirsten had embroidered with a pair of doves. "You simply could not see, Matthias. I'll have a word with your father. You're to rest this weekend, at least until your head stops hurting."

Matthias clambered aboard the mare's broad back and leaned down along her neck, which disturbed the horse not at all.

"You've done this before," Daniel said, "paid a call on Lady Buttercup when your spirits were low."

"You tell us to visit the stable when we're not feeling quite the thing, and it works. Buttercup is ever so patient and strong. I visit Freya too."

Daniel slipped the offending glasses into his breast pocket. "If you don't mind, I'd like to bide here for a moment. Back to the house with you, and go in through the kitchen door."

By way of Cook's belief that biscuits and boys were meant to be together.

"May I attend tea with Lady Kirsten?" Matthias asked, balling up the handkerchief and stuffing it in a pocket.

Tea! Daniel had forgotten entirely about Kirsten's obligation to the boys. "Yes, you may, but I'm keeping the glasses."

Matthias slid off the horse and gave her a final pat. "You'll talk to Papa, sir?"

"I'll send him a note this evening and ask him to call on me when lessons are over on Friday." Assuming Daniel still had his post by week's end.

"That's all right, then. Thank you, Vicar!"

Matthias pelted out the door, while Daniel remained sitting in the straw next to the mare, studying a pair of paternal spectacles that had nearly turned a smart boy blind, stupid, and hopeless.

                            ❦

The trays were in readiness—three of them, for six boys could impersonate a plague of locusts—and the teapots were full of a weak gunpowder blend, while Kirsten's nerves would not arrange themselves in any order at all.

Daniel, her Daniel, the father of her child, was very likely still *married*.

"Looks very pretty, milady," the housekeeper said. "You'll make gentlemen of those boys yet."

"Thank you, Mrs. Castle, but they already are gentlemen." That was Daniel's influence, for manners and decorum were only the outward trappings. The kindness and honesty of a true gentleman were best learned by example.

Ralph tapped on the open parlor door. "Beg pardon, milady, Mrs. C. The scholars have come to call, if your ladyship is receiving?"

Why wouldn't—? Oh. Because she'd stormed out of the schoolroom near tears and as upset as she could recall being. Because of Daniel's dratted, scheming, perishing wife.

"I'm always happy to see our scholars, Ralph. By all means, send the children to me."

The boys trooped in—hands scrubbed, hair neatly combed—and arranged themselves on the sofas and chairs. None of the usual jostling took place to sit closer to Kirsten, or to the tea cakes.

"Gentlemen, a pleasure to see you again."

Glances were exchanged among the six boys, but they said nothing as Ralph withdrew.

"Matthias, where are your glasses?" Kirsten asked. He set great store by them and was seldom without them.

"Vicar says the glasses make it harder for me to see. We want to talk to you."

An expensive, elegant pair of spectacles did not make it harder to see. The boy was confused. Kirsten held out the plate of tea cakes, then recalled she'd told the boys that sandwiches always came first.

Not a single boy reached for the sweets.

"Am I in trouble?" Of course Kirsten was in trouble, in the most vulgar sense and in ways she couldn't even name. Daniel had needed her support and she'd run out on him.

"We think you *have* troubles," Danny said, "but nobody will tell us what they are. Papa went to the stable to visit with Beelzebub. You should go visit your mare."

"He's right," Digby said. "And try not to shout at Vicar, for he's the best fellow, and he can't shout back."

"Because he's the vicar," Thomas added. "He mustn't curse either, unless Beelzebub stands on his foot, which would be an accident, of course."

"Maybe," Frank said, nudging the tea cake tray a few inches toward his hostess, "you should apologize."

"Or you could polish your boots," Fred suggested.

"I was very upset when I raised my voice," Kirsten said. "I'm still upset." But how she loved these boys and their earnest care for her and Daniel.

Matthias passed her a handkerchief that looked quite familiar. A pair of doves cooed along one edge.

"Vicar's still in the stable, Lady Kirsten. He doesn't mind when we're upset."

Yes, he did. Daniel minded, he *cared*, he tried to help, and he was still married to that awful woman.

"You're right," Kirsten said, rising. "Mattie, if you'd pour out, and, Digby, you can be in charge of the sandwiches. Thomas, you pass the tray of cakes; Fred, you do the plates; and, Frank, you mind the silver and the linen. Danny, you're in charge of leading the conversation, so try to think of things to talk about besides the weather."

"We'll talk about the Acts of Union," Danny said. "Though they happened more than a hundred years ago."

Kirsten left the scholars in her mama's best parlor, six perfect gentlemen, asking one another to "please pass this" or "would you like a bite of that." She was still crying when she reached Beelzebub's stall, and descended into open sobbing when she found it empty.

Eighteen

DANIEL HAD NEVER BEFORE HEARD KIRSTEN Haddonfield weeping, but he recognized the heartbroken lamentation that echoed the misery in his own heart. He left the earl's mare napping in her bed of straw, brushed himself off thoroughly, and turned Kirsten by the shoulders in Beelzebub's empty stall.

She sagged against him, her dignity abandoning her utterly. "Oh, Daniel, the b-boys said I mustn't raise my voice, but you're married and I love you, and it isn't right."

A fair, if lachrymose, summation.

"My dearest lady, please cease your tears. I'd give you my handkerchief but mine has gone astray." Daniel unknotted his neckcloth—one of the old, soft, mended ones—and dabbed at Kirsten's cheeks.

"*I* have your handkerchief," she wailed, "but I want your heart. I want your future. I want your children and all your rotten, perfect boys. Daniel, I can't let that dratted woman have you."

Gone was the pragmatic creature who'd confronted Daniel in the schoolroom, gone was the rational aristocrat who'd briskly ended two engagements. In her place was a woman who loved passionately.

Who *was loved* passionately.

"I'll marry you," Kirsten said, leaning into him. "Let Olivia disport with her cousin, let her pester you for funds as often as she pleases. My settlements are generous, and she can have—"

"No." Daniel kissed Kirsten's cheek, tasting the salt of her tears. "Olivia is like a pernicious illness. She starts as a slight ache in the joints, and if you do not rout her at that stage, she soon steals all vitality and will from the patient short of killing him bodily. We cannot be married as long as she can plague us."

Kirsten pulled away and paced several yards down the barn aisle, turning with a swish of her skirts, then turning again, like a horse pacing her stall.

"Nicholas can likely have her transported," she said, "and you and I can remove to the Hebrides. Except only Presbyterians can tolerate the northern isles. I'm willing to become a Presbyterian, Daniel, but I cannot abide—"

Kirsten halted, her hems brushing her boot tops, her hands fisted at her sides. "Daniel, I am so frightened."

He met her in the middle of the aisle, knowing she'd often endured fear, but she'd likely never confided her anxieties in another. Truly, the vows were irrelevant when a commitment of such magnitude had already been made.

"Concern is warranted," Daniel said, though so was faith, "because we're opposing a foe without honor, but that might be to our advantage."

He'd remained sitting in the straw near the big,

placid mare, considering every aspect of the situation and mentally refining on boys who spent too much time viewing the world through their father's lenses.

Where despair had been, determination took root, and hope along with it. Daniel's situation had merely wanted a change in perspective.

For Papa—stern, rigid, unbending Papa—had been right after all.

"I could call Olivia out," Kirsten said, her embrace growing fierce. "Women have fought duels over slights as petty as an insult to a lady's hat."

The slight Olivia was prepared to deal to Kirsten, Danny, the unborn child, and Daniel far exceeded slander to mere millinery.

"We can send her to the antipodes," Daniel said, stroking his thumb over Kirsten's damp cheek. "We can run away to Cathay, we can remove to the wilds of Canada, and I would still be married to Olivia."

"I want to marry you," Kirsten said. "I need to marry you, I long to marry you, and I shall marry you."

Daniel kissed Kirsten's cheek, for as bleak as their situation was, her outburst vanquished the last doubts he'd harbored about their engagement—about himself. He was not merely an acceptable alternative to a life of spinsterhood, he was Kirsten Haddonfield's dearest love.

As she was his. A dearest love was worth fighting for.

"I've been plagued by snippets of Scripture all week," he said, shifting Matthias's glasses from his breast pocket to a side pocket, lest they come between Kirsten and her intended's heart.

And a little child shall lead them...

"Aren't you usually plagued by snippets of Scripture?" Kirsten asked, arranging Daniel's somewhat damp and thoroughly wrinkled cravat around his neck and tying it loosely.

"The occasional passage will occur to me, but this week I've been deluged. Elijah, the Gospels, Proverbs... They've all been flying at me in odd moments. As I sat among the beasts here in the stable, one passage resounded more loudly than the others, but I've only now realized its significance."

Kirsten's gaze turned wary. "If it's the bit about adultery—"

"I don't believe in an Almighty Barrister, exalting the letter of the law above the spirit, my dear. An elaborate ruse was undertaken to make me believe I was a widower, and the resulting sin rests with the deceiver, not with the deceived."

While the miracles were his and Kirsten's to keep.

An after-shudder from her bout of crying passed through her. "I hate Olivia, Daniel. If you're preparing to spout pieties about loving the sinner, I will decline your spiritual guidance. Olivia is a menace and a plague and she must be stopped."

"Ephesians," Daniel said, love for his intended flooding him. "'Be angry and sin not, let not the sun go down on your wrath, neither give a place to the devil.'"

Kirsten untied his neckcloth and retied it more neatly. "*That's* your great insight? Be angry and sin not? We need a miracle, Daniel, not a sermon."

What they needed was faith, trust, and a bit of cooperation from their friends and family. Across the aisle, the earl's mare rose up from her bed of straw and shook vigorously.

"I love you," Daniel said. "You are my miracle too. I will be married to you and no other, and that's all that matters. Come sit with me in the garden."

Daniel's beloved cast him a look that suggested he was half-daft, which he was. He was also, eternally and entirely, hers, though beyond that, he had few answers.

Kirsten led Daniel out to the gazebo, which was now surrounded by beds of pansies and by rosebushes straining to bloom. The boys were probably plastered to the parlor windows, tea cakes in hand, and that was fine.

Daniel kept Kirsten's hand in his as they settled on a bench in the gazebo, and Kirsten rested her head on his shoulder. He prosed on about the details of the wedding—a special license would allow them to marry outside the church building proper—and occasionally paused to enjoy the scent of his intended or the exact feel of her silky hair against his cheek.

He did so without an iota of guilt, because Kirsten was, after all, the woman to whom he would soon be wed.

❧

The parties assembled in Belle Maison's best formal parlor, each person in appropriate finery and the bride's siblings looking particularly pleased. The scholars had picked the bride's bouquet, though they were off enjoying their parents' weekend hospitality, with the exceptions of Digby and Danny.

Bishop Reimer was in cheery humor, shaking

hands, smiling, and generally looking friendly and genial. In addition to Kirsten's brothers and sisters, the wives were present as well—Beckman's Sara, Ethan's Alexandra, and George's Elsie.

Nita had not yet returned from her travels with Mr. St. Michael, but she'd sent warm wishes and a lovely wool counterpane from Germany as a wedding gift.

The kitchens prepared a feast worthy of the old earl's funeral, and the house was scrubbed within an inch of its cellars. The neighbors, who'd arrive when the gathering in the formal parlor had concluded, would be shown such generous hospitality that nobody would go home hungry and few would go home sober.

The stage being lavishly set, the family grew quiet, and when the parlor door was closed, Reimer cleared his throat and signaled the earl that one more round of libation was in order before matters got under way.

❦

"He did it," Bertrand said, tossing his hat and gloves onto the sideboard. "Damned fool vicar married his lady, and half the shire is blathering about the bride being radiant and the groom besotted. I hope you're happy."

Bertrand was happy, because anything that moved Olivia closer to her goal moved her closer to the day when she'd have to get on with her life.

A life that included him.

"They're married?" Olivia asked as the butler closed the door. "You're sure?"

Not "how was your journey," "you must be tired,"

or "thank you, dear Bertrand, for going to so much effort." Not from his Olivia.

"No, my dearest," Bertrand said, moving down the corridor to his office, because some discussions ought not to take place before the help. "I am not sure. I was not in attendance at the nuptials. The couple used the special license to have the ceremony in the earl's formal parlor, and I was, alas, not invited. Maybe bishops go jaunting out to Kent for their health, and earls beggar their exchequers feeding the peasantry for the hell of it."

The gouty old man at the Queen's Harebell had sung the praises of the bridal punch in terms usually reserved for saintly visions.

"They're married," Olivia said, no longer a question. "I knew it."

As Bertrand closed the office door behind her, she warmed to her topic.

"Daniel is too handsome, too sweet, too saintly not to need a woman tending to him. He thinks the world is full of people just as virtuous as he is. Marriage to him was the biggest mistake I could possibly have made, but now all will come right."

Or all go to hell.

Bertrand poured himself a tot of brandy to wash the dust of the road from his throat, because the woman whom he'd fed, clothed, sheltered, and swived couldn't be bothered to offer him that consideration.

"Are you admitting that you should have married me, Olivia?"

She appropriated his drink and took the first sip. "You were another village boy with more ambition than sense and hands that wandered at every opportunity. Of course I should not have married you." She passed the drink back. "Not then."

Not *then*. Hope, useless and stupid, washed through Bertrand along with the warmth of the spirits.

"Have you considered how you'll confront Banks now that he's a bigamist, Livvie?" Poor, saintly sod.

Olivia threw herself onto the sofa where Bertrand liked to stretch out of an evening.

"The courts might not see it that way," she said. "The courts might think you tricked him, and thus he's not to blame. I can still cause a glorious scandal, and that's all that really matters."

No, that was not all that really mattered.

You tricked him. Bertrand topped up his drink and took a place leaning on the mantel, the better to watch Olivia when she realized she should have married him after all.

"You think to implicate me because I sent Banks word of your supposed death?" Bertrand asked.

"Don't turn up difficult, Bertrand," she said, arranging expensive silk skirts. "You've been a dear, and Daniel probably hasn't even kept your little note."

The note Bertrand had sealed and signed while Olivia looked on.

"Doubtless, the vicar threw my epistle straight into the fire as grief overcame him," Bertrand said, "but I know something *you* have signed, many somethings, in fact." More and more every week.

"I haven't corresponded with anybody," Olivia shot back. "I'm supposedly dead. Shopgirls who do fittings won't identify me as Daniel Banks's late spouse, so stop annoying me."

"Annoying you is amusing." Annoying Olivia was also satisfying on a level so petty, the village boy in Bertrand was ashamed. "You sign the bills at the shops, Olivia. Silk, satin, lovely wool blends, all manner of embroidery and finish work. Shoes, hats, gloves, stockings, nightgowns… You have impressive taste, but your bills are impressive too, and you kept right on signing them as Olivia Banks after your supposed death."

Bertrand didn't begrudge Olivia those excesses. When he'd first come into money, he'd overspent too, on the biggest coach, the most impressive teams, the best tailoring. After about a year of such foolishness, he'd settled down.

Olivia would never settle down. She needed a keeper, for her own good and the good of the king's peace.

"The bills are sent to you, Cousin," Olivia said, sticking out her right foot, which was adorned with a gold slipper. "The shops are very pleased to have my custom."

She wiggled her toes and lay back against the sofa cushions, a woman very much in charity with herself.

Bertrand swirled his brandy, enjoying the bouquet and the moment. "Olivia, how will you pay those bills?"

The golden slipper disappeared from view. "You'll pay them. That's how it's done, Bertrand. You impose yourself on a lady, and then pay her bills."

"You're not a lady. You're a scheming, common, married woman. You commit adultery with me, Olivia, for which you can be divorced."

She rose and patted his cheek. "Divorce would see Daniel hounded from the church, and while that might be delightful to watch, I wouldn't get my money that way, would I? Daniel will never divorce me."

She was magnificent in her selfishness and determination, but Bertrand was determined too.

"If I don't pay your bills, then you could well go to jail. They keep you there until the debt is paid, you know. Perhaps your impoverished spouse can pay your extravagances, because you're still legally his responsibility—unless he claims his wife is deceased. There was a funeral after all."

But nothing from a medical man documenting Olivia's "death" in London. All rather complicated, but the constables would toss Olivia in jail first and sort out the details later.

"Bertrand Carmichael, are you threatening me?" Olivia's voice held a novel and gratifying hint of uncertainty.

"I'm offering you a friendly warning, Olivia. You may insult Banks freely when no one is on hand to contradict you, but your scheme hasn't borne fruit yet, and it might never. I can toss you out this minute and you've no claim on any man save Banks, whom you plan to defraud of his wealth and his happiness. Your wifely devotion gives a prudent man pause. Do you want to know the sum you owe to the various shops?"

Olivia wanted to slap him. Bertrand could see fury in her gaze, feel rage vibrating through her along with all the old resentments and frustrations. The thought of debtor's prison had curbed many a foolish impulse, though, and Olivia's hands stayed at her sides.

Bertrand gave in to a foolish impulse of his own and kissed Olivia's cheek.

"We're friends, Olivia, and you must not take your friends for granted. If you want me to arrange this confrontation with Banks, if you want my assistance in your daft plans, then you will show me the appreciation and respect I am due."

He held his glass up to Olivia's lips, and with murder in her eyes, she obediently drank the last of his brandy.

༄

"So now what?" Fairly asked, and Daniel was relieved at the question. Kirsten shot him an encouraging look across the breakfast table, which was as close as they'd been to each other since yesterday's nuptial gathering.

"Now," Daniel said, accepting the rack of toast from Lady Della, "we wait." They dined without benefit of a footman at the sideboard, most of the staff having been given a half day in light of yesterday's overindulgences.

"How long do we wait?" Bellefonte asked from the head of the table.

An Old Testament question with immediate relevance.

Nobody was happy with Daniel's scheme, nor was he overjoyed with it himself. Even if they managed to thwart Olivia, many questions remained unanswered, such as how Daniel would support his family when the church had tossed him aside.

"We wait as long as it takes," Kirsten said. "I am an earl's daughter, and if I say the vicarage needs new wallpaper before I'll bide there, nobody will say anything about it. Not every couple goes to housekeeping immediately after the wedding. Della, the butter usually follows the toast."

Della obliged without comment, suggesting the tension in Daniel's gut was shared by the entire family. The scholars would have a week's holiday, but then the schoolroom routine was to resume, to the extent Daniel could support that farce.

"It's as if there's a war raging nearby," Lady Della said. "We have no idea when the enemy will march in this direction, but the best spoils are here, so a battle is inevitable."

Fairly appropriated the teapot. "Well put. Letty, some tea?"

Daniel's sister had been quiet yesterday, and she looked none too cheery this morning.

"I wish we could confront Olivia," Letty said as her husband poured out for her. "She thinks she has the element of surprise on her side, but why wait until the time and place of her convenience? She took months to embark on her mischief and she might wait years to spring her trap. Daniel could be a bishop before Olivia pounces, and where does that leave Lady Kirsten?"

Letty knew well how tenacious and relentless Olivia could be—and how mean.

"I agree with Letty," Kirsten said. "If we confront Olivia, we choose the time and place, we choose who accompanies Daniel and what strategy to bring to the engagement."

Daniel set down the fork he'd been using to chase his eggs around his plate.

"I hadn't thought to bring anybody with me. Olivia might be devious but she won't—"

The entire table regarded him as if he'd gone daft.

"I was the one who spoke vows with the woman,"

Daniel said. "Her grievances are with me, and mine with her. I don't see any need to further involve—"

Kirsten sat back and folded her arms, one eyebrow lifted ever so slightly. Their children would come to dread such an expression from her.

That thought reminded Daniel that time was of the essence, after all.

"Daniel, we have family to consider," Kirsten said. "What do you tell the scholars about riding out, even over familiar ground?"

A telling shot. "Travel in pairs," Daniel said, another of his biblically based admonitions, for the apostles had gone forth in pairs. "Take a groom or a friend, but don't ride out by yourself if you can help it."

The earl spoke up, though to appearances, he addressed the teapot. "You set a bad example in that regard, Banks, when you charge about on your demon steed. Time to mend your ways, methinks."

Fairly's expression was both sympathetic and determined. "Lady Kirsten is right. We are your family, and that gives us certain privileges."

A vicar celebrated the service facing the congregation. As a result, he saw the glances that passed up and down the pews and across the aisles. Entire arguments, gossip, complaints, and sympathies were often traded right under his nose as some martyr was scripturally thrown to the lions.

Martyr. To the lions.

A look passed between Letty and Kirsten, who were nominally sisters by marriage.

"Well, Banks?" the earl asked. "What shall it be?"

Last week in the stable, sitting in the straw with

Buttercup, Daniel had come to a startling insight: be angry and sin not.

He took that to mean he had a right to address the wrongs done to him and his loved ones, that piety did not condone wrongdoing. A warrior's version of virtue that appealed more strongly than the meek, humble, accommodating version Daniel's father had tried to pound into him.

Papa had been a lonely man. As Daniel had trudged through his late father's old journals and fading correspondence, a paradox had emerged. Papa had known Scripture and theology, and every verse to every hymn ever penned by the pious hand of man, but he hadn't known love. Warmth of the heart had bewildered the old man and left him bereft of words.

And yet Papa would approve of what Daniel had planned for Olivia, and Papa's scathing assessment of her—rendered in writing, many times—would be Olivia's downfall.

"I will appreciate any and all help our family sees fit to give me," Daniel said. "If I might have the butter?"

Kirsten smiled. Fairly patted Letty's hand, and the earl took up the newspaper that had been folded by his elbow.

God was in His heaven, and all was right with Daniel's world—almost.

❧

"I don't like this holiday business," Fred said, flopping down into a pile of straw. "We've nothing to do but read the Bible, and all our sisters talk about is the assembly. Vicar makes the Bible ever so much more fun."

"Or they blather on about their infernal dresses," Frank lamented.

Digby could sympathize with that sentiment. His mama had taken to prattling on about her dresses since she'd remarried. She'd complained of having to let her seams out for some reason.

From below the haymow came the sounds of the livery's horses contentedly munching hay, but other than that, all around the shady village green was quiet. Haddondale was still recovering from Saturday's merriment at Belle Maison. Even the lending library hadn't opened yet, which every boy had agreed was an affront to their scholarly ambitions.

"Was Lady Kirsten very pretty?" Thomas asked. He sat cross-legged nearest the ladder, because Thomas was the best lookout.

"She's always pretty," Digby said. "Vicar was handsome too, but he's always handsome. The men had to wear knee breeches, and satin, and rings and stuff."

"Formal attire," Danny said, the way Digby's mama might have described a muddy dog asleep on her best sofa. "The dower house isn't the same without you fellows. Maybe Alfrydd would take us out for a hack."

Matthias had his nose in a book, though any mention of riding usually provoked a recounting of his great steeplechase on Buttercup.

"Mattie, what are you reading?" Digby asked. Matthias hated to read usually.

"The Latin grammar," he said, not bothering to look up. "*Puer* and *puella*, *amo*, *amas*, *amat*."

"Boy and girl, I love, you love, he loves? We covered that weeks ago," Frank said. "Infernally boring too."

Everything had gone *infernal* with Frank. Last week's word had been *diabolical*.

"I can *see* it now," Matthias said, putting the book aside. "I have an idea for how we might liven up our holiday."

"Does this idea involve toads?" Digby asked, because Mattie Two Eyes—his new nickname—was quickly regaining his former nimbleness of mind.

"Not toads, you Hun. Flowers. We're to pay a call on the newlyweds. Ladies like flowers, and there will be lots of tea cakes left over from Saturday."

"Not a bad idea," Danny said. "I don't think Papa has much to do without scholars to teach, and he can't have Lady Kirsten all to himself. Sharing is a virtue."

Howling greeted that pronouncement, for bending the virtues to one's own use had become a game among them.

"Fine then," Frank said, getting up and beating vigorously at his straw-covered trousers. "We go on a biology walk through the churchyard's flower beds, then pay our call. Everybody clean out your pockets first, in case Lady Kirsten tells us to take an extra cake or two for later. Then we'll ask Alfrydd to take us on a hack, but this week will be the most diabolically boring, infernally long week of my scholarly life."

❧

The most diabolically long, infernally boring, nerve-racking week of Daniel's life ensued while the scholars went on their holiday. During that week, Lady Kirsten was overheard remarking to all and sundry that work yet needed to be done at the vicarage before she'd set up housekeeping there.

Her ladyship was not quite telling a falsehood, for the vicarage had no nursery.

"You're brooding," Kirsten said.

Daniel rose from his desk in the dower house, sweetness, anxiety, and grief colliding in his heart at the sight of her.

"How long have you been spying on me, my dear?" he asked.

Kirsten slipped her arms around his waist. They embraced frequently, but the kissing... By tacit agreement, the kissing would have to wait.

"I stood in that doorway for several minutes, Daniel, and you were elsewhere entirely. Are you having second thoughts?"

Daniel was having regrets.

"I wish I'd told my father that I respected him," Daniel said, looping his arms around Kirsten shoulders. "He wanted my respect, and he had it, but I didn't know enough to give him the words." At twenty, Daniel had known only that Olivia would marry him, a vicar needed a wife, and Papa was a curmudgeon.

"So what did he write about?" Kirsten asked, brushing Daniel's hair back from his brow. "The poor man filled journal after journal, and it can't all be sermons and theology."

All of their touches now were for comfort, none for arousal, though desire plagued Daniel relentlessly. The tenacity of his carnal interest in his lady was a backhanded source of reassurance, for all else was in tumult.

"Papa wrote his true feelings. I'd thought he considered me a young fool, and he did, but he also respected my academic accomplishments, and he liked that I thought for myself, even when I reached the wrong conclusions."

"He loved you," Kirsten said.

Her words brought an ache to Daniel's throat, a not entirely sad ache. "He loved me. I love you, my lady, so very much."

Daniel kissed Kirsten then, a soft, lingering press of lips. A kiss of shared regrets, not a little weariness, and endless longing.

Footsteps sounded on the stairs. Daniel felt the moment when Kirsten heard them, and felt her fling aside the impulse to break apart from him. When Fairly came prowling down the corridor, Daniel was the one to end the embrace.

"My lady"—Fairly tossed off a crisp bow—"Banks, good day. The meeting has been arranged for tomorrow morning as you suggested, and my traveling coach awaits your pleasure. As far as Carmichael knows, my own dear viscountess spotted Olivia earlier this week while out shopping in the wilds of Mayfair. Per your instructions, my note to Carmichael intimated that I'm prepared to pay a large sum if a certain irregularity in my brother-in-law's circumstances can be kept quiet."

"Thank you, my lord," Kirsten said. Her voice was calm, but her grip on Daniel's hand was quite snug. "I'll fetch my cloak."

She kissed Daniel's cheek and hurried away, and abruptly, the waiting was over.

This scheme Daniel had concocted was as worthy

of a rotten boy as it was of a bishop, and that combination—of creativity, conviction, and strategy—was as peculiar as it was…appropriate.

Papa would have been proud of him, a fortifying notion. Kirsten was proud of him, and Daniel was even a little proud of himself.

"You were right, Banks," Fairly said when Kirsten was out of earshot. "Bloody, exactly, goddamned—excuse my language—right. Money, and the notion that you're in severe difficulties was all we needed to lure Olivia from the shadows. She has been shopping too. Buying out half the modistes and milliners in Mayfair."

Bills for which Daniel, technically, was responsible. Ironic, that.

"My thanks for your efforts," Daniel said, and now, when he should be racing full tilt for London, he was reluctant to leave the dower house.

"Must you be so confoundedly calm, Banks? We're about to catch a demon brewing her mischief, about to thwart her foul schemes and put her to rout, true love will triumph and all that, while you are the soul of sober manners."

Fairly had a bit of the demon in him too, a bit of the avenging angel, while what awaited in London left Daniel calm. Simply…calm.

Did she but know it, Olivia was the one about to enter the lion's den.

"Let's be on our way," Daniel said. "Kirsten's family will want to discuss matters yet again when we reach London, and Kirsten needs her rest."

Fairly was a physician, and his own dear lady was in

need of frequent rest of late. He didn't argue Daniel's point but stalked off toward the head of the stairs.

"I don't understand you, Banks," he said as Daniel took one last look at the study where he'd planned his lessons and finally read his father's journals.

"I'm a man in love," Daniel said, closing the door and joining Fairly on the steps. "Love can require sacrifices."

Love offered gifts too, though. Wonderful, precious gifts that made all the sacrifices worthwhile.

"Love requires that you seize your joy when it befalls you," Fairly said, his stride purposeful. "You're getting the woman of your dreams; she gets you. Her settlements are handsome enough, and Danny is doing well. If you can't make a happily ever after out of that, you're not trying hard enough."

"I'll miss the boys," Daniel said as they reached the bright sunshine of the back terrace. "Kirsten and I will be happy—very happy—but we'll both miss the boys terribly. Both are true, the happiness and the sorrow."

Be happy, even in the midst of heartbreak.

Be angry and sin not.

Nineteen

"OLIVIA, YOU'RE LOOKING WELL."

Such was Daniel Banks's inherent virtue that, to Nick's ears, the compliment to Mrs. Banks was sincere. Not relieved, not resentful, not ironic, simply sincere.

With his civil greeting, Banks had cordially saluted an opponent across the space of a dueling ground. He'd also spoken accurately, for the fair Olivia appeared to be in the pink of health.

"Who are *they*?" she asked, aiming a glance at Nick and Fairly.

Fairly was in good form this morning, looking both dapper and menacing in his London finery, an avenging angel between celestial errands of divine wrath. Nick had attired himself in similar lordly splendor while Banks was simply…Banks.

A sober suit of brown, plain black waistcoat, the same riding boots he'd worn to Haddondale months ago, and yet Banks was also different.

His hair had been trimmed, his clothing fit him perfectly, nothing mended or patched, and his cravat was for once expertly starched and tied.

He looked, in other words, taken in hand. Cared for. Married.

Loved. Also determined as hell.

In the middle of Fairly's peacefully blooming London garden, Banks obliged with introductions.

"Olivia, may I make known to you Nicholas, Earl of Bellefonte, and David, Viscount Fairly. His lordship to my left holds the living in Haddondale; his lordship to my right has the honor to be my brother-in-law. You were well acquainted with his present viscountess, my sister Letty, when she shared a household with us."

Ah, a gratifying hint of uncertainty passed through Olivia's eyes, a nervous hand smoothed over her skirts, while Mr. Carmichael—a man to be pitied, according to Banks—said nothing.

"Shall we be seated?" Fairly asked, though in fact he was giving an order, and Carmichael, at least, knew it. Fairly was married to the woman whom Olivia had blackmailed, the woman whose child had endured Olivia's indifferent variety of mothering.

"We're to remain out-of-doors?" Olivia asked.

Had she wanted to gawk at Fairly's commodiously appointed town house?

"I'd rather you not set foot in my home," Fairly said, his rebuke chillingly pleasant. "Nor will I offer you food or drink."

"Come, Olivia," Banks said, gesturing toward a wrought iron grouping beneath a pair of stately plane trees. "Our discussion should not take long, and you and Mr. Carmichael can be on your way."

His Saintliness was apparently amused at Fairly's posturing, while Nick was impressed with Fairly's restraint.

Banks, Olivia, and Carmichael took chairs beneath the maples, while Nick and Fairly each assumed a post standing at Banks's shoulders. Nick affixed a serious expression on his features, mentally folded his guardian angel wings, and prepared to enjoy himself.

"What do you want from me, Olivia?" Banks asked.

His tone was merely curious, and again, Mrs. Banks appeared to have enough sense to be uncertain. Daniel was not a fellow in anticipation of felony prosecution, not a man alarmed by the prospect of blackmail or scandal, and she must have perceived this.

"You can have what you want, Daniel," Olivia said, all sniffy graciousness. "I won't stand in your way, but I'm your lawfully wedded wife and entitled to your support for the rest of my life."

Not a bad opening, also probably not the fanfare of threats and bullying she'd planned.

"Olivia is prepared to be reasonable," Carmichael said, sending the lady a look that said she'd best heed that guidance. "A sum certain in exchange for her willingness to leave you in peace, Banks. A civil bargain. Everybody can go about their business."

"Unmolested and undisturbed," Banks murmured, plucking a daffodil from beside his seat. "What sum certain had you in mind, Olivia?"

While Banks sniffed his posy, Olivia courted utter ruin. Letty, Viscountess Fairly, would have enjoyed this exchange.

Olivia named an impressively greedy figure. Carmichael found it expedient to study the leafy canopy above.

"And you believe that sum will sustain you for the rest of your days?" Daniel asked.

"She does," Carmichael interjected into the small, telling hesitation from Olivia. "Installments over time will serve; you needn't pay it all at once."

"Olivia, I will pay you nothing for your silence," Daniel said gently, so very gently. "You betrayed me, my flock, and my loved ones, and I will not be further victimized by your greed."

If Nick recalled his catechism accurately, greed was a deadly sin.

"You will pay me," Olivia hissed. "I put up with you for years, and we're married, and you owe me support. That's the law. The law also says you can only be married to one woman at a time, Daniel, and I'll tell the entire world what you've done if you turn up stubborn now."

Daniel took another sniff of his flower, a lovely specimen though a prodigiously late bloomer.

"My father castigated me for stubbornness when I announced my decision to marry you," Daniel said, "and he was right. I was determined to wed you, and maybe the resulting years were penance for my disregard of his advice."

"I want my money, Daniel. I can make trouble."

Slowly, Daniel twirled the daffodil. "Papa was worried about me, you see, so worried he confided his fears in many letters to his friend, Bishop Reimer. Papa documented his reservations about our marriage night after night in his journal. I would not listen, Papa claimed. I was willful and misguided. The union did not have his blessing, though Papa would always pray for my happiness and my eternal soul."

Carmichael, a businessman according to Fairly,

shifted back in his chair, but Olivia did not yet sense her looming defeat.

Nick resisted the urge to scratch his nose and instead flexed his fists.

Olivia's lily-white hands were fisted as well. "Your father was a theological drudge, Daniel, and I wish you the joy of the same fate. If the Church finds out that you've committed bigamy, your only pulpit will be in a jail."

"Banks hasn't committed bigamy," Fairly said evenly, "despite your attempt to shove him down that path. Banns were cried, a gathering held, a special license procured. No ceremony. No bigamy."

The twirling of the daffodil stopped.

"We drank some excellent punch, though," Nick volunteered. "Consumed a quantity of first-rate victuals. Got to see all my relatives and lark about in my silk knee breeches. No wedding, though."

Olivia was off her chair, storming away to the fading lilacs. "*You lied to me, Daniel? You misrepresented? Made a farce out of a holy sacrament?*"

The lady's indignation was as genuine as it was laughable. Her scheme required that Daniel be stupid and predictable in his piety, that he come along like a sacrificial goat into the wilderness of Olivia's choosing.

Fairly put a gloved hand on the back of Olivia's chair. "Madam, I suggest you compose yourself."

Even the meanest, scuttling hedgehog had instincts in the direction of self-preservation. Olivia was no different. She resumed her seat, perching on the very edge.

"You were always honest, Daniel. Even when

dissembling would have been in your interest. Even with the boy, you never told anybody in Little Weldon outright that he was your son, you merely allowed the assumption. And now this."

"Honesty is a virtue," Nick said into the yawning silence. His observation provoked more silence but for a pair of robins, chirping enthusiastically in the branches above. Probably on the nest, spring having arrived in all her glory.

"We're still married," Olivia said, her chin coming up. "Unless you reach an accommodation with me, Daniel, you will always live alone. All it will take is a word from me in the ear of the right bishop—"

Banks raised a hand rather than allow Olivia to spin that fancy. "I married you against my father's wishes. I was twenty years old, and thus not of age to marry without my father's consent. Our union is being annulled, Olivia. The evidence has been submitted, and the decision a foregone conclusion when my father's position was made clear to one of those very bishops whom you'd seek to manipulate."

Carmichael, oddly, looked pleased with this development. Had Nick been sitting beside Olivia Banks—was her name Banks?—he might have scooted his chair back.

"*An annulment?*" Olivia whispered. "You're having the marriage annulled, Daniel? Our marriage?"

"Very likely a fait accompli," Fairly said, "certain donations having been cheerfully made to certain charitable interests. Banks is not liable for your debts; he's not liable for your support. You are a woman cast out of the vicarage to fend for yourself as best you can. My wife, whom you sent to the same fate, did not counsel further retribution, though believe me, madam, her counsel is all that stays my hand."

Daniel passed Fairly the daffodil, which earned him a blink of mismatched lordly eyes, while Nick endured a wave of sheer affection for his relations. Whatever this meeting was, it was the opposite of a mess.

"I received good counsel from a lady as well," Daniel said, drawing a packet from an inner pocket. "She advised me that mercy was in order, so this is a bank draft, Olivia. If you're prudent, it will last you a good while or pay off a portion of the debts you've accumulated buying fripperies. Your fate is in your own hands, and you may say whatever you like to whomever you choose. I wish you well."

His final sermon delivered, Reverend Daniel Banks rose, bowed, and simply walked into the house. Nick wanted to applaud, but that would have been un-angelic of him.

"I'll see your guests out, Fairly," Nick said. "And I'll lock the garden gates behind them."

Fairly sent a curt nod in Carmichael's direction, spared Olivia the king of all ironical bows, and took himself across the garden.

"Olivia, come," Carmichael said, extending a hand down to her. "There's nothing more you can do here."

"Nothing more she can do without ending up in jail herself," Nick said pleasantly. "We have your little epistle, Carmichael, the one condoling Daniel on Olivia's supposed death. We have the testimony of the Great Weldon vicar, whom you retained to perform an internment of an apparently empty coffin.

We have all the evidence of fraud and conspiracy to commit fraud—"

"I have a commodious estate far to the north, your lordship, and the weather has moderated. It's time I looked to my acres. Olivia, *come along.*"

She sat staring at the bank draft. The funds were not enough to keep her in any style, not enough even to pay off the exorbitant bills she'd run up clothing herself in new finery.

"You could take ship," Nick suggested. "Start over in India. A woman of enterprise might manage there well enough."

If the diseases, perils, and general lawlessness didn't put a messy end to her.

"Olivia, bestir yourself," Carmichael said. "It's over and you've lost. If you'll marry me, I'll take you north."

The poor fool was sincere. Daniel had predicted this, having known Carmichael as a lad.

"Madam, your welcome here is at end," Nick said, because the damned woman had started to cry. "Carmichael, must I signal the footmen?"

Nick would not put his hands on Olivia Whoever She Was, lest he pitch her over the garden wall like the contents of last night's chamber pot.

"Daniel didn't remarry," Olivia croaked. "You *told* me he'd married that woman, you *said* the entire village was celebrating, and now all I have is this, this—"

"You have an offer of marriage," Nick said, sending a meaningful glance in the direction of the house. "You have some funds, you apparently have an ally in Mr. Carmichael. I suggest you tour the north permanently, because Fairly would see you hanged but for his lady's merciful nature. The viscount has the means and the meanness to do it too, and Banks would not stop him."

That got Olivia's attention. She was on her feet in the next instant, her hand lashed around Carmichael's arm.

"Bertrand, take me away from this place. Daniel has deceived me, and I'm well rid of him."

Her own greed had deceived her, had led her to view the world through her own avaricious lenses, while Daniel had simply been wise. Carmichael ought to put Olivia on the first ship bound for Cathay.

They left the garden arm in arm, the bank draft peeking out of Olivia's reticule, the birds overhead having for some reason gone silent.

❦

"I am not very happy with Bishop Reimer," Kirsten said, whipping Daniel's cravat into a tidy mathematical. George had taught her a half-dozen knots, and Daniel preferred the simplest. Kirsten liked it too, for it was simple to *un*do.

"This parting from your pulpit by degrees has to be agony," she went on. "Of all the curates starving in all the rural parishes of England, he couldn't find one willing to come to Kent on short notice? Isn't there one who—"

Daniel kissed her, and as always, his kisses made Kirsten stop what she was doing as gratitude had its moment. Gratitude was a fine way to start the day, to end the day, to middle and between the day.

They were married now. A quiet ceremony in

Reimer's parlor, a few family members in attendance, some late daffodils clutched in Kirsten's hands.

She and Daniel were married, and they could kiss whenever they pleased.

"I'll wrinkle your cravat," Kirsten said, subsiding against her beloved. "Will you tell the boys today?"

"I thought telling my pastoral committee would be the worst," Daniel said, looping his arms around her. "I thought Reimer would have some disappointed sermon to inflict on me. I thought—telling the boys will break my heart."

"Your rotten boys put that heart back in you," Kirsten said. "Of course telling them you're leaving the church will be awful."

More kissing followed, because in the ledger book that had become their new life—joy to one side, grief to the other—the pleasures of their shared affection brought much comfort.

Daniel's tongue came calling, and Kirsten's exhortations to uncooperative bishops flew out of her grasp. She tucked herself closer, body to body, marveling at the ever-evolving fit between them.

"My breasts—" she muttered into her husband's smile.

"Are more glorious than ever," Daniel said.

"I'm weepy," Kirsten said, sliding a hand over Daniel's falls and finding evidence of impending marital bliss. "I fall asleep in the pantry. I can't think—"

Daniel's hands, slow and knowing, were working Kirsten's skirt up as he walked her back against their bed.

"Think later, my lady. Love now."

"You'll be late to the schoolroom," she said, starting on the buttons of his falls. "You have so few days

in the schoolroom left, so few sermons left to give."
Then Daniel was to become steward of one of Fairly's
smaller estates, while Kirsten was at risk of becoming
a good Christian.

Marriage to Daniel had done that.

"You aren't ashamed to become a steward's wife,"
Daniel said, sinking to his knees before Kirsten could
get all of his buttons undone. "It's a quiet life, but we
won't be far from family."

"Stewarding an estate is not that different from
shepherding a flock, Daniel. If I can be a vicar's wife,
I'll learn to be a steward's wife." The simple, almost
irrelevant truth. Of course, she'd turn her every ability
to making a success of their new situation.

"What matters," Kirsten went on, smoothing a
hand over Daniel's hair, "is that the boys will lose you,
and you will lose them. That isn't right, Daniel. That's
not fair, it's not what—"

More kisses, and clothing strewn in all directions,
and tickling, and then quiet, miraculous loving.

Daniel had become a fiend between the sheets. He
brought a vicar's endless self-restraint, a headmaster's
stamina, and a rotten boy's wiliness to his lovemaking.

Also a husband's devotion.

"I love this part," Kirsten said as Daniel slowly,
slowly joined his body to hers. The quiet of a beautiful morning surrounded them, the scent of lavender
rose from thoroughly rumpled sheets. "I love the part
where the two become as one flesh."

Daniel's thumbs brushed over her palms, a caress
as tender as it was intimate. "I love you. I will always
love you."

He gave her the words often, he gave her the deeds now. Kirsten surrendered to the joy and the pleasure, even as she worried for her husband, who knew nothing about stewarding the land and everything about looking after the tender, vulnerable human heart.

❧

"Don't worry," Daniel said when he could again form complete sentences. Telling his wife what to do was an exercise in wasted breath, though. Kirsten worried because she cared.

"I will try not to worry about you," she said, smoothing a hand over Daniel's naked chest. "But the boys, Daniel. I think of the boys losing you, and I want to weep."

She did weep. A lot. Brusque, self-contained, pragmatic Kirsten Haddonfield Banks had become a watering pot who cried at the sight of kittens in the barn, Matthias's first perfect examination, and Daniel's letter of resignation, tidily penned and sitting on a corner of his desk down the corridor.

"We'll live only a few hours away," Daniel said, "and Digby is family. He and Danny will visit back and forth."

Change was a part of life, in other words. Daniel understood the words his father had occasionally muttered, understood much about the old man he hadn't when Papa had been alive.

Kirsten's hand moved lower, over Daniel's middle, and he spared a glance at the clock on the mantel.

"You're late," Kirsten said, her hand pausing. "Ralph can entertain the boys for only so long. Let's get you dressed."

Ralph's forced cheer was another trial, for he'd become attached to the boys, and to the notion of being part of a vicar's boisterous, unpretentious household with his Annie.

"I've had a revelation," Daniel said, tying Kirsten's sash a few minutes later. They'd become proficient at dressing each other—also undressing each other.

"What's your revelation?" Kirsten asked, passing him his hairbrush when he'd finished with the sash. She had a positive genius for disarranging his hair in certain situations.

"Faith is not a matter of sticking to the rules, reciting the Commandments or the small talk by turns, and staying on the well-lit path," Daniel said, "but neither is it a matter of adhering to selfish impulses in the face of opposition and calling that bravery."

They never referred to Olivia by name. Fairly had confirmed that she was now Mrs. Bertrand Carmichael, late of Rural Obscurity, Cumbria. Daniel hadn't asked for details and probably never would.

Kirsten took the brush from him and gave his hair the last wifely touches. "So what is faith to you now?"

"Faith is love. Faith is waking up beside a steward's wife when I'd thought always to wake up beside a vicar's wife, possibly even a dean's or a bishop's. Faith is saying good-bye to the boys, telling them I'm proud of them, and knowing a few months here, a few Latin verbs, will stand them in good stead."

Kirsten wanted to protest—Daniel knew the look in her eye—but her kind heart got the better of her logic.

"Mattie can see now," she said. "Thomas no longer

sits on anyone. Danny has friends and plays as noisily as a normal boy. They can all manage their ponies, the Blumenthals haven't put a toad anywhere but the terrarium in weeks."

"Exactly. No stirring sermons, no great ecclesiastical brilliance; just a handful of boys a little happier for living in here. I cannot change water into wine, can't pretend I didn't marry disastrously the first time, but I can be happy with you, and with a life outside the church. That's what faith requires of me. Joy and courage, not misery over a past that can't be changed or a future that can't be controlled."

The clock ticked; the morning breeze brought country air through the bedroom.

"You worked this out with Beelzebub, didn't you?" Kirsten asked. "All those mad dashes you went for after the wedding."

"No, actually. I went for those mad dashes because I love to gallop my pony. I worked this out when I was faced with the choice of a life with the woman I love or a life with the church. Even my father— maybe especially my father—would have wanted me to choose love."

Kirsten's kiss was a benediction. Her smack on Daniel's bum was pure Kirsten.

"Go inflict Latin on the innocents. Even if you must end their school year early, Daniel, you owe them that pony race."

Kirsten had a natural talent for cheering him up. The pony race was half of what the boys talked about, and even their fathers had apparently started offering strategy and advice.

"See you at luncheon," Daniel said, kissing his wife's brow. "Ask Cook if we can picnic in the garden."

Kirsten thrived on activity, and picnics took planning. Daniel parted from her at the head of the stairs, he turning to the schoolroom, Kirsten toward the kitchen. He exercised a besotted husband's prerogative and admired her retreating form until she turned, shook her finger at him, and blew him a kiss.

He blew her a kiss in return and headed off for a day in the schoolroom, one of his last.

And that hurt. All vicarly blathering about faith and courage aside, leaving the boys was breaking Daniel's heart. They were such good boys, good boys as only rotten boys could be. Full of fun and curiosity, given to laughter and honesty at the oddest, most touching moments.

Daniel paused outside the schoolroom, letting the heartache have its due, because that was part of faith too. A man whose first marriage had been annulled could remain at his pulpit—Reimer knew of two such fellows, though they were in very obscure, poor parishes—but what sort of example would Daniel be?

An odd thought came to him: a man who'd stumbled badly might be a very good inspiration to the faithful. Moral perfection wasn't the subject of any scriptural passage Daniel could recall, but forgiveness, compassion, and self-acceptance were often mentioned.

"To do justice, love mercy, and walk humbly with my God," Daniel paraphrased old Micah. Perfect marks weren't required on that exam, but parting from some dear, impressionable, rotten, perfect boys remained unavoidable.

❧

"I never thought I could hate Vicar," Fred observed as the most recent William of the Week croaked softly in Digby's pocket.

"I don't hate him," Frank said as they trooped along toward the stream running through the mares' pasture. "But I wish he wasn't leaving. The third declension looks beastly hard, and Vicar would have made it understandable."

"It's not so bad," Mattie said from Fred's other side.

To Digby, every Latin declension and every conjugation was hard, and no wonder the language had died out long ago. French and English didn't bother with all that folderol and they were still doing a brisk business. Papa had laughed when Digby had trotted out that observation.

Digby and his friends weren't laughing much at all lately.

"Vicar can go if he must," Thomas said, "but why can't Lady Kirsten stay here? Haddondale is her home. I'm going to ask the earl to make her stay, and then maybe Vicar will stay too."

Danny wasn't with them, having been whisked off early to his titled relations. Already the cracks were forming in their little school, and Digby hated that.

"What I can't figure out," Digby said, "is why Vicar would rather spend his days counting sheep and goats when he could be with us here. What does hiring the shearing crew or rotating the crops offer that could be more fun than Roman battles, Mattie's French jokes, or picnics in the garden?"

They'd picnicked earlier that week, exactly the

sort of unplanned enjoyment that made the history of Hanoverian Germany bearable. Lady Kirsten had told them about making her bow before the Regent, whom she said was quite stout.

He probably needed to hunt toads more often, for Vicar said a healthy body contributed to a—

"Mattie," Digby said, "are you thinking up another French joke?" For Mattie had come to a stop several yards before the stream. William, who could probably smell his home nearby, had fallen silent.

"Vicar likes solving problems," Mattie said.

"Like he figured out your stupid specs?" Fred asked. Among the boys, they were never anything but the stupid spectacles, the infernal glasses, the diabolically dumb eyepieces.

"Like that," Mattie said, gaze on the stream, which was rushing happily along, "but also like Thomas's penmanship, which Lady Kirsten helped him tidy up. Like Fred's mixing up the royal succession. Like Danny isn't so good at maths."

"Nobody's good at everything," Digby said. William stirred in his pocket, probably anxious to see his family.

"I like solving problems too," Mattie said. "Vicar leaving is a problem. We'll go back to birch rods and boring lectures in cold schoolrooms. No more William of the Week, no more picnics, no more great battles in the stable yard, no more pony races."

Sorrow passed through the group. The pony race was to be held next Saturday. Classes would finish up Tuesday, the boys would go home, and then a pony race and a picnic would be held on Saturday to celebrate a school year that ought not to be ending so soon.

"We have to do something," Thomas said. "We can't be Vicar's best boys, his scholars, if we don't solve his problems the way he solves ours. Lady Kirsten would agree."

Digby agreed. The Blumenthals nodded. William croaked. Mattie smiled.

"I have a plan," he said. "It will take a lot of work, and we must be prepared to sacrifice, to endure beatings and scolds, and to go without our pudding."

"That's exactly what we endured before Vicar started teaching us," Thomas said, absently rubbing his backside. "And exactly what we'll have if he leaves us for some sheep farm."

"William can't go home just yet," Mattie said. "And we've a lot of work to do. First thing we'll need is two buckets each."

❧

"Greymoor doesn't steward just any race, you know," Fairly said, swinging up on his mare. "The result of today's mischief will be a tribe of horse-mad young men—in addition to a lot of broken bones."

"Which is why," Daniel said, from Beelzebub's saddle, "a trained physician is on hand, to ensure the best medical care for any scrapes and bumps. These boys are good riders, Fairly, and they're on sound, sensible ponies."

"There is no such thing as a sensible pony," Fairly retorted. "Demon spawn, the devil's handmaidens, Lucifer's boot boys, dastardly apprentices to the Fiend, the model of how not to create a horse, worse than——"

Fairly's jaw snapped shut. Kirsten, Elsie, and Letty pulled up in an open barouche, Kirsten at the ribbons.

"Ladies, good day," Daniel said, though the smile Kirsten gave him confirmed that for her, too, the day held some grief. "The boys will be along shortly. Fairly was just telling me how much fun he had as a boy, racing his pony all over the shire."

"Indeed I was," Fairly said, patting his mare and producing a fond smile. "Nothing a boy likes better. Ah, here come the jockeys now."

Fairly cantered off, for it fell to him and his mare to lead Loki to the starting line. Bellefonte and Buttercup were doing the honors for Frank Blumenthal, while Squire Blumenthal had a fractious exchange with Fred's pony.

"Shouting is never a good idea at the starting line," Daniel said. "I do believe the third Commandment is imperiled. Ladies, you'll excuse me."

No less personage than Andrew, Earl of Greymoor, one of Fairly's in-laws, was in charge of the start. He rode a black about the same size as Beelzebub, though somewhat calmer for having hacked over from Surrey the previous day.

Daniel sorted out the Blumenthals, though the squire managed a muttered, "A word with you later, Mr. Banks," before he trotted off and left Daniel to deal with Fred's rambunctious little gelding.

The ponies lined up—George had practiced this with the boys many times—and the boys and ponies all settled.

The scholars would recall this moment, and it would be a fine memory. Daniel lifted his gaze past the neighbors who'd come out to cheer on the boys, past the row of carriages and carts sitting well behind the finish line. Off to the southwest, the Downs were clad in benevolent green, summer beckoning the sun closer.

I will lift up mine eyes unto the hills…

Kirsten met Daniel's gaze, blew him a kiss, and waved her handkerchief. She would recall this day too, when their little scholars had galloped off to meet life's next challenge.

Daniel would miss these boys for the rest of his life. They'd sorted him out and given him a shove toward his own next challenges. He'd worry over them, pray for them, write to them when they were older, even visit them when he called upon the earl.

If their parents allowed such familiarity. At any point, the situation with Olivia could become common knowledge, and scandal might erupt. A steward could endure scandal more easily than a vicar could, which was to say, a steward could endure scandal while a vicar could not.

Daniel had shared the facts with his pastoral committee, and despite their protestations, as soon as Reimer identified a successor to St. Jude's pulpit, Daniel would step down.

If Daniel loved his rotten boys, and he did, then he'd go gratefully to the post Fairly offered.

Greymoor walked before the six ponies, nominally inspecting bridles and saddles, patting a pony here, admiring a shiny stirrup iron there. Freya stamped her foot, which Matthias, like the budding equestrian he was, ignored.

"Gentlemen, on your marks," Greymoor said calmly. "Get set, and GO!"

❧

Kirsten had never been so proud, nor so sad, as when she beheld six perfect little gentlemen in their saddles, trying so hard to pay attention to the strutting earl, when each boy, to the marrow of his sturdy bones, wanted nothing more than to send his steed tearing across the countryside.

And Daniel, sitting calm and smiling on Beelzebub, a little apart from Nicholas, Fairly, George, and the other papas.

Her heart broke for Daniel, who'd taken a pack of rotten boys and turned them into scholars and gentlemen.

"We need to talk to you."

Elsie recovered before Kirsten or Letty. "Sally, May, and Nancy. Hello," Elsie said. "A pleasure to see you."

The three oldest Blumenthal sisters were looking quite fetching—and quite furious—in spring bonnets and shawls.

"Might we talk after the race?" Kirsten said. "The boys will be coming back around the woods in about ten minutes." Unless somebody was injured, somebody went astray, somebody's pony bolted from the pack, or somebody came off and couldn't catch his pony to climb back on.

Many things could go wrong in a boy's first race.

"What we have to say won't take long," Sally said. "But if you don't listen to us, we'll commit murder by sundown. Two murders, and Mama will help us."

"Papa might too," May added.

"And the servants," Nancy muttered. "The Webbers too. I don't know what Vicar has been doing with our brothers these past months. They seemed to be making such progress, until they came home on Tuesday. Mr. Banks has apparently taken reasonably decent little boys and turned them into demons."

"My boys have become demons?" Kirsten said. "The dearest little scholars ever to spill their milk on each other and botch their French, *demons*? Surely you are mistaken."

Elsie was smiling an odd smile, as was Letty. Kirsten passed Letty the reins and climbed down unassisted, for it seemed her rotten boys had turned up perfect just when their decorum counted most.

❧

"You can't imagine the shrieking," Squire Blumenthal said, while his gelding snatched at the grass. "The entire complement of Egyptian toads has taken up residence at the Grange, Banks, and it will not serve. Did you *teach* those boys the fine art of toad catching?"

Well, yes, Daniel had. "Boys have a natural aptitude for such things, sir, normal boys. I'm sure the twins are simply glad to be done with their studies."

Blumenthal blotted his forehead with a white handkerchief while his horse's bad manners went uncorrected.

"Banks, these are not simple high spirits. I know my boys, despite what you might think, and they have their mother's determined nature. They were doing well with you, mastering everything from sums to how to converse in something other than an angry shout. Since Tuesday, I've feared to cross my own threshold of an evening."

Denton Webber ambled over on a smart, lean gray. "Banks, a word with you. Blumenthal, you might want to join us. What is this nonsense about you leaving the church, Banks? My wife is threatening to leave *me* if I can't find somewhere to send the boys, and the only place the boys are willing to go is back with you."

Blumenthal stuffed his handkerchief back in his pocket. "You *asked* your own children what they wanted, Webber?"

"They tell you what they need, what they want," Daniel said, "if you pay attention, the same way you know how your horses or your flocks are going on."

"Matthias isn't as subtle as all that," Webber said. "He's bold once he sees an objective. Mrs. Webber and I are worried he'll turn into his cousin, a thoroughgoing rascal who can get 'round any tutor ever born. I've been meaning to talk to you about the cousin, but first, Banks, I am charged to ask: Leave the church if you wish to, but what must we pay you to keep your school open?"

Twenty yards away, Kirsten had climbed out of the barouche and been taken captive by the three Blumenthal sisters of a marriageable age.

"Keep my school open?" Daniel asked. Any minute, the boys should come thundering around the edge of the trees, and now was not the time—

"Keep my school open?" Daniel repeated more softly as the sense of Mr. Webber's words sank in.

"Mrs. Blumenthal would want me to ask you the same question on the same terms," the squire said. "Since the boys came home a few days ago, my kingdom has been at war, Banks. My wife won't speak to me unless it's to ask if I'll send the boys off to public school on Monday. My daughters were heard discussing how to implicate their brothers in offenses serious enough to merit incarceration."

Webber took up the chorus.

"My housekeeper is threatening to give notice. The boys trapped the pantry mouser in with the clean linens. The lot was no sooner laundered and refolded than it happened again, with the stable tom added for good measure. Perhaps we can't pay what Lord Fairly has promised you, but I've spoken to my brother about his boys—he has two, and they're the despair of his every dream. Nobody likes to speak of a boy who can't be managed, but you could fill that dower house with them."

At some point, Nicholas and Fairly had joined the circle forming around Daniel.

"You could take on several dozen at least," Nicholas said. "The dower property sits empty otherwise, and I've rather enjoyed having rambunctious scholars on the premises. Gives Belle Maison a proper cachet, to have an academy right across my garden."

"You have room for plenty more juvenile miscre—scholars," Fairly said. "Might have to add on to the stable, though."

Daniel's heart started pounding amid all the reasonable tones and casual suggestions—pounding or breaking.

"I'm very flattered by your opinions of my teaching ability, but I can no longer… That is to say, my vocation, my religious calling—"

"Who says you must wear a collar to teach a pack of unruly boys?" George asked—and where had he come from? "If you expand your enrollment, you won't have time for vicaring in any case. One must learn to be flexible, Banks. The boys need you; their families need you. That business with the cat in the linen closet is intolerable."

The business with the cat in the linen closet was a sure sign of collusion, of cooperation among a shrewd and determined pack of scheming little—

"I'd be happy to help," Ralph said. He was unmounted, and his presumptuousness had turned his ears red. "Annie likes working at the dower house too."

"Baskets every week," Blumenthal added. "Missus suggested it. The girls will sew you all the curtains you need."

Mrs. Webber had joined the Blumenthal ladies in an earnest discussion with Kirsten, and over the kettle-drum thumping in his chest, Daniel wanted to shout for his wife to rescue him from these mad fools—

"Here they come!" somebody yelled, and a cheer went up along the line of conveyances and picnic blankets.

The thunder of little hooves pounding for home in a flat-out gallop joined the pounding of Daniel's heart as Kirsten broke away from the women to stride in Daniel's direction.

She was upset. Those dratted women had upset Daniel's beloved and these men had upset Daniel. Kirsten needed him; Daniel needed her. Nothing else mattered, and nothing would serve but that he go to her.

Fairly was blathering about scholarships when Daniel nudged Beelzebub forward. The circle of fellows fell to cheering the contestants on, but Daniel had eyes only for his wife.

"They made you cry," he said, climbing off his horse. "Those infernal women made you cry."

"I don't want to leave the boys," Kirsten blurted out, falling against Daniel and lashing her arms around his waist. "Daniel, I never thought I'd have any children to love, and that has made me overly susceptible—I *cannot* leave our rotten boys, and they don't want to leave us either. I'm a bad wife and a terrible helpmeet and a rotten Christian, but *I want to keep our boys*. Tell me you can solve this, Daniel, because it's b-breaking my h-heart."

The cheering grew louder, the pounding hooves closer. Six horse and rider pairs streaked safely over the finish line to mad applause.

"I cannot solve this," Daniel said, hugging his wife indecently close. "I could never have solved this. Thank all the merciful powers and six little scamps, somebody else already has."

Epilogue

"I asked at the Queen's Harebell, because the vicarage stands empty," Patrick Warwick informed the woman who'd opened the door. "I was told I'd find Reverend Banks at the Belle Maison dower house, though why the minister—was that a toad?"

"That was the William of the Week," the woman said, opening the door wider and stepping back into a gleaming front hallway. "You'll have to pardon our Charles. He's not as fast as the other boys at catching toads—not yet, but he's wily and tenacious, and we have high hopes for him. Won't you come in, sir?"

Wily, tenacious boys were seldom viewed with such great good cheer—Patrick had been one—and this woman was not a housekeeper. A man of the cloth learned to read people, though no parson's instincts were needed to reach that conclusion. She was not attired as a housekeeper, and she was too pretty.

Also far too pregnant. Patrick followed her inside, out of a late summer afternoon.

"I am Patrick—"

A small, dark-haired boy came pelting around the corner.

"That way, Charles," the lady cried, pointing down the corridor. "William is tiring. Don't give up, and you'll soon have him."

The child snapped off a bow and dashed away.

"You encourage toad catching, ma'am?"

"I can't have toads loose in the house, now can I? The boys decided no toad could endure a week without taking any air, so our William goes for a hop about the house at least once a day. A boy learns stamina and strategy when he's assigned to toad duty. The responsibility is much-coveted among the new arrivals. Do I take it you're Patrick Warwick, late of Dewey Close?"

"I have that honor," Patrick said, offering a bow more polished than young Charles had attempted.

"I'm Lady Kirsten Banks," the woman said with a bit of a dip that might have been a curtsy. "Daniel is trying to explain to the youngest boys why the Regent, as head of the Church of England, gets away with ceaseless gluttony and intemperance. The older boys are trying very hard not to laugh. Theology is a frequent trial to their composure."

Patrick was hot, dusty, tired, and too honest for his own good. "Theology is a frequent trial to my own composure."

"Marvelous," she said, hanging Patrick's hat on a hook and taking him by a dusty sleeve. "Daniel says you've vexed the bishops with your outspoken sermons and liberal politics. The only fellows I like better than those who think for themselves are hungry, thirsty fellows who think for themselves."

Another boy went by at a thundering gallop.

"Try my parlor, Harold," Lady Kirsten called after him, "and consider that one doesn't catch a rabbit by making noise."

Just like that, the small fellow slid to a halt and tiptoed in the opposite direction of the toad catcher.

"Rabbits teach quiet?" Patrick hazarded.

"And speed," Lady Kirsten said, drawing Patrick into a sunny dining parlor. "We've been expecting you for a week. Sally Blumenthal in particular has been practicing her soprano solos, so to speak. You're probably used to that sort of thing by now."

"Speed, stamina, and strategy are skills every vicar must call upon occasionally," Patrick said, because to this smiling woman, a man might admit such truths.

"Daniel will like you very well," she replied. "I'll have some ale sent up and tell Daniel he must leave off instructing the scholars long enough to greet his successor. If you see a rabbit or a toad, summon one of the boys in French, Latin, or Greek."

"Because that teaches…?"

"It gives the quarry time to get away. Charles is the fidgety sort and afternoons in the schoolroom are hard on him. A good steeplechase through the premises helps him stay out of trouble.

"I'd just made up a snack for my husband," her ladyship went on, "but he'd want you to have it." She lifted a cover from a plate and revealed two sandwiches, ham and cheddar peeking from between slices of pale bread. A plate of sugar-dusted biscuits sat near a glass of lemonade, and sliced peaches filled a glazed bowl.

"I've only had peaches once before," Patrick said, which wasn't exactly polished repartee. His mouth watered at the very sight of the glistening fruit though. Peaches were ambrosial, the nectar of the gods, and more than a delicacy in the wilds of the North Riding. For a cold sliced peach, Patrick might well have joined Adam and Eve in their fall from grace.

"My brother grows them over in Surrey," Lady Kirsten said. "We have plenty. Enjoy your snack, and I'll free Daniel from the lions."

This was a snack? But then Reimer had said Banks was leaving the church to be headmaster at some establishment the titles were keen to send their heirs to. *This* establishment, apparently, and boys— especially boys who spent afternoons racing about— were prodigiously accomplished at eating.

Lady Kirsten swished away, moving at a rapid clip for a woman approaching her confinement.

Patrick was halfway through his first sandwich and his lemonade when a tall, dark-haired man accompanied her ladyship into the dining parlor.

"Mr. Banks," Patrick said, rising to offer a bow. He'd not turned loose of his sandwich and had to switch hands with it to shake Banks's hand.

Banks smiled at that faux pas, an expression of humor, commiseration, kindness, and mischief. His smile belonged on the face of a confident, merry young boy, but also looked exactly right on him.

"So glad you've arrived, Mr. Warwick. Your safe travels have been in my prayers for weeks."

Clergy were always throwing around references to prayers, playing piety games with each other, half in jest, half in earnest. Patrick had the sense that Banks was simply being honest.

"Shall we sit?" Lady Kirsten suggested. "I've left the door open out of respect for the fugitives, but I can close it if the noise will bother you."

The noise being the occasional scampering boy or gratuitous shout.

"I have three younger brothers," Patrick said. "This is not noise."

Husband and wife sat, one on either side of the table, while Patrick was positioned at the head.

"You must have your brothers come visit," Lady Kirsten said. "We like boys."

"Girls too. Girls have a better grasp of strategy," the vicar observed with a fond smile for his wife. "We'll add a program for girls in a few years. How did you leave Reimer?"

Abruptly, Patrick wished he'd not listened to the directions of the good fellows at the Queen's Harebell, wished he'd kept riding right down to the coast, then taken ship.

"Reimer despairs of me," Patrick said. "I've offended the men who've held the livings at my last two posts. I criticized their politics. This is my last chance."

A glance went across the table, volumes of unspoken conversation between man and wife, between two conspirators who colluded with rabbits and toads in the name of scholarship for rambunctious boys.

"Well, that's a pity," Banks said, all gentle consternation, "because you are absolutely, utterly, indispensably needed here. I'm run ragged trying to maintain my church duties and look after the boys. Lady Kirsten will soon have new duties that must have her complete attention—though we haven't chosen a name yet—and prior to my arrival, this parish hadn't had a dedicated pastor with any real vocation for years."

"You cannot abandon us," Lady Kirsten said, smoothing a hand over the bulge of her belly. "Daniel and I have taken on more than we ought, with the boys and their education. They're special boys, you know, every one of them. If you will not make a go of this position, Daniel will be asked to wait for yet more months while Reimer dithers over a replacement."

Men left the church. Younger sons inherited titles, other men inherited means and even businesses or land. Still others were quietly encouraged to find another calling before their vices caused the church embarrassment, but none of those factors seemed to apply here.

And Reimer did dither. He was a first-rate ditherer, and he flirted with his help.

Patrick studied his lemonade, rather than peer at his host. "May I ask why you're stepping down?"

"I was married before attaining my majority, and without my father's consent," Banks said in the same tone of voice a man might refer to having once ridden a piebald despite a preference for bays. "The union was annulled earlier this year after a period of separation from my first wife. My flock knows my circumstances, and has invited me to stay on, but the situation gave me an opportunity to evaluate my choices. Kirsten and I will be happier and can make a better contribution if I'm a headmaster rather than a vicar."

So simple. Patrick liked simple, honest answers far better than the convoluted High Church nonsense.

"The lemonade is very good," he said. The company was too. *Kirsten and I*, Banks had said, as if their happiness were a conjoined entity.

"Daniel loves the boys, and they love him, and I love them all," Lady Kirsten said, setting a pitcher of lemonade by Patrick's elbow. "You'll have far too much room for one person at the vicarage, no matter how much you might enjoy solitude. You must visit us often, lest you get lonely."

Patrick *was* lonely, had been ever since his uncle had told him to choose the church, the military, or the New World.

A rabbit loped softly into the room, a pretty gray bunny with a wiggly little nose. A large brown toad hopped in after her.

Neither Mr. Banks nor his wife spared the creatures more than a glance, and the corridor was silent. Something eased in Patrick's chest. Hunger and thirst addressed, toad and rabbit accounted for, and at least one offer of friendship already extended.

"I shall love it here," Patrick said, offering the plate of biscuits around. The three adults—and one rabbit and one toad—sat for nearly an hour discussing the parish, the boys, the genial earl who held the living.

And *not* the weather. By the time the conversation wound around to the choir, Patrick felt as if he were talking to his two, or possibly four, oldest friends.

Little boys came through to scoop up the animals;

a dinner bell sounded from somewhere distant in the house.

"You will join us for dinner," Lady Kirsten said, scooting her chair back. "The boys will want to look you over and offer suggestions for how to go on in Daniel's place. Our boys are very helpful, and often have excellent ideas."

Mr. Banks was around the table to hold her ladyship's chair as quickly as any of the boys might have been, and when she rose, Lady Kirsten kissed Banks's cheek and leaned into his chest.

Right there in the parlor, with Patrick unable to look away, husband and wife cadged a happy little snuggle.

"Don't be scandalized," Lady Kirsten said. "The boys ignore us, and the help laughs at us. I'm besotted with my husband, Mr. Warwick. Maybe Sally Blumenthal will one day behave the same way with you."

A queer feeling came over Patrick, the urge to laugh accompanied by a little chill. He had yet to meet the lovely Miss Blumenthal, but he adored a confident soprano and was abruptly hopeful he might adore his position as the Vicar at St. Jude's.

As it happened, he lasted five years, before becoming the first instructor at the Haddondale Academy to teach Latin to the young ladies, and the first to suggest that every scholar be permitted to participate in the year-end horse race.

The girls were fiendishly good on horseback, and at chasing toads and rabbits. They disdained to chase boys...

Kirsten and Daniel's five children learned beside the other scholars, who included various cousins, in-laws, and neighbors' children as well the occasional titled heir whom some public school had nearly wrecked.

Even the near wrecks came right. They all came right, even if they never mastered the fifth declension nouns or the proper form of address for a retired archbishop. They came right because regardless of the subject matter, the curriculum taught was one of kindness and honesty, compassion and tolerance, hope and forgiveness, love without end.

Amen.

Read on for a sneak peek at the next book
in the True Gentlemen series

Will's True Wish

"WE WERE HAVING A PERFECTLY WELL-BEHAVED outing," Cam said, though Cam Dorning and perfect behavior enjoyed only a distant acquaintance. "Just another pleasant stroll in the pleasant park on a pleasant spring morning, until George pissed on her ladyship's parasol."

The culprit sat in the middle of the room, silent and stoic, tail thumping gently against the carpet.

"Georgette did not insult Lady Susannah's parasol all on her own initiative," Will Dorning retorted, for he knew Lady Susannah Haddonfield was adept at avoiding all notice. "Somebody let her off the leash."

"Lady Susannah wasn't on a leash," Cam shot back. "She was taking the air with her sister and Viscount Effington, and his lordship was carrying the lady's parasol—being gallant, or eccentric. I swear Georgette was sniffing the bushes one moment and aiming for Effington's knee the next. Nearly got him too, which is probably what the man deserves for carrying a parasol in public."

Across the earl's study, Ash dissolved into whoops

that became pantomimes of a dog raising her leg on various articles of furniture in the Earl of Casriel's London abode. Cam had to retaliate by shoving at his older brother, which of course necessitated reciprocal shoving from Ash, which caused the dog to whine fretfully.

"I should let Georgette use the pair of you as a canine convenience," Will muttered, stroking a hand over her silky, brindle head. She was big, even for a mastiff, and prone to lifting her leg in the fashion of a male dog when annoyed or worried.

"I thought I'd let her gambol about a bit," Cam said. "There I was, a devoted brother trying to be considerate of *your* dog, when the smallest mishap occurs, and you scowl at me as if I farted during grace."

"You do fart during grace," Ash observed. "During breakfast too. You're a farting prodigy, Sycamore Dorning. Wellington could have used you at Waterloo, His Majesty's one-man foul miasma, and the French would still be——"

"Enough," Will muttered. Georgette's tail went still, for the quieter Will became, the harder he was struggling not to kill his younger brothers, and Georgette was a perceptive creature. "Where is the parasol?"

"Left it in the mews," Cam said. "A trifle damp and odiferous, if you know what I mean."

"Stinking, like you," Ash said, sashaying around the study with one hand on his hip and the other pinching his nose. "Perhaps we ought to get you a pretty parasol to distract from your many unfortunate shortcomings."

Casriel would be back from his meeting with the solicitors by supper, and the last thing the earl needed was aggravation from the lower primates masquerading as his younger siblings.

More aggravation, for they'd been blighting the family escutcheon and the family exchequer since birth, the lot of them.

"Sycamore, you have two hours to draft a note of apology to the lady," Will said. "I will review your epistle before you seal it. No blots, no crossing out, no misspellings."

"An apology!" Cam sputtered, seating himself on the earl's desk. "I'm to apologize on behalf of your dog?! I didn't piss on anybody."

At seventeen years of age, Cam was still growing into his height, still a collection of long limbs and restless movement that hadn't resolved itself into manly grace. He had the Dorning dark hair and the infamous Dorning gentian eyes, though.

"Shall you apologize to Lady Shakespeare or to Effington's knees?" Ash asked. "At length, or go for the pithy, sincere approach? Headmaster says no blots, no crossing out, no misspellings. I'm happy to write this apology on your behalf for a sum certain."

Ash had an instinct for business—he had read law— but he lacked the cunning Cam had in abundance.

"Ash makes you a generous offer, Cam," Will said, stowing the leash on the mantel and enduring Georgette's But-I'll-Die-If-We-Remain-Indoors look. "Alas, for your finances, Ash, you'll be too busy procuring an exact replica of the lady's abused accessory, from your own funds."

"My own funds?"

Ash hadn't any funds to speak of. What little money

Casriel could spare his younger siblings, they spent on drink and other Town vices.

"An exact replica," Will said. "Not a cheap imitation. I will inspect your purchase to be complete by the time Cam has drafted an apology. Away with you both, for I must change into clothing suitable for a call upon an earl's daughter."

Into Town attire, a silly, frilly extravagance that on a man of Will's proportions was a significant waste of fabric. He was a frustrated sheep farmer, not some dandy on the stroll, though he was also, for the present, the Earl of Casriel's heir.

So into his finery he would go.

And upon Lady Susannah Haddonfield, of all ladies, he would call.

❧

"A big, well-dressed fellow is sauntering up our walk," Lady Della Haddonfield announced. "He's carrying a lovely purple parasol. The dog looks familiar."

"That's the mastiff we met in the park," Susannah said. "The Dorning boys were with her." A trio of puppies, really, though the Dorning fellows were growing into the good looks for which the family was famous.

"Effington said that mastiff was the largest dog he'd ever seen," Della replied, nudging the drapery aside. "The viscount does adore his canines. Who can that man be? He's taller than the two we met in the park."

Taller and more conservatively dressed. "The earl, possibly," Susannah said, picking up her volume of Shakespeare's sonnets and resuming her seat. "He and

Nicholas are doubtless acquainted. Please don't stand in my light, Della."

Della, being a younger sister, only peered more closely over Susannah's shoulder. "You're poring over the sonnets again. Don't you have them all memorized by now?"

The genteel murmur of the butler admitting a visitor drifted up the stairs, along with a curious clicking sound, and then…

"That was a woof," Susannah said. "From inside this house."

"She seemed a friendly enough dog," Della replied, taking a seat on the sofa. Della was the Haddonfield changeling, small and dark compared to her tall, blond siblings, and she made a pretty picture on the red velvet sofa, her green skirts arranged about her.

"She's an ill-mannered canine," Susannah said, "if my parasol's fate is any indication."

Though the dog was a fair judge of character. Lord Effington fawned over all dogs and occasionally over Della, but Susannah found him tedious. The Dornings' mastiff had lifted her leg upon Lord Effington's knee, and Susannah's parasol had been sacrificed in defense of his lordship's tailoring.

Barrisford tapped on the open door. One never heard Barrisford coming or going, and he seemed to be everywhere in the household at once.

"My ladies, a gentleman has come to call and claims acquaintance with the family."

The butler passed Susannah a card, plain black ink on cream stock, though Della snatched it away before Susannah could read the print.

"Shall I say your ladyships are not at home?" Barrisford asked.

"We're at home," Della said, just as Susannah murmured, "That will suit, Barrisford."

She was coming up on the seventy-third sonnet, her favorite.

"We can receive him together," Della said. "If Nicholas knows the Earl of Casriel, he very likely knows the spares, and Effington fancied that dog most rapturously."

"Effington fancies all dogs," Susannah said, and he fancied himself most of all. "But you'll give me no peace if I turn our caller away. Show him up, Barrisford, and send along the requisite tray."

"I've never drunk so much tea in all my life as I have this spring," Della said. "No wonder people waltz until all hours and stay up half the night gossiping."

Gossiping, when they might instead be reading. Was any trial on earth more tedious than a London Season?

"Mr. Will Dorning, and Georgette," Barrisford said a moment later. He stepped aside from the parlor door to reveal a large gentleman and an equally outsized dog. Susannah hadn't taken much note of the dog in the park, for she'd been too busy trying not to laugh at Effington. The viscount prided himself on his love of canines, though he was apparently fonder of his riding breeches, for he'd smacked the dog more than once with Susannah's abused parasol.

Barrisford's introduction registered only as the visitor bowed to Susannah.

Will Dorning, not the Earl of Casriel, not one of the younger brothers. Willow Grove Dorning himself. Susannah had both looked for and avoided him for years.

"My Lady Susannah, good day," he said. "A pleasure to see you again. Won't you introduce me to your sister?"

Barrisford melted away, while Della rose from the sofa on a rustle of velvet skirts. "Please do introduce us, Suze."

Della's expression said she'd introduce herself if Susannah failed to oblige. The dog had more decorum than Della, at least for the moment.

"Lady Delilah Haddonfield," Susannah began, "may I make known to you Mr. Will Dorning, late of Dorset?" Susannah was not about to make introductions for the mastiff. "Mr. Dorning, my sister, Lady Delilah, though she prefers Lady Della."

"My lady." Mr. Dorning bowed correctly over Della's hand, while the dog sat panting at his feet. Like most men, he'd probably be smitten with Della before he took a seat beside her on the sofa. Only Effington's interest had survived the rumors of Della's modest settlements, however.

"Your dog wants something, Mr. Dorning," Susannah said, retreating to her seat by the window.

Mr. Dorning peered at his beast, who was gazing at Della and holding up a large paw.

"Oh, she wants to shake," Della said, taking that paw in her hand and shaking gently. "Good doggy. Very pleased to make your acquaintance."

"Georgette, behave," Mr. Dorning muttered, before Susannah was faced with the riddle of whether manners required her to shake the dog's paw.

Georgette turned an innocent expression on her owner, crossed the room, and took a seat at Susannah's knee.

Presuming beast, though Georgette at least didn't stink of dog. Effington's endless canine adornments were the smelliest little creatures.

"My ladies, I'm here to apologize," Mr. Dorning said. "Georgette was in want of manners earlier today. We've come to make restitution for her bad behavior and pass along my brother Sycamore's note of apology."

"Do have a seat, Mr. Dorning," Della said, accepting a sealed missive from their guest. "At least you haven't come to blather on about the weather or to compliment our bonnets."

Bless Della and her gift for small talk, because Susannah was having difficulty thinking.

This was not the version of Will Dorning she'd endured dances with in her adolescence. He'd filled out and settled down, like a horse rising seven. Where a handsome colt had been, a warhorse had emerged. Mr. Dorning's boots gleamed, the lace of his cravat fell in soft, tasteful abundance from his throat. His clothing *fit* him, in the sense of being appropriate to his demeanor, accentuating abundant height, muscle, and self-possession.

Even as the man sat on the delicate red velvet sofa, a frilly purple parasol across his knees.

"This is for you, my lady," he said, passing Susannah that parasol. "We didn't get the color exactly right, but I hope this will suffice on short notice to replace the article that came to grief in the park."

Susannah's parasol had been blue, a stupid confection

that had done little to shield a lady's complexion. That parasol hadn't made a very effective bludgeon when turned on the dog.

"The color is lovely," Susannah said, "and the design very similar to the one I carried earlier."

Susannah made the mistake of looking up at that moment, of gazing fully into eyes of such an unusual color, poetry had been written about them. Mr. Dorning's eyes were the purest form of the Dorning heritage, nearly the color of the parasol Susannah accepted from his gloved hands.

Willow Dorning's eyes were not pretty, though. His eyes were the hue of a sunset that had given up the battle with night, such that angry reds and passionate oranges had faded to indigo memories and violet dreams. Seven years ago, his violet eyes had been merely different, part of the Dorning legacy, and he'd been another tall fellow forced to bear his friend's sisters' company. In those seven years, his voice had acquired night-sky depths, his grace was now bounded with self-possession.

Though he still apparently loved dogs.

"My thanks for the parasol," Susannah said, though she might be repeating herself. "You really need not have bothered. Ah, and here's the tea tray. Della, will you pour?"

"Georgette likes you, Susannah," Della said as she poured the tea. "Or she likes that parasol."

The dog had not moved from Susannah's knee, though she was ignoring the parasol and sniffing at the sonnets on the side table.

"Georgette is shy," Mr. Dorning said, "and she's

usually well mannered, save for occasionally snacking on an old book. Her mischief in the park was an aberration, I assure you. Lady Della, are you enjoying your first London Season?"

For the requisite fifteen minutes, Della and Mr. Dorning made idle talk, while Susannah discreetly nudged the sonnets away from the dog, sipped tea, and felt agreeably ancient. Without Nita or Kirsten on hand, Susannah had become the older sister suited to serving as a chaperone at a social call.

"I'll bid you ladies good day," Mr. Dorning said, rising.

"I'll see you out," Susannah replied, because that was her role, as quasi-chaperone, and having Barrisford tend to that task would have been marginally unfriendly. Mr. Dorning, as the son of an earl, was her social equal, after all.

"Georgette, come." Mr. Dorning did not snap his fingers, though Effington, the only other dog lover in Susannah's acquaintance, snapped his fingers constantly—at dogs and at servants. He'd snapped his fingers at Della once, and Susannah had treated Effington to a glower worthy of her late papa in a taking.

Georgette padded over to her master's side, and Susannah quit the parlor with them, leaving Della to attack the biscuits remaining on the tea tray.

"You didn't used to like dogs," Mr. Dorning observed.

"I still don't like dogs," Susannah replied, though she didn't *dislike* them. Neither did she like cats, birds, silly bonnets, London Seasons, or most people. Horses were at least useful, and sisters could be very dear. Brothers fell somewhere between horses and sisters.

"Georgette begs to differ," Mr. Dorning said as they

reached the bottom of the steps. "Or perhaps she was making amends for her trespasses against your parasol by allowing you to pat her for fifteen straight minutes."

Susannah took Mr. Dorning's top hat from the sideboard and passed it to him. "Georgette ignored the new parasol. I think my wardrobe is safe from her lapses in manners, though the day your dog snacks on one of my books will be a sorry day for Georgette, Mr. Dorning."

Despite Susannah's stern words, she and Mr. Dorning were *managing*, getting through the awkwardness of being more or less alone together.

"You're still fond of Shakespeare?" Mr. Dorning asked as he tapped his hat onto his head.

A glancing reference to the past, also to the present. "Of all good literature. You're still waiting for your brother to produce an heir?"

Another reference to their past, for Mr. Dorning had confided this much to Susannah during one of their interminable turns about Lady March's parlor. Until the Earl of Casriel had an heir in the nursery, Will Dorning's self-appointed lot in life was to be his brother's second-in-command.

"Casriel is as yet unmarried," Mr. Dorning said, "and now my younger brothers strain at the leash to conquer London."

He exchanged his social gloves for riding gloves, giving Susannah a glimpse of masculine hands. Those hands could be kind, she hadn't forgotten that. They'd also apparently learned how to give the dog silent commands, for at Mr. Dorning's gesture, Georgette seated herself near the front door.

"I'm much absorbed keeping Cam and Ash out of trouble," he went on, "while allowing them the latitude to learn self-restraint. Apparently I must add my loyal hound to the list of parties in need of supervision."

The dog thumped her tail.

Did Will Dorning allow himself any latitude? Any unrestrained moments? He'd been a serious young man. He was formidable now.

"We'll doubtless cross paths with your brothers, then," Susannah said, "for Della is also determined to storm the social citadels." Once Della was safely wed, Susannah could luxuriate in literary projects, a consummation devoutly to be wished, indeed.

"You have ever had the most intriguing smile," Mr. Dorning observed, apropos of nothing Susannah could divine. "Thank you for accepting my apology, my lady. I look forward to renewing our acquaintance further under happier circumstances."

Having dispensed such effusions as the situation required, he bowed over Susannah's hand and was out the door, his dog trotting at his heels.

An *intriguing* smile? Susannah regarded herself in the mirror over the sideboard. Her reflection was tall, blond, blue-eyed, as unremarkable as an earl's daughter could be amid London's spring crop of beauties. She *was* smiling, though…

❧

"Our younger brothers are in awe of you," Grey Dorning, Earl of Casriel, said as Will's mare was led out. "Over their morning ale, they ridicule me, a belted earl with the entire consequence of the house

of Dorning upon my broad and handsome shoulders.
You, they adore for strolling down Park Lane swinging a purple parasol as if it's the latest fashion edict
from Almack's."

Rather than reply immediately, Will took a moment
to greet his bay mare. He held a gloved hand beneath
her nose, pet her neck, and before Casriel's eyes, the
horse fell in love with her owner all over again.

"I took Georgette calling with me," Will said,
scratching at the mare's shoulder. "She can be both
charming and menacing, which is why Cam and Ash
like to take her to the park. She impresses the fellows
and attracts the ladies, rather like *you're* supposed to do."

The stable lad led out Casriel's gelding, a handsome black specimen whose displays of affection were
reserved for his oats. The groom gave the horse a pat
on the quarters, and the horse wrung its tail.

"Don't scold me, Willow," Casriel said, climbing
into the saddle. "The Season is barely under way, and
an earl must tend to business. The impressing and
attracting can wait a few more days."

"Your only prayer of avoiding matrimony evapo-
rated when Jacaranda married Worth Kettering," Will
said, taking a moment to check the fit of the bridle
and girth before mounting. "Without a sister to serve
as hostess, you are doomed to wedlock, Casriel. Marry
for the sake of your household, if not for your lonely
heart. Dorning House needs a woman's touch if the
staff isn't to continuing revolting twice a quarter."

"You are such a romantic, Willow," Casriel replied
as their horses clip-clopped down the alley. "I can
barely afford to educate our brothers, and that rebellious

household must eat. I will marry prudently or not at all. How did the visit to the Haddonfield ladies go?"

That question ought to deflect Will from sermonizing on the need for every unmarried earl to take a wife posthaste, though like many questions put to Will, it met with a silent reception.

They reached the street, where the surrounding traffic meant Will would remain civil, despite an older brother's well-meant goading, so Casriel tried again.

"Did Lady Susannah receive you? She has an entire litter of siblings, doesn't she?" Casriel did too, but lately he felt like a stranger to even his only full brother.

"Lady Susannah was most gracious," Will replied, "as was Lady Della. Lady Della has the misfortune to be the only petite, dark-haired Haddonfield in living memory."

"A runt, then, in your parlance. If she's a pretty, well-dowered runt, nobody will bother much about her shortcomings." Will was partial to runts, perhaps he'd marry the Haddonfield girl.

"Our own runt has taken to gambling," Will said. "Though if Cam keeps growing, he might soon consider a career as a prizefighter."

Sycamore, for shame. "All young men attend cockfights."

"No, Grey, they do not. Duchess of Moreland coming this way."

Casriel tipped his hat, the duchess waved. Her Grace—a pretty, older lady with a gracious smile—probably knew Casriel's antecedents back for six generations, but without Will's warning, Casriel would have been hard put to recall he'd seen the woman at the previous evening's musicale.

Financial anxiety played havoc with any man's concentration. No wonder Papa had retreated to the conservatory and the glasshouse rather than take the earldom in hand.

"How do you keep it all organized, Will?" Casriel asked. "How do you keep track of Cam's mischief, the duchesses, the purple parasols, the stewards?"

"A purple parasol is rather difficult to lose track of," Will replied, possibly teasing. One could never tell for sure when Will was being deep and when he was being ironic as hell.

"Am I to worry about Sycamore's gambling?" Casriel would worry, of course, about the sums lost, and about Sycamore, who well knew the family had no coin to spare.

"Yes, you should worry," Will replied, "though not about the money. I've bought Cam's vowels, and will deduct a sum from his allowance from now until Domesday. You should worry because he was at a bearbaiting, because Ash could not stop him, because last week it was the cockfights. The company to be had in such locations is abysmal."

Cam should be at university, in other words. All young men in the awkward throes of late adolescence should be at university, though finding tuition for such an undertaking was three years of a challenge when more younger brothers were busily inspiring insurrection among the maids back in Dorset.

"What does Ash say?" Casriel asked.

"That he can't control Cam, so he simply keeps an eye on him. This is how young men become spoiled or worse. My Lady Heathgate, her sister-in-law Lady Fairly beside her, with the matched chestnuts."

"Wasn't there some scandal involving Lady Fairly?" Casriel asked when his hat had been dutifully tipped.

"She was a vicar's daughter taken advantage of by a scoundrel," Will said in the same tones he'd report on a play seen the previous evening. "She managed Fairly's brothel, though she never entertained clients, and he's since divested himself of that business. The titled ladies in the family treat her as respectable, though she and Fairly live very quietly."

"Willow, no wonder the boys are in awe of you. Thank God our papa forbade me to buy any commissions, or Wellington would have turned you into an intelligence officer and shortened the war considerably."

Will drew back, allowing Casriel to ride first through a gap between a stopped curricle and the walkway.

"I would never have managed in the military," Will said. "Bad enough they kill boys who've barely learned to shave, but they also kill horses by the thousands."

This was the problem with Cam's bad behavior. Not that the youngest Dorning brother was wasting money, for an earl's younger son was bred to waste money, and not that he was making friends in low places.

Earls' sons did that too.

From Casriel's perspective, the problem was that Cam sought entertainments involving harm to animals. Blood sport was supposed to be part of a young gentleman's diversions, true, but Will had no patience for entertainment based on inflicting misery on animals.

Cam had known that from the cradle.

"I can send Cam back to Dorset," Casriel said, "but

we're better off keeping him where we can supervise him." Where Will could supervise him.

"He might be trying to get sent back to Dorset," Will replied as the green oasis of Hyde Park came into view. "One of the Dorset housemaids had her eye on our youngest brother, and has had her hands on him too."

"Angels deliver me," Casriel muttered. "We don't dare leave him in Dorset without one of us to watch over him, and yet I'm not about to turn off a housemaid simply because Cam can be lured into the butler's pantry."

"Younger siblings grow up more quickly than heirs and spares," Will said. "I'll think of something." He tipped his hat to a flower girl and tossed her a coin.

The girl was pudgy, plain, and her apron streaked with damp and dirt, but her smile was radiant as she passed Will a bouquet of violets.

"Thank you, Ellen," Will said, bringing his mare to a halt. "Can you spare a posy for his lordship too? He must make himself agreeable to the ladies who are thronging the park."

The flower girl shot Casriel a dubious look, then selected a nosegay of lily of the valley. She handed the flowers to Will, who passed them over.

"Excellent choice," Will said. "Good day to you, Ellen."

The mare walked on, while Casriel dealt with holding a batch of delicate blossoms in addition to four reins.

"What am I to do with these, Willow? Carry them between my teeth? Why does that flower girl look familiar?"

"I've hired her to supply flowers for the house. She rarely speaks because of a stammer, but she's quite bright, and has the best prices. An earl's home must be maintained according to certain standards, which of course, a countess would see to."

Oh, of course. The fate of the earldom rested on flowers Casriel probably could not afford, but stammering street vendors would have a fine Christmas. Whatever was amiss with Will, it was getting worse.

The closer they drew to the park, the more crowded the streets became, so the horses could move only at the walk. Willow deftly braided his batch of violets into the mare's mane, where they somehow did not look ridiculous. Casriel, by contrast, felt the veriest fool riding through Mayfair, flowers in hand, and horse likely to turn up mischievous at any moment.

"The Duchess of Moreland's two nieces," Will said quietly. "Miss Bethan and Miss Megan Windham. Their cousin, Lady Deane, the duchess's youngest daughter, at the ribbons."

"How in God's name do you keep them all straight?"

"Flowers to the elder," Will murmured. "Miss Bethan, sitting on the outside."

Miss Bethan Windham was a lovely little creature with whom Casriel had not danced. He would have recalled that red hair, and those green eyes, and the smile that blossomed when he passed her the flowers. The ladies flirted and teased and generally made a man forget which direction the park lay in, and then traffic shifted, and Will cleared his throat.

"Ladies, good day," Casriel said, for he was as well

trained to Will's cues as any hound. "My regards to your family."

"You can be charming," Will said when the carriage had pulled away. "Don't pretend you can't. Those flowers will end up pressed between the pages of the lady's journal, and the scent of lily of the valley will always make her think of you."

"Is that how it works?" Will seemed very convinced of his theory, and yet to the best of Casriel's knowledge, Will had never fancied a specific lady. "How is it, Willow, you know the names of all the women, right down to the flower girl? You earn the undying loyalty of horses and dogs, both, and impress our brothers daily, but the females never seem to notice you?"

Willow had the knack of becoming invisible, in other words. He'd had this ability since boyhood, had slipped through university on the strength of it, and still used his invisibility to good advantage in ballrooms and gentlemen's clubs.

"My objective is to ensure the ladies notice *you*," Will said. "One of them might even notice Ash, who is a good-looking, friendly devil, and knows his way around figures. Once I get you two married off, I can enlist your wives to assist me in finding ladies for our other brothers."

Papa had despaired of Willow, though the late earl and his second son had had much in common.

"As usual, Will, you have an excellent plan, though I detect a serious flaw in your scheme."

They crossed Park Avenue at a brisk trot, and not until they were well within Hyde Park did Will take the bait.

"What is the flaw in my plan?" he asked. "You and Ash are both handsome and sons of an earl. I see to it that you're well dressed when it matters. You're passable dancers and considerate of women. With all the bankers' daughters looking to marry into the nobility, all of the viscounts and baron's daughters or even widows—what?"

Willow had doubtless made lists of these women, another worry added to Casriel's endless supply.

"I know you mean well, Will, but Ash and I can find our own ladies. The flaw in your plan is that you've made no provision for finding *a lady of your own*. Give me those violets. This park has become overrun with women, and an earl-without-countess must defend himself with whatever weapons he can find."

"The park is always overrun with women at the fashionable hour," Will said, "but as it happens, I have my own use for these flowers."

Will cantered off in the direction of a gig driven by a blond woman with a petite brunette at her side. The Haddonfield ladies?

Casriel trotted after, for this moment would go down in Dorning history as the first encounter with a proper woman to which Willow Grove Dorning would arrive bearing flowers.

Two

"DELILAH HADDONFIELD, IF YOU DON'T STOP TWIRL-ing my parasol," Susannah said, "I will use it to smack you. You'll scare some gallant's horse, and he'll be ridiculed, and then talk will start that you like men to notice you."

The parasol slowed. "I am in my first Season, Suze. I am a legitimate by-blow, and my name is Delilah. If I encourage the notice of the men, I'm fast. If I don't encourage the notice of the men, I put on airs. As it happens, I am trying to attract the notice of somebody."

Effington often rode in the park at the fashionable hour, else Susannah would never have subjected herself to two outings in a single day. After the morning's debacle, Delilah was doubtless nervous of his lordship's regard.

"It's early in the Season," Susannah said, maneuvering around a stopped phaeton. "You needn't attract anybody's notice. Simply enjoy a pleasant outing in the company of your devoted sibling."

"I love that about you," Della said. "Behind your spectacles and sonnets, you're tenacious and loyal."

When Susannah wanted to slap her hand over Della's mouth, she instead nodded cordially to the Duke of Quimbey, a jovial older fellow who could still gracefully turn a lady down the ballroom.

"You will please not mention my spectacles." Spectacles were for the elderly, for clerks, and men of business. For people who had trouble reading, not women who devoured literature by the hour.

"Mr. Dorning," Della said, snapping the parasol closed and resting it against the bench. "A pleasure to see you again. What a lovely mare."

Susannah didn't intend to draw the carriage to the verge, but to the verge the horse did go, and there halt. Perhaps their gelding needed a rest, or had an overly developed sense of the social niceties.

"My ladies," Mr. Willow Dorning said, touching his hat brim. "I'm happy to see the new parasol put to use. I will refrain, however, from commenting on either bonnets or weather."

Della's brows drew down at Mr. Dorning's grave tone, but Susannah understood teasing when she heard it.

"See that you don't, sir," she said. "Has your dog been denied the privileges of the park for her earlier indiscretions?"

Susannah noticed Georgette's absence, for the mastiff was a part of Will Dorning's ensemble, like a carved walking stick or a particular signet ring, only larger and more noticeable. Susannah wasn't sure what the violets in Mr. Dorning's hand were about, though for the past seven years, violets had reminded her of his eyes.

And of his gallantry.

"Willow, you are remiss," said a fellow trotting up on Will's left. The newcomer rode a handsome black horse, had the Dorning violet eyes, and felt entitled to an introduction.

The earl, then. Susannah hadn't seen him for years. Beside her, Della preened, fluffing her skirts and twiddling her bonnet ribbons, exactly as a young lady might.

Exactly as Susannah never had.

"My ladies, this presuming lout is my brother," Will said. "Grey, Earl of Interruption and Casriel. Apparently, we're about to be joined by my younger brothers as well, for which I do apologize."

The last was aimed at Susannah, more drivel, but Mr. Dorning's eyes said he was also commiserating with her on the entire topic of siblings. More introductions followed, for Mr. Ash Dorning, and Mr. Sycamore—"though he will ignore you unless you call him Cam"—Dorning.

The earl seemed content to sit back and allow his younger brother to manage the entire encounter. Other carriages tooled past, other gentlemen rode by, and for the first time, Lady Della Haddonfield was seen to hold court in the park.

Della teased Ash Dorning about the fancy knot in his cravat, while Susannah tried not to stare at Mr. Willow Dorning's violets.

"Thank you," Susannah said, beneath the banter of their siblings. Will Dorning was the most perceptive man Susannah knew, for all he lacked charm. She needn't say more.

"You're welcome," he replied just as softly. "I have my own motives, though."

Something Della said caused the other three brothers to laugh, and up and down the carriage parade, heads turned. The Earl of Casriel smiled at Lady Della Haddonfield, ensuring the moment would be remarked by the women over tea and by the gentlemen over cards.

"We each have our own motives," Susannah replied. Shakespeare had made the same point in a hundred more eloquent turns of phrase.

Mr. Dorning fiddled with his horse's mane. "It hasn't grown easier, then? You haven't learned to love the dancing and flirting and being seen?"

He'd predicted she would. He'd been wrong, or kind, or both.

"I am content," Susannah said, which they both knew for a lie. She had never needed to dissemble with him, so she amended her statement. "I will be content, rather. Della has already attached the interest of Viscount Effington, and that portends a successful Season for her."

This merry, impromptu gathering in the park surrounded by four handsome fellows improved those odds considerably.

"May we call upon you, Lady Susannah? You and Lady Della?"

The question hurt. A childish lament—*I saw him first*—crowded hard against loyalty to Della. Willow Dorning had been honorable toward Susannah before she'd comprehended how precious such regard was.

He'd make a wonderful brother-in-law, damn him.

She smiled brilliantly. "Of course you must call upon us, you and however many brothers or dogs you please. We're always happy to welcome our friends." A slight untruth, for Susannah resented any who interrupted her reading.

"Willow!" the earl called. "Didn't you bring those posies for the lady?"

Della Haddonfield, who could wield truth like a rapier and silence like a shield, *simpered*, and Susannah's heart broke a little.

A nuisance, to have a heart that could break. Susannah had thought herself beyond such folly.

"The violets go with his eyes," Cam Dorning said. "Willow is partial to violets, you see."

"As am I," Della said. "Such a delicate fragrance, and so pretty."

Violets did not last, though. Susannah had reason to know this. The horse in the traces took a restive step and shook its head.

Time to go.

"I am partial to ladies who forgive us our minor lapses," Will said, presenting the violets in a gloved hand.

Della reached for the bouquet, and the moment might have turned awkward, but Susannah realized at the last possible instant that the flowers were not for Della, *they were for her.*

She passed the reins into Della's hands as if the movement were choreographed, and accepted the violets.

"Thank you, Mr. Dorning. I'm partial to violets as well. I don't want these to wilt, though, so I'd best get them directly home."

Della recovered with good-humored grace as the men made their farewells and cantered away.

"Shall I drive us home, Suze? Your hands are notably occupied."

Susannah's heart was occupied too, bemused with feelings of pleasure and uncertainty. She was once again sixteen years old, growing too quickly, and terrified of tripping on the dance floor.

"Hold these," Susannah said, shoving the flowers at Della and taking the reins. "You can drive next time."

They left the park for the busy streets of Mayfair, Della holding the flowers, and occasionally—say, when a carriage full of young ladies passed—raising them to her nose as she waved or smiled.

"You are awful," Susannah said, proud of her sister's guile and pleased with the day. "The entire battalion of Dorning brothers has asked permission to call on you, you know. There's a handsome, eligible earl in the bunch, and he seemed taken with you."

A reassuring thought, for reasons Susannah would examine once she'd put those violets in water.

Della waved to another group, this time holding the violets aloft. "The earl is probably ten years my senior, Suze, but they're a fine group of fellows. Effington is titled, and he and I get on well enough."

For all Della was smiling furiously, and beaming gaiety in every direction, her words were tired and hard.

"You'll have other choices." A woman always had choices, though often, she hadn't any good ones. "Give it time."

"He fancies you," Della said, touching a fragile

violet petal. "Mr. Will Dorning fancies you, Suze. You might have choices too."

⁓

"What was that all about in the park, earlier today?" Casriel asked. He was the most inquisitive older brother ever to inconvenience a busy younger sibling. "All that gallantry beneath the maples and flirting among the infantry?"

"You will accuse me of trying to marry you off," Will replied, and the accusation would have had some merit.

The waiter bustled over to their table. Casriel ordered his usual beefsteak, Willow a plate of fruit and cheeses, because Georgette harbored a special fondness for the club's cheddar.

"Please recall," Will went on, "that you intruded uninvited on my conversation with the Haddonfield ladies. I was making amends for Georgette's misbehavior."

Mostly, and being a little sentimental too.

"You bought the woman a replacement parasol and hand-delivered a written apology. What amends remained to be made?"

Casriel thought in terms of crops and ledgers, sums owed, and acres fallowed, so Will explained. He would explain as many times in as many situations as it took for Casriel to learn to think like an earl, rather than a country squire.

"Lady Della is in her first Season, Casriel. Her escort this morning—a handsome, eligible viscount— was nearly pissed upon by my dog. The worse damage was not to the parasol."

The earl wrinkled a nose euphemistically described as aristocratic. On Will, the same nose was a sizable beak. Ash and Cam had been spared the worst excesses of the Dorning nose, as had their sisters, Daisy and Jacaranda. The remaining three brothers had yet to grow into the family proboscis one way or the other, though they had the Dorning eyes.

"Suppose the lady's consequence might have suffered," Casriel said, considering his glass of wine. "From what I heard, Effington delivered a sound beating to Georgette on the spot. I'm surprised she didn't dine on rare haunch of viscount for his presumption."

So was Will. Georgette was a peaceful soul, but she took a dim view of repeated blows to the head.

"The whole incident makes no sense to me, Grey. Georgette has better manners than our younger brothers. Something must have provoked her to misbehavior."

"Cam would provoke a saint to blaspheming. Will you join me for tonight's rounds?"

The Miltons' ball, a soiree at Lord and Lady Hamilton's, perhaps a round of cards back here at the club. Casriel had to be let off the leash at some point, and those were safe gardens for him to nose around in.

"I think not," Will said. "If you make yourself agreeable to the hostesses, they'll ensure you're introduced to all the ladies interested in becoming your countess. Don't dance with any of the marriageable women more than once, don't leer down their bodices no matter how they trip against you or lean too closely on the turns. If you must, smoke a cheroot on the balcony or eat some leeks, and breathe directly on the more presuming ones."

Casriel was handsome, and he'd make a loyal, if somewhat distracted husband. Like Will, he indulged the manly vices rarely and discreetly. He was not wealthy, however, not compared to what many of the ladies on offer were accustomed to, and Dorset was not the most fashionable address.

Grey Birch Dorning was a good man, though, and Will was proud to call him brother.

"Willow, one fears for you," Casriel said, keeping his voice down. "The point of tonight's outing, the point of this entire sortie among the Beau Monde, is to secure the charms of a well-dowered lady. Without your excellent counsel, I won't know one of those from the impoverished sort when they get to leaning or pressing or any of that other business."

Weariness dragged at Will. Weariness of the body, weariness of the fraternal spirit. So many brothers, and Jacaranda was too enthralled with her knight to be of any use getting those brothers married off. Will's other sister, Daisy, was knee-deep in babies, and had her hands full with her squire back in Dorset.

"You will be married to your countess quite possibly for the rest of your life, Casriel, or for hers. If birds can mate for life without recourse to intelligence officers, belted earls ought to be able to manage it too."

The food arrived and conversation lapsed. When Will had eaten half of his selection of cheeses, and wrapped the other half to tuck away in his pocket, he excused himself and repaired with a newspaper to the card room. Cam and Ash were probably once again losing money at some gaming hell or cockfight, and that was so disappointing as to be nearly sickening.

Perhaps the earl could sort them out. Will was growing tired of trying.

⤝⤞

"Playing a bit deep, aren't you, Effington?"

The question was friendly and infuriating. Frankincense Godwin Emeritus Effington, Eighth Viscount Effington, rearranged his cards, then put them back in their original order.

"The Season is upon us, Fenwick," Effington drawled. "I must have my diversions, and your pin money too. What say, the loser of this hand goes directly to the Milton ball and submits himself to the mercy of Lady Milton and the wallflowers of her choosing."

"High stakes, indeed," Fenwick said, amid a chorus of "Done!" and "Hear, hear!" though the other four men around the table were smiling. Two were married, the other two were wealthy. They could afford to be amused at the ordeals of the impoverished, titled bachelors.

Two minutes later, Fenwick threw in his hand. "A plague on your luck, Effington. Perhaps I should start carrying around a little dog, and my cards would improve."

"Having a well-behaved canine prepares a man for the companionship of a well-behaved wife," Effington said, stroking a hand over the homely little pug in his lap. "Both must be pampered, fed, taken about, cossetted, and occasionally disciplined for naughty behavior, isn't that right, Yorrick?"

The dog looked up at mention of his name, but knew better than to bark. They all learned not to bark, eventually. A lap dog made winning at cards ever so much easier, drawing attention from a man's hands at opportune moments.

"I heard your well-behaved lady was laughing in the park with no less than four Dorning brothers in attendance," Fenwick remarked as he downed the last of a drink. "The Dornings are prodigiously handsome, and Lady Della Haddonfield is too pretty for you by half, Effington. If she didn't have so many strapping, devoted brothers, I might pay my addresses to her."

Effington had got word of the scene in the park from one of the many who'd seen Lady Della tooling home, all smiles, and brandishing violets under the very nose of Polite Society. Fenwick was moderately handsome, in a rough, dark way, and said to be connected to one of the northern earls.

Some ladies were attracted to that rough, dark lack of refinement. Della Haddonfield apparently had better sense.

"Lady Della resides with only the one brother," Effington said, gathering up the cards. "The newly minted Earl of Bellefonte, who needs to take his womenfolk in hand, if you ask me."

"Is that what you were doing with Dorning's dog this morning?" one of the other fellows quipped. "Taking the beast in hand by beating at it with a parasol?"

If the women hadn't been present in the park, Effington would have done much more than swat at the damned mastiff. The dog had wanted a firm hand, but alas, the women *had* been present.

"I should have had Yorrick with me," Effington said, grabbing his dog's nose and giving it a waggle.

"He would have defended the pride of the house of Effington."

Or Yorrick would have been reprimanded for his cowardice.

"The ladies do like a friendly dog," one of the married men observed. "Don't understand it m'self. If a beast can't chase down vermin, what good is it?"

Effington ought to have burst forth into an aria about the wonders of canine companionship, for he'd cultivated his public devotion to dogs assiduously. Alas, the hour grew late, and more pressing matters required his attention.

"I will share something with you gentlemen in confidence, for our conversation has unwittingly touched on a sensitive matter," Effington said, tidying the deck into a neat stack. He shuffled the cards, when he'd rather have flung them into the fire.

For the last hour, he'd been winning. For the hour before that, despite Yorrick's slavish cooperation, he had lost.

"I'm for my penance," Fenwick said, rising. Had an inconvenient decent streak, did Fenwick. No uninvited confidences would keep him awake later tonight. "Gentlemen, good night. Yorrick, pleasant dreams."

Fenwick patted the dog, and earned Yorrick's signature hopeful look, which was doomed to failure, of course. Yorrick would do the job he'd been trained for until Effington no longer had a use for him.

"We spoke earlier of Lady Della," Effington said, dropping his tones to the regretful register as Fenwick departed. "I favor the lady with my attentions because she's burdened by unfortunate antecedents, and most of Polite Society treats her accordingly. As an earl's daughter, they can't ignore her, but she's in truth her mother's by-blow, and the ladies will never let her forget it. One feels compelled by gentlemanly honor to champion such a creature."

Sympathetic murmurs followed, for women in search of a well-placed husband were not permitted unfortunate antecedents.

"Good of you to take notice of her," one older man said. "She should be appreciative."

"Her family probably is," another noted. "Not so easy to find a match for the bastards."

"You will keep this in strictest confidence, of course," Effington murmured, thus guaranteeing that every man present told at least one other fellow and two women by morning.

"Of course," came the general reply. No one questioned where Effington had come by this "confidence," which was fortunate. Lady Della's dark coloring, her petite stature, and her siblings' protectiveness had fueled some unkind talk, and the rest was nothing more than nasty speculation.

"Then I leave you," Effington said, rising with the dog in his arms. "And bid you all good night. Yorrick, my darling, it's past your bedtime."

Effington made his exit, stroking and patting his dear little doggy, and kissing endearments to the top of Yorrick's head, while nobody seemed to recall that the evening's winnings and losings had yet to be totaled.

The other men were probably too preoccupied deciding where to share the juiciest gossip of the evening. Well done, if Effington did say so himself.

About the Author

New York Times and *USA Today* bestselling author Grace Burrowes's bestsellers include *The Duke's Disaster, The Captive, The Laird, The Heir, The Soldier, Lady Maggie's Secret Scandal, Lady Sophie's Christmas Wish*, and *Lady Eve's Indiscretion*. Her Regency romances and Scotland-set Victorian romances have received extensive praise, including starred reviews from *Publishers Weekly* and *Booklist*. *Darius* was an iBooks Store Best Book of the Year for 2013. *The Heir* was a *Publishers Weekly* Best Book of 2010, *The Soldier* was a *PW* Best Spring Romance of 2011, *Lady Sophie's Christmas Wish* and *Once Upon a Tartan* have both won RT Reviewers' Choice Awards, *Lady Louisa's Christmas Knight* was a *Library Journal* Best Book of 2012, and *The Bridegroom Wore Plaid* was a *PW* Best Book of 2012. Two of her MacGregor heroes have won KISS awards.

Grace is a practicing family law attorney and lives in rural Maryland. She loves to hear from readers, and can be contacted through her website at graceburrowes.com.